I NEVER PLAYED CATCH WITH MY FATHER

a novel
based upon a true story

ACKNOWLEDGMENT

When I Never Played Catch With My Father was first published, in hardcover in 1996, the World Trade Center served as the setting for the business office headquarters for the main character. Following September 11, 2001, we considered editing the manuscript to reflect a different location. However, we decided to maintain the integrity of the original manuscript, leaving the setting as it was intended. We honor those Americans who lost their lives on that day and are sensitive to all that thereto pertains.

A SPECIAL ACKNOWLEDGMENT

My deepest thanks to *Ms. Oprah Winfrey* who, thanks to my publicist, Nancy Eddy of Novato, California, read and recognized the value and impact of this epic novel. To my lasting surprise, she invited me to appear on The Oprah Show. I am eternally grateful for her well-recognized love of books and authors.

—Gene Cartwright

Publisher's Note Inviting Feedback

Report Errors & Make Comments

Although books undergo thorough editing, errors can still slip through the cracks, even in older releases of The Bible, like the King James Version. One example is the omission of the word "not" in the seventh commandment, "Thou shalt not commit adultery." Famous authors like James Joyce and J.K. Rowling have also been known to make mistakes in their works. We value your feedback and encourage you to reach out to us if you come across any errors or have any comments to share. Please send us a note at: feedback@falconcreekbooks.com

I NEVER PLAYED CATCH WITH MY FATHER

For mothers and daughters; fathers and sons.

Based upon a true story

By

Gene Cartwright

Published by Falcon Creek Books

Second Edition – Softcover Cover
Library of Congress Cataloging-in-Publication Data Library of Congress Control Number:
Cartwright, Gene
I Never Played Catch With My Father: a novel/by Gene Cartwright —
1st ed. p. cm

ISBN: 0-9649756-7-5
ISBN: 978-0-9649756-7-5 (13 digit)
Title: 1098765432

GMW
LA-TX-DC

Published by Falcon Creek Publishing Company – Falcon Creek Books

Printed in the United States of America

Original 1st Edition Comments from Real People

Congratulations on a wonderful story

—**Gene Autry**

Late, former owner of the California Angels, now the Los Angeles Angels baseball team, and famed Westerns hero.

"Seldom does a first novel overflow with such emotion, such realism, and power. The second reading was even better.

*—**Lance Brown**, CA*

"This is a story about family, about baseball, about the enormity of seemingly small things. It is a story every parent should read; every son and daughter should read. It brought back so many memories. If this book doesn't touch your heart, you don't have one.

*—**William Sheffield,** CA*

"I cried my way through this book. It was so real. It made me think about my own mother and father—my own childhood. The author must have read my diary.

*—**Pat Sherrard,** Texas*

There comes a time when the search for meaning in this human opera, called life, supplants the search for fame and fortune. For James Theodore Phalen, that time has come.

The world knows Phalen as a bright, Harvard-educated, post-baby boom billionaire from rural Texas who has it all. What the world does not know is that he is at war with personal demons, struggling with childhood memories of his strict, uncompromising, God-fearing father, and facing a tragedy he could never have imagined. He is also harboring a secret he can no longer contain.

More titles by Gene Cartwright

In Her First Life
Half Moon, Full Heart
The Widowmaker
Fire Night
Dying for Love
The Promise Road
The Drammen Code
The Water Line
The Value of Small Things (non-fiction)
Staying Alive: A Woman's Essential Guide to Living Safely (non-fiction)
Quietkill
Still Dreaming
Nowhere, Texas

Forthcoming

The God War
Harold
Edenland

Dedication

To my loving father Elmer, who more than a half-century ago, following only two months of courtship, had the great wisdom and enormous good fortune to marry my sainted mother, Marie. If there are angels in heaven, they are now amongst them.

Forethought

I am almost certain I recall the moment of my birth, though mercifully not in scarlet detail. I have thought about this a lot. For as long as I can remember, I have recalled the sensation of suddenly emerging from a world of muffled sounds and comforting darkness into one of offending noise and unbearable light. What else could it be, except the moment of my birth?

The days and months immediately following my traumatic arrival are blank, and ages one and two remain a swirling blur. However, I have a reliable recollection of ages three onward. I especially remember age seven. It was then my simple, Leave It to Beaver life, and my simplistic view of the world changed for all time.

A Poem for My Father

My Father's Son

WHO AM I?
I am my mother's child,
plucked from her womb, bathed in her blood,
wrapped in her warm love, unending.
I am the tree planted by the river's edge.
I am a jewel in the crown of all creation.
I am my mother's child.
But I am my father's son.

WHO AM I?
I am my mother's child,
nurtured from her breasts, cloaked with her care,
soothed by her sweet voice, unfailing.
I am a seed sown deep in rich, black sod.
I am the rich harvest of past generations.
I am my mother's child.
But I am my father's son.

When I have walked in dark, foreboding places
and stood in danger's path, my mother's calming voice
comes to me on the wings of the wind and I am at peace.

WHO AM I?
I am my father's hope,
born in his shadow, held in his grip,
heir to his iron will, unbending.

I am either a force for good or a tool for evil.
I will regale in praise or suffer damnation
I am my mother's child.
But I am my father's son.

WHO AM I?
I am my father's hope,
keeper of dreams he yet dreams,
imbued with his faith, affirming.
I am the rainbow arching over green meadows.
I am day unmasked by the sun's revelation.
I am my mother's child.
But I am my father's son.

When I have walked in dark, foreboding places
and stood in harm's way, father's silent strength
comes to me like quiet thunder—and I am not afraid.

WHO AM I?
I am my mother's child.
But I am my father's son.
Yes, I am my mother's child.
But, I am my father's son.

Rosedale, Texas

July 6, 1960

Chapter One

I Remember

"Dear God, I am only seven, but I have already decided what I am going to be, and what I am not going to be. The rest is up to you and me, but mostly you."

On the day I turned seven, my world became a different place. Instead of making wishes and blowing out candles, I closed my eyes and made two solemn vows. One was to someday become a major league baseball player; the other was to never be poor. Even then, I knew have was better than have not. While my first vow was the stuff of every boy's dream, my second was born of a tragedy I still wish I could forget.

During the night before, a transient family, apparently seeking shelter, trespassed onto the abandoned Devereaux farm, about four miles from ours. In the early morning hours, an oil lamp fire raced through the dilapidated structure burning it to its frame. Everyone inside perished in the raging inferno.

Authorities reported finding the charred remains of a man, woman, and three children huddled inside, only five feet from the front door. They came so close to getting out. Tragically, it appeared thick, choking smoke obscured the main escape route and overtook them.

The stunning news was delivered to us by a neighbor, Mr. Jules Stimpe, at about 8 am that morning. Our family of five had just finished downing a Texas-sized, country breakfast of ham, eggs, grits, hash browns, and homemade biscuits. I was looking forward to later opening gifts, blowing out candles, and stuffing myself with five-layer, double chocolate birthday cake.

Normally, we Phalen kids would have been ushered from the room before grownups began *serious* talking. But everything happened so quickly. An emotional Mr. Stimpe, winded and wild-eyed, blurted out the jarring words, the minute he bolted through the front door.

"Y'all heard, yet?" He yelled out. "Y'all heard?"

We all gazed at each other with wonderment. None of us had any idea what he was squawking about. Before anyone could ask what he meant, Mr. Stimpe continued apace, gesturing frantically. His plate glass-thick eyeglasses tumbled from his bearded face, saved only by his ample midsection. He seemed about to burst with whatever it was he was trying to say.

"The ol' Devereaux place caught fire, last night!" He said. "Five people burned up inside the main house; man, woman, three kids, they think. Hard to tell. God help 'em." His voice cracked.

"Oh, my god!" Mother shrieked, thrusting both hands to her flushed face. That did not slow Mr. Stimpe one bit. He kept right on going, nonstop.

"Poor folks didn't have a chance in the world. Probably just put up there for the night, I reckon. No 'lectric or nothing up there. They think an 'ol oil lamp was the cause of it. Likely found it in the barn. Used it to eat by and all," he said.

My heart leaped to my throat. I felt it thumping so fast it scared me. I knew what I had heard, but it just...it just did not seem real to me. It was so incredible. What added to the weight of the moment was Mr. Stimpe himself. Here was a somber man—a church elder and all—normally so slow and deliberate, he was the butt of jokes amongst some of us kids. We called him Mr. Mo, short for molasses. Now here he was pacing in our living room, tripping over his words and waving his arms around.

"You saying they all dead? You know that for sure?" Father asked, hoping there was some mistake. He drew to within inches of his friend.

"There is no mistake, J.Q.," said Mr. Stimpe. "I wish there was. God knows I wish there was."

A long, pained silence followed.

"Think they were anybody we know—anybody from around here?" Father asked. Mr. Stimpe shook his head several times.

"No, don't think they was from roun' these parts. From what I hear, an ol' beat-up car with Okie plates was found parked outside."

I knew father frowned upon use of the term, Okie. He sighed a bit, but let it ride this time. This heart-wrenching news had our rapt attention. We were all struck dumb by it. Seeing mother so emotionally overwrought brought tears to my own eyes. I had never seen her this way. I did not know what to think.

Mr. Stimpe rambled on. Father kept trying to get him to slow down; had him take a deep breath, repeat everything more slowly. It was only after he had stopped to take the much-needed breath, that mother noted we were still in the room. By then, it was too late to have us leave. We had heard everything.

I am not sure when I found my voice or was able to stir from where I stood. I do know I instantly lost my appetite and could not eat at all the rest of the day. Mother just stood there in the middle of the living room. I can still see her, especially her eyes. Tears streamed down her face. She shook her head from side to side, mumbling something I could not quite make out. Whatever it was, she kept saying it over and over again—some mournful mantra, as I recall.

I found it impossible to even imagine the terrible thing we had heard described. My big brother, Carter, and I wondered aloud how something so awful could happen to real people. I trembled, just thinking how much this poor family, especially the children, must have suffered. Carter and my sister, Rosie, both older and slightly more composed, tried to comfort me as best they could. Truth is, we were all awash in tears.

As soon as Mr. Stimpe left, a somber father summoned us all into the living room. Neither he nor mother thought it necessary or had the presence of mind to explain to us the horror we had just learned about. I had so many questions but held them inside. I was not sure I fully understood the reality of human death. Of course, I had seen dead farm animals, but I had never seen anyone cry over them.

Father stood near the large bay window and read several scriptures. Moments later, we all prayed for the deceased family. We did not know them, but that did not matter. Afterward, mother gave us all especially long and powerful hugs. Her salty tears fell on my upturned face. I remember her chest heaved with every sob, while she held us close to her. She seemed reluctant to let go.

Father did not say much. After praying, he strode out onto the long front porch, lingered there for a time, gazing in the direction of the Devereaux place. I quickly followed and stood a couple of steps behind him, shrouded in his shadow. I recall seeing a dark, smoky haze in the distance and remember the acrid smell of smoke that hung heavy in the morning air. Aware of my presence, father turned to me and noted my pained expression.

"Go on back inside, son," he said. "Go on."

"Can I stay here with you?" I asked.

"Got things to do directly," he said. "Stay here with your mother. I'll have some of your birthday cake when I get back. Go on, now."

"Where you going?"

"Can't go with me this time, son."

"How come?" I asked him. "I won't get in the way."

Father gazed down at me, tousled my hair with his right hand, and again insisted I go back inside. That was not what I wanted to hear. I felt so safe, standing next to him, hearing the rumble of his deep voice, feeling the protection of his towering presence. I did not want to leave his side.

A half-hour later, Mr. Noah Peetson, another neighbor and a reserve deputy sheriff, pulled up in his prized, black Packard automobile and honked twice. I was not at all happy to see him. I even tried to wish him away, without success. Father soon left with him, after whispering something to mother and planting a gentle kiss on her forehead. I assumed he and Mr. Peetson were headed to the Devereaux place, to see the destruction for themselves.

Moments later, a strangling, suffocating feeling engulfed me. I could not stand being inside the house. My breathing became labored; beads of prickly sweat covered my brow. It seemed the four walls were closing in on me. Carter must have noticed my distress. He turned toward me, caught my eye, and nodded for me to follow him. I did.

The two of us hurried through our rambling ranch-style house and onto the back porch. We bounded down the steps and struck out across rolling, green fields, toward the towering 'Man O' War' oak tree, on top of Heritage Hill. That is where we always went when no place else seemed big enough.

There was a very personal reason for the depth of my sadness. Purely by chance, I had seen that family the day before, while in town with father. They were riding in a clanking, smoking, 1954 Desoto bearing Oklahoma license plates. The old car was the only family possession to survive the flames, unscathed.

I recalled the soiled faces of three children: two girls and a boy, peering out of the car at ogling townspeople, including me. We glared back at them, as they chugged through town. The young boy appeared to be about my age. He seemed saddest of all. In spite of only a fleeting glimpse, there was something about his eyes that struck me; they were distant yet piercing. His stiletto gaze seemed to slice right through me. My connection with him was instant and eternal.

I stood in front of Stoddard's Five & Dime, staring, as they limped out of town. Nauseating smoke spewed from the rickety old car's dangling exhausts. It made a god-awful noise, drawing derisive laughter from some. I was sure they did not feel welcome to stop. If only I had smiled, I later thought, or given a friendly wave.

Carter and I reached the old oak and stood there in stony silence. There was little need for words. I wondered about the boy. What was his name? What kind of life had he lived? Did he like chocolate cake? Did he have friends—great friends like mine? Of course, no one else could possibly have had friends quite like Duncan Stoddard, Peetie Simpson, Jed Stimpe, Iggy Davenport, Twenty-one Smith, and the rest of the guys.

Had this boy ever gone fishing, jumped logs, skipped rocks, picked wild berries in summer, or played baseball? I prayed he had at least experienced the latter. It would have been a shame to die never having played baseball.

For months thereafter, my nights were filled with recurring dreams, not nightmares, but dreams filled with images of this family. In those dreams, everything always turned out differently. Everyone survived. They were all able to escape the flames, scramble into their old car and flee to our farm.

In my dream, we took them into our home, fed them, gave them new clothing. After a few weeks, with their old car repaired, the family left for Dallas, where the father had been offered a job. The day they left, the boy and I exchanged baseball gloves and promised to stay in touch. Then, I would always awaken, just as they were driving away. I would sit up with a start and realize it was all a dream. That always saddened me, because I wanted it to be real, not some silly dream.

One night, I awoke to find mother standing by my bed gazing down at me. Apparently, my fitful sleeping and my crying out during the dream had awakened her.

"What's wrong, James? What's wrong?" I remember her asking. Surprised to see her standing there, I did not answer right away. Mother moved closer. Coaxing me from bed and taking me by my hand, she led me into the kitchen. There, she poured me a glass of milk then sat stroking my face and watching me drink.

"It's the fire, isn't it," she said.

I glanced up quickly. She knew. I had not told anyone about how I felt, but somehow, she knew. "Yes," I whispered. "Yes."

"I figured as much. You haven't been the same, since all this happened. You haven't been my same little baby boy," mother said.

"I am not a baby, mom," I protested mildly.

"You will always be my baby," she said, smiling. "But I have a feeling there is more to all this—more than the fire. Listen son, you can tell me anything. Mother understands. And it's alright to feel whatever it is you're feeling inside. I'm sad too. We all are. I want you to know you can tell me whatever is troubling you. Don't hold it inside."

I insisted there was nothing more, but mother knew better. Call it intuition or whatever, but she had a sixth sense when it came to things like that. Finally, with her gentle insistence, I told her all about seeing the family in town the day before they died. I told her about my dreams and we both cried. Mother put her arms around me and assured me I had nothing to feel guilty about; that I was in no way responsible for the insensitive actions of stupid adults.

A half hour later, I was much calmer. I even finished the milk, except for a swallow or two. I could never drink a full glass of anything, even to this day. Just as we were about to leave the kitchen, we heard father stirring. I jumped to my feet and wiped my eyes.

"Mom, please don't tell father about any of this. You have to promise," I said. "You have to."

"Why, son?" She asked.

I swallowed hard, trying to think of some way to avoid answering. Mother waited patiently, pinning me with her gaze.

"I don't want father to know I was crying about it. I don't want him to think I'm still a kid, 'cause I'm not. I'm seven, now. I'll be a man, soon. And men don't cry like children. Daddy never cries. Only babies and sissies cry," I said, using a term that now makes me cringe.

Mother appeared stunned, taken aback by my wordy response. I even surprised myself. She gripped my hand and stared into my eyes. Before she could say anything, I darted for my room as fast as I could. The subject never came up again.

To this day, thirty-five years later, the vivid memory of July 6, 1960, haunts me. Every single birthday I have had since has reminded me of that fateful morning. Saddest of all, no one ever claimed the remains or reported such a family missing. Dental records were never located. How was it possible a family of five could perish and not be missed by someone? It was as if they never existed.

Three weeks later, it was discovered the car they were driving had been abandoned a year earlier by its Tulsa owner. Exactly one month after the fire, all were buried together in a single, Crawford County, pauper's grave. Father read a brief passage of scripture. Elder Johannsen prayed. Mother and Mrs. Stimpe placed flowers next to the simple marker, which read:

A FAMILY THAT LIVED AND DIED TOGETHER.
JULY 6, 1960

So, even as I celebrated my seventh birthday, grieved, and shed tears for members of a family whose names I never knew, I made my two vows. Despite my youth, it was clear to me, had this family not been poor and homeless, their fate would likely have been much different. They would not have been at the old Devereaux place.

As traumatic as this experience was for me, it was atypical of the normally predictable, carefree, storybook realities of my small-town life. I suppose that is why it made such an indelible impression upon me. I felt forever bound to this family. And it was by no means the only tragedy I credit with altering my view of life.

In 1994, while I sat in my World Trade Center offices, a stunning event, which I will detail later, cemented a decision that altered the course of my life. The winding path leading me to that pivotal decision was fraught with numerous twists and turns. Many events combined to force me to face the truth about my past and myself. I had no idea such a journey lay before me.

To explain it all, I have to go back to those innocent, memory-filled days spent as a child. I often wonder how I got here. How did New York City become my home, my throne-room, my gulag? Before I answer these and other questions, there are many things you should know about me.

For an impressionable seven-year-old, the horror at the old Devereaux farm presented a powerful lesson in life and death. For the first time, I realized just how fortunate I was. I even looked at Carter and Rosie in a more endearing way. The experience also foisted upon me an awareness of the terrible effects poverty can have on the life-choices the poor are forced to make.

I began wondering how and who decides to whom one is born. Who determines which of us begins life rich or poor, healthy, or infirmed? It all seemed such a toss of the dice. I could have been that boy. I could have been any boy—even a girl, for godsakes. I could have had entirely different parents. Only I would not have known I was someone else. That was the jumbled way I thought about it, then.

In my small, north-central Texas hometown of Rosedale, I saw the pity and scorn some heaped upon poor people. I witnessed their piteous struggle for esteem. They always seemed so...so sad, so isolated, even shunned. I also learned of the poverty suffered more than a generation earlier by my own family. I wanted no part of it.

With divine intervention, I have at least kept one of those vows made thirty-five years ago, long before experiencing the onslaught of fame, fortune, and heady publicity. My journey to success has been an amazing ride. I have basked in the notoriety; the celebrity status; the peer praise; but enough is enough. I am no longer flattered being constantly referred to as one of America's wealthiest men, although it is true. I now cringe at the very sound of those words.

So, I will state for the record, I am a rich man—a very rich man able to satisfy virtually any material desire. Being a humble farm boy, from rural Texas, I cannot describe the feeling of awe, and the sense of responsibility, the realization inflicts upon me. I do not overstate when I say this success has exacted a significant price, as you will learn.

Despite the temptation these days for the media to reduce every issue to sound bites, every public figure to simplistic caricature, there is more to me than the numbers used to define me and quantify my wealth.

In 1993, President Clinton named me, and a dozen others to a panel invited to the White House to discuss budget and economic issues. My first inclination was to decline the invitation. I did not relish the possibility of being drawn into partisan politics. However, I reluctantly agreed. After all, it is not every day that one gets a personal call from the President.

Shortly after arriving in Washington, D.C., my worst fears were realized. The moment I stepped into the Rose Garden, following our initial meeting, I was singled out for pummeling by the press. Amongst other things, they were bent on determining my party affiliation and my personal appraisal of the President's economic policies. One reporter even asked my views regarding Whitewater. I simply ignored him and recognized another eager inquisitor.

I was further bombarded with unrelenting questions about my personal wealth, not my ideas regarding the nation's economy.

"Mr. Phalen, is it true you recently made 800 million dollars in a single day, as the result of an international currency transaction? And how much do you give to charity, annually?"

"Mr. Phalen, has the President or his people approached you to contribute to his legal defense fund? And do you think he's been candid in response to the various allegations?"

"Mr. Phalen, how much did you pay in taxes last year, and may we see your personal returns?"

I was aghast. It was truly amazing to witness. How anyone can survive in such a shark-infested environment is beyond my understanding. I have no plans to show my face in Washington again anytime soon. I do not need it. You have to be a masochist, a lobbyist, a journalist, or a special prosecutor to survive in such an environment.

I have been fortunate to have a few great friends who help keep me humble and anchored to reality. With even the most modest of egos, it is sometimes difficult to not be personally affected by all the hype regarding one's own brilliance and well-doing. These are friends not impressed by my social standing or balance sheet. They can be and usually are brutally frank.

On a cold December 22 last year, I experienced lunch at the New York Ritz-Carlton, with just such a friend, Miss Melody Ann Melford—a remarkable woman. We met five years earlier when her red Jaguar she was driving clipped the rear bumper of my vehicle. Unfortunately, we were both trying to exit the driveway of the Ritz at the same time. She was ninety-eight then but exhibited the energy of a spirited sixty-year-old.

Miss Melody exited her car, wearing a blue, designer business suit, and approached the limo so quickly I hardly had time to get out. She assured me this was the first auto accident she had ever had and did not want to blemish her perfect driving record. Standing less than a foot from me, and staring into my eyes, she said if I was as nice as I was handsome, I would not call the police. What could I do? She was so charming and apologetic I was totally disarmed.

The memorable incident gave birth to a very warm and lasting friendship. I only wish I had met her years earlier. Sadly, Miss Melody died three weeks ago, at the tender age of 103. Her charm, her feistiness, her quick wit had no equal. She had doleful eyes that twinkled, possessed a knockdown sense of humor, and had chutzpah to spare.

During last year's lunch, I recall asking Miss Mel to what she attributed her long life, her youthful spirit, and her boundless energy. She did not miss a beat.

"Several things," she said with an elfish grin, easing her fingers through her elegant white hair and leaning closer to me. "For one thing, I never eat, drink, or put anything into my body that I wouldn't give a 10-year-old. That's one of the reasons I still have my own teeth," she boasted proudly.

"What about your occasional glass of wine?" I asked, displaying a wide grin and a "gotcha" look on my face.

"Mind your own business, Phalen," she said with a wink and feigned punch, "My wine is purely medicinal." I had no choice but to agree. "Second, I never worry about money at all," she said. "Never wanted so much of it as to have to stay awake nights trying to figure out how to keep it. And I have never lost the child in me. If the child in you ever dies, you are already dead as a doornail. It just takes a while for them to bury you."

That is what I meant by *experiencing* lunch with Miss Melody. She was a captivating spirit, a tireless spinner of tales, and a self-described admirer of healthy young men. And although she had buried three husbands, she insisted on being called Miss.

Miss Melody declared each husband was special. However, her one complaint was that she was yet to find a man who could match her IQ, creativity, and physical stamina. The latter she boasted with a sly wink and naughty smile. I did not ask what she meant. I feared she would tell me.

Miss Melody's views about money and the way it colors life, forced me to think seriously about my own rewarding, yet often harried existence. Do not misunderstand; I never considered taking a vow of poverty. I simply reflected upon her passionately held views. It was impossible to ignore anything she said, especially when she clutched your hand, leaned into your face, and shook her finger at you.

Some mornings, I lie awake in the master bedroom of my Park Avenue apartment, gaze up at the muraled, ten-foot ceiling, and wonder if I have been fantasizing about my success. I say success because I draw a clear distinction between success and wealth. I believe one can be successful and not be especially wealthy. However, I am blessed to be both.

Do not be put off by my candor. I am no braggart. To the contrary, I am humbled, just being able to honestly make such statements. When I was eight or nine years old, father read a passage of the bible to me that said:

"It is easier for a camel to pass through the eye of a needle than for a rich man to enter heaven."

After hearing this, I wondered just what was so wrong—so inherently evil about wealth. Should I not aspire to be rich, so my odds of entering through the Pearly Gates would not be diminished? Was I to understand the only virtuous people were the poor, who somehow tended to lead more righteous and circumspect lives? I think not. The more I have lived and observed many peoples, the more I have come to see that sin and evil are not exclusive to the privileged class.

I now understand the passage father quoted suggests the rich tend to have more faith in themselves and their money, and less in the Almighty. Father said they preferred having their heaven here and now, rather than in some sweet by and by. I concluded if that were true, then poor people must be suffering their hell here on earth, and therefore inclined to believe their heaven would come later—a deferred plan of sorts.

Regarding my own wealth, while I am not exactly a Bill Gates or a Warren Buffett, if I never earn another dime and happen to live a thousand years, my lifestyle will not suffer. I realize I am living an incredible dream afforded few.

Notwithstanding all this, I remain astonished at the wealth existing in this country. I marvel at the opportunities to accumulate great wealth for those, who either by circumstance of birth, good fortune, or dint of will, get to play the game. And believe me, the frenetic drive for success and fortune can be a deadly, high-stakes game—a war, with battlefields strewn with casualties.

For me, getting into the game certainly was not due to the circumstances of my birth, unless you count the limitless love I inherited, and I do. All I have is a product of great luck, very hard work, a fearless spirit, and my reliance on faith infused in me by my parents. I confess this reliance on faith has tended to both soar and crash over these years, yet it remains an integral part of my life.

Still, I often ask: "Why me? Why have I been so fortunate? Why not the homeless people standing on street corners begging for spare change? Why not millions of others who are smart, work hard, pay their taxes, and barely make ends meet?"

Again, I do not mention my wealth to boast. So please do not think me lacking in modesty; there is a point to my belaboring the fact. I know there are extremes of wealth and poverty still existing in America. I do much to help those who are less fortunate. Because of the values my parents instilled in me, I feel a deep sense of responsibility to be a good steward of all I possess.

Yet, in one significant respect, I too am a poor man. I say that, because despite my finances, despite the honors, the peer praise, the ego-stroking, and things used to keep score, I cannot purchase at any price the one experience lacking in my otherwise enviable childhood—a playful moment with my father. I cannot recall a single one. And believe me, I have tried, stopping just short of inventing such a recollection.

This may strike you as odd, perhaps incredulous, but for such a moment, I would gladly pay a million, a hundred million dollars. I would pay any amount. After all, what value should one place on such priceless memories, which I believe help form the foundation of genuine happiness? I can always make more money.

Still, I am only a man—a mere mortal. And like you, I am unable to capture lost moments or alter the past in any way. I wish I could. I have to laugh when I hear some call me powerful. I am not taken in by that hackneyed characterization. By powerful, they simply mean I am filthy rich. I detest the moniker. It suggests I am who I am, solely because of limitless financial resources that alone grant me this so-called power.

Filthy rich or powerful or not, it is regarding the absence of certain childhood memories that my perceived power fails me. All my influence, all my successes, all my ability to control people and events do not matter one whit. I cannot summon to mind memories of events that never occurred. I cannot rewrite the history of my childhood, to fill in the missing pages with moments I only wish I had known. I cannot turn back the clock and change the fact that...I never played catch with my father.

Even as I write these words, I find myself wishing the truth were different. Unhappily, it is not. Although baseball was my all-consuming childhood passion, I never experienced the joy of sharing it with father. It is surprising, but of all the things in my life that could matter to me, this seemingly insignificant fact most defines my disappointment, quantifies my poverty.

While I truly miss not experiencing this hallmark event with father, my regret goes far beyond not having tossed some ball back and forth with him. There is much more to it than that. The fact we never did typifies the absence of a deep heart and soul connection so vital to fathers and sons. Neither wealth nor success is a substitute. This bond is irreplaceable.

So, when people make erroneous assumptions about me, analyze me, probe my life, and wrongly conclude I have it all, they are wrong. What does "having it all" really mean anyway? Whoever really has it all?

When I was growing up, I frequently felt the sting of disappointment, whenever father chose to do more important things. At the time, I had no idea these and other fatherly absences and omissions would come to mean so much to me. I simply accepted the realities.

Kids seldom forget things that truly matter to them. If you are a parent, ask yourself which you would most regret in twenty years: missing another boring meeting or not witnessing the look of ecstasy on your kid's face when he or she spots you at a school play or little league game?

Should I publish this book, I realize some will read the foregoing paragraphs and think: How dare this rich WASP complain about such trivial, personal matters, when countless poor kids are doomed to live in urban squalor never even knowing their fathers.

I understand the cynicism. However, all things are relative to individual circumstances. Of course, my own disappointments pale when compared to hunger, homelessness, Aids, and other regrettable human conditions. It is because of my own experiences and awareness of my blessings, that I spend money and time trying to improve the lives of kids and adults in New York and elsewhere.

I refuse to be branded with guilt for having enormous wealth. I make no apology for my success and reject personal responsibility for elevating all unfortunate souls. I recognize that like others, some wealthy people can be insensitive and disgusting. I have even met and on occasion associated with some of these people.

However, beating up on the rich seems to have evolved into some sort of blood sport in this country. I for one refuse to be a casualty. My broad-based philanthropy speaks for itself. Besides, I would much rather be my brother's employer than *my* brother's keeper.

Forgive me for sounding my own siren. In some respects, I feel I am debating myself. That is not my intent. I am whom I am, as cliché as that sounds. The horror stories of others do not diminish my disappointment, regarding experiences many consider rites of passage. It is no trivial matter to me.

However, I am perplexed that at this stage of my life this still weighs so heavily upon me. Surely by now, all this would have long ago faded into the foggy domain of lesser things. Yet, it is seldom far from the surface. It evokes deep sadness; a feeling of eternal loss, not anger. I feel that loss, each time I see a father tossing a ball toward the outstretched hands of a young son eager to prove himself his dad's equal.

Whenever I catch a game at Yankee Stadium, I nearly always spot a beaming father and his hotdog toting young son. They are often outfitted in Yankee caps, pinstripe jerseys, carrying gloves and determined to bag that elusive foul ball.

On the heels of an exciting play, the father leans over and explains what happened, in details that would put Vin Scully or Harry Carrey to shame. That is what I mean, when I refer to lasting memories that help form a solid foundation for life.

I sit there, my mind goes back, and I could not care less about the bulls and bears of Wall Street. A lump forms in my throat; my eyes grow moist, and, for a time, I am no longer aware of what is happening on the field.

For a moment, I indulge myself. I imagine I am that young boy, that the man is my father, the moment belongs to us, and the experience is ours to share for a lifetime. It is all quite real to me. And though I feel I am an intruder; I permit myself to bask in the warmth of that delusion for only a moment—a fleeting moment.

My name is James T. Phalen, and I find myself at a crossroads. A perplexing change is enveloping my life and, frankly, I do not feel so damn powerful and in control. Where is all the invincibility others have attributed to me?

I have come to a time and a place in my life where the road long traveled seems dark, twisted, even impassable. Certainty has become uncertainty. Supreme confidence threatens to succumb to debilitating doubt. This is not like me. This is not the world I know. Worst of all, is the feeling of not being in complete control.

This kind of affliction can strike anyone; rich, poor, black, white, brown—anyone. No one is immune. It is seldom something that happens abruptly. There are no lightning bolts, no big bangs, no earthquakes. It happens subtly. One day, everything seems to swirl around you, even as you are standing still.

Why is this happening to me? Perhaps all this introspection is a result of my being forty-plus, advancing through middle age, and facing questions of life and death. Perhaps.

One day, one awakens to find the old notions and familiar landmarks have somehow shifted, or disappeared altogether, and no one bothered to tell you. The old rules no longer serve to guide or direct. Long-held, once revered assumptions and perceptions of what is important, of what gives meaning to life are no longer enough.

When the mask that often adorns us all is stripped away, we are left naked—left to discover we have perhaps never really known ourselves, let alone anyone else. Such self-appraisal does not come easily. It can be scary.

Having wallowed for so long in a world of greed and self-fulfillment, I had grown to think myself immune to such emotional mumbo jumbo about time and place and roads long traveled. It seemed a bit too esoteric for me. As long as I had my cellphone, my fax machine, my computer, my Gulf Stream Jet, my motorcar, my money, my credit cards, and myself, what else could I possibly require? You may say I was self-consumed.

Forget all this New Age, self-god crap hyper-promoted by self-anointed gurus preaching auto-evaluation, while hawking fake crystals on home shopping networks. I was already focused inward. I did not need some spiritual imposter taking my money; in return for convincing me I was my own center.

I riveted my focus on the big, shiny, gold ring; forget brass. And when my goal was reached, my focus was fixed on the next one and the next one. I kept moving. One thing was certain; I would not die in place; no standing still and offering the grim reaper no challenge whatsoever.

Success became a fix, as addicting as heroin or crack, only without the social stigma. Indeed, our society celebrates and even demands such success. Failure (anything below first place) is not tolerated in America. If you doubt this, tell me where I can find all those monuments erected in adoration of General George Armstrong Custer's silver medal-winning finish.

Now, to my wonder, I am at a crossroads I had not expected to reach so soon, if at all. It is a place where fame and fortune are not enough. I find this circumstance painful, sobering. At times, I feel stupid acknowledging my difficulty explaining or coping with this. After all, I have been socialized to believe and to act as if men can, and should be able, to deal with anything.

More and more, I find myself brooding about life and death, about this complex and brutal world around me, and my place in it. So, what if I have amassed a trove of grownup toys, trinkets, and treasure? A hundred years from now, who will know or even care that I was here? What positive contribution will I have made? Why should I care?

The intoxicating elixir of attaining enormous personal success, the adrenaline rush that comes from playing the 'game' well, seems unable to satisfy me as before. I feel an emptiness that grows daily. Why is this?

In the midst of my day-to-day madness, I long for simpler times and at day's end am left with only my longing. More and more, I am drawn to lingering thoughts of my childhood, and those stilted, unresolved memories of father. But why has this surfaced now… why at all?

I am under no illusion. I am no writer—no professional writer. I have no intent of trying to pen a 700-page encyclopedia of my life. What follows is simply an open letter to me and to father, whose watchful gaze I still feel upon me. After all these years, I feel the undeniable urge to move beyond private thoughts and whispers, to speak aloud, even if only to me. I feel a need to empty my overflowing heart; something I have never taken the time to do before. It never seemed manly enough, not enough coarseness, danger, sweat, derring-do, grit, grime, and Lava soap.

I have always felt that if I ever took the time to write, it would be about Wall Street. I would likely pen some exposé with sordid details of shameless acts committed by seedy characters with choirboy facades, thousand-dollar suits, respectable titles, pricey European motorcars, and tastes for fine wine and women with first names only. However, here I am turning the probe inward. It is long overdue.

Look, I was not always the person I am today. I had a wonderful childhood, despite the few though lasting regrets. I had a life, long before this. I had joy and sadness, laughter, and tears, just like you. Who I am now, both public and private, is a result of that life and that childhood.

While I would be happy, if this book strikes a resonant chord with millions of readers and makes me a best-selling author, that is not my primary goal. I would write this book even if I was the only person on earth.

If I am lucky, writing this book will help me resolve lingering questions about my childhood. Heaven knows I could use that, because I have been in denial regarding aspects of my past. I have long realized I held a view of father not clear or wholly endearing. To escape confronting these realities, I have maintained a state of perpetual motion, not permitting myself more than a moment to pause and reflect, until now.

Chapter Two

Father

Understand one thing: I truly loved father. John Quincy Phalen was a man unlike any I have known. Nothing about him was the least bit ordinary. His stature was imposing; his countenance fear-inspiring, his voice like thunder summoned on command. Adults forget what it is like to be three feet tall, straining to peer up at someone more than twice as tall and upset by something you have done. The word intimidating comes to mind.

Father's eyebrows were so thick they sometimes cast their own shadows on his stoic face. This produced an even darker and more brooding expression than customary; at least it seemed so to me then. I would not say I was afraid of him, but on the rare occasion when he smiled at me, I felt great relief and wondered what I had done right, so I could do it again in exactly the same manner.

Father was not a man to trifle with. He could simply stare at me disapprovingly and my heart would race. I wanted to please him and felt bad and frightened, whenever I angered him. That was true of Carter and Rosie, as well. Often, mother would intervene, stepping in and attempting to deflect father's wrath with a lighthearted comment. Sometimes it worked; frequently it did not.

It was shortly after an occasion where father found it necessary to both scold and take his leather belt to me, that I began having this recurring nightmare. The very thought of it still makes me recoil slightly. I was not sure why it began. I refer to it as my never-ending dream. It occurs still.

The dream is strange for many reasons; not the least of which is the fact it finds me in a small city, not a wisp of a town like Rosedale. I know it is I in the dream, though I feel I am a composite of several entities. That feeling persists until the end when I have no doubt the 10-year-old boy being frightened to death is me.

It all starts shortly after midnight, in a modest, but declining middle-class neighborhood shrouded in dense fog. I find myself on a quiet, empty street lined with quaint little houses, barely visible to me. Every living thing seems either asleep or vanished, except for me.

I move slowly along the damp, uneven sidewalk, fighting the fright swelling inside me. In the poor light, my feet are hardly visible. Despite my attempts to soften their impact, my steps reverberate in the thick, moist, night air. I do not know why, but it always begins at this exact spot. The haunting feeling of being completely alone is overwhelming.

Our family lives at the far end of this street in an old white house surrounded by a chain-link fence. The rickety gate makes a squeaky noise whenever it opens and closes. In my dream, the house is always completely dark inside. However, from the front porch, I can always make out the faint sound of laughter coming from the Jack Benny show on the radio. Strange.

I do not know where I am coming from—perhaps a friend's house. I do know I am starting for home much later than ordered. Father had made it clear he wanted me home before 10 o'clock. I have no doubt he will be waiting for me with his leather belt, ready to tan my hide. Clenching my jaws, I resolve to take it like a man, cover my sore butt with petroleum jelly and crawl into bed.

Above me, through the canopy of fog, I can make out the ghostly outline of a crescent moon. Using its scant light, I make my way along the narrow sidewalk, desperately trying to avoid stepping on the cracks. Someone told me stepping on cracks can break your mother's back, or some such childish silliness.

I figure I am halfway home when I am certain I hear footsteps behind me. They echo in the distance, so I quicken my pace. So do the footsteps and I freeze. I should start running right away, but I freeze. Just then, two more steps crash against the concrete and halt. My heart pounds against my chest walls. I am not imagining things after all. With trembling fists clenched, I glance quickly over my right shoulder and bolt ahead.

Immediately, the steps behind me are quicker than my own. This is not a good sign. Seeking to calm myself, I keep thinking I am being ridiculous, that there's nothing to be afraid of. I actually tell myself I am dreaming. It does not help. A shudder courses my spine and I shake, as a thousand horrible scenarios invade my consciousness. Flush with contrition, I wish with all my heart I was snuggled warmly and safely in my bed, but I am not.

My pulse soars. Instinctively, I break into a respectable trot and almost trip over a raised portion of sidewalk in front of an abandoned house. Fearing what may now inhabit the eerie place, I dare not even look toward the creepy structure. Recovering from my misstep, I race past, glancing anxiously over my shoulder into foggy nothingness. Who or what could be following me?

Whoever or whatever it is, my determined stalker seems right on my heels. I can almost feel its hot breath scorching my neck. I desperately want to wake up but cannot. Why can I not awaken? Any minute I expect to feel cold, clammy hands with topical veins and gnarled fingers reach out and sink long, pointed fingernails into my shoulders.

My fear explodes like a Roman candle, causing my eardrums to quake. Confessing to every past sin, I swear to never disobey father again, for as long as I live. "Just get me out of this," I mutter aloud. But I realize I have to first survive this ordeal, in order to honor this latest vow.

Finding the trot respectable but much too slow, I break into a full-fledged, no-holds-barred sprint—pride be damned. Within an interminable minute or so, I reach our gate, fumble briefly to open it, dash through, and slam it shut. The metal-on-metal clanks, echoing more loudly than ever before. It reverberates through the darkness, like a hammer striking an anvil.

I streak to the front porch and leap onto it, without touching the steps. Sweating profusely and trembling badly, I thrust my right hand into my front pocket. To my horror, I discover there is no key to the front door!

A throbbing lump fills my throat; I almost die. My fists feel like lead, as I pound the door. I can hardly lift my arms and my feeble effort barely makes a sound. Although I am beating as furiously as I can, my efforts seem futile.

Suddenly, the gate creaks open. "My god!" I think, "Please let this be a dream!" I command myself to wake up, but things only worsen. The panicked voice in my head screams at me to get off the porch, run to the rear and try opening the back door—anything.

Heeding the voice, I struggle to reach the end of the long porch. My feet feel like concrete blocks, but somehow, I keep moving. I leap to the ground and sprint toward the rear of the house, as fast as my legs can carry me.

All the while, I hear the demon and sense my would-be tormentor gaining on me. I hear its heavy breathing, its low guttural rumblings. An awful stench fills the thick air, stinging my nostrils. The ground shakes under its fearsome weight. This is a bit much for a ten-year old, I think. Why could I not just dream about baseball or something?

Just as I reach the corner of the house, I trip over a snarled water hose father asked me to put away the day before. Now, my disobedience is making it possible for this...this thing to gain on me. I start to stand and realize I have twisted my ankle badly. The pain is excruciating, but there is no time for self-pity. As the approaching footsteps grow ever louder, I grimace with pain; I grunt loudly, scramble to my faltering feet and manage to yank myself onto the back porch.

The front of my head aches fiercely and my mouth feels like parchment. I feel as if I am swallowing sand. In near panic, I try to say the Lord's Prayer but can hardly remember a word.

"Our fa..." is all I can manage to utter. Surely, I am being chased by the devil, his minions—all things evil. Where in the world am I? Why is this happening to me, I wonder.

With great fear and trembling, I finally reach the screen door and yank on it with all my waning strength. Despite my efforts, my tortured motion is slow and feeble. Still, I persist. Finally, the door gives way. It is not latched. "Thank God!" I whimper. Flinging open the door, I grasp the entry doorknob frantically. If it does not open, I am done for. It does open. Thank God!

In my panic to get inside, I collapse, exhausted, onto the cold, damp linoleum floor. From out of nowhere, a huge rat scampers across my forearm, bringing a shrill shriek from my cracked lips. Scrambling madly, I vault to my feet and immediately slam the door shut.

Sweat streams from my throbbing brow, as I labor to catch my breath. With my shaking body leaning against the wooden door, I clutch the inside knob with one hand and reach to turn the lock with my free hand. Cold, prickly sweat still covers my brow, but I dare not release the doorknob. My only hope is to lock the door as fast as I can. I know I only have seconds to act.

Then, without warning, this...thing crashes onto the back porch, causing the whole structure to shake violently. I have never known such fear in all my life. Seconds later, the doorknob begins turning in my tiny hand. There is no way I can counter this awesome force. There is no way I can hold off the inevitable. My nearly sapped strength is failing fast.

I try desperately to scream out to father, but scarcely a whimper escapes my lips. The horror gripping me is unimaginable. I nearly wet my pants. Suddenly, I feel the weight of someone, or some "thing" much larger and more powerful than I. Whatever it is, it is forcing the door open. I cannot hold it. My feet begin sliding backward on the slick, slimy floor. Summoning all the physical and mental strength I can muster, I give it everything I have, but it is not enough.

Then, just when I lose this battle of strength, I awaken, never knowing whom or what my demon is. It always ends this way. All I know is that in a few days or a few weeks, I will dream this dream again. And I will again awaken and wonder what it all means.

The only person I have ever told this dream is Rosie. That was more than thirty years ago. Now, a few million others will know of it. Rosie reasoned it all had to do with my fear of disobeying my father and my imagined punishment for those transgressions. She assured me it was just my overactive imagination gone berserk. Rosie was always so wise and insightful. I recently learned she, too, had her own private thoughts and fears, regarding father. Not long ago, she shared some of these with me.

Many years into my adulthood, I discovered I loved father in a way I could never have imagined as a child or young adult. Children tend to harbor unflattering views of their parents. They often see them as relics or dinosaurs, incapable of entertaining a single contemporary thought. Many seem to think their parents leaped feet first from their mothers' wombs directly into adulthood, bypassing childhood altogether. Some parents act as if that is true.

It gets worse, as kids become wizened teens brimming with newly acquired knowledge. Their jaundiced views of their parents give way to expressions of pity and resignation. They become convinced that what afflicts parents must surely be some untreatable disease warranting quarantine or worse.

I grew up near Waco, in bucolic Rosedale, Texas, where both city limit signs were practically on the same post. There were moments in my impetuous youth when I felt contempt and even scorn for father.

I recall sometimes being very angry with him and mumbling customized epithets under my hot breath. However, I had the good sense to make sure I was well out of his earshot, before displaying a single frown or uttering a single mutinous word. I cherished life and wanted to live as long as the Almighty permitted me.

Tell me, what boy, upset and angry with his father for reasons real and imagined, has not muttered cuss words, or even voiced momentary hatred for him? What young boy has not pounded the air with clenched fist, ground his teeth, and either wished himself three feet taller or his father three feet shorter or both? Not many, I am sure. And I was no different.

This did not happen frequently; yet recounting it here brings specific instances to mind. Still, I respected father. I honored him, and I definitely obeyed him. Father pointed out Ephesians Chapter 6, Verses 1-4 to us often enough:

Children obey your parents in the Lord for this is right. Honor your father and mother, which is the first commandment with a promise, that it may go well with you and that you may enjoy long life on the earth. Fathers, do not exasperate your children; instead bring them up in the training and instruction of the Lord. - NIV

Of course, when father read us the part about enjoying long life, that did it. We took that to mean, live forever. When you are a child, not only do you want to live forever, but you are also naive enough to really think you will. Besides, there was no reason to think anyone who could create heaven and earth would not be able to deliver on such a promise.

Father and I were products of very different times, separated by many, many years. He had grown up during the Great Depression. Father had seen the tragedy of economic devastation and human misery firsthand; he lived it, here in his beloved America.

In this land of plenty, death from the ravages of hunger became an ever-present occurrence. Painful complications from diseases resulting from severe malnutrition caused the death of father's oldest brother, Isaac. Father was devastated. He told mother that the day they buried my uncle, grandfather had to physically remove him from his brother's grave.

For more than 20 years, his grief-stricken mother and father blamed themselves, until their deaths only three days apart in 1953. I am saddened, when I think of the pain father surely felt, experiencing the deaths of both his parents within the same week. They died three weeks before I was born.

All this family history came from my mother. Father never once spoke about it. It must have had a profound and devastating impact upon him—turned him inward, made him more introspective, less inclined toward frivolity. I am sure that is when he lost his ability to smile.

I recall seeing a frayed, faded, black and white photograph of father's family: his parents and two brothers. It was taken by a young photographer who later became famous for his depression-era photos. His name escapes me now. I only saw it a couple of times, but that was plenty for me. I got the point.

Mother showed it to me when I was no more than seven or so. It gripped me like a vise. That is when I first came to understand and know the image of poverty and hunger in a personal way. It was there in father's face, in his eyes and in those of the others.

I recall complaining bitterly about having to eat a dinner of chicken, corn, and mashed potatoes two days in a row. Just imagine that. Today, such insensitivity on the part of a parent could land them in court or even worse, on a talk show.

Mother did not say a word. She went to her bedroom, returned with the photo, and handed it to me. Even now, I can still see those gaunt, pencil-thin images, the sunken cheeks, the deep-set eyes, the hopeless expressions, and the thousand-yard stares.

I looked at the youthful face of my father and imagined him to be about my age. It occurred to me that little boy would have given anything to have a heaping plate of chicken, mashed potatoes, and fresh corn. He would have eaten every morsel and sopped the gravy with the last bit of bread.

Father sat at the far end of the dining table, staring at his plate, and barely eating. He saw mother return with the photo. It must have spawned a horde of painful recollections. I felt so ashamed; I promptly gobbled down my dinner and asked for seconds. I never complained again—about dinner.

I have come to understand the Depression became a defining experience in father's life, as it did for millions of other Americans. It explained his rabid intolerance of wastefulness, his never taking prosperity for granted. Father always admonished us to not put more food on our plates than we could eat. That was one surefire way to incur his wrath. "All things, in moderation, son. If you want, you can always get more," he would say.

By comparison, I had only known plenty. I honestly cannot recall a single instance when we lacked anything we truly needed. We Phalens were by no means rich, but I never had to wonder where my next meal would come from, where I would sleep or if I would survive the week. If we did not wear shoes, it was not because we had no shoes to wear. In summer, we chose to go barefoot.

Several times a year, our church would sponsor a food and clothing drive for poor families in Crawford County. We would all donate something. Father and mother told us to give more than things we had outgrown, but to also select at least one item we cherished and give it cheerfully. That way, we would know the true joy and blessing of giving. I questioned the notion but obeyed, mustering as much cheerfulness as I could.

Furthermore, father fought in World War II, the war that was to have ended all wars. It did not. I grew up with the specter of my dying in Vietnam a very real possibility. That scared me to death. Anyone approaching draft age then, who claimed otherwise, was either lying, crazy, or both.

I remember many of my friends wishing they were old enough to go fight and kill some gooks. When I reminded them that as high school juniors, they would soon have their chance, their boyish bravado quickly faded into silence.

The Tet Offensive and other key battles made American flags scarce in Texas and almost every other State. On at least three occasions, flags lowered to half-staff honored Rosedale native sons who lost their lives in Vietnam.

The death of any Rosedale son affected the entire town. It was as if every family had lost a son—a son too young to vote, but not too young to die. You could see it in the faces of those you passed on the street—hear it in their wavering voices. It was inescapable.

As a young male, I felt as if a flaming arrow had landed at my own feet. Mother must have had those same dire thoughts. One look at her or any mother with young sons and you could see the fear in their eyes.

Further honor included the etching of the hero's name on a granite marker in the Town Square and the placement of his photo on the front page of the Rosedale Courier newspaper. Alongside the photo would appear the history of the young life. In all cases, there simply was too little history in the short life of a 19-year-old to take up much space.

During these painful episodes, a mournful mood descended upon Rosedale like a violent Texas rainstorm. The grief-stricken family began receiving visits from friends and neighbors. They were offered condolences and assurances their son died serving and protecting his country. I wondered if the family believed that. I also imagined my parents being informed of my own death, should I someday wind up face down in a Vietnam rice paddy.

In my junior year in high school, the nation's draft machinery was churning out raw recruits in a steady stream. I knew that short of obtaining a college deferment, my turn would come. I would have to put my life on hold and go off to war to defend what? My country or the macho sensibilities of lying politicians bent on erasing their mistakes with the blood and sinew of their young.

Thankfully, the war officially ended, four years after I graduated from high school. Many prayers were answered, though not soon enough for more than 58,000 Americans, and more than 2 million of the enemy and civilians. Had I not obtained the education deferment, I definitely would have been expected to volunteer.

You have to understand something. There was absolutely no hint of an antiwar movement in Rosedale. Not a chance. Bumper stickers reading: America: Love It or Leave It, were as plentiful as bumpers themselves, and as permanent as rifles in the windows of Cowboy Cadillacs—pickup trucks.

Anyone who did not share that view knew to keep his or her thoughts private. It is not that such a person needed fear being physically accosted. It is that they would have been unwelcome at the bank; the grocery store; the service station; the hardware store; the restaurant; the department store; the clothing store; the shoe store; the septic tank company, and the one funeral home, most likely.

Our heroes could not have been more different. Father's heroes were World War II Generals George S. Patton and President, Dwight D. Eisenhower. However, father later grew less enamored of Ike, following the President's speech warning of the evils of an unbridled military-industrial complex. He felt Ike had grown a little soft, after spending eight years in the White House and much of that time on golf courses. Yet, he hated to see the old warrior go.

Richard Nixon had not impressed father at all, either as Ike's Vice-President or as a man. I overheard him telling mother there was just something about the man he found unsettling. Even so, he seemed touched by the former President's recent death and the outpouring of sympathy for his daughters, Julie, and Tricia.

Father thought John Kennedy was too liberal. I heard him say Kennedy would likely try to change things too fast, especially in the South. Even then, I knew he was referring to African Americans, Blacks, Negroes—Colored, back then.

Father was by no means, a racist. Like most white people in the South, (I recognize most Texans do not like being lumped in with the rest of the South. It is not that they have anything against Southerners; they just see themselves as a breed apart.) I am sure father simply felt comfortable with the status quo.

Such a view was at best selfish and at worst insensitive. In all my childhood, I never heard him make a single disparaging remark about anyone. The handful of nonwhites—blacks and Mexicans—in the county stayed in their places and lived by the rules set for them. That was just the way of things, then.

There were no Negroes in our church or school, a fact I was aware of even during my young years. I had many questions then, but I mostly kept them to myself. I remember wondering if segregation existed in heaven and hell too. We gathered in our white churches to praise and worship what, a white God? I often speculate about what would have happened if a black family had walked into our church on a Sunday morning.

Mostly, I found myself thoroughly confused. Then I learned in school that Egypt was the cradle of civilization. I knew Egypt was in Africa and wondered about all the emphasis placed on the contributions of Europe and Europeans, to the exclusion of others.

As for the election, I am sure father voted in 1960, but to this day I have no idea for whom he voted. And he had no reaction to Kennedy's election that I can recall. Whether he liked it or not, JFK was the President and he respected that.

My heroes were former President Harry S. Truman, Elvis, and Stokely Carmichael. President Truman was bold and resolute, and Elvis represented youthful rebellion. But why Carmichael, of all people? Why a black, 60's radical whom many considered an antisocial rebel bent on destroying America? Well, I figured had I worn his shoes, I likely would have done the same things. He was resolute and showed no fear. I looked at people like him, H. Rap Brown, and others and thought it must have taken an awful lot of courage and anger to stand toe to toe with good ol' boys with badges, guns, and hemp rope.

During that period, it was very easy for the majority to narrow the argument to one of law and order vs. lawlessness and disorder. The British most likely made similar arguments back in the 1700s.

To this day, I wonder where my heretical thinking came from. I am not aware of anyone in Rosedale ever voicing remotely similar sentiments. I suppose I took seriously the Constitution and the notion that God created us all equal. No one bothered to tell me it was all theoretical.

Of course, I have never told anyone this before. Fair-haired young white boys were not and are not raised to think this way. And even if one dared harbor such thoughts, he certainly was not going to tell anyone on planet earth.

At the age of eight, I overheard a local merchant, in Rosedale, tell a customer there was only one thing worse than a nigger: a nigger lover. I cringed and stood still, over behind the canned food section. I am not certain they knew I was in the store until I walked up to the counter. Most likely, it would not have mattered if they had known. The men spoke and asked about father and all. I answered as politely and calmly as I could, paid for my half dozen Windmill cookies, and hurried out of the store. I told absolutely no one what I heard.

The experience savaged my lofty opinion of the merchant. This man was a member of our church and highly thought of. I remained silent. I did so because I did not relish accusing grownups—pillars of the community—of such behavior. Besides, I could not be certain his harsh words would have earned him condemnation by many in Rosedale. I reasoned, that if he felt this way, and the man he was speaking to seemed to share his view, there was a strong likelihood others did as well. Applying what I had learned from my years of faithful churchgoing and bible reading, I wondered if the merchant's comment referred to God as well. After all, father had taught us God loved us all.

Today, I confess I no longer have heroes. I suppose that is because I have seen so-called heroes up close and am all too familiar with us mortals, and our failings, including, or perhaps especially, my own. It is said we are products of our times. It is true. Father's life and his ideas were shaped by his parents, his childhood, his fears, his joys, his pain, his successes, his failures, his world—the whole of it. He was who he was. I often wonder if he turned out to be the person he truly wanted to be.

Whenever I see that famous car scene in the movie, On The Waterfront, where Marlon Brando is yelling and screaming to Rod Steiger about what he could have been, I think about father. I see Marlon Brando, but I hear father's booming voice.

Like him, I am a part of the bittersweet harvest reaped from seeds sown in my own generation. And what a generation that was and is. My generation either witnessed, produced, suffered from, or aided and abetted the birth, promulgation, and or the demise of the following: Rock N' Roll, Elvis, Jimi Hendrix, The Beatles, Little Richard, the Vietnam War, race hatred, the 1968 Democratic Convention in Chicago, the Alabama Church Bombings; the assassinations of Medgar Evers, John and Robert Kennedy, Martin Luther King, Jr., Chaney, Schwerner and Goodman, Viola Liuzzo; James Reeb; Haight-Ashbury, Kent State, Timothy Leary, Twiggy; Woodstock, the Black Panther Party, J. Edgar Hoover, Spiro T. Agnew, Richard Nixon, Tiny Tim, Laugh-In, Ed Sullivan, George Wallace, and many more, too numerous to mention, although I tried.

However, I have no right to neither boast nor complain. I am white, male, well educated, very successful, wealthy beyond dream, living in America, and free of prostate cancer. Contrary to opinions frequently voiced on talk shows, I am not part of an endangered species. We white males are not on the brink of extinction.

While I fully understand the individual plight of some of my mal-affected brethren, I blame those of us who kept silent in the past and enjoyed the spoils from past sins of our fathers. Now, after enjoying the whole pie for so long, many of us are indignant that others have the unmitigated gall to demand a slice. That attitude comes from being a member of what has always been an exclusive and protected species.

Back to the subject of heroes. I suppose my only real hero—the man I viewed as a giant capable of slaying all dragons, a man able to do all things—was father. And therein lies my dilemma. How could the man I love and respect, the man I revere, the man who was and is my only real hero also be responsible for creating a single disappointment that endures to this day?

I often wonder if father wanted children at all. Perhaps his fathering us was merely adherence to what he believed to be his Christian duty to replenish the earth. Perhaps he was only being obedient to the scripture or only suffered us as some atonement for earlier sins. Then again, perhaps I am making too much of the way father drew clear lines between himself, as a parent, and Rosie, Carter, and me, as children.

Chapter Three

Not My Father

(a year ago)

Having lived for more than forty years, I have arrived at that moment when one's parents belatedly take on an aura of sainthood. In retrospect, it seems mine possessed the wisdom of Solomon and the patience of Job. Normally, such a revised view results from having to rear one's own children. Although I have no children of my own, I have nevertheless come to view my parents in this way.

Sadly, I can no longer express to my father how I have come to view his strict, uncompromising parenting. My dear mother, Bonnie, assures me that somewhere just beneath his unfocused gaze, his frail, unsteady body wracked by a severe stroke, the father I knew still exists. Perhaps.

The fact is, I will never see that father again. I fear he is gone forever, and all that can be said to him, and understood by him, has been said and understood. This is not a fact I accept easily. It does not seem possible, that a day that once seemed an eternity away could have arrived so soon, and with such devastating impact. This is something that happens to other fathers, other families. You only read about these things; you never experience them personally.

All I have now are memories of the man father was. And I feel a deep sense of guilt for thinking of him in the past tense, while he remains clinically alive. I cannot help it. I now see him as two individuals: the man he was and the shadow of a man he has become. As painful as that is, I cannot escape the reality of his physical condition.

It is difficult to accept that the vibrant, energetic father of my youth can no longer feed himself, perform the simplest hygienic tasks, or control bodily functions. Father is also unable to consistently engage in meaningful conversation.

Seeing him this way is sheer torment. The picture is indelible. Even the deepest slumber offers me little refuge from the image seared into my mind. At times, I pretend it is not real, that father's condition is something I dreamed up in some horrible nightmare. However, it is all too real.

I will never forget it was 9:23 A.M., on a gloomy, overcast Tuesday two years ago. My secretary and friend Ruth Wiesenthal took the call and mother informed me father had been stricken. Ever since I have been a different person. The awful news brought that sinking feeling that hit me right in the pit of my stomach. It left me gasping for breath and feeling empty.

Any of you with elderly parents know the fear an unexpected phone call can bring, especially in the middle of the night. Although this call came early in the day, the look on Ruth's face told me it was not a call I would welcome. I did not.

Within eight hours of getting the call, I had canceled all appointments, ordered my jet readied, and flew to Houston's famed Medical Center and St. Luke's Hospital. I had father flown there, after doctors in nearby Summers County and in Waco determined they could do little for him.

Mother was devastated. Every conversation I had with her was emotional and tearful. She kept saying father had been fine, until the very moment the stroke occurred, within minutes of his lying down to take a short nap.

Earlier that morning, father had repaired a section of fence just east of Heritage Hill and had not complained of any discomfort. One instant all was well. In the very next breath, he fell stricken.

Choking back my own emotion, I struggled to assure mother that father would be alright. I reminded her of his tenacity—his iron will. I spoke boldly as if I had the full faith and credit of God Almighty behind me. Yet, my words sounded impotent, even to me.

After I hung up the phone, I just stood there numbed, gazing blankly out of the window into endless nothingness, wondering when I would awaken. I summoned a tearful prayer to my parched lips, even as I doubted God would listen to me.

I arrived at Houston Intercontinental Airport and went directly to the hospital on Holcombe Boulevard. My older and only sister, Rosie, arrived the day before. She shared a suite with mother at the Sheraton Grande Hotel in the Post Oak area. Rosie had taken leave of her position as Principal at a Dallas elementary school. Rosie's second husband, Robert, an Executive Vice-President of one of H. Ross Perot's companies, remained in Dallas with their 5-year-old son Robert, Jr.

For the time being, Carter stayed on in Rosedale to look after the farm and his Chevrolet/GMC dealership I had finally persuaded him to let me purchase for him. Having long since made his peace with a tragic event in his life, Carter had readjusted, gotten married, and was father of a 2-year-old son, William. He was enjoying life.

The second I entered St. Luke's front doors a pall came over me. I truly hate hospitals. I have always, and perhaps unfairly, viewed them as way stations dotting the highway en route to the grave. I have improved my view, as I have gotten older and more likely to have some need of their services.

It did not take long to reach father's hospital wing. Rosie and mother decided to wait in the modest but comfortable waiting room at the end of the corridor. I took the long walk to father's room alone. My mind was awhirl with fear and dread, regarding what I would find.

One of the most difficult things I have ever done was enter the eerie stillness, the disturbing coolness, and the unnatural whiteness of father's room. The silence was broken by the creak of the door closing, and the faint mechanical whirl of equipment keeping father's condition stable. Digital readouts on the various bio-electronic devices produced a ghostly glow.

There was father—prone, silent, very still—his head heavily bandaged. An intravenous tube was attached to his left arm. In his nostrils were clear plastic oxygen tubes, with little green connector things on them. I felt weak. Momentarily I braced myself against the entry wall. Hearing mother describe father's condition on the telephone was one thing but seeing it for myself was entirely different.

It is impossible to describe how I felt. This man who lay before me, helpless and disfigured—his mouth twisted to one side, his right hand curled inward, could not possibly be the man I had known all my life. I had obviously entered the wrong room.

The father I knew was tall, strong, resilient, deep-voiced—always in control. His deep blue eyes seemed capable of piercing steel like a laser. This man I stood staring at, as tears slowly formed in my eyes, must surely be an impostor, I thought.

Then it occurred to me, I had never seen father lying in bed before. All those years, and this was the first time. It was something you never really think about, under normal circumstances.

I touched father's hand, but there was no response. I remember standing there for the longest time, holding his hand, wondering where the father I knew really was. His deteriorating physical form was lying there in bed—this bed with its neatly creased sheets and perfect hospital folds. But where was his robust spirit? Where was father?

I said a prayer and stood there cemented to the spot, unable to move. I cried. I could not remember the last time I had cried, but I cried that day. Tears rolled down my face and collected underneath my chin. I clenched my teeth and shook my head from side to side, as if by doing so I would awaken, and all would be well. It was not to be.

A few moments later, a nurse cracked open the door, peeked inside, smiled at me, and closed it again. I backed away from the bed, turned, and stepped lightly to the window where I opened the blinds, slightly. I did so quietly, as if I was being careful not to awaken father. In truth, I wanted to yell out to him, scream at the top of my voice, shake his bed, cause him to sit up with a start, and bawl me out for waking him from his nap.

Outside, the day was beautiful and sunny. The trees and grass were the greenest I had ever seen, other than in Rosedale, that is. If father was condemned to spend nights in a hospital bed tethered to tubes, sensors, and monitors, I saw no reason he should be condemned to endure days without sunlight. I opened the blinds all the way and stood at the window, gazing down at the ground-level entrance, not focusing on anything.

I started to turn away, then saw an elderly man in a wheelchair. He was being taken by a woman of twenty, or so—probably his granddaughter—to a red Mustang convertible waiting at the curb. He was smiling. I watched until he was safely in the car and driven out of view.

I envied this man. He was sufficiently well, sitting upright and apparently going home to his family. I was happy for him, but I envied his good fortune. At the same time, I was envisioning that scene for father in a few days or weeks. Regardless of the present situation, we had to remain positive.

I remained in Houston with mother and Rosie for ten days. Most of that time was spent at the hospital, though I persuaded mother to let me take her on a brief tour of the city. She reluctantly agreed. Yet, it was obvious to me, her mind never left St. Luke's and father.

By the end of my time there, father began showing steady improvement, although he still had not fully regained his ability to speak. I remember the day he opened his eyes and was able to grip my hand. It startled me.

Certain he was aware of my presence, I quickly called Rosie and mother into the room. We stood around the bed embracing each other. All felt that perhaps father had begun the long, tough journey back. There were hopeful smiles all around and joyous prayers of thanks. Soon, a cheerful, soft-spoken nurse entered the room and advised us to let father rest. We did so, happily.

Rosie was due back in Dallas in a few days. Mother confessed she would rather be near father than nestled in some hotel room, no matter how fancy. So, I arranged for a spouse's suite at the hospital. There, she would be only steps away from the man with whom she had spent all her adult life.

It appeared to work. Mother, who had been solemn and withdrawn, seemed much more upbeat, so I returned to New York. A week later, she informed me father had improved enough to gain release from the hospital. It was great news. Mother took him home and I arranged for twenty-four-hour in-home nursing care; a certified dietitian; a cook, and a housekeeper.

For mother, who had never permitted another woman except Rosie into her kitchen, all this help took some getting used to. At first, she complained of not having much to do. However, she soon began enjoying having someone around who looked after father, pampered her, and took orders without giving her sass.

Everything seemed to be going well. Then, father suffered two mild strokes within a month. Doctors had warned this may happen. Still, it was hard to cope with the reality. We had permitted ourselves to bask in the euphoria of his well-doing. Each passing day had seen our prayers answered. The dreaded news of father's relapse was quite a blow, for me and for all of us.

Six months later, father was up doing light chores and plodding around with the help of a walker. We were all astounded. His fierce determination was evident—a fact that should not have surprised us. Mother complained of having difficulty keeping him from overexerting himself. I was ecstatic.

Seven weeks later, father had abandoned the walker and had begun taking on a few minor carpentry jobs. Mother threatened to take him over her knee before he turned down a contract to supervise construction of a VFW hall in northern Crawford County.

Father and I enjoyed frequent, though brief telephone conversations. I could barely detect slurred speech, although his voice lacked its customary resonance. I would call to speak to him, he would chat for about a minute, then say: "Son, you want to talk to your mother?" That was my clue he had said about all he cared to and was eager to get off the phone.

This was nothing new. Father was never one for idle conversation. I was simply thrilled he was alive and apparently on the road to recovery. It was what I had prayed for. The thought of losing father was something I did not want to think about. A part of me even denied the possibility he would not always be there.

Until the age of six, I thought people lived forever, as long as they ate their spinach and broccoli, and obeyed their parents. When I found out differently, I was very upset. Since then, I have come to dread the possibility of growing old, and the certainty of dying. Each seemed an unfitting reward for a life well-lived.

So, while I remained deeply concerned about father's long-term health, I was able to refocus myself and plunge back into my burgeoning schedule. Yet, each call from mother gave me fits, until I could gauge the tone of her voice and determine all was well. She seemed to sense my anxiety and would preface her conversation with assurances father was alright. I would thoroughly quiz her—she called it interrogation—until I was convinced, she was not trying to shield me from the truth.

Chapter Four

Into The Looking Glass

Months later,
with father's health again in decline, I am a different man, both in mind and spirit. I had allowed myself to feel things could somehow be as before. Perhaps it was merely a son's wish that his father could be the father he had always been. I think of the song, "Everything Must Change," and realize this includes me and father as well. Reality can be cruel and merciless.

I am not certain father's suffering is entirely responsible for sparking my heightened awareness, although I am certain it has played a determining role. Perhaps the change was inevitable. What is undeniable is the great extent to which events have forced me to engage in self-appraisal, to gaze into the looking glass in search of the real James Theodore Phalen. I regret it took this tragic circumstance for me to stop and take a hard look at my life.

Alise, my girlfriend of three years and a very successful author, was and is a source of great strength and understanding for me. I hope I have given her half as much as she has given me. Thank God, for Alise. She sees the change in me, in ways even I am not aware of, and suffers with me. Alise understands I am anguished because my father is slipping away and little more can be done for him.

Perhaps I feel more mortal, more vulnerable, less invincible than before. I pretend I am the same, and struggle to be as dispassionate and focused on business as always. However, that grows less and less possible. I no longer derive the same pleasure—the same gratification from my things; my techno-toys; my pursuits, my diversions as I once did. I cannot quite get back to where I was before this tragedy. And I question if I should even want to.

This uncertainty disturbs me. My aim has always been to either limit or eliminate uncertainty. I did not get to where I am by accepting circumstances with a benign attitude things will work out on their own. Things need impetus, push, initiative, and direction. Still, uncertainty blankets me.

I ask myself what is going on with me. Perhaps the answer is I cannot divorce myself from this dilemma, as I normally would. I am an integral part of what is happening. This time, it is not some faceless family facing a heartbreaking dilemma. It is my family and me. There is a world of difference when the hand of fate knocks at your own door.

Whenever I speak to Rosie, as I have done each week since father became stricken, I can sense her mounting frustration. It grows out of her not reconciling her feelings about father, her childhood, and her first pregnancy. Rosie regrets not talking to him years ago when father could have comprehended and responded to her.

Whenever I speak to Carter about father, he always deflects the conversation, refusing to even acknowledge the seriousness of his condition. Carter always says:

"Jimmy, you know our ol' man is as tough as nails. He ain't goin' nowhere 'fore he's ready to go." He then laughs nervously and launches into diversionary conversation about sports or anything else that comes to his mind. Still, I think Carter is much more affected than he lets on perhaps even more than Rosie or me. He sees father every day. All these years, he has witnessed his decline from close-up.

In many respects, of the three of us, Carter is most like father. He generally responds with silence, even when screaming is the only natural, if not logical response. And he is not one to share his feelings easily. Although he was never a genuine extrovert, I do not recall him being quite this way when we were growing up. Lately, I have done a lot of thinking about those growing-up days.

Early last week, while sitting alone in the living room of my twenty-third-floor apartment overlooking this oft-reviled, oft-adored urban Stonehenge called New York, I removed a dusty album of childhood photos mother gave me during my first year at Harvard. I suppose the gift was her way of helping me stay connected to home while living in a foreign land, as she put it.

It required diligent effort to retrieve the album. I had all but buried it beneath file boxes of college memorabilia, old newspapers, and journals. I do not know why I felt compelled to risk slipping into a melancholy retrospective. For years, I had been avoiding that, seeing little profit in raw emotional exercises.

Several times, taking note of how big a task digging out this bulky collection of memories was becoming, I decided to abort the effort. Minutes later, submitting to its lure, I soon sat holding it in both hands. For the longest time, I stared at the album, trying to decide whether I wanted to peer into the rearview window it represented.

For years, I had been content remembering my childhood with a peripheral glance not requiring me to focus sharply. If I opened this album, I would have to look backward with a steady gaze. I was certain this would bring a geyser of mixed emotions rushing to the surface—some desirable, some not so desirable. I was not so sure I wanted this.

Moments later, I was still sitting there—silent, brooding, sipping on a glass of Chardonnay. It occurred to me there were more productive things I could be doing. Still, I stared blankly at the album, pondering the possible emotional consequences of my next move. Should I? Should I not?

The words: Phalen Family Album stood out in bold relief. I ran my fingers over them, back and forth. I drew a deep breath and slowly lifted the engraved cover. The die was cast.

I thumbed through the first few pages then flinched, gripped by one photo I have not been able to get out of my mind since. It was a picture of our family taken in 1958, after Sunday services at New

Redeemer Christ Church. New Redeemer is a small, A-frame, white clapboard, country church where my father remains a church elder.

I was five years old and skinny as a rail. My knees were bony lumps separating my lower legs from my thighs. I wore this dumb sailor suit as every little boy in America found himself forced by law to wear back then. If ever there was a national uniform for boys, that was it.

Even worse, I had to wear the little matching sailor hat—the one with the blue tassel hanging to one side. I remember buxomly women at New Redeemer smiling, hovering over me, patting my head, pinching my cheeks, and telling my mother how cute I was.

They were right, but I hated that. I cringed whenever they came near me because I knew what was coming. I swore that if I ever had a son, I would never do that to him. There would be no sailor suit, no sailor cap, and no cheek pinching. Since I have yet to marry, and as far as I know have not fathered children of any gender, I have kept my promise.

In the photo, father is resplendent in his best black suit, black string necktie, and black hat he bought the day before at Paine Brothers Men's Store on Main Street. I do not really know why the store was called Paine Brothers. I never knew any other Paine, other than Mr. Finneas Paine. If he had a brother, he either died years before or lived far away and was not on speaking or visiting terms with his brother, Finneas.

I loved accompanying father to Paine Brothers Men's Store. Perhaps because the sign outside said Men's Store, plus the fact I entered unchallenged had something to do with it. Besides, the place had a certain look, a certain smell to it. The merchandise was displayed just so. There was all this men's stuff, and it made me feel more grownup, in an inspiring sort of way.

Still, I expected any moment some SS Officer would demand to see my credentials and finding them fraudulent would have me tossed from the train. Maybe I had read too many Agatha Christie novels.

Mr. Paine was a friendly, affable sort who always found something to be happy about. If it was a beautiful sunshiny day, he would say: "It sure is a beautiful, sunshiny day." I would smile and nod agreement, then scurry as fast as I could to catch up with father who was already several strides beyond us. If it were a rainy day with lightning-filled skies, he would say: "It sure is a beautiful, sunshiny day!"

The first time Mr. Paine said that to me was on a stormy Saturday afternoon. I stared at him as if he were nuts. He continued: "High above the clouds, that is. Gotcha, didn't I? Sun's always shining, and the skies are always blue way up there, you know." I would nod yes and again hurry to catch up with father.

I enjoyed following father around the store, trying to match his footsteps. I often fantasized about someday coming in as an adult and buying clothes just as he did. Mr. Paine would probably have me stand on the riser in front of the mirror. He would adjust my cuffs; ask me how that looked or how comfortable this or that felt. I would not answer aloud, because father never did. Father just nodded his head or grunted. I figured it was some special language unique to men. After all, mother never grunted.

Mr. Paine, who always wore a cloth tape measure around his neck and a wristband filled with pins, seemed to know what the grunts meant. He would mark the areas with chalk and pin the material.

Mr. Paine was a very funny man. He loved telling wry jokes. He was the spitting image of Floyd, the barber from the old Andy Griffith Show. I swear, he looked just like him. He wore the same type of eyeglasses, had the grin, the voice and everything. I would crack up just listening to him.

No matter how ill-fitting a suit looked on you, Mr. Paine would make you think you looked like a million dollars. He figured whatever he needed to do to make you happy could be accomplished with scissors, needle, thread, a smile, and a pat on the back.

Returning to the photo, father looks so tall...like a giant redwood with arms. He stands erect, gripping his worn bible, staring sphinx-like, straight ahead, displaying no emotion. I remember him looking that way often, even when he was not having his picture taken.

Mother stands next to him with an arm around the shoulder of my seven-year-old sister Rosemarie. Rosie's hair is braided in those twin pigtails she wore until she was about eleven or so. I cannot see them, but I can see the braids. They start at the front, on the sides of her head, and continue all the way to the back. She hated them…thought they made her look like a little girl. They did and she was.

I am just in front of the two of them, restless, hungry, wondering just how long we were going to stand there waiting for Elder Johanssen to snap the picture. I figured I would be a grownup with kids of my own, by the time he figured out which button to push. I am sure he was a smart and righteous man, but photography was not his strong suit. As I look at this photograph, I am sure the Almighty had a hand in how well it turned out.

Carter, then 9, stands next to Rosemarie. I chuckled, as I stared at the picture. There was Carter with his chest all puffed out, holding his breath, clenching his fists, hunching his shoulders. He was trying to look more mature and muscular than he was.

Carter was very proud of his muscles then. Mother, without father's knowledge, let him order a $7.95 bodybuilding kit he saw advertised in the back of a Superman comic book a friend loaned him. Mother paid for it from her stash of "in a pinch money," which she kept in a Mason jar on the top shelf of the kitchen cabinets (She did not know we all knew where she kept it).

Week after week, Carter waited for the mailman to bring his miracle device that was going to convert him from a puny, nine-year-old to a powerful, muscle-bound wonder-kid. I wondered if that were possible but did not say anything. I believed whatever my big brother said. He would race home from school every day, find mother, and ask if the kit had come. I made up my mind, if it worked for Carter, I would sneak and use it too.

After Carter's daily inquiry went on for so long, mother took to heading him off at the door the instant he entered the house. She would shake her head sadly and say: "Not today, son." A frowning, disappointed Carter was not fit to be near for an hour. I steered clear.

We all breathed with relief, when the kit finally came from a faraway place called New York. Sadly, it was not at all what we thought it would be. The good news: Carter stopped driving us nuts. This contraption had two shortened broomstick rods that slipped through holes cut out in the two, rectangular, metal bars. The bars were attached to the rods by tightening a screw into them. That was it. Even I could have made the thing.

Carter exercised whenever he could. One day, father walked into the barn—the unofficial gym. He found Carter bare-waisted and working out feverishly with his makeshift barbells. Father stood looking at him...never said a word. He just watched for a second or two then turned and left.

Carter soon lost interest in his bodybuilding, especially after the screws broke. The cheap metal bars cracked when he dropped them on the floor. I am sure he could have fixed them, but that meant using father's tools. That was not about to happen. Father prized his Craftsmen tools. No nine-year-old kid was going to get his clutzy hands on them, not in father's lifetime.

The other choice was to ask father to repair the barbells himself. I am sure father would have fixed them if Carter had asked. And Carter probably would have asked, if he had thought father would have taken the time to do it.

From the very beginning, mother made a point of telling Carter how well he was developing and how proud of him she was. I am sure he welcomed that. What he really wanted and never got was father's notice of him. How could he not notice him?

As I write this now, it dawns on me that Carter's intense interest in bodybuilding was likely his way of trying to measure up to father's dominating physical stature and gain his approval. He always looked up to him, as did I.

The fact is, when you are a boy, you see your father as a muscle-laden, all-powerful he-man with no limitations. In reality, he can be a 110-pound weakling, but you do not see him that way. To a son, his father can do most anything. He can take on just about anyone at any time and emerge the victor.

Carter took to doing push-ups and tugging on big rocks we would find half-buried in the dirt. He would stand in front of the mirror flexing his biceps and walking around looking for things to pick up, just to show how strong he was. He was fairly strong.

Big brother even sprouted patches of underarm hair. I seriously doubt that was the result of his workouts. Carter thought it proved something. I do not know what, except he would have to start putting extra soap on the towel and scrubbing a little harder when he bathed. At least that is what mother told him. Then, when he would fail her sniff test, she would make him bathe again.

In one of his many attempts to exhibit his strength, Carter once tried to lift me over his head. I yelled for mother and kicked and screamed for him to put me down. He will kill me for writing this, but while he was lifting me, he strained so hard he passed gas. I do not mean one of those harmless little tweaks. This thing sounded like a dozen foghorns going off in a tunnel and smelled absolutely awful. When mother came into the room, he quickly put me down. We all beat a hasty retreat, including mother. I still laugh when I think about it.

Carter was more than a brother. He was at times my teacher and always my friend. He still is. My big brother is often introspective. He is a thinker whose quiet touch belies his intensity and depth. It was Carter who taught me to catch, using a worn tennis ball he found at school.

He was also fiercely protective of both Rosie and me. He once trounced one of the town bullies who normally feasted on little kids like me. I was very proud. Carter asked I not tell father, but word got around anyway. Father must have heard about it, though he never let on.

My big brother was very protective of mother as well. When he was twelve, we kids somehow learned that he had been a difficult birth. Mother almost died. After learning this, Carter changed a lot. He became conscious of mother's every ache and slightest discomfort. Once, she came down with a bad cold. Carter hardly left her side, except for school. Father had to assure him she would be fine, before he relinquished his constant vigil.

Strange, how looking at a single photograph can evoke so many memories. I recall the hot Sunday afternoon the picture was taken, as if it were yesterday. It happened to be Testimonial Sunday at New Redeemer. That is when we would all sing hymns, acapella-style. The adult faithful would tell how blessed they were...what God had done for them and all. It was also the last Sunday I wore that dumb, navy-blue sailor suit.

On the way home, while climbing into the rear of our old 1954, 4dr. Ford Sedan, I split the seat of my pants. They ripped loudly.

Everyone turned, looked at me, then each other. Rosie snickered and pointed at me. I immediately took a swipe at her. That earned me a stern, over-the-shoulder look from father. Message received loud and clear.

Mother never got around to darning the outfit and I never wore it again. Whatever happened to it, I do not know. Father suspected I had split them intentionally and said as much. I really had not. I have no doubt mother still has them stored away somewhere. Perhaps I will have her dig them out at some point in the future. I doubt it, however.

I sipped more Chardonnay, peered at the aged photo, and observed something I had never noticed before. Everyone was smiling, except for father. He stood staring straight ahead with laser intensity. It was as if someone had told a joke and he was the only one who had not gotten it.

Father was always so serious and purposeful. Looking back, it seemed as if we were all time-travelers, and father was the stern Wagonmaster determined to get us to the 'Promised Land', even if it killed us.

In Rosedale, and indeed much of Texas, father was well known and highly respected. The Phalen name is as much a part of Texas history as any you can mention. My great grandfather Silas Phalen III, a burly blacksmith and self-styled poet, whom legend has it could fell a horse with a single stroke, rode with the General Sam Houston. He did so, carrying a rifle in one hand and a pen and quill in the other.

As for father, he was a carpenter by trade and a preacher at heart. He was a stern, no-nonsense man who knew the Bible better than nearly anyone, save the Apostles themselves. Everyone said he was the best carpenter in the whole state of Texas. They were right. There was virtually nothing father could not build, from houses to barns, churches to country stores, courthouses to coffins. He had a hand in either building or remodeling half the buildings in Rosedale. That was and is a source of great pride for me.

When I was a kid, my chest swelled with pride whenever I walked into one of father's buildings. I practically felt a sense of ownership. I even pretended they belonged to us. In a way, it made me feel as if Rosedale owed father a special debt of gratitude. In reality, our family owed a huge debt to Rosedale and its citizens, for keeping father with steady work all those years.

There was a saying: J.Q. Phalen keeps you covered, from the cradle to the grave. Texans have a saying for just about everything. There is even a saying that goes: If a situation comes up and there ain't no sayin' for it, a real Texan will make up one right on the spot and make you think it has been around a thousand years.

One thing is for sure: father put the fear of God into us at an early age. He never passed up a chance to quote the bible's admonition to parents to:

Bring up a child in the way he should go, and when he is older, he will not depart from it.

We soon learned God's eyes were always upon us. He knew and saw all we did. Just imagine that. For a young mind, this was a scary notion indeed. It meant one could never have complete privacy, whether you were hiding in the woods, in the closet, under the bed or even hunkered in the bathroom.

Of course, according to father, one should find great comfort in that. A true believer always desires to walk in the security and comfort of God's constant watch. Still, we were often made to feel that if we as much as spat on the ground, God would condemn us to eternal hell-fire—a frightening thought.

We Phalens were always either on our way to church, at church or coming home from church. We were some very churchly people. I suppose one view is that if we were in church, we could not be stealing plums from Mr. Summers plum trees, planting dead fish under the front seat of Mr. Hemphill's pickup truck, scaring poor Widow Tibbs while she washed dishes near her kitchen window at night, or worse. Please understand; we Phalen kids would never dream of such unchristian mischief.

While such intense devotion to church attendance and Bible study were not exactly electives, I am sure it did not harm us any. It likely did us a world of good. None of us grew up to be mass murderers, pedophiles, prostitutes, pimps, pornographers, or politicians.

I suppose I am one to talk, considering I am, amongst other things, a lawyer. However, I would like to think those of us who toil in the corporate domain are not deserving of the scorn and loathing so often visited upon our other brethren.

Father was a walking repository of Bible verses. He studied the Good Book more than any minister I ever heard of. He applied its teachings to his daily life, often saying: "My desire is to walk upright before the Lord."

I marveled at father's ability to quote chapter and verse and apply them to almost any real-life situation. We had weekly home Bible study that would always conclude with Bible drills. Father had us stand with our Bibles closed and would call out a verse. For example: Psalms 42:1-5. Carter, Rosie, and I would quickly whisk through our Bibles to find the verse. She was usually the faster of the three of us. One of us would find the verse and begin reading:

1. As the deer pants for the water brooks,
2. So pants my soul for You, O God.
3. My soul thirsts for God, for the living
God. When shall I come and appear
before God?

That would go on for a half-hour or more and a winner was declared, usually Rosie. As time went on, we all became quite proficient at these drills. We knew many of the verses without looking and could locate a particular book and chapter on first opening.

The Bible and family prayer played a very prominent role in the Phalen household. At the dinner table, you did not dare think of taking a bite of food without first offering prayer and reciting a verse. That just was not done unless you wanted to be made an example of.

It soon became a joke amongst us kids, that if we wanted to eat hot food at dinner, it was best one of us offered prayer of thanks, before father had a chance. Father's Grace, or asking of blessings, had a way of becoming sermons, while stomachs growled, food got cold, and our eyes rolled back in our heads. Our blessings would sound something like:

"Father in Heaven, we thank you for the food we are about to receive for the nourishment of our bodies, for Christ's sake, Amen."

Father's would begin: "Father in heaven, we come before you at this hour with our heads bowed and our hearts humbled before your throne of Grace. We realize all our blessings..."

By then, we knew we were in serious trouble. Mother, sensing our anguish, knew exactly how to bring things to a speedy conclusion. Just when father was beginning to get wound up, mother would softly say: "Now, Father." That seemed to always do it. Within another sentence or two, father arrived at Amen, and we voiced our own thanks, both to God and to mother.

Father was very big on the book of Revelations. Personally, it always scared the devil out of me. Maybe that was father's intent. For as long as I can remember, people were saying we are living in the end times and the Second Coming was near.

In my mind, I envisioned beasts, flying white horses, flaming swords, rivers of blood, and could almost hear the screams, moans, gnashing of teeth and everything. It all made any sane kid think that if you did not obey your parents and do all the Good Book said, you would spend eternity roasting like a pig at a luau.

Thanks to father, television was one intrusion that never interfered with our education or bible study. We never owned one, until I was thirteen years old. Father felt television was the tool of the devil, in many respects. According to him, even Ed Sullivan was going to hell. My god, I wonder what he would say today. Until his stroke, he still refused to watch television, except for CNN, occasionally.

Rosie, Carter, and I desperately wanted a television set. At school our friends often talked about TV shows they had watched. We could contribute nothing to those conversations. We did everything we could to convince father that having a set would not lead us to sin and sedition. Mother was on our side, but father had the final say.

To try and convince him, we were on our best behavior. We performed chores with precision and without having them pointed out. We went above and beyond the call of duty. Beds got made; shoes were put away; the barn was cleaned; the front yard cut, and the grass bagged without a word of instruction. I even ate all my collard greens, without complaint. If you knew how much I hated collard greens, you would understand what a sacrifice I made.

While we were always good students, we studied even harder and made even better grades. To even mother's surprise, we were the first dressed and ready for church every Sunday morning. We wanted the television set.

The closest we ever came to watching television was during weekend trips to town on Saturday mornings. If we were lucky, we got a chance to watch cartoons, westerns, and other Saturday morning fare, on the TV sets in the display windows of the local furniture-appliance store. Unfortunately, we were seldom able to watch an entire program. Father had a way of showing up just before the big climax.

On Christmas Day 1966, we got our first television set. It was a Magnavox. We were all ecstatic. All our hard work and best-laid plans were finally rewarded. However, the thing came with 1001 rules, not for operation but for viewing. Father laid down the law, regarding when we could watch and mostly when we could not.

There was to be no TV viewing during the week, except for programs like: Playhouse 90, Victory At Sea (WW2 documentary series) or anything famed journalist Walter Cronkite did. Weekends were fine, except on Sundays when we were permitted to watch only between 6 P.M. and 8 P.M. after evening church. That meant Lassie, and Ed Sullivan, as long as no female performer revealed skin above her calf—Lassie excluded.

To our surprise, father sometimes watched particular programs with us. He would point out those things he felt needed explaining, in a good versus evil context. At the time, we felt annoyed by that, but in retrospect that is what all parents should do, especially with their young children.

One of father's favorite shows was Bonanza. He easily identified with the family patriarch, Ben Cartwright and loved Hoss like a son. As for the violent gunplay, father pointed out that sometimes it is necessary to counter evil with force. He used the same rationale, during the several times he took a belt to our backsides.

Of course, we already knew about good, evil and force. The bible is replete with examples of horrific violence. We kids had these discussions amongst ourselves, but never mentioned any of it to father or mother.

Regarding television, we soon learned that if we wanted to watch our favorite shows, we had best make some plausible excuse to go to a friend's house to study. The trouble was, we would all want to go study on the same nights. There was not much chance of that happening. We had to compromise. It worked, until father caught on and put an end to our little scam. He said if we wanted to study with friends, they had to come to our house.

Chapter Five

Deeper Into the Looking Glass

I drew a labored breath and leafed through more timeworn photos of Rosie, Carter, and me. There we were at church again, at a town parade, another of us on the front porch at home.

Home. Our patch of earth was like Shangri-La, perfect for adventuresome kids like us endowed with vivid imaginations. We lived on a farm, though it was not really an all-out working farm like Mr. Orlo Tinfaddle's place up the road or the Cragen Miles farm. Theirs were truly mammoth operations.

Father planted a few acres of corn, mustards, collards, turnips, okra, squash, tomatoes, onions, peppers, and watermelon every year. We also had a few cows, chickens, horses, and the like. In return for taking their fill at harvest, extra farmhands were always in abundant supply.

We also owned healthy groves of apple, pear, plum, and pecan trees that got along just fine without our meddling and fretting over them. I think father's suffering through the Depression had a lot to do with growing all those vegetables every year. He was determined that no matter the nation's economy, he would always be able to feed his family. However, our crops were so bountiful, we would end up giving almost three-quarters of it away.

What I recall most fondly about our land was the abundance of wide-open space and big blue sky. We had endless room to run and run we did. If you have never known the thrill of running at breakneck speed through boundless fields, with the summer wind in your face, the smell of bluebonnets or sweetgrass in your nostrils, and no speeding car to watch for, you have my deepest sympathy.

The mere thought of it all takes me back there. Suddenly, I am breathless again, struggling to keep up with my older and faster siblings who playfully threaten to run away and hide from me. I do not mind their teasing. I know no matter how far we roam, I can always find my way home, I think.

My sister Rosemarie could run faster, jump higher, and climb trees better than any boy I ever saw. She never once scraped her knees. Unlike me, she never fell from the fence and dislocated her kneecap. Such mishaps occurred during summer, more than any other time. As the school year neared an end, mother would always stock up on first aid supplies. Carter and I usually made sure they did not go unused.

Rosie, Carter, and I lived for the summer. Those storybook summers of our youth were truly golden. They were magical, filled with time and space for matchless adventure. We were Tom Sawyer, Becky Thatcher and Huckleberry Finn come to life. When the school year neared an end, you could sense a change in the way you felt inside. It seemed the cage door was about to open. We would at last be free.

I often draw comfort and peace from memories of those days. There was never a thought they would not last forever. Perhaps my recollection of those times is distorted a bit. Things often take on a more romantic hue, when viewed in retrospect. Yet, I am sure I am understating just how wonderful and innocent it all really was.

I especially remember the sky was so big, so bright, so blue back then, like the way Montanans speak about Montana sky. It even seemed a lot higher—more of it. Back then, every place was like Big Sky Country. It just had that feel to it. Nowhere was the beauty of nature more evident than in the middle of a sprawling green field, surrounded by flowers, the smell of the earth and tall Sweet Grass.

I am sure we took it all for granted, and rightly so. When you are a kid, you should be able to take those things for granted. Sadly, that is not true today. I often say I am glad I was born and raised during the period I was.

We did not know zip about CFCs, ozone depletion, or the greenhouse effect at all. We had no idea what was really happening to the environment. You might say we were blissfully ignorant. If that is true, then I still would not change a thing about our perceptions of our little corner of the world. Our world looked like the canvas of a master artist with an immeasurable imagination. According to father, such was indeed the case.

I also recall cool, crystal-blue lakes and streams with water so clear you could see the fish swimming three or four feet below the surface. We would often jump in barefoot and join them, without the slightest notion regarding the water's effect on our health. I remember we even drank some it.

When I close my eyes, I see us skipping stones across the water, one right after the other. We did not have a care in the world. It was heaven. And we assumed every kid in the world enjoyed that same heaven.

Some days, we would lie on our backs in picture-book fields, staring up at puffy, floating clouds and pointing out ever-changing animal shapes. We would quickly turn to telling of what we wanted to be when we grew up. I had no doubt I was going to be a major league baseball player. Carter was certain he would be a sea captain and sail his very own ship. Rosie wanted to be a racecar driver.

When Carter and I heard that, we snickered and told her she had to choose something else. Everyone knew girls could not be racecar drivers. We were not being mean to her. We were only reflecting our prejudices and accepted societal conditioning. Still, Rosie seemed deeply hurt and saddened by our reaction to her.

"Why not?" She asked.

Fact is, we had no real answer to give her, at least none that made sense. Carter and I gave each other a couple of dumb, blank looks and shrugged.

"Because," we both chortled in unison. "Because."

An interminable silence followed. Rosie stood and, with head down, walked alone across the field and back to the house. We simply watched her, shook our heads, and wondered what we said to upset her.

At other times, while staring up at the sky, we would spot airplanes flying at enormous altitudes. They were often so high, we could not hear the engines. We would wonder what was keeping them up there; why they did not falright back to earth. Then we would spend the next twenty minutes guessing where the plane was going and what it would be like flying in an airplane.

The closest we ever got to a real plane was about five hundred yards from Mr. Diboll's loud, old single engine, smoke-belching crop duster. It made a god-awful sound and had a faded picture of a big bumble bee painted on either side of the fuselage. Whenever Mr. Diboll swooped down over the fields, the plane's wings looked as if they were going to falright off.

Then, there were those spectacular southwestern sunsets. I loved those sunsets. They were indescribably beautiful. Mesmerizing. Whenever we looked out over the gentle slope of those sprawling fields, it appeared the earth was practically swallowing that big fiery ball. The sinking sun spewed flaming pinwheels of dancing color, forcing the surrounding clouds, fields, buildings, and everything to take on a strange and beautiful glow.

I recall being very disappointed, when the sun began to sink below the horizon. It did so much too quickly for my liking. I suppose it was a bit unreasonable to expect it would reach land's end and pause there for an hour, just for me.

When we were not running, jumping, climbing, lying on our backs staring up at the sky, watching Mr. Diboll's old crop duster, admiring sunsets, or skipping stones, we explored the woods. I loved roaming the woods, leaping over hollow logs, pretending the old man who lived in the trees was chasing us. Legend was, he ate little kids who failed to pay toll to pass through.

The three of us would romp with reckless abandon all the way through Crescent Woods. It had to be over a mile across. Maybe a million…a gazillion. Every time we went through, it seemed to get bigger.

We would exit the woods, near Devil's Fork and strike out across still more fields. Later, we would end up sauntering barefoot down winding country roads until dusk and beyond. Often, darkness would overtake us, and we would scare ourselves silly with wild imaginings of being followed by ghosts and other creepy creatures.

We did this without fear of being accosted or molested or worse. No bad guys with an array of dysfunctions waited behind trees and fence posts poised to pounce upon us and do horrible things. Our lives were uninhibited by such concerns that so adversely affect children today. It all seems so long ago now.

When I think back, I ask myself whether I really and truly enjoyed those glorious, carefree moments as much as I might have. Does any child? Can any child? Probably not. Did I take it all for granted? Probably. Still, I remember and regret those wonderful times passed so quickly.

Mother would often join us in our exploits and explorations. I suppose the one thing I have always loved about her is the little girl in her she has never outgrown. She has never lost those childlike qualities: a playfulness, an ability to quickly forgive, an eagerness to face tomorrow, an inner joy that serves to keep her young both in mind and spirit. I am certain that more than anything, these qualities are responsible for her eyes that still dance and her continuing zest for life.

I believe we begin to truly grow old, when we lose our ability to play like children. Mother has never lost her playfulness. Her face, now wrinkled and lined, still exudes love and sincerity in a manner that is purely angelic. You only have to be around her for a moment, to understand what I mean.

Still, I suspect that deep inside, mother has thoughts about her life as a wife, mother, and woman…thoughts she keeps to herself. We all have our private place inside us. I find myself wondering just what her dreams and expectations for her life were. Did she ever lie on her back in a field, stare up at the sky and dream of what she wanted to someday become? Had she realized those dreams?

Rightly or wrongly, mothers tend to bury their personal aspirations and dreams, in deference to those of their husband and children. They did then. I wonder how many lawyers, doctors, scientists, engineers, politicians, and writers were lost to the old notions of where women belonged. I am saddened to think I played even a small part in mother not being all she might have been. Yet, I am happy she chose the indispensable professions of motherhood and housewife. She was and is the world's best—my prejudices notwithstanding.

Mother frequently took us fishing. During the summers, father and his crew went off to work and we did our chores as fast as we could. Afterwards, we would grab our poles, lunch baskets, empty pails and bait and head straight for Crawford Lake, about a mile and a half from our back porch. Along the way, we would often stop to pick blackberries, using knotted oak sticks to fend off an occasional rattlesnake. Carter wanted to bring along father's rifle for protection, he said. Mother would have none of it.

When we reached the secluded pier at the lake, we would all feast on the juicy berries not devoured during the walk. Our purple lips, tongues, and fingers would remain so for days afterwards.

I remember once convincing mother, against her better judgment, to join us in an old boat that sat tied to one of the creosote pilings supporting the pier. It looked safe enough. She finally relented and we all scurried into the shallow water and examined it very carefully, or so we thought. No sooner had we all piled into the wreck than it began springing serious leaks.

The empty boat had looked fine, until our combined weights forced the leaks below the water line. It was hilarious. We scurried from the boat like rats abandoning a sinking ship, jumping up and down in the water. We were thoroughly soaked. It was so much fun, I asked mother if we could empty the boat and do it again.

I do not remember father ever engaging in what he called 'such foolishness and nonsense.' He would always say:

When I was a child, I spake and acted as a child.
When I became a man, I put away childish things.

I am almost forty-two, but those words still ring in my ears.

When father was not busy working, he was, as the Chief Elder, busy tending to church business. There was always plenty of church business. I mean no disrespect whatsoever by my tone. Some things stay with you a very long time, maybe forever.

I suppose he felt that acting like a kid and joining with us in play would diminish his parental influence. On that score, he believed in maintaining a wall of separation. Once, we all overheard him verbally chastise mother for playing with us. He lectured that her dignity suffered and would lead to our not respecting and honoring her. Nothing was farther from reality.

As a boy, I never climbed onto father's back and played horsey. We never playfully tumbled on the floor or engaged in any of the many things fathers do with sons, except work. Virtually every conversation we had was serious and not a real conversation, not even the mildest give and take. They were more like sermonettes or directives. If there was an exception, I do not recall one.

When Carter was thirteen, I lost my best buddy to father's need for an extra pair of hands on his building sites. I will never forget the look in my brother's eyes, shortly after turning thirteen. Under most circumstances, reaching thirteen would have been a time of celebration and joy at finally attaining teenagehood.

Carter probably felt that joy, but it was tempered by the further heaping of adult-like responsibilities upon his young shoulders. The effect was a severing of him from the unfettered joys of childhood.

Carter seemed to take it all in stride. I was the one angered. I had lost a running buddy. Rosie was great to play with, but the three of us had always been together. I did not want Carter to have to work. My turn came a few years later.

I now understand father was not being cruel. He simply harked back to his days as a boy. When he was only four or five, he worked the fields, tending animals alongside his father and siblings. He later credited those experiences with his growing up to be a man. He was taught to bring pride and dignity to his work, whatever it happened to be.

In his mind, father was only instilling the same work ethic in his sons. He was impressing upon them a sense of responsibility, and a duty to carry one's own weight. He would often quote a short passage of scripture that says, paraphrasing:" Those who do not work do not deserve to eat." It was only considerable time later I came to employ this genius bit of adult rationalization. As a child, I thought the whole thing stank.

Chapter Six

The Big Game

...and on the 8th day, God created baseball.

Another faded photo—a treasure I had not seen in over twenty-five years—stirred more emotion in me than I could have anticipated. It was I at age 9, dressed in my first Little League baseball uniform, on the first day of my first season. Seeing the picture caused a wellspring of memories to erupt.

"Just look at that little kid," I thought. "Is that really me?"

I wondered what happened to the uniform, the shoes, and the cap. The memories came flooding back in torrents. On that remarkable day, my excitement was uncontrollable. My chest burst with pride. I was on the team! I recall saying it aloud, trying to prove I was not dreaming.

To merely say I loved baseball would be the ultimate understatement. I lived baseball. It was in my blood. Eating, sleeping, and breathing were things I had to do. I had no choice. Playing baseball was something I wanted to do more than anything.

When I was not at baseball practice, I was constantly pestering Carter to play catch with me. It did not matter whether in the front yard or on the side of the barn, I wanted to play. After sunset, we would turn on the porch light and keep playing, until mother made us quit and come inside before mosquitoes embalmed us.

I was seldom more than arm's reach from my ball and glove, even when I slept at night. Carter would tease me about it, but I did not care. When I was in the major leagues someday and he would have to pay to see me play, he would take it all back.

I kept gawking at the photograph. Compared to the size of my teammates, I was a runt in baggy pants. Today, that look is fashionable, but back then I was odd man out. The outfit swallowed me whole. I later received one that fit better, but on that day, this was all I had to wear. "My god! I was such a runt then," I whispered again.

Our team was called The Rosedale Dodgers. I remember my jersey so engulfed my tiny body, the word DODGERS on my chest spelled DOERS. The excess material folded over, obliterating the middle "D" and "G."

For a moment, I felt I was inside the picture looking out. Tears filled my eyes, blurring my vision. I brushed them away. I was there again, reliving one of the most exciting days of my life—the day I finally got a chance to play real baseball.

I was on top of the world that Saturday. Mother was nearly as excited I. She wanted to starch and iron my uniform and put creases in the pants. Thankfully, Carter convinced her if I showed up like that, my teammates would laugh me off the team. To my great relief, she relented and ironed them lightly. Carter had saved me again.

I turned away from the picture, to get a firmer grip on myself then turned back again. The overwhelming memory of that summer day was too powerful to resist. I took a few more sips of my Chardonnay, leaned my head back, and closed my eyes. From that moment on, it was as if someone had dimmed the lights and turned on a projector.

It surprised me father let me to play baseball at all. He never had much use for sports...thought it took valuable time away from more productive pursuits. I loved sports, but I hated football with a passion equaled only by my love of baseball. That was not something I would have said aloud, not in Texas.

In Texas, football is a religion. To this day, voicing hatred of football is absolute heresy for any red-bloodied Texas boy. There is probably a law against it. In Texas, football was and is number 2, running a close second only to God himself, that is when God is looking. However, King Football is number one, if God so much as blinks. And in Texas, God blinks a lot.

I do not really know when I first fell in love with baseball. When I was a little kid, Texas did not have a Major League baseball team. Still, I remember Carter and me sneaking father's old Philco radio from the living room into our bedroom and listening to Texas League games. Carter was reluctant to do it, but I would call him chicken, make clucking sounds and he would give in. I could have sneaked the radio into the room all by myself, but I wanted a partner in crime —an accomplice. In case we got caught and ended up in the big house, I wanted a cellmate.

Sometimes, on weekends, when father was not at home, mother would allow us listen to the Major League Game of The Week. Notwithstanding the excellent play-by-play, called by the great Dizzy Dean, Carter would explain the games to me. He would even sketch diagrams on paper to help me understand it all. What other big brother in the world would go to such trouble?

Closer to home, I recall the Houston baseball team was called the Buffaloes or Buffs for short. They were a part of the old Texas League. We would listen to the exciting play-by-play of Guy Savage and Gus Mancuso. These guys really knew the game. They made us feel as if we were right there at the ballpark. We could almost smell the hotdogs.

One could practically feel the ball hit the bat or pop into the glove. I itched with excitement, as I lay stretched out across the bed, munching on crunchy macaroon cookies, and drinking milk. Of course, I made sure not a single crumb remained on the quilt. Mother did not play that.

I have long since forgotten the names of the Buff's players, except for two: Bob Boyd and Whitey Reese. Several years later, the Houston Colt .45's came along, then the Houston Astros. Texas finally had its own major league team.

Still, my favorite team was the Brooklyn Dodgers. The players' names roll of my tongue as easily as saying my ABC's: Jackie

Robinson, Duke Snider, Pee Wee Reese, Gil Hodges, Carl Furillo, Roy Campanella, Junior Gilliam.

Then there was the incomparable Willie Mays. He and Hank Aaron are the only non-Dodgers I ever idolized. Mays was a true Giant, in every sense of the word. He was my all-time favorite. Man, he could hit, he could catch, he could fly, and amazingly he seemed to have eyes in the back of his head. It seemed to me, he would watch a deep drive and intentionally stand still for a split second, just to give the ball a fair chance. The truth was, he took off at the crack of the bat.

God, I wanted to be like Mays. I still do. I have hours of old sports reels on video showing his awesome talent. Above all, he always seemed honest, friendly, and straightforward. To this day, when you see him in television interviews, he leads off with a smile. I am sure his smile was not what inspired fear and anguish in the pitchers of his day.

The people of Rosedale, the good members of New Redeemer Christ Church and even my own father would have fainted, if they had known I believed in reincarnation and the reason I did was my hope that when I died, I would come back as Willie Mays. I am sure it would please Willie to know that. Of course, he would likely suggest I not rush his departure from this dimension.

As for Hank Aaron, I do not think even baseball people fully realize just how remarkable a human being he is and how incredible a baseball player he was. Sure, everyone knows he broke Babe Ruth's record of 714 homeruns then went on to hit an unbelievable 755 homeruns, before retiring. Few know Hank set more major league records than any player in baseball history.

Many have forgotten the absolute hell he went through, given the actions of racists and bigots who did not want an African American to break Ruth's record. Hank received numerous death threats and horrible letters; some threatened his daughter with kidnapping.

I watched his remarkable career, first at Milwaukee and later Atlanta. It is unlikely his remarkable feat of 755 homeruns will ever be broken in my lifetime. I know that is a dangerous thing to say, regarding athletic records, but just think about it.

Today, a homerun slugger would have to stay healthy and play every season for at least twenty years, while hitting no fewer than 35 homeruns each year. Even so, he would only have 700 and would be 55 short of tying Hank's record. It just ain't ever gonna happen, not legitimately, anyway. You can laminate that page of the record book and move on.

I look at many African American players such as Aaron, Mays, Robinson, Bob Gibson, Reggie Jackson, and countless others and cannot help remembering that until Robinson broke the so-called color line in 1947, modern baseball was reserved for whites only. This was even after blacks had fought and died in every U.S. War, including two World Wars, fought to secure freedom for Europeans and others.

When one looks at many of the amazing stars of the old Negro League, including Satchel Paige, Josh Gibson, and others, one realizes that many of the white Major League stars of their day would have been riding the bench, had blacks not been excluded. There I go again, committing heresy. The truth is, I wish the game had been open to everyone. Just imagine how much more amazing baseball would have been then. It would have truly been America's Game.

When I was eight and a half, I finally got father's permission to play baseball, only provided it did not interfere with church or school, and in that order. I vividly remember the Saturday morning he drove us into town. He took me to Mr. Vonner's Western Auto and bought my very first baseball glove. I was thrilled right down to my KEDs. I stood staring at what must have been two-dozen baseball gloves—a huge inventory for a town as small as Rosedale.

The smell of genuine cowhide hung heavy in the air, as I stood at the glove display with mouth agape. I slipped my small hand into at least a half dozen gloves, before I found the one I wanted. It had Mickey Mantle's autograph on it. Never mind that Mantle was more famous for his hitting than fielding and was a Yankee to boot. That did not matter. I was getting my first glove. However, I do remember asking Mr. Vonner why they did not have a Willie Mays glove. He smiled rather awkwardly but did not answer.

Father looked at the $7.99 price tag and nodded to Mr. Vonner, who gently patted me on the head. I hated when people did that, but I was much too happy to dwell on it. We followed him to the sales counter. Mr. Vonner, keen to observe my uncontrollable excitement, asked if I wanted to wear the glove or have him put it in the bag. He already knew the answer.

As for the glove, I later bleached out Mickey's name and wrote Willie Mays' name in its place with mother's bluing pencil. I meant no disrespect to Mickey, whom I saw a couple of years ago on a TV news magazine show. He spoke about his career, the death of his son, and his stint at the Betty Ford Clinic where he battled alcoholism. I really empathized with him, and the problems caused by his addiction. His liver transplant surgery had a whole country pulling for him. Mickey's death saddened me.

As I watched his '93 television interview with NBC sports personality Bob Costas, I felt saddened by his inability to come to terms with his self-doubt, regarding his place in the hearts and minds of baseball fans. Hey, Mickey! We loved you. If I could have spoken to him, I would have asked him to forgive me for erasing his name. I was only nine years old. If I had it to do all over again, I would find a glove with Willie's name on it from the very start.

I thanked father for that glove. He truly seemed to enjoy buying it, as much as I enjoyed receiving it. Yet, to my lasting disappointment, he never came to see me play, not once. And I never understood that. I confess I still do not understand it. Even at my young age then, I was certain the God we worshipped would not have punished him for missing a single elders' meeting. Why could he not just say an extra prayer, I wondered, or put a few extra dollars in the collection plate.

I must tell you about the first game in which I ever played. Nothing compares to it. I recall it was a bright and cloudless Saturday—a day as close to perfect as any day I have ever seen. I could hardly wait to get to the ballpark. I was a tangle of nerves and had no appetite for breakfast that morning at all. Mother said I had something called the heebie-jeebies.

The night before, I slept with my baseball glove tucked under my pillow and dreamt of hitting the winning homerun, as the crowd went wild. Okay, so the dream was not an original. The truth was, there was only a small chance I would even get a chance to play. I was good, alright, or so I thought. It is just that most of the other guys were a little better. Alright, a lot better.

That did not really matter, because the coaches always tried to let every kid play. However, in a tight game, that plan could easily go out the window. The idea was to win. Even at nine, I knew that. Arriving at the ballpark, dressed in my uniform, and looking no differently than the starting nine players, was thrilling enough for me. We all had a chance to go through warm-ups in the outfield, whether we were in the starting lineup or not.

The diamond sparkled, thanks to groundskeeper, Mr. Noah Peetson, and his two talented helpers. During the week, Mr. Peetson was a Sheriff's deputy. He also owned a small pig farm a few miles from Duncan Stoddard's place.

Mr. Peetson was very proud of his work, the baseball field, not the pigs. It was a work of art. The baselines were the whitest white and as straight as arrows. The green grass was perfectly manicured. Each blade looked as if it had been cut to exactly the right height. The dirt around the bases, and along the base paths, was raked in a pattern. It was then lightly dampened with fine a mist. Too bad we had to destroy it all by playing on it.

The instant I crossed those white lines, I felt instantly set apart from the rest of humanity. I was a baseball player! I had done what every great baseball player had done at this stage of their lives: I had taken the field on game day. Never mind I had yet to officially field a ball or swing a bat. I was a baseball player. No one could take that away from me.

Although I did not realize it then, I think what made baseball so special to me was the fact it required nothing extraordinary from me. I did not have to be tall, muscular, or especially strong. I did not really have to be smart, although it helped, I was. Jed Stimpe was not a smart kid, and he was a star player. I should hasten to add that Jed grew up to be a brilliant fellow and is an Associate Justice of the Texas Supreme Court.

For most of the game, I hugged the far end of the bench, rising only to cheer the play of my teammates and to duck a screaming foul ball that almost took my head off in the top of the second inning.

I was not alone on the bench. There was Duncan Stoddard, a tall, gangly, awkward-looking kid, who had enormous promise as a pitcher. He was an awesome southpaw with an unorthodox windup and a contorted kick that made it look as if his leg was going to fly right off. Once he released the ball, he would all off toward the side of the mound, reminiscent of the legendary right-hander, Bob Gibson.

Duncan's coiled left arm would come flailing out of nowhere. Before you knew it, the ball was simmering in the catcher's glove. His control was doggone good, as well, to the dismay of most opposing batters.

Of course, Duncan could get a little wild sometimes. His control would go out the window, but that was rare. When it did happen, Peetie Simpson, our rather robust catcher, would trot out to the mound, with his belly flopping over his belt, and try to calm him down.

Peetie looked a lot like late Yankee catcher, Thurman Munson, even then. He had a good-natured personality. I could look at him and break out laughing for no reason. I often wonder what happened to Peetie. For a long time, I wondered what those two would talk about out there on the mound. It struck me as strange that Duncan would burst out laughing, just as Peetie turned and headed back to home plate.

Duncan finally told me Peetie would tell him a different dirty riddle every time, yet he never told me what any of them were. He said he did not want to ruin the innocent mind of the Chief Elder's son.

Whatever Peetie said worked, though. Duncan would settle down and his blazing fastball or sinking curve would do the job. Of course, the coaches did not encourage a lot of curve balls, although Duncan had a natural curve. They warned that too many young kids were throwing their arms out, trying to pitch curve balls. Seeing as how fastballer Nolan Ryan pitched forever and had such an amazing career, I guess they had a point.

Duncan had the potential to be a great pitcher. However, he had one, very serious problem. Whenever he became nervous, he would vomit and become incontinent; he would pee all over himself. Pee would run right down his leg, soaking his socks and everything.

The guys would go nuts with laughter. Poor Duncan: puking and peeing at the same time. Even the coaches, including our manager Mr. Leon McCloud, had a hard time keeping a straight face. I really felt so sorry for my friend and said a special prayer for him on Sundays, and before each game in which he was to pitch.

Duncan and his family left Rosedale when we were both 11 years old. We soon lost touch. Sadly, I never saw or heard from him again, but I pray he has had a wonderful life. I am sure he outgrew his problem. Anyway, he was to have pitched this game, but he became just a little too nervous and, well.

As the game neared an end, I had all but decided my baseball debut would have to wait. At least mother would not have to launder my uniform for the next game. Except for the seat of my pants, it still looked as fresh as it did at the start of the game. The important thing was I was on the team. Of course, that was pure baloney, but I had to tell myself something.

Finally, my big moment arrived. In the top of the sixth and final inning, with our team leading by two runs, Mr. McCloud put me into the game at third base. I thought I had died and gone to Ebbets Field. I heard him call my name sure enough, but I thought I was dreaming. Mr. Mac called for me a second time. I jumped to my feet.

"Me?" I asked, pointing to myself.

"I mean you," he barked, continuing to chomp on the wad of chewing tobacco tucked in his right jaw.

My heart was pounding like a jackhammer. I grabbed my glove, tugged at the waist of my pants, and almost tripped over a blade of grass, as I took the field. I felt more excited than ever in my life and swore to stop every ball that came my way.

I took my position, went through the short warm-up, and stood pounding my glove like all the pros do. Mother, Rosie, and Carter kept yelling out to me—cheering me on. Although I temporarily lost track of exactly where they sat, I doffed my cap cockily, pretending I was the epitome of cool.

Yet, I was anything but cool. My poor stomach was churning and bubbling fiercely, but I did not care. If I did not pull a Duncan Stoddard, I figured I would be alright. I was in the game. I was in the game!

With every pitch, my heart skipped a beat. I watched the ball, from the pitcher's windup to his delivery and its arrival at home plate. I was ready. Later in the inning, having yet to field a ball, I was much more relaxed. There were two outs with runners on second and third. The count was full: three balls, two strikes. One more out and the victory would be ours.

I again glanced into the stands at my own private cheering section. I even envisioned myself crossing the third base line and tossing my glove high into the air in victorious celebration. Of course, I would not have had a turn at bat, but that was okay.

On one hand, I wanted the ball to come to me, so I could prove how good a player I was. I kept telling myself if the ball came my way, I would glue my eyes to it and keep it front of me at all costs. On the other hand, I prayed the ball would go anywhere else but to me.

Then the unthinkable happened. My family's cheering briefly distracted me, causing me to be completely unprepared for a hot ground ball that bolted toward me like a shot. I remembered everything Mr. McCloud had told me. I fixed my eyes on the ball, bent my knees, bounced on my toes, and prepared to stop the grounder. The thing blasted straight between my legs.

Suddenly, everything became a blur. My heart sank to my heels. I had blown it. I had failed my team; shamed my family; embarrassed my town, my country, North America, and planet Earth. I would have to leave the solar system for sure. Darth Vader, here I come!

I thought I would die right on the spot. The fat butt, third-base runner, with his pug-nose and pigeon toes, practically walked home. The buckteeth second base runner, flashing a cocky grin, streaked toward third with no intention of stopping. I wanted to trip him, just for the heck of it. However, I had a ball streaking into short left field to worry about. Everything was in a haze. Everyone was yelling at me, screaming at the top of his lungs.

"Jimmy! Jimmy! Get the dat-gum ball, 'Jimmy!"

I wheeled around and dashed into short left field. I almost slipped down, as I got to the ball. Fortunately, the thick grass had slowed its velocity. I reached down, grabbed it, and winced. It felt more like a fifteen-pound shot put than a baseball. My arm felt weak, like a string of spaghetti. Somehow, I found my strength, wheeled around, and saw the second-base runner rounding third base and streaking home.

At the same time, I saw the hitter rounding first and barreling toward second. I do not know why, but instead of throwing home, I hurled the ball toward second base. Summoning all my strength, I drew back and uncorked one as hard as I could. A loud grunt gushed forth and I fell. I never saw the ball arrive at its final destination.

They tell me it was a dead strike, clothesline, screaming rocket to the first base side of the second-base bag. The runner slid right into the tag, two seconds before the tying run dove for home plate.

He was out! Game over! We had won! Everyone went hog-wild. You would have thought we had won the Little League World Series or the Major League World Series. Grownups were jumping up and down in the stands like kangaroos. Folks were hugging each other and screaming at the tops of their voices.

My ecstatic teammates piled on top of me, sending me crashing to the ground under their weight. At least my uniform was no longer clean. With considerable effort, I managed to crawl from the pile. The guys then lifted me onto their shoulders and marched around the field as if I was some conquering hero. It was embarrassing.

Still, I felt like Brooks Robinson… like Willie Mays. The crowd kept cheering so wildly the ground practically shook. No one wanted to go home. Even now, the cheers still ring in my ears. I did not want that magical moment to ever end.

I do not know exactly when it happened, but it soon dawned on me something was missing. This unbelievable moment was not whole. My immeasurable joy was tempered by my realization that father had not been there to witness my heroics. Strangers had been there; the opposing team had been there. People I neither knew nor cared about had been there, but father had not. How could I ever make him know what happened? How could I make him truly want to know? I stood there, whispered his name, and lowered my head. Mr. Mac asked me what was wrong. "Nothing," I said. "Nothing." I lied.

Sure, I loved the crowd; the wild cheering, the fact my mother, sister and brother were all very proud of me. I even survived Mr. McCloud's bear hug. I loved the pats on the back and the fact my teammates awarded me the game ball. But father was not there. Nothing could ever change that; not then, not now, not ever.

I knew even then, if I lived a hundred years, the thrill of that moment would never be repeated. And father was not there to see it. No verbal account could ever come close to painting the picture for him. No reenactment could possibly capture the tenor, the verve of the actual moment. One had to have been there. Ironically, what turned out to be one of the most thrilling days in my life, also held a major disappointment for me. Mother said it would pass.

As time went on, I took note of the fact other fathers offered their time at practice. They provided Station Wagons for trips, their moneys for uniforms and equipment. At some point in my first season, I began pretending father was at my games. My teammates had fathers who never missed a game; most never missed a practice. So, I figured if nothing else, I could at least pretend father was there.

And so I did. I would stand at home plate or in the field and stare at a spot in the bleachers I chose for him. No matter who sat there, I would always pretend father was right there, pointing at me proudly, cheering me on.

Following each home game, mom treated me to a celebratory visit to the local Dairy Queen. Later, I would arrive home and attempt to tell father all about the game. It turned out to be quite a chore. He would listen, impatiently, for a moment or two, then dismiss me quickly—his mind always somewhere else. I felt as if I was keeping him from something important. I felt crushed.

There are two things a kid can spot faster than anything else: inattention and insincerity. I soon learned to share my excitement only with mom, Rosie, and Carter. I did so to avoid feeling ignored, hurt, and becoming angry with father.

That is the way it was. What hurts even now, in recalling all this, is the fact father was not being intentionally callous and insensitive. The truth is, I think I could have dealt with that much better. The fact is, he simply never appreciated what it all meant. He never understood.

Throughout my high school years, although I lettered in baseball, father never saw me play. And I was good. I was doggone good. Mr. McCloud, and other older men, who loved the game, assured mother she had a potential Major Leaguer on her hands.

During my junior year, our team reached the State Playoffs for the first time in our history. We had an excellent opportunity to win the baseball title in Class 2A. The whole town shared in the excitement. Local merchants posted banners in their stores, wishing us well. Days at Crawford High were virtually one continuous celebration. Classes often erupted into spontaneous pep rallies. The game became almost anticlimactic.

Finally, the playoffs were held in Corsicana. Father was not able to come on the Saturday we were to play, owing to his duty to help prepare Sunday sacrament. Mother, Carter, and Rosie accompanied us, traveling on one of two buses chartered for the dozens of supporters.

Our team was in complete shock, witnessing such support. We had seen that kind of excitement for football, but never for baseball. We lost our semifinal game 10-7, but none of us were disappointed. We were so thrilled with our success, we celebrated more than the winning Gladewater team.

By the time I began my final high school baseball season, I was no longer reserving a seat for father. I still loved him, but I had resigned myself to the realities I had lived with for so long. He would never see me play baseball and that was that. Mother, sensing my disappointment, would take me aside and say, as she had for years: "Your father loves you. He cares about what you're doing. It is that he is a very serious person—never was into sports and things." I nodded yes, as if I understood. The truth was, I did not. I still do not.

Chapter Seven

Moving On

At last, I turned to another forgotten page in this abbreviated catalog of my life and discovered two poems I had written. The ruled, loose-leaf pages, which I had not seen in decades, had yellowed, and become brittle around the edges. I handled them as if they were the original Declaration of Independence or The Magna Carta. I read them, anxiously.

For a moment, I felt I was somehow violating the privacy of the person I once was—the young kid who had, on some long-ago day, bared his soul, emptied his heart, and moved on. Now, here I was prying into the remains of moments long forgotten.

I wrote a lot when I was in junior and senior high school. I not only felt I had a gift for writing; I felt a need to write. Writing was my way of expressing thoughts I could never disclose to a real person. Even if my ideas were not fully formed, I could still enjoy being uninhibited and free to vent my emotions. It was like singing to the wind, with only an echo to offer a critical review.

At that time, I did not write with the hope of becoming a poet or an author. I simply wrote to give voice to those things I was feeling as a kid—a kid experiencing life anew each day. I wish I had kept all those poems and short stories I had written. I would give anything to see them in one big pile on my dining room table.

I looked at these two and read them over and over. The words leapt off the page, transporting me back in time. It was so strange, reading the tender thoughts—words emanating from my mind at the age of fifteen.

SHADOWS

Shadows fall, this way and that.
Trees and spires account for some.
But those that could never be cast by
trees, where do they come from?
A lonely, broken heart
must help to darken the night—
some poor wretched soul
with no will, no might.
A million sleepless minutes,
gathered and bound in one,
cast a long, dark shadow
that falls in silence upon the ground.

I read Shadows repeatedly and found myself wondering just what it was that led me to write this poem. What was going through my young mind? Where was I? Who was I thinking about?

Then I remembered. It was a dark, rainy school day. The skies bulged with dark storm clouds and crackling lightning bolts. I sat in Miss Lewis' second period English class with about twenty-five other classmates. The lights in the entire school had gone out twice and all the students received word to remain in whatever class they were in. It was exciting and at the same time frightening. Some kids screamed, each time the lightning crackled.

As was often my custom, I took a seat some distance away from the others and began writing. There was something about dark, brooding, inclement weather that appealed to a particular side of me. It prompted certain passions to bubble to the surface. To this day, I find beauty in threatening skies, dark clouds and violent rain whipped by a frenzied wind. I am drawn to it, like metal to a magnet.

I sat there writing, closeted in my own little world. I felt set loose from my chains—free to fly, free to soar. I was still in the classroom, but I was not in class. The thoughts, the words, the emotions were pouring out.

Rain fell in torrents. The wind strained to lift the roof. Lightning erupted like cosmic explosions, flashing with a thousand tentacles across a brooding sky. An hour later, during a break in the storm, students were dismissed for the day. I was disappointed.

Without a noise or faintest sound,
a silent cover comes creeping down.
It's like the sound of little cat-feet
that never seem to touch the ground.
All around, the light is fading
from this cover's quaint persuading,
and most appalling is the falling
of shadows on the floor.
Yet there's no need for arms ascending,
it's only the night slowly descending,
hence the day will soon be ending
from the plains to the shore.

I do not know why I never gave this poem a title. For a moment, I considered titling it then decided against it. That would have been like defacing it. I did not want to change anything about either one. And I suppose my Edgar Allen Poe influence is apparent in the latter piece.

I sat running my finger over the page, breathing a silent thanks to mother for saving this part of my past. Moms often have an indiscriminate way of clearing things out. Many a valuable baseball card and other collections have ended up lining a landfill somewhere.

I could not help thinking that somewhere in the old steamer trunks and apple crates, at mother's there must be still more stored memories. I would look someday. Maybe I would also be able to find the eighty or so pages of an unfinished novel I began writing halfway through my freshman year in high school.

~

My High School Seniors' photo caused me to bring out my small magnifying glass. I leaned over the page, gazed at all those youthful, hopeful faces, and found myself whisked back through time. I drew a deep breath.

There we were, frozen in the moment for all eternity. There, none of us ever grew older; never died; never stopped smiling; and never disappeared, not to be heard from again. We were right there in the photograph, unchanged after all those years.

Photographs have a way of halting the aging process, capturing a nanosecond of life, and magically preserving it for all eternity. I remembered the day our Seniors' photograph was taken. We all assembled in the auditorium. Most of us were scattered in small groups around the room, talking, laughing, and generally having a great time.

At one point, I walked up onto the stage and stood gazing out at the gathering. One by one, I singled out each of my fellow students and saw them in a way I never had before. In my mind, everything grew silent. I heard none of the noise, none of the talking and laughing. It was as if I was making a mental record of how we all were that day, at that point in our lives. Inside, I knew we would all soon be scattered to the four winds, never to assemble like this again. I regret not having a camera.

I sat staring at the photo, for what seemed an eternity. Before I realized it, I found myself humming the words to our school song:

Dear Crawford High,
We love thee true.
We place thee o'er all others
and see you safely through.
Our love for you remains
unchanged through time.
We'll ever love thee,
cherish thee
dear Crawford High.

High School graduation, and indeed my entire senior year, was both the happiest and saddest time of my life. We all found ourselves suddenly at a junction in our lives where responsibility for our future was, for the most part, on the verge of becoming our own.

Most of us looked forward to graduation with heightened anticipation and a healthy amount of anxiety. It was a little scary. An event so long cloistered in the distant future was at last upon us. When I think about it, it was like being caged for all one's life then having the door swing wide open.

What exactly would the future hold? What would we do with all this freedom? How would our lives turn out? What was this adult world we had long aspired to inhabit really like? How would the expectations match the realities?

I recalled our Commencement night, the painful good-byes to lifelong friends uttered through smiles and tears. Of course, only the girls cried. We guys made sure real tears never got past our eyelids.

There were all those sincere promises to stay in touch, although we knew we would likely never see each other again. The place we had been so impatient to leave, teachers whose classrooms we had longed to close the doors on, suddenly seemed an inviting sanctuary from a world that loomed both ominous and alluring.

Even now, I find myself wondering whatever happened to most of those kids in that photo. I wonder where they are; what happened to them; how their lives turned out. Did they find success and happiness?

We never had a high school reunion to speak of. Five years after my graduation, our school merged with a larger school in the county. Crawford High became a kindergarten and elementary school. It was heartbreaking. They even changed the name. That saddened me greatly. It was a sacrilegious act if ever there was one.

All the trophies and awards proudly displayed in a showcase in the front entrance, were boxed and carted to some musty warehouse. The weathered outlines of the letters spelling out 'Crawford High School' stood as silent testimony to the dastard deed. It made me feel as if we never were. There was no visible testament to our having ever existed. That hurt. Tampering with roots and history can be an awful thing.

Ten years after graduation, several of us spoke by phone, attempting to organize a big reunion. However, our efforts were not too successful. Only fifteen out of a class of sixty-five students attended the event held at the Hilton Hotel in Waco.

At least twelve members of my graduating class are deceased, a large number for such a small class. Three are in prison. One is a transsexual living in Provo, Utah, of all places. I have no idea what has happened to most of the others. Someday, I hope to account for them all. I have also decided that as soon as possible, I will do whatever it takes to return Crawford High, my alma mater, to its rightful place of honor. Recounting all this now has cemented my resolve to finally act.

I confess that at my core, I am, and have always been, a sentimentalist. I find a certain painfulness in remembering very special moments that can live on only in your memory. I suppose I have always felt this way, even when I was a kid. However, over the years I have been far too goal-obsessed to schedule time for fond remembrances or anything that did not contribute to my balance sheet. Success has a price.

You see, with success comes a responsibility or perhaps a need to improve upon the earlier success. The question is never: What have you done?" It is always: "What have you done today?"

Until now, anything that stood in the way of my riding that never-ending success-go-round fell to a lower level of importance. Admittedly, it is a cunning trap that can be the undoing of high-strung, success-driven A-types who fail to negotiate the curves.

However, I have always known in my heart of hearts, I am not the fire-breathing capitalist with ice water for blood. I am not one who stops at nothing to achieve a financial objective. I have had to summon that fiercely competitive quality that makes it possible for me to walk among the heathens and not become one myself.

So, I find these recollections both stirring and quite difficult. I cannot believe almost twenty-five years have passed. I am at once blessed and cursed with perfect memory of those times of my life. No other period holds the same meaning; generates the same intensity of emotion, nor creates the same longing to revisit as does those high school years. I regret having wished them to pass so quickly.

During the summer, before my final undergrad year at Harvard, I spent a week in Rosedale. One afternoon, I found myself walking the vacant campus of Crawford High. I had not returned since that long ago Commencement night. The place was haunting and deserted, except for a lone maintenance person locking the building up when I arrived.

I am sure I walked every square foot of those grounds, remembering long ago days, and months and years spent there. I peered through the windows into familiar classrooms, now furnished with much smaller chairs and desks. Approaching a locked door at one end of the main building, I stared through a glass pane down a long, empty hallway bathed in evening shadows.

I stood there for the longest time, unable to move away. For a moment, I could almost see childhood friends walking the hallway; rummaging through lockers; playfully jostling each other. I could hear their voices and the reverberations of their footsteps against the highly polished concrete surface. I cupped my hands to the sides of my head and peered in even more intently.

For a brief time, I could almost make out faces in the distance. These faces looked so young, so immature, and so happy and carefree. Even the teachers appeared youthful. I suppose they really were. It is hard to accept that I am now older than many of my teachers were then.

I was there, too—with Rachel, walking side by side with her, feeling ten feet tall. I kept gazing and realized I was having a spiritual experience that affected me in a way I had not expected. The place seemed hallowed, almost shrine-like. It was as if, without moving an inch, I had suddenly been transported back in time and space. My feet seemed rooted to the spot. My eyes were fixed. I found it difficult to move, even harder to leave.

I know this must sound more than a little melodramatic, but there is a sadness in moving beyond memorable mileposts, knowing you can never go back and can seldom take with you those you care about. It is all about moving on, starting anew and often alone.

Every now and then, both in nightdreams and daydreams, I return to that summer afternoon. I am still standing there staring, peering into the past. I return to my beloved Rosedale, to those halcyon days spent at Crawford. I hear the voices. I see the faces. I close my eyes tightly and I am nearly there again, staring down that long hallway, hearing the laughter, feeling the moment. In reality, I am thousands of miles away. Still, I am there. I am always there.

Chapter Eight

Sweet Rachel

My fondest and most treasured memories are of Rachel Summer; beautiful, soft, angelic, regal, petite, strong, yet fragile Rachel. Rachel happened into my life at the age of sixteen, changing it forever, stirring within me emotions I had no idea existed.

I first met her when I was a high school sophomore at Crawford. She arrived in Rosedale quite unexpectedly from Beaumont, Texas the summer before, to live with her uncle and aunt, Doyal and Maureen Summers.

Rachel proved herself a brilliant student. She was soft spoken, quietly alluring and possessed the most beautiful eyes I have ever seen. I felt certain she could see right through to my soul. I was certain if I gazed into them long enough, I would find myself hypnotized. I did and I was.

Even now, whenever I close my eyes and think of Rachel, I can still smell her sweet, intoxicating aroma. I can feel her softness and her gentle touch. I even hear the melodic sound of her angelic voice. The years have done nothing to dim those memories.

I do not intend this to read like the opening page of some cheap, dime-store romance novel. I honor my memory of Rachel far too much for that. I had taken close notice of girls long before, but none captured my imagination or stirred my blood as did she. She had no peer.

I should say right now, we never made physical love to each other. I have long felt had we done so, it is inconceivable the gratification could have surpassed what Rachel and I felt for each other every day.

I am not saying I did not think about making love to Rachel. Lord knows I thought about it. I am saying we just never did it physically. To be honest, I would not have known quite what to do anyway. I remember thinking should the moment ever arise with Rachel, or any other girl and I did not instinctively run away, I would figure everything out.

When I learned Rachel was in my homeroom, it reaffirmed my belief in God, Almighty. However, when she was assigned a seat right next to mine, it cemented by belief there was a heaven, and it was in my homeroom.

At first, I was too shy to even look directly at Rachel, let alone say something to her. It was she, who finally broke the ice and began talking to me. The moment our eyes met, something connected. There was a *knowing*. Soon, Rachel and I were having lunch together every single day. We talked about everything you can imagine.

Of one thing, I was certain: I did not want her to think of me only as a male friend. There was nothing wrong with that. It is just that I did not want a relationship where she only regarded me as a buddy. I already had plenty of buddies. I wanted to occupy that special place in her heart.

We were also both Honor Society members, and nearly always studied together. Two days after she arrived at Crawford High, our resident football hero, George 'Moose' Strunk, decided he should lay claim to the school's most beautiful girl. I think he had the idea of marking his territory.

I recall the day he first approached Rachel, as the two of us were talking in the hallway just outside Miss Lewis' classroom. He stepped right into our space and introduced himself like he was some god.

"Hi there! I'm George Strunk," he said, and waited for Rachel to melt. Rachel, having obviously been forewarned about Moose, looked up at him and said: "Congratulations." She then placed her arm inside mine, tossed her head back and the two of us walked away leaving Moose nonplussed, embarrassed and twisting in the wind.

I resisted the temptation to instantly turn around and laugh at the dumbfounded look on his face. Instead, I stared straight ahead. Rachel gripped my forearm and briefly leaned her head against my shoulder. From that moment on, I was hopelessly in love. My feelings for Rachel had really started the day I first saw her.

When I ventured a glance back, 'Moose' had disappeared, dragging his tail behind him. My heart was pounding a hole in my chest. My pulse raced. My vision blurred. I was fully aware of stares and whispers of the kids we passed in the hallway. I was certain I had never, ever felt this way in my life. It felt good—unbelievably good. I cannot tell you how good. I tingled all over and knew I wanted to feel that way every day.

Although we never used the words, girlfriend and boyfriend, Rachel and I shared a wonderful, magic-filled relationship that lasted until she suddenly left halfway through our senior year. I was heartbroken.

Rachel and I had been inseparable. Other than at school and school events, we saw each other at town events and every Sunday at church. I now confess Rachel was the main reason I never complained of having to go to church every Sunday. I also used every bit of creative thinking I could muster, to find a way to accompany father to the hardware store on Saturdays.

It so happened Mr. Summers and his wife also had a custom of visiting the hardware and other stores on Saturdays. I would walk around town while father shopped. Rachel did the same and so we would have our time together. It would always end far too soon, and Sundays would come far too slowly.

I recall having many hushed conversations with Rosie about Rachel. Rosie knew and understood what I knew, which was that father would not have approved of the relationship. It was best I not suggest Rachel and I were any more than friends.

Then I came up with what I felt was a brilliant idea. I asked Rosie to befriend Rachel and to invite her over as often as possible. She agreed. I would also accompany Rosie, whenever she would visit Rachel at the Summers' place. While I do not think father was ever the wiser, I have since learned, though I suspected as much even then, mother was not at all taken in by my scheming. May God bless mothers who know and do not tell, and fathers who are often too busy to notice some things.

Rachel was not in the photograph I had in front of me. She left Rosedale the day after Christmas and a few months before the picture was taken. To my continuing regret, the only photos I have of her are those in two earlier yearbooks. The best image I have of her is the one I carry in my heart.

At the time, I did not understand why Rachel went away. Her aunt, Mrs. Summers died suddenly. And someone decided it would not be fitting and proper for a young girl to live alone with an older man, not her real father. There were the inevitable small-town rumors to avoid.

I went into deep mourning, feeling empty, betrayed, and confused by the whiplash of emotions. I even wished we had never met. I lost interest in almost everything and desperately wanted to leave town with her. It is said that kids our age then do not have a clue about love. However, that experience tells me otherwise. I know I loved Rachel and she loved me. We did not need FDA approval or parental blessings to know what we felt.

That year, Christmas Day church services meant a few precious hours under the same roof with Rachel for the last time. I could not keep my eyes off her and honestly do not recall hearing a single song or a single word spoken throughout the entire service.

We both managed to sneak into the cafeteria before everything was over. I remember holding her hand and kissing her, as we both stood at the water fountain fumbling for words. Rachel had tears in her eyes, and I shook all over. We were more afraid some grownup would happen upon us than anything else.

"Why are you crying?" I asked, stroking her tears away while struggling to keep my own eyes dry. Rachel forced a smile but did not answer. I already knew the answer. A sadness consumed both of us, the day she told me she was going away and would not be coming back. At first, I thought she was teasing, but it was soon clear she was not. Until then, I had never felt such a feeling of helplessness in all my young life.

"This could not be happening," I thought. Especially now that I had begun to exit my cocoon and was learning that my heart was not just some organ that pumped blood throughout my body. Not now that I had found something, and someone, I loved as much or more than baseball. Just why Rachel left Rosedale so abruptly baffled me.

It was the worst Christmas I ever had. Normally, the holidays were a time filled with excitement, great expectations, and joy at not having school for a couple of weeks. Our home was filled with the smell of pine from the tree, and stomach-tingling aromas from mother's cooking. Stockings hung neatly over the fireplace. At night, moonlight bounced off a puffy blanket of snow that covered the countryside, as far as one could see.

However, this year was different. All the usual trappings of Christmas were the same. I was different—inside. I was heartbroken. The most difficult part of all was knowing Rachel and I could not spend all of Christmas Day—our last day, together.

The day after Christmas, Rachel was gone forever. I knew I would likely never see or speak to her again. It devastated me to my core. I had never felt that kind of pain before. It consumed me. The thought I would never hear her call my name, feel the touch of her hand, and have my nostrils filled with her aroma again was unbearable.

"Why had God forsaken me," I whispered. No one ever said James the way she did. Rachel refused to call me Jimmy and did not like it whenever others did. She would always say:

"Your name is James. You should be called James. That is what your mother named you. No one has a right to change it." She could have called me whatever she wanted. I would have answered.

Rachel was rumored to have gone back to live with an older and newly divorced sister in Beaumont. Whether she did or not, I never knew. It was later rumored she left to go live with an aunt somewhere in Nebraska or Iowa.

I once asked Mr. Summers where she was. He seemed reluctant to answer. Finally, he told me that as far as he knew, she was in Beaumont. He then gave me an address scribbled on the inside of a matchbook cover with two matches left in it. He ripped them out before giving it to me. I have since wondered if Mr. Summers felt he was preventing some irresponsible juvenile act on my part. The cover was later destroyed when I left it in my jeans and mother washed them. Fortunately, I had memorized the address.

I must have written a hundred letters to that Beaumont address. None were ever answered or returned. I imagined someone was intercepting them and throwing them away. Or worse yet, someone was reading them. The very thought of someone other than Rachel reading my heartfelt words of love and longing was unbearable.

To this day, although I never received a letter from Rachel, I have never thought it was because she did not want to stay in touch with me. I never doubted she missed me as much as I missed her.

Until I graduated from Crawford, no one ever replaced Rachel in my life. No one could. I owe Rosie so much for helping me maintain my sanity through it all, but I decided not to go to my senior prom. I suppose I was still grieving my loss. I would not have had fun anyway and it would not have been fair to my date.

So much has happened since those days. Yet, after all the living I have done, all the turns I have taken, and the women I have known, I find it hard to understand why I still think of Rachel as warmly as I do. On occasion, I imagine inhaling the fragrance she once wore. I wheel around, half expecting to see her. That amazes me.

I often wonder whatever happened to Rachel—if she is still alive. More than likely, she went to college, got a degree, and is enjoying a successful career. She probably got married, has one or two kids, and likely lives in the Midwest somewhere.

I wonder if she remembers and still thinks of me from time to time. Four years ago, her uncle, Doyal Summers died. I asked mother if anyone resembling Rachel came to the funeral.

"Rachel who?" Mother asked. There was no reason she should remember Rachel as well as I did.

"Rachel Summers," I said. She was his niece, remember? She came to live with them for a while, then left just before..."

"Oh! I remember! I remember!" She interrupted. "Rachel was a very beautiful girl. The two of you were real good friends." I am certain mother's understatement was intentional. "No, I didn't see her then," she said. "She wasn't there."

After that, neither of us spoke for quite a while.

A few months after Rachel left and took my heart with her, graduation came and went. Still heartbroken, I looked forward to college, though my scholarship to Harvard would not take effect until the following June. They said something about funds not being committed until mid-fiscal year. That posed a problem regarding my draft deferment. To maintain it, officials at Harvard accepted my September enrollment and officially delayed my class enrollment until June the following year. That was fine with me.

I do remember wondering if Harvard had a real baseball team. For a brief instant, I entertained the notion of playing baseball in college. However, that silly notion soon passed. Besides, whether Harvard had a team or not, I was not aware of them having produced a single major league player.

Except for the scholarship, I would most certainly have chosen to attend the University of Texas, Texas A&M, or some other Southwest Conference university with a strong baseball program. I was certain I could have been an academic all-American baseball player and had a good chance of being drafted into the majors.

However, when you receive a full academic scholarship to a university such as Harvard, you do not say "No thanks, I would really rather play baseball." And you especially do not say that, if your father's name is John Quincy Phalen and you value life. Who could have blamed him?

As for my brother Carter, following his graduation four years earlier, he somehow escaped the claws of Selective Service for two years. He then landed a coveted two-year stint in the National Guard. He was extremely lucky. Everyone and his brother were after those slots in the Guard. Even those spouting hawkish rhetoric were trying to get in the guard. Anyway, when Carter's tour of duty ended, he was placed on active reserve, subject to immediate call-up.

My brother had never expressed any desire to go to college. He once told me that everything he needed to know, he learned in mother's womb. Carter was not smiling when he said that. He was dead serious.

Rosemarie had successfully completed her freshman year and would soon begin her sophomore year at the University of Texas. Following high school, she had spent more than two months at a Church mission in Brownsville, working with children on the Mexican border. The experience touched her very deeply. You could hear it in her voice, in the way she spoke of being blessed to be an American. That is the way Rosie was—giving...always giving.

During that last summer, I shared many of my secret thoughts, my dreams, and fears with Rosie. I spoke often of Rachel… how much I still loved and missed her. For me, it was healing, to be able to talk about her and to speak Rachel's name aloud. I also discovered that as close as Rosie and I had been as children, I never knew much about her private world—her inner self. All that would soon change.

Chapter Nine

Rosie

I suppose in most families, it is the youngest child most often favored or spoiled in some way. While none of us Phalen kids were really favored or spoiled, Rosie was, is, and will always be, very special to me. It is Rosie and my mother who are responsible for my view of women as equal or superior to men, in all the ways that truly matter. Whether physically or intellectually, there was precious little Carter, or I could do that Rosie could not do as well, and most often better.

Mother could wield a mean hammer, power a chainsaw, or impart jewels of wisdom, in a manner worthy of a revered philosopher. As I mentioned earlier, she could fish and hunt berries with the best of them. The one thing she never mastered as well as father was the manly art of taking a strap or branch to us. She believed in talking more than did he. That was enough to nominate her for sainthood.

I remember my sister Rosie with great warmth, deep affection, and moist eyes. Only a few years ago did it dawn on me that Carter and I were blessed with something Rosie never had: a sister. Everyone should have a sister, especially a sister like Rosie. Sadly, she never experienced that joy.

Of course, mother treated her more like a sister than would have most mothers. Yet, I am certain it was not the same. Sure, we had our minor sibling differences. And I am not going to stretch credulity by suggesting we never fought. Still, I would not trade a single one of our childhood moments together for anything in the world.

Rosie and I had a special bond strengthened by the fact mother gave her certain responsibilities, regarding my care. She loved playing big sister, practicing, and developing her mothering skills at my expense. I was her willing, if perhaps unwitting guinea pig, and suffered no lasting damage as a result. Sis fed me, bathed me, changed my diapers; she even bandaged my frequent cuts and scrapes.

According to mother, when Rosie was three years old, she even made a thankfully unsuccessful attempt to nurse me. We both share laughs about it to this day. It came about so innocently.

Having seen mother perform this task with such ease and having seen the calming effect it had always had on me, Rosie decided she would try to nurse me too. However, there was one important matter she did not take into consideration. At less than one year old, I was already weaned. Some may wonder how I came to be weaned at the exact age of eleven months, sixteen days, thirteen hours, and twenty-two minutes. It came about quite suddenly.

My mother has always been ambivalent when recounting the events of that unseasonably cool summer afternoon. She was sitting in the swing, which still hangs from one end of our long front porch, cradling me securely in her lap. I was hungry, crying, and had been causing quite a commotion for some time. Finally, she concluded I needed feeding.

She had no sooner sat down and began to breastfeed me than I promptly chomped down with my tiny front teeth, right into her left breast. She let loose with a pained, primal scream unlike any heard before or since in that part of Texas.

A second later, having carefully rescued her nipple from my vice-like crunch, she shot to her feet, made a beeline into the house, straight to my baby bed. There she deposited me rather unceremoniously. From that moment on, I lost all my accustomed dining privileges and was forced, cold turkey, to eat with utensils like everyone else.

I assure all that I have suffered no long-term ill effects, because of the abrupt cancellation of my mammary dining privileges. The spoon diversion program I entered seemed to have worked just fine and I can attribute no lasting dysfunction to the event.

I am certain that a visit or two to a therapist would, through regression therapy, yield some horrific emotional crisis from which I would never recover. That of course would lead to a huge lawsuit, jail time for my mother, years of counseling for me, a movie-of-the-week, a tour of the talk show circuit, including a segment on Hard Copy and the destruction of my family. No, thank you.

Apparently, Rosie forgot mother's traumatic episode or had not taken it to heart. One day, a couple of months later, owing to my screaming and raving, she decided to emulate mother. Her chest was as flat as mine, but that did not stop her from making a valiant, if ill-advised, attempt.

Fortunately for her, mother walked into the room just in time and saved her from a fate worse than death. She has since, on countless occasions, expressed her eternal gratitude to mother.

To father's consternation, Rosie was always more comfortable wearing Levi's, cowboy boots and mixing it up with Carter and me. She had little use for fancy, frilly, lacy things that made her feel more like a doll than a real living person. Except for church and school, she always wore whatever we wore.

When she got her hair washed, got dressed up in her best dress and shoes, Rosie was really something to see. I did not realize it at the time, but when she dressed up in girl stuff, Carter and I treated her differently. We were more deferential; allowing her to get into the car first; opening doors for her; pulling her chair out at the dinner table; saying excuse me if we stepped on her toes and not socking her when she teased us or made faces.

Father wanted Rosie to be more ladylike, versed in the social graces, and less vocal—much less vocal. He often scolded her severely, telling her she was as rambunctious and noisy as were us boys. Father said she was destined to never be considered a lady if she did not mend her ways. He blamed mother for most of that.

Whenever he would scold Rosie soundly, for that or any other reason, Rosie would always fall into a state of abject silence for what seemed like days. She became someone else, like a mute. I marveled at her ability to take and maintain this vow of silence with the determination of a resolute P.O.W. She would 'go within', and only days later come out and be herself again. We would miss her during those times she was away. When it was all over, she would not speak about it to anyone.

Rosie was not permitted to wear high heels or use makeup. Father insisted no daughter of his was going to live under his roof and parade around like a hussy or some Bourbon Street floozy (My apologies to Bourbon Street).

Mother did not wear high heels or even use makeup. Father felt she looked just fine without them. I am sure mother's avoidance of cosmetics was due to father's insistence, although she would surely deny it.

It was not until Rosie was a freshman at the University of Texas that I recall seeing her in heels and a small amount of lip-gloss. I do remember she seemed a bit awkward in the shoes, although she struggled to appear at ease.

And of course, boys and dating were completely out of the question for Rosie. Father reasoned there would be plenty of time for things like that after she graduated high school. A casual conversation with a boy at the church picnic was fine if the boy maintained a respectable distance and did not try to take things beyond gentlemanly conversation.

Father lectured Carter and me that as loving, responsible brothers, we had a duty to always protect our sister's honor. I took that to mean we were to at least spy on her, and at worst deal with any boy who did not give her respect.

It was for her senior prom that Rosie was permitted her first and only date. His name was Jonah Beck, Jr. We called him J.B. His father, an elder at our church, was well respected throughout Rosedale and Crawford County. Mr. Beck owned the local hardware and grain store.

Before J.B. could officially ask Rosie to go to the prom, he had to first ask father. Carter and I would later joke that J.B. asked dad to the prom. Rosie just went along. That was not too far from the truth and was not the least bit funny.

The night of the prom, J. B. arrived in his dad's blue and white, 1955 Buick Roadmaster. He was all decked out in a black tuxedo and carrying a corsage for Rosie. Mother had spent hours helping her get dressed. Rosie looked gorgeous. She even sneaked a little Vaseline onto Rosie's already pink lips to give them a glossy appearance. Rosie looked so beautiful, we asked her what happened to our real sister.

J.B. was clearly nervous. He kept stuttering and fumbling with his hands. Beads of sweat covered his forehead like morning dew. Every now and then he would take a deep breath, expel it loudly, and wipe his forehead with the back of his hand. Mother handed him a Kleenex. Seconds later, he needed another. She decided to hand him the whole box. I suppose it did not help that Carter and I kept passing through the room and staring at ol' J.B.

Finally, Rosie was ready. So was father. He had decided, without a word to mother, Rosie, or anyone, to drive the two of them to the prom. He would return later, to chauffeur them back to our house. And that's exactly what he did.

I felt so embarrassed for Rosie. Her expression fell with a loud thud, as an audible sigh of disappointment escaped her lips. Father sprang all this on her at the last possible moment. There she was, on the cusp of womanhood and being treated as if she was incapable of going to a prom without her father parked between her and her date.

If Rosie felt hurt, she tried hard not to show it that night. She later confided to me that father's presence did not really bother her until they arrived at the school. Several kids spotted her. A couple of them sneered and snickered. Rosie ignored them. Ever since grade school, we had grown accustomed to kids teasing and calling us church mice or worse. Rosie decided nothing was going to spoil the night for her. She was willing to suffer almost any indignity to see it remained, for the most part, her night.

I have come to suspect Rosie's being so sheltered was the main reason she was not exactly boy-wise when she arrived in Austin at the University of Texas. By the time Christmas break of her freshman year rolled around, she was pregnant.

Poor Rosie. Her very first sexual encounter and she got pregnant. It was a truly horrific period in Rosie's life. I too, would not want to relive one second of that time. Father was devastated, convinced he and mother had failed as god-fearing parents. He felt especially humiliated, as a father and head of household.

Publicly, he was embarrassed. Father seemed to feel his moral authority had been dealt a death blow. How could he ever hold his head high again and command the respect of townspeople he had known all his life? After all, he reasoned, he was an elder in the church—the Chief Elder. He had long justified his strict parenting by pointing to the bible and insisting results would prove him right.

Now, this...this stain, this blight on the family name appeared to have undone all he had achieved. It must surely be the devil's work, he seemed to feel. Mother was practically silent—much too silent for my liking. I understood it was in deference to father, but I did not think she owed him her complete silence. I wanted her to step out of father's shadow and be herself.

Of course, mother engaged in no verbal chastisement of Rosie. She did what any caring mother would do; she put her arms around her and cried with her and for her. We could all see the pain in mother's face and hear it in her quivering voice.

Mother's pain and sadness came more from feeling she had not explicitly counseled her young daughter in the ways of the world. There had never been this no-holds-barred kind of conversation with Rosie or any of us, for that matter. I mean, sex was something one did not discuss with their children back then. I suppose in father's mind, a discussion of sex would have been akin to encouraging it.

In the Phalen household, sex was rarely mentioned. When it was, it was only referred to in biblical terms. During our family bible-gatherings, father would warn us of a host of sins to avoid. Fornication—never defined but generally understood—was only one of them. I looked up the word and understood well what it meant from a purely intellectual perspective. Of course, sex, and the very natural and often premature pursuit thereof, is anything but an intellectual exercise.

Why most parents, particularly my parents, avoided the discussion I will never understand. For god's sake, we lived on a farm. Sex was all around us. The horses did it. The bulls and cows did it. The dogs did it. Bees did it. My mother and father did it. After all, the good-fairy or Federal Express had not left us on the porch. So, go figure.

Rosie later confided she had agonized terribly, before finally informing us she was pregnant. I could not imagine the pain and anxiety she had gone through. She chose to tell everyone, during her first night home for Christmas break. It took a great deal of courage for her to do that, knowing what she knew about father. I have often wondered if I would have had the strength to confront the stark realities as she did.

From the moment I saw Rosie, I knew there was something different about her; I do not mean physically, although she did look like a Vogue model to me. It was not that I harbored any suspicions, but there was something strange and aloof in her spirit, her eyes, her voice. It troubled me a lot. I mentioned it to her.

Twice, I asked her what was troubling her. She did not answer and did not look me directly in the eyes. Before I could repeat my question, Rosie slowly raised her right arm across her chest and held it there. That simple movement had a very special meaning to Rosie, Carter, and me.

When I was seven, the three of us kids had made a promise. We would never lie to each other; no big lies; no little lies; no white lies. We agreed that if something was ever seriously wrong and we could not answer truthfully, we would place our right arm across our chest. Without uttering a word, we would each know and understand that more love than words was needed. The words could always come later.

So, I watched with a sinking feeling, as Rosie placed her arm across her chest. I saw tears in her eyes. That frightened me. Before I could say or do anything else, she wiped away the tears and smiled broadly.

"I'll be alright," she assured me, placing her hand on mine, and changing the subject. Earlier, Carter had noticed something too.

A full month before Rosie revealed her dark secret, mother was aware something was not right. She later told us of dreaming she was at Rayfield's Department store one Saturday morning, buying baby clothes. When she awoke, Rosie's name was on her lips. The dream had been more a vision than a dream.

Christmas Eve night, after we returned from church services, Rosie broke the news to us. It was the most electric, riveting and numbing moment I had known. Father grew physically weak and had to sit right away. Mother went to him, to make sure he was alright. Carter and I rushed to a tearful Rosie, put our arms around her and told her how much we loved her.

For the longest time, except for Rosie's sobbing, there was dead silence. No one spoke. It was one of those awful moments when you wish time would pass quickly. It creeps. You wish yourself well beyond where you are. Time stands still. Minutes later, father composed himself, asked mother to get his bible and told Carter and me to leave the room.

That Christmas was unlike any we ever experienced before or since. Rosie's shocking revelation had barely lost its echo, when I learned Carter had his own, no less stunning secret to share. He proudly informed us he had volunteered for the Marine Corps. My mouth fell open.

"Say what?" I screamed at the top of my voice. At first, I felt hurt and disappointed he had not told me. We had all suspected he would be called up eventually, but I never thought he would up and volunteer, not for the Marines of all things. I had always heard Marines were the first in and the last out, often in body bags. I knew all about that Semper Fi stuff, but this was my brother!

When I finally gave him a chance, Carter explained the anticipation of being called up had driven him nuts. He just wanted to get it over with on his own terms. He told me he feared if he had told me earlier, I might have persuaded him not to enlist. I certainly would have tried.

Now, I had to hurriedly come to grips with the fact Carter would soon be leaving for boot camp at Parris Island, South Carolina. I had heard bone-chilling horror stories about that place.

It was scary to think that within a few months, he could be wading through some rice paddy in Vietnam with incoming artillery going off above his head. How was he ever going to survive without Rosie and me to talk to and play with? How could he possibly survive without mother's home-cooking and father's stern direction?

Did Carter's enlistment, Rosie's unwanted pregnancy and my leaving for Harvard all mean we were no longer kids? Did this mean that days of lying on our backs and staring up at funny-shaped clouds, jumping logs and skipping rocks were gone? I feared the answer was yes.

As startling as Carter's news was, Rosie's appeared to affect father more than his son's volunteering for the Corps. He seemed more upset by Rosie's pregnancy casting a shadow over his good name, than the terrible danger inherent in Carter's certain tour of duty in Vietnam.

I hope I am not being too harsh or unfair in my assessment of father's reaction. All I know is that we were all in a maelstrom. This was all happening so fast. One day, all was well. We were going about our lives, enjoying our friends, each other, the land, the predictable, albeit boring security of country life.

Then, everything changed with warp speed. We were all struggling to find our way. It was a predicament we were all unaccustomed to being in. Somehow, it had always seemed that real serious problems only afflicted other families, not the Phalen family.

Father somberly insisted we all pray, both as a family and as individuals. We did. There were moments when it seemed someone had died—that we were in mourning. The rest of us made a conscious effort to avoid laughter at all costs. I suppose we felt laughter would be an affront to father, who seemed to wallow in his deep hurt and disappointment. I had a feeling of powerlessness. Was this what adulthood was all about? Was this really just a harbinger of things to come?

Suddenly, my own words, expressing a youthful longing to be grown up, were beginning to haunt me—even mock me. You know the words. You've said them yourself. As a kid, you find yourself under the boot of so-called parental oppression, relegated to your place and say to yourself: "I wish I were *grown." And* you mean it. You sincerely long for adulthood. I wish I had a dollar for every time I have uttered those words. At the tender age of sixteen and a half, I was already beginning to long for the past.

Chapter Ten

The Wages of Sin

Rosie lost the baby.

In her third month, she miscarried. A week later, she attempted suicide. We were sent reeling. Rosie? Suicide? No, not Rosie, I thought. Not our family. Such a thing just was not possible. Our world turned inside out, upside down, twisted like a pretzel. That was my initial and admittedly selfish appraisal.

My sister Rosie, whom I had known and loved all my life, had tried to take her own life. The very thought of it was incomprehensible for me. It remains so, to this day. Even now, I have to say the words aloud, just to reconfirm the fact it really happened.

Surely God had forsaken us, I thought. Scared out of my mind, I dreaded to think of what new tragedy each succeeding morning would bring. It was a terrible beginning of a new year. I prayed for Rosie as I had never prayed for anyone else before.

It was not long after her suicide attempt, that Rosie slipped into what we now know was a deep state of depression. She desperately needed psychological help, but that was out of the question. It was bad enough she had gotten pregnant, lost the baby and attempted suicide. If word ever got out that Elder Phalen's daughter was seeing a shrink, father may as well leave Texas. Even I could not reach Rosie. Carter tried desperately to get through to her, until the day he packed, and we drove him to the Greyhound Bus depot, next to Stoddard's Drug Store and Five & Dime.

Three other nervous-looking kids were making the same trip to South Carolina that day. All were very close friends of Carter's. He expressed to me the hope they were not joining because of him. I was certain they were, though I never told Carter I thought so. I guess he did not want to feel in any way responsible, should they never make it back home alive.

I remember taking an especially hard look at the four of them. Would they ever return home? Would I ever see my brother again, I wondered. Plain and simple, I was scared. My mind overflowed with questions:

"Why in God's name did all this have to be happening to our family? Why did there have to be a Vietnam War, anyway? What in the devil were we doing there? Where was the Gulf of Tonkin and where was the proof of an attack on our ships?"

By now, America had grown too accustomed to seeing the war delivered into their living rooms during the dinner hour by Walter Cronkite, Chet Huntley, and David Brinkley. At no time in its history had such a conflict been made such a personal part of our everyday existence.

I looked at Carter and saw a boy who suddenly appeared taller, stronger, and much more grownup than I had ever seen him. I suppose when you stand to lose your life in a war, one deserves to be viewed through a different lens—a more mature lens. Yet, it struck me as odd that grownups, who were only days earlier referring to these kids as boys, were now calling them men.

What suddenly made them men? Was it the fact they would soon be in harm's way? Was this honor hastily bestowed as a way of soothing the consciences of old men too old or too unwilling to fight? Maybe these boys really were men.

However, in the many years that have followed, as I have looked at old video clips of these fierce fighting men, their youthful appearances amaze me. They should have been wearing baseball or football uniforms. They should have been worried about S.A.T. scores, not the latest manipulated casualty figures. I now look at their fighting gear and it occurs to me these boys must surely be playing dress-up in their fathers' war outfits. They were not.

Even now, I feel a significant degree of guilt at having been bright enough, resourceful enough, blessed enough to obtain a college deferment. I understand what must have been going through the mind of a young Bill Clinton, though I do not condone his later lack of candor about it. I too, was not eager to go to Vietnam.

Meanwhile, so many dutifully answered the call and ultimately went to their deaths. They asked no questions. My decision was not without its consequence. Who was I? I was not a congressman's son. I was not a Senator's son. I was not a child of privilege. What made me so special? What made them so special?

I gave my dear brother an especially long and powerful embrace, while patting him on the back repeatedly. I kept saying something like: "You take care of yourself. You hear? And hurry back home, too."

Patting on the back as you embrace is something men tend to do. You seldom see women do that. Men cannot permit themselves to hug another man, even their own brother, in a firm and still way. Do not ask me why. We just do not.

I did not allow myself to cry either. After all, I was for all practical purposes a man already. All that crying and emotionalism were for women, I thought. Father did not cry, and I was not going to break down either. I would wait until I was back home and standing alone in the middle of those rolling fields we had played in so much as kids. I would hold out until I had reached the crest of Heritage hill and stood in the shadows of the towering Man of War oak tree, that I later renamed Carter Oak. For me, it became a living monument to my brother. I would wait and cry then.

Rosie hardly spoke at all, as we waited. She insisted on standing some distance away, staring blankly at Carter, with her arms folded. Minutes before the final call crackled over the public address system, Carter walked over to her and put his arms around her. Rosie hesitated at first, then embraced him tearfully, burying her face in his chest and shaking. Mother, her eyes also filled with tears, joined them and the three soon returned to where father stood watching.

Within minutes, we were all accompanying Carter to the bus door. Just before he climbed aboard, father said his good-bye, with one hand clasping Carter's hand and the other gripping his shoulder. I remember watching and wanting so badly for him to embrace Carter; that was something I had seldom seen him do to any of us before. I tried to will it to be.

I peered deeply into father's eyes and hoped for even a hint of a tear—just one. It was not to be. I am sure he felt the sadness we all felt. He simply had his own way of showing it. Father was not a man to vent his emotions in a graphic way. That is just the way he was. Mother told me years later, that was the way his father was.

Once aboard the bus, Carter placed his stuffed garment bag into the overhead and plopped down onto a window seat. We stood there waving at him, trying to read his lips. That failing, Carter took an index finger and drew an outline of a large valentine on the window. He then pointed at us. That touched mother deeply. She really started crying then.

Rosie began shaking. I put my arms around her, as the bus started to pull away. With the gnarled, oft-broken fingers of his right hand pressed lightly against his brow, father came to attention and snapped Carter a sharp salute. He then returned the hand to his side and turned away quickly.

The riveting images from that emotional day seared themselves in my mind like a branding iron. I can see them as if I were still standing there. Long after Carter's bus disappeared, we remained there, staring silently into the dust-filled distance.

No one wanted to move, but there was nothing more to say. Father was the first to break the spell, when he turned and started for the car. He took long, lumbering strides that none of us could match. He held his head down as he walked. The unusual sight struck me, because father always walked so proudly, his head held high, shoulders erect, eyes straight ahead. I wondered what was going through his mind. What was he feeling deep inside, where only he and God knew?

The short trip home without Carter was the longest I had ever taken. In the several days and weeks following, Rosie began to come around slowly. She became more and more spontaneous, initiating fitful conversations with mother and me. She avoided father as much as possible.

Around 6:30 one Saturday morning, the two of us rose and had a quick breakfast. Minutes later, we took poles, bait, and lures in hand, then headed for our secret pier at Crawford Lake. Along the way, as the morning sun crept above the hills, Rosie and I reminisced about how many times the three of us had made this trek.

As we talked, she became more and more emotional, though she tried hard to sound calm. This continued long after we reached the pier and sat with bare feet dangling over the cool water.

We sat talking for hours on end, not caring what time it was or where we were. The lures were untouched, the hooks never baited, and our lines never cast. We sat there talking candidly, revealing things each of us never knew.

I had not known that, as a young girl, Rosie felt very lonely; at times unwanted; convinced that she did not really fit in. She felt lonely, not having a sister to confide in as only sisters can. Rosie also told of having a diary named Carrie she pretended was her sister. I never knew that. I do not think even mother knew. I felt deeply honored she shared that part of her life with me.

Rosie revealed having always believed she looked homely and not the least bit attractive. I was stunned. She had always been a very beautiful girl and had grown up to be a very beautiful woman, my prejudices aside. Rosie explained it was in part because of this unspoken view of herself, that she chose to dress and act like a tomboy. By so doing, no one would expect her to look beautiful. Her tomboy facade was her mask.

As I listened, Rosie's words resonated in my head. I could not help wondering how she managed to closet her true feelings and thoughts so thoroughly. Then came my turn. I confided to Rosie that I once considered asking that I be given away to H.L. Hunt, the late billionaire. I had read he had two sons whom he adored and spared no expense to satisfy. I envied them and concluded were I one of H.L.'s sons, I could do anything I wanted, including sharing my good fortune with Carter and her.

Rosie laughed, saying had she known of my secret, she would have joined me in insisting I be given to Hunt for at least a year or two. It was good to hear Rosie laugh, if only for a few brief seconds.

It was nearly noon, before our conversation turned to her pregnancy and the loss of the baby. I treaded lightly. It was clear by her wavering voice and teary eyes, it was still too fresh in her mind. Nonetheless, she clearly wanted to talk about it.

The most touching thing I remember was Rosie telling me she had named the baby James, after me. No one else knew that. I was speechless. I still get a slight chill thinking about it now. She made me promise not to tell anyone and only released me from this promise, when she learned I was writing this book.

During our conversation, Rosie gave me the distinct feeling she blamed father for James' death. I tried to argue reason, but she would have none of it. Rosie suspected father had, as she put it, prayed mightily that the stain be removed. There was no doubt in her mind he had importuned God to intervene, and God had done so. Nothing I said seemed to have a chance of changing her mind. I understood the depth and sincerity of her belief.

This traumatic event in Rosie's life caused her to question even God. She felt guilty about that. For her, it had become a matter of pain layered with guilt and disappointment. Again, I felt powerless to change anything. I have since learned that my listening and being there for Rosie mattered very much to her.

Three months passed. Carter called and informed us he had completed boot camp but would not be coming home prior to being shipped out, as he put it. He had gotten his orders and would be heading for Vietnam within ten days, with a brief stopover in Okinawa. We had all been praying he would come home first. It was not to be.

Carter also explained his classification was 0311. The more I learned its meaning, the more frightened I became for him. You see, 0311's, also referred to as *grunts*, were the foot soldiers; they were considered fodder. In chess terminology, they were the pawns and were naturally plentiful. They had to be. They were the expendables. They were the ones who were not only *on* the front lines; they *were* the front lines.

Grunts drew enemy fire and engaged the enemy. They drew them out, while Generals remained in the rear with their maps and pushpins. I asked Carter why he had not tried to go to OCS (Officer Candidate School) in Quantico, Virginia. He chuckled.

The fact was, being a first or second Lieutenant in Vietnam was no free lunch either. He'd heard the life expectancy of a First or Second "Louie" in Vietnam was about as bad as being a grunt. They received instructions to either tape over or black out their shiny Lieutenant bars before they set foot on the tarmac.

I was the last to speak to Carter that night. I listened to him talk and was impressed by how much older he sounded. My god, only three months had passed, and he sounded as if he was five years older. Yet, despite the bravado, that is part of the standard equipment issued to young Marines, I could sense his fear. He was reading the headlines, just as we were.

I remember asking Carter questions about boot camp. We talked about all the things we would do when he returned home. I did not want to let him go and did so only when I heard others in the background hounding him to get off the phone.

After, he hung up I had this gnawing feeling of guilt. I felt guilty I was not there with my brother. We should have been together. We had always done everything together; shared everything, talked about everything. The feeling persisted for days. And again, I felt powerless and unable to change things.

By the beginning of May, against mother's persistent pleading, Rosie had returned to the University of Texas and was preparing to pour herself into her studies. She grew more determined than ever to become an elementary school teacher. Yet, in our many conversations and letters, it was clear she was in pain and still mourning for her son.

I doubted she could concentrate on her studies and tried desperately to refocus her, to no avail. It concerned me that given her grief, she might fail her courses and fall prey to renewed depression. At some point, our conversations would always turn to father.

I do not believe Rosie ever hated father. I just think she felt profoundly hurt and disappointed in some of his actions and, more significantly, some of his inactions. She often spoke of the fact he never put his arms around her. He never once attempted to understand and console her. Rosie knew that in father's mind, she had attempted the ultimate sin—suicide. Still, why could he not have embraced her just once, wiped her tears away and assured her everything would be alright?

I cried for Rosie and for myself. I was going to be an uncle. Finally, I had thought, there would be a Phalen kid younger than me. I cried for Rosie because I loved her. Whatever hurt her hurt me too. I was also angry that Rosie ultimately had to confront her demons alone. I suppose we all have to face our demons alone. More than anything else, I wanted to do more than feel sorry for her; for myself; for all of us.

During this awful time, father's demeanor was that of the consummate elder. "It is the will of Almighty God," he insisted in an unemotional, unwavering voice. He had always referred to the baby as it, not he. It was as if the baby and Rosie's pregnancy were never real to him.

The last thing Rosie wanted to hear was that the baby's death was God's will. For a time, she confessed, she stopped praying; she stopped believing in God altogether. How could God take her baby, while the likes of Charles Manson and other pond scum were still breathing and living on taxpayer's money?

Rosie was never really the same again. None of us were, but she was lastingly traumatized. I miss the Rosie I knew before all this happened. She lost her bubbly, effervescent personality that had always been infectious. One could not have been around the old Rosie and remain despondent or moody. It just was not possible. If you wanted to brood, you had to make sure Rosie was not around, or take yourself a long walk deep into the woods somewhere.

Over the years, she went through frequent periods of being moody, distant, withdrawn, and silent. Still, she was able to confide in me and I in her. The two of us had always talked about things, pondered imponderables, mused about age-old questions of life and death, what-ifs of every kind, wondered where God came from, why he made man in the first place.

Once, I came up with the brilliant deduction that, with all due reverence, God had to have been on some monumental ego trip back in the beginning. Just think about it. Suppose you were that all-powerful and had just completed a magnificent creation called the Universe. I mean, you had really outdone yourself.

You looked all around at this astounding, ever-mushrooming, infinite work and said Wow! All this had never been done before. It would never be done again. Then you realized you were alone. There was no one else around to share your Wow, no crowd in the bleachers cheering and doing the Wave. What would you do?

You would likely use your god-power to create someone with whom to share all this mind-bending awesomeness. I think I would have. Rosie conceded my deduction, though a bit sacrilegious, was probably as reasonable as any she had heard. We laughed until tears streamed from our eyes.

Those distant, wonderful days we spent as children, those innocent times, those precious moments children can never fully comprehend or appreciate, now belonged to the ages.

Chapter Eleven

The Homecoming

I graduated high school with honors, was valedictorian and earned a 4.0 g.p.a. To my folks' great delight, I received many academic scholarships, coveted designations as a National Fellow, and a National Merit Scholar—major honors bestowed upon only a few high school students across the country. I did not feel like a nerd or an egghead, but I suppose I was. However, I would like to think I did not look the part.

Meanwhile, Rosie was back at The University of Texas. After several months of waiting, I was only days away from heading to Harvard. I had aged considerably during those past few months and had lost a considerable degree of my innocent view of my world.

We were being told the Vietnam War was moving slowly toward, to quote the euphemistic Nixonian phrase, Peace With Honor. Then we received a dramatic, heart-stopping phone call. Carter, who had enlisted in the Marines a few months earlier, was returning home, for medical reasons. We were thrilled. At first, it did not matter what those medical reasons were. Carter was coming home.

I remember father, mother and me going to town to meet his bus. The day was brooding; the skies were dark and ominous looking. It had threatened to rain all day, but not a single raindrop had fallen.

Hardly anyone spoke at breakfast. Mother was so nervous and excited; she could hardly sit still. Father barely touched his food and soon left the house to take a long walk. I ate sparingly, walked outside, and stood on the back porch watching father head across the fields toward the old Man of War oak—Carter Oak.

Father took long, gangly strides—his hands dug deeply into the pockets of his faded blue coveralls. I stood watching, until he had almost disappeared. I wondered what he was thinking, what emotions he was permitting himself to feel, with only the gaze of God and his young son upon him.

A few hours later, the time had come for us to leave for the depot. I waited in the living room with mother. She sat rocking back and forth in the rocker given her decades earlier by her mother. Minutes later, with his brow deeply furrowed, father emerged from their bedroom.

To my shock, he wore this tattered, faded, dusty-green WW2 army jacket. It was festooned with campaign ribbons and bore a bronze star. My jaw dropped. Father had been awarded the Bronze Star? I had never known this. Not even a hint had ever been revealed regarding this medal. A matching soft army cap sat atop his head. He wore a pair of starched and pleated khaki pants with cuffs.

Both mother and I were floored. We stared at him for a full minute, with eyes bulging and mouths agape. In all my eighteen years, I had never seen any portion of this old uniform, let alone father wearing it. Only once had he ever spoken about the war, and particularly his service in Italy.

I felt a lump in my throat and knew I was seeing a side of him I had never seen before. Father stared straight ahead with shoulders squared, eyes unflinching, and headed for the front door.

Mother rose slowly. The two of us looked at each other with wonderment. Tears formed in her eyes and trickled down her cheek. Mother wiped them away with a small white handkerchief clutched in her right hand. She then followed father out onto the porch.

On the way to meet Carter, no one spoke. There was no need for words. Mother clutched her purse tightly with both hands and softly sang *Amazing Grace*, while rocking her head from side to side. I can still hear her singing—her voice breaking frequently. She would clear her throat and continue humming.

Amazing Grace, how sweet
the sound
that saved a wretch like me.
I once was lost, but now I'm
found....
Was blind, but now I see.
Hmm-hmm

Finally, her voice trailed off into silence. Father stared fixedly at the narrow road ahead, looking neither to the left nor the right. I sat quietly, polishing the chrome-plated inside door handle with the tip of my index finger. For a moment, I sat humming Amazing Grace, along with mother. I then caught myself, took a deep breath, and sat watching the countryside go whizzing by my side window.

I could sense the mounting excitement and anxiety in all of us. My heartbeat furiously, as I kept thinking about Carter coming home. We all knew he had been wounded and would likely be on crutches. However, the fact he had survived, when so many tens of thousands had not, was all that mattered. I would get a chance to see him before I took off for Boston.

I remember wishing Rosie was there. We would all be together again, just the way we used to be. For some reason, which I can no longer recall, she was not able to leave Austin right away. She would arrive the following weekend. By then, I would be on my way to Harvard. I would not see her for some time.

I kept wondering what Carter would look like, how he would look in his dress-blue Marine Corps uniform—the ones in all the posters and television ads. I guessed it would take only a couple of hours before the two of us made a beeline for Crawford Lake.

We would sit there fishing and munching on the goodies mother would pack in a wicker basket. I would catch him up on all the things that had been going on in Rosedale. Of course, that would not take much time to do.

I knew he would probably have more than a few questions about Mary Lou Danfield, an attractive but stout girl whom he had had a crush on since his freshman days in high school. I would have a hard time telling him that a week after he left, she got married to one, Butch Canfield and soon moved to Houston. Rumor had it she now had a baby boy, who reportedly looks just like Butch's first cousin, Fenton Brooks.

It then dawned on me that after all he had been through, all that probably would not matter very much to Carter. He was a man now, not some kid home from summer camp. Far from it. Carter had witnessed the horrors of war and had stared death in the face and lived to talk about it. Others had not.

When we arrived on Main Street, the bus was only blocks away from the depot. A large crowd was gathered out front, including Mayor Howard Bertram Stennis III, members of the VFW, and several members of the Daughters of The American Revolution (DAR). Carter was going to have a real homecoming celebration.

Knowing him as I did, I figured he would be more than a little embarrassed by all the fuss. He was never really an extrovert and had always shunned the limelight.

I remember occasions when we would all have to memorize speeches and perform in various activities at church or school. Carter could remember his lines with almost a single read. I envied him, in that respect. Still, he would have done anything to just stand behind a curtain and not have to face hundreds of faces, each with a pair of eyes trained upon him.

This day, he would again have to face the crowd—a friendly crowd. You see, in Rosedale and perhaps in only a handful of other Rosedales across the country, returning Vietnam veterans received hero treatment. There would be no name-calling, flag burning, urine-tossing, phlegm-spitting, feces-hurling protesters, and no antiwar speeches.

It is not that the townspeople did not believe in free speech. I observed that in Rosedale free speech meant one was free to pledge allegiance to the flag, free to sing God Bless America, free to engage in school prayer, and free to threaten to hang anyone who objected to any of the above.

We parked in front of Dunphy's Diner and soon joined the others standing on a small platform erected the night before. It looked a little rickety to me, and then there was the sign— the

Welcome Home sign hanging from the roof. It was crooked and the letters were uneven, but that did not matter much.

Moments later, the bus eased up to the depot. A small contingent from our small school band struck up America, The Beautiful. The fact they were slightly off-key did not matter much either. They were almost always off-key.

We quickly made our way to a place near the front of the crowd and waited as the bus came to a stop. The door soon opened, and passengers began disembarking. Most were civilians clearly surprised by Rosedale's show of warmth and hospitality. They soon discovered they were not the honorees.

I watched as, one by one, the passengers seemed to take forever descending the steps. There were four soldiers in army uniforms greeted with cheers. The mayor placed a ribbon around each of their necks. A member of the D.A.R. (Daughters of The American Revolution) handed each a rose and planted a kiss on his cheek. Dozens of camera flashes went off.

All honorees were immediately escorted, by another D.A.R., to Dunphy's world-famous dining establishment. There, a bannered and ribbon festooned banquet room awaited. All this was done to honor the young men and their families. Sadly, this kind of reception was the exception for scores of returning Vietnam veterans.

We continued waiting, anxiously. Almost everyone had gotten off the bus. Where was Carter? We grew more than a little concerned. I looked at Mother. She looked at me. Just then, the driver stepped to the ground carrying a wheelchair. Mother turned toward me, gasped, and clutched her chest. We watched with pounding hearts.

Finally, looking thin but resplendent in his dress-green uniform, Carter appeared in the doorway, supported by two crutches. Relieved, surprised, and thrilled, I let loose a yelp and broke toward him with arms outstretched. It was then, I saw.

In a flash, I saw something I had not seen the instant before. Carter's left leg was missing. My brother had only one leg! My heart nearly stopped. I called out his name and reached out to help him down the steps. He took a deep breath and squared his shoulders.

"Hold on, little brother," he said, sternly, waving me off. I held my ground and waited. Father and mother stood next to me. Mother tried valiantly to contain her shock. Suddenly, Carter's right crutch slipped. It took all the restraint I could muster, to not rush to his side.

When he stepped to the ground, everyone but father embraced him. Mother and I tried very hard to control us. It seemed mother would never loosen her grip on him. She had her arms around him, with her head pressed against his chest for the longest time. I looked on, gripped by a scene I knew I would never forget. By contrast, father stood straight as an arrow. He snapped a sharp salute, which Carter returned, clutched Carter's hand, and squeezed it firmly.

"Welcome home, soldier—my son," he said. His voice cracked slightly, as he gripped Carter's right shoulder firmly and stared into his eyes. For the first and only time I can recall, I saw a lone tear trickle slowly down father's right cheek. It surprised me. Mother noticed it too and hurriedly wiped it away. I wanted to take a picture of it instead.

We had all known Carter had received a serious leg wound, though no one informed us just how severe it was. Word had come late one evening after we returned home from midweek prayer service. All we knew was he had received a leg injury. Seeing Carter step from that bus with a leg missing was a terrible shock but had to be put into perspective.

It was years later, that mother explained the tears she had shed that day. She explained they were for all those grieving parents whose sons and daughters had arrived home in coffins at Dover Air Force Base. These were mothers and fathers, she realized, who would have given anything to have had their sons and daughters return with only a limb missing. I know she was right, but it was more than just Carter's missing limb.

It did not take long for me to realize Carter had changed in ways not immediately apparent. He looked more or less the same, except for something about his eyes; his glance was distant. Carter had sprouted more facial hair and at times his voice had an unfamiliar resonance—a fitful cadence.

My attention was also focused on Carter's outer appearance and too little on his heart, mind, and soul. All that quickly changed. It was soon clear to me he bore little inner resemblance to the brother I had known and loved all my life. It seemed one Carter had left home and another Carter had returned.

The very first night he was home, I found it virtually impossible to engage him in a sustained conversation. While that alarmed me, I reasoned anyone who had seen the human destruction he had seen, however briefly, could not return home as if he had only been on a quick trip to the 7-11.

However, in all the days that followed, things worsened considerably. There were times I would sit talking to him and he appeared to be staring straight through me. I felt transparent. Carter would not answer questions or respond within the normal ebb and flow of things.

More often than not, a reply would come minutes later, after I had moved on to something else entirely. Carter had this faraway look in his eyes. At times he appeared completely disconnected from the present. It both concerned and scared the hell out of me.

At one point, during a conversation I was having with him, he suddenly grabbed his crutches, stood, and stalked out of the house onto the back porch. I followed quietly, observing him from a distance, through the screen door.

Carter stood for the longest while, leaning against the center column and staring down at his one foot and the two crutches. Momentarily, he raised his head and began staring out over those familiar fields far in the distance. He had to have been remembering glorious days we all spent out there playing. I am certain he remembered our daydreaming and wondering aloud about the future.

Then, in apparent disgust and frustration, Carter began banging his crutch angrily against the column. I wanted to rush to him right away, but held back, wanting to give him the space and time he needed.

It was then, I knew all the things I had imagined we would again do together would have to be indefinitely postponed—perhaps forgotten. Later, Carter returned inside and continued the conversation, as if he had never left the room.

I spoke to mother, expressing my feeling that Carter probably needed psychological counseling. What in the world did I do a fool thing like that for? I knew there might be a little discomfort with my suggestions. I had no idea. The notion anything other than something physical could be ailing Carter met the kind of resistance not seen since Columbus first asked Queen Isabella for a few lousy ships and a handful of sailors.

Nevertheless, mother reluctantly raised the taboo subject with father. He would have none of it. He insisted forcefully, that the power of prayer and supplication to God was sufficient to cure whatever ailed Carter. Furthermore, what I was suggesting be done was unholy and worldly. He insisted what was needed was prayer. I believed in prayer too, but I wanted backup. Poor Carter had little to say about it.

For a time, I was afraid of being thrust prone on the altar as a burnt offering to the Almighty—an Old Testament atonement for my blasphemy. Father made it clear he felt psychologists, psychiatrists (whom he still called Alienists) and their ilk were akin to practitioners of witchcraft, paganism, idolatry, and Satanism. One might say he had very strong feelings about the subject. So, to avoid tarring and feathering and being run out of town on a rail, I figured I had better set sail for the east coast as soon as possible.

Perhaps my folks were right in suggesting all Carter needed was a little time to rest, get his bearings, and try to forget what had happened in Vietnam. I could agree with the part about resting and getting his bearings, but I had not heard of anyone with a life expectancy sufficient to forget Vietnam. Besides, the war still raged. No one truly believed the end was in sight. Nixon, like Johnson, had lied before. The name Cambodia comes to mind.

Before leaving for Boston at week's end, I spoke to Carter about counseling as a way of dealing with his reentry into civilian life. For the first time, I was thrust into the awkward position of offering advice to my older and wiser brother. I did so on the condition that he not mention the nature of our conversation unless he agreed with me. My desire was not to lobby unduly for my view, though I felt I was right. I simply wanted Carter to at least listen to what I had to say, and seriously think about it.

That was not to be. Carter assured me he was fine and that all he really needed was time to rest and reorder his life. I prayed he was right and felt there was little else I could do. After all, he was still my big brother. I believed what he said. I had always believed him.

Chapter Twelve

From Rosedale to Boston

Harvard. Me, at Harvard?

The youngest son of John and Bonnie Phalen—with eyes straining to take in sights never before seen, and fresh cow dung still clinging to the soles of his boots—in Boston?

Right! And may God have mercy on his country-soul. Being a bright but somewhat naive farm boy from Texas, and suddenly thrust into the lofty, nosebleed environs of Boston academia, inflicted quite a shock to my culture—a shock from which I have yet to recover. As I should have expected, I received constant reminders that I had a slight Texas twang and the mannerisms of a cowpoke.

That did not bother me. What did annoy me was the fact these pointed reminders came from Bostonians who looked malnourished, tight in the britches, soft around the edges and strange sounding to me too. I should point out that these individuals were the exception, not the rule. I found a way to deal with most of these cultural differences. I ignored them.

I enjoyed my years in Boston and at Harvard. I feel I adapted about as well as could have been expected. I confess my personality did undergo a blossoming of a sort. I became more of an extrovert than when I first arrived. Still, I traveled in a small circle, choosing to bury my head in the books. As a result, my performance placed me in the upper ten percentile of my class. I succeeded.

What most amazed me about Harvard was the fact a great number of my fellow students were not the egghead types I had wrongly expected. They were often as irreverent, raucous, antiestablishment, and as prone to imbibe as any I had heard of.

In the wildly, successful years that followed, I earned degrees in law, economics, and business (MBA) and entertained suitors from half the Fortune 500. I later found myself on Wall Street, touted as an eligible, bachelor-whiz-kid destined for fortune and fame. I reasoned I could do without the fame, but the fortune part suited me just fine.

I worked hard, paid my dues, and was soon making mega-deals and mega-money in the go-go eighties. I mean really big money, very large money. I even made money in the late seventies, too. High-interest rates and inflation were very, very good to me.

Those experiences were dizzying, electric, intoxicating... seductive. It was an E-ticket to Wonderworld. I became a successful arbitrageur, investment banker, lawyer, and wheeler-dealer. I say that proudly, without hesitation. There was nothing whatsoever to be ashamed of.

It was all very heady stuff. I brokered scores of high-stakes, high-drama deals that made me more money than I knew existed. I got caught up in the ether. It was truly inebriating. Thoroughly addicting. I was a junkie for sure.

If I had not fathered a new deal within a couple of weeks, I felt like a has-been. I needed a fix and kept them coming. It was nothing to go through 48 hours getting less than six hours of sleep total, with the help of a caffeine I-V and an endless adrenaline rush. Some of my fellow-masochists were making it on much harder stuff.

A major Wall Street player, whose name anyone on the planet would recognize, once sat behind his desk during one of those marathon sessions that stretched into the early morning. He pulled open a desk drawer and removed a silver box. It looked like one of those large gourmet cookie tins, only there were no Denmark windmill designs on this thing.

He calmly opened it. The container was brimming with cocaine. I almost dumped in my pants. My eyes rolled up in the top of my head, as he helped himself and offered a round to about six of us who were in the room. I was stunned by his matter-of-fact attitude and his assumption he would have willing takers. It seemed like business as usual, for him.

However, only one other guy took him up on his offer. This particular clown was such a brown-noser he would have given the guy a tongue-bath if he had wanted one. This guy later went to work in the upper levels of the Treasury Department in the Reagan and later Bush administrations. I was happy for him. He later did me a few favors, following my inadvertent reference to that night in New York.

Of course, I never mentioned those events in any way. And I never elicited any quid-pro-quo from this fellow. That would have been illegal. I think the guy just had a guilty conscience and was trying desperately to salve it in any way he could. I simply helped him assuage his guilt.

Anyway, Mr. Big, whose cocaine it was, grew quite nervous when only one of us accepted his offer. He buzzed in one of his flunkies who took the container and quickly left the room with it.

All was well in my life, I thought, and with good reason. I was riding high. I was hob-knobbing in the same circles with the likes of Carl Icahn, T. Boone Pickens, Michael Milken, Ivan Boesky, and others.

I even had an occasion to swap tall tales with The Donald, during a highbrow party in his Plaza Hotel penthouse. It was the most boring party I have ever attended, until Trump arrived. I had made a point of going to these things alone. That way, halfway through it, I had no compunction about disappearing and leaving the Hauté Société people to themselves.

During that period of my life, I did not have time for serious relationships, let alone the thought of marriage. All that would just have to wait. Oh, I had gorgeous girlfriends with whom I satisfied my basic instincts and primal urges. There were the big parties, the country clubs, the extended European vacations. Ironically, these found me spending more time on the phone and using fax machines than reposing on white-sand beaches.

Year in and year out, my income, influence and addiction to hedonism skyrocketed. I was not flaunting my wealth, but I was not playing the hermit either. Alise can attest to that. I was alive, witnessing tremendous worldwide events, trying to make sure I profited from them.

And why should I not? Everyone else was. At the close of the eighties, the Soviet Empire collapsed, the Berlin Wall crumbled, the Warsaw Pact disintegrated and I sub-totaled my considerable winnings. Caution was the password, but it was clearly time for capitalism to move east, albeit cautiously.

It was then, that order in my life turned to disorder. Why does it happen this way so often? Just when you are soaring high, like an eagle, something happens to bring you tumbling back to earth like a rock.

For me, it was more a crash than a tumble. Father was stricken with a powerful stroke that left him only a shell of the man I had known. Even after I had seen him at St. Luke Hospital in Houston, I could not accept the reality of his deteriorated condition. Father was seventy-five and barely able to speak. Yet in my mind, father's dying was not within the realm of possibilities. He was my father. Parents do not die, I remember thinking. All I had to do was will it not to be.

I find myself at a crossroads, unable to decide which way to turn. I had not expected this to happen to me. Why should I have? But I am now determined to do as I have always done. Deal with the realities and move on. I have always taken pride in being able to do that. But this is far different from any other traumatic circumstance I have had to face. There are no strings I can pull, no phone call I can make to either set things back on track or cut my losses.

Within a year of father's first stroke, his health was steadily declining. I kept in constant touch with mother, speaking with her several times a day. On at least two occasions, during father's re-hospitalization in Houston, I met them there and spent a couple of days. The last time was a little less than six months ago.

At that time, mother had resigned herself to the fact father would likely not get much better. I still had not reached that point. I kept hoping one day mother would call and inform me he was walking unaided and talking up a blue storm. The call never came.

Meanwhile, all my business ventures were proving more and more profitable. I ran my enterprises from a suite of offices at World Trade Center, located on one of the floors of Sarrazin, Jacobs, and Carrazzo, one of the largest law firms in the country. Ours was truly a symbiotic relationship. I had gone to work for them, a few years out of Harvard.

At the same time, I began making investments and learning the investment banking business from the owner of one of the firm's largest clients, Simon, Wachtler and Evans. In a few years, I was making more money from my investments and deals than all the firm's partners combined. That kind of success did not go down well with many people.

When I started becoming the subject of whispered conversations around the water cooler and of lengthy articles in scores of financial publications, I decided it was time to move on.

However, at that time I purchased controlling shares in a booming, leading-edge, high-tech Silicon Valley firm, a phenomenal software company, and several support businesses from California to Massachusetts. My other financial holdings were tracking upward at considerably better than average rates and showed no signs whatsoever of correcting.

There were more financial magazine articles. I turned down request after request to appear on television with talking heads interested only in ratings. I did not want the public notoriety. I could see what high visibility had done and was doing to people such as Trump and others. I wanted no part of it.

From a business standpoint, things could not have been better. I made sure I exited the junk bond market at the right time and was careful to play the game by the rules, whether I liked them or not. The SEC and other agencies had spies everywhere who seemed to catch only those they wanted to catch.

The political climate was changing in Washington, but that was really of little concern to me. Of course, I had my own philosophical and political views, but I was no rigid ideologue. I never let those things interfere with sound business decisions.

For years, I had followed my own dictum to position myself financially, so that it would not matter who was in the White House. From a purely business standpoint, Elmer Fudd could have been elected President in the eighties for all I cared. Some might argue he was. I am not one of them.

Despite all I had, there was one achievement I still sought. I wanted very much to attain a principal position within the legal profession. I had not formally practiced law and certainly did not need the money. Still, I had this notion that since I had worked hard to become a lawyer, I should at some point be one in more than name only.

I was also enjoying a very close, monogamous relationship with a very beautiful, intelligent, and successful woman. To say she was beautiful and leave it at that would do an injustice to her beauty. To simply say she was smart would hardly tell the full story. I have never had difficulties interacting with strong women who have a real sense of themselves. I prefer strong women who are not shrinking violets, women well-aware of their femininity.

Alise was and is such a woman. I recognize that she wants a more permanent relationship. So do I, at some point in the future. The question is whether either one of us is ready to alter what was a wonderful relationship already.

Chapter Thirteen

Alise

I met Alise Tomei at a Christmas Party, three years ago. She was introduced to me by one Sy Scarborough, a fellow lawyer and fellow member of the board of directors of Simon, Wachtler, and Evans. Sy confessed to having designs on her but figured she probably preferred someone with hair and a social security number larger than three digits.

Alise, who had just written her second, number one, nonfiction best-seller, No Time for Fears, was and is truly a vision to behold. What was so captivating about Alise was how soft-spoken, non-pretentious and perceptive she was and still is. Whenever she looked at me, I always got the feeling she was peering right through to my soul. At first, I found it impossible to hold her gaze. That disturbed my ego considerably, but I soon got over it.

Alise had doleful eyes that made words unnecessary, the kind of presence that made time insignificant. We began spending more and more of it together, enjoying each other more and more as well. What was happening between us was the birth of something special—something undeniably wonderful. I did not have to wonder about it. I could feel it.

Alise felt it too. When we were not together, we were calling each other and making plans to see each other. Without any designs on our part, our bond grew rapidly. Soon, we were beyond simply meeting each other for dinner, plays, and movies; we met for the pure joy of being in each other's presence.

When Alise was not on a book tour, making the network morning shows or researching a new book, she shared my Park Avenue apartment. We soon discovered we had a lot in common. We shared a love of quiet moments in front of fireplaces with snow falling outside. Many such moments were spent together at a charming little place I purchased in Connecticut and another in the Hamptons.

Alise become a source of great comfort for me, as I struggled with my distress over father's condition and my deepening concern about mother. She insisted everything would be alright and that I should stay positive and upbeat for my mother. In a way, Alise became my conscience—my link to myself.

She confronted me about the fact I had not returned to Rosedale and spent the time necessary to make sure all was as well as it could be. She was right. I found myself wondering why I had not done just that. There was little need for concern about being out of touch, from a business standpoint. However, just as I would agree with her, she would tell me how much she missed me, whenever we did not see each other for a few days.

Alise and I loved New York at night. The city takes on an indescribable character after the sun goes down. Carriage rides in Central Park under a moonlit night were something we did as often as we thought about it. Hardly a Broadway show came and went without the two of us gracing the best seats.

We frequented exclusive restaurants with such regularity, we had our own tables all over town. Yet, after a time we delighted in cloaking ourselves in anonymity and dining in nondescript little places with great food and crates of atmosphere. There is just so much I can take of plastic smiles, phony how-do-you-do's and obnoxious, saccharin-soaked servility.

Other times, I would call the limo on a Friday night, and we would take a nighttime ride to my little place in Connecticut for an extended weekend. It was on such a night, while the fireplace roared, that I looked into her eyes and read something I either had not seen before or had not wanted to see. I saw a questioning look that would not go away.

Later in bed, Alise turned and stared at me with those big, gorgeous eyes of hers and asked point-blank:

"How long do we do this?"

At first, I pretended I did not understand what she meant, but that could never work with Alise. She knew me too well.

"How long?" She asked again.

"As long as you want to," I said.

Alise continued staring in silence. I vowed I would not be the next to speak. She kissed me softly and asked the same question again, this time even more softly. I took a deep breath and gave the same answer, knowing full well the point of her question. She smiled and caressed my face with both hands.

"We'll see," she said with a naughty smile and locked her legs tightly around my waist.

A month later, at 2:45 one morning, the limo drove us slowly through the water-soaked, deceptively quiet, tame-looking streets of Times Square. The wetness yielded a contorted reflection of the sea of neon and other light emanating from surrounding buildings. Except for a few cabs, commercial vehicles, an occasional siren, and sightings of requisite creatures of the night, we were as alone as one can be on the streets of New York.

A short time later, after an hour of devouring each other and almost passing out in the shower, sleep came easily to both of us. Alise, who normally complained of my inordinate stamina, voiced no objection when I fell asleep within seconds of my final mournful effort.

It had been quite a night for us. We had seen Andrew Lloyd Webber's Sunset Strip for the second time in as many nights, and after declining an invite to dine with Alise's parents, had gorged ourselves on seafood and wine at one of our favorite haunts.

All evening long, Alise seemed unusually probing, both in her gaze and in her conversation. It was as if she had some unformed question she wanted to pose and felt unsure about what the question was. Though I sensed this, I nevertheless pretended not to be aware of it. I am not sure I know why I did so. Perhaps I did not want to assist her in formulating some question I either could not or did not want to answer. I thought, why be a party to my own undoing?

The next morning, I awoke earlier than usual. I glanced over at the clock on the nightstand. It was 5:26am. I had slept only a couple of hours. I glanced at Alise who was still fast asleep, appearing every bit the angel, she was. I felt exhausted. Yet I knew it was not from the torrid activity Alise and I had enjoyed hours earlier. It was more like mental fatigue I had not been aware of the day before.

As I lay staring at Alise, then peering up at the ceiling, I felt a surprising swell of emotion that brought moisture to my eyes. For the life of me, I could not understand why. What was it? Searching for an answer, I tried to recall what if anything, I had dreamed about.

Minutes later, all I could come up with was a faint recollection of having once again dreamed my never-ending dream, the one I recounted to you earlier. I have no insightful reason for why it persists to this day.

Once I was fully awake, I realized I was dripping with perspiration. I felt weak, my heart was beating rapidly, my right ankle ached from having tripped over the water hose. This was far too real for me. I do not know why I even mention it here, except for my desire to exorcise this from my mind for all time. Fat chance.

Chapter Fourteen

Man in My Mirror

As I lay watching Alise and recalling my dream, it dawned on me this was my forty-first birthday—the day I would be named a full partner in one of the largest, most prestigious law firms in the country. I should have been euphoric.

Yet, even at this early hour, the day already had a certain feel to it—a certain character. Everyone experiences this at one time or another. You awaken and already the day displays a personality that impacts you either negatively or positively.

Some mornings you feel you have the strength to slay dragons. Then there are days you want to pull the covers back over your head and wind the clock backward. I was not yet sure which one of those days this was. It would not take me long to find out. Part of my melancholy feeling was undoubtedly due to my reflections on the family that died at the Devereaux farm on my seventh birthday. The two events were eternally linked.

I opened my eyes and glanced at the clock again. It was 6:47. I had apparently fallen back asleep. I looked at Alise again who was by now curled in the fetal position, her beautiful, taut, tan presence was staring me right in my still blurry eyes. I reached out and pulled the sheet over her, raised myself to a sitting position, and massaged my lids.

I had grown concerned about the early morning, blurry vision thing. I wondered if old age predictions were catching up to me. I pondered that disturbing thought for a moment, then became aware of a strong physical manifestation of sexual arousal. Thank God not all the predictions relating to aging were accurate.

A few minutes passed before I eased out of bed and quietly made my way to the bathroom. I had no sooner closed the door than it struck me. I was still not feeling as euphoric as I had anticipated feeling on this long-awaited day. Perhaps, I thought, after my usual constitutionals, I would feel differently. I am normally a fast starter and almost always have a positive slant the instant my feet hit the floor.

This morning was different. Naturally, I thought about father and wondered how mother was coping. Both were undoubtedly still asleep. Eastern daylight time meant it was almost 6 am in Texas. During his pre-stroke days, father rose at about 4:30, and had his early morning devotional reading and prayer. By 6 am, he would be ready for breakfast and a third cup of coffee.

Mixed with that recollection was the image of father lying coiled in tubes inside that sterile hospital room in Houston. I suppose I will always see that image in my mind. I shook my head as if doing so would clear my mind. It did not.

I opened the cabinet doors, removed my shaving cream, and razor, and prepared to shave. I applied the foam without looking, having done it so many times. A few minutes later, I finished shaving and stood patting my face dry.

Suddenly, I was riveted with astonishment. Gripped by the image in the mirror, I stumbled backward, then eased closer. What I saw floored me. It did not make sense. What stunned me was the image of my father staring back at me from the mirror. It was he in every conceivable detail: the wrinkled brow, the bushy gray eyebrows, the piercing gaze. There he was, as plainly as if he were staring into the mirror himself.

I thrust both hands to my face, then removed them quickly. The image was gone, leaving me to wonder if it was my mind that was gone. I was as frightened as I have ever been in my life—more frightened than my nightmare had ever made me. Surely father had died, I thought, and his spirit had come to me for that one brief instant. I considered calling mother, then hesitated, fully expecting the telephone to ring. It did not

I washed my face again, dried and stood peering into the mirror. For the first time, I realized I had begun to look more like my father than ever before. I do not mean as distinctly as the earlier image. This time it was me—my own image. I saw his eyes, the way his lips turn down when he concentrated on something, the way one bushy brow is slightly higher than the other, a slight line across my brow. My god! I was becoming my father.

From older men, I had heard stories of one day arriving at that moment when a son begins to take on the mannerisms and even the physical characteristics of his father. I am certain it happens to women too. Women perhaps feel men do not think about these things, but we do. It is just that we do not talk about them as freely.

When this transformation takes place, there is no magical line one crosses to mark the event. There is no predetermined day one can cross off the calendar and prepare for. No alarm bell goes off, nor do those who experience it always acknowledge the event. It just happens.

Moments earlier, as I prepared to shave, the face I saw looked just as it had the day before, the week before, the months and years before. What happened? Did some invisible hand reach down from heaven and strike me? Had my eyes failed to transmit this visual information to my brain earlier? Had the change only just now taken place, even as I stood there looking?

There was never any denying I was my father's son, but I was not my father. My belaboring this is not because I do not think my father is and always was a handsome man. He was. It is just that, this revelation signifies more than I care to accept. It means I have crossed some line over which I can never retreat.

What it says to me is that perhaps a mere thirty-five years earlier, my father likely stood gazing into a mirror. Similarly, he may have observed his own father gazing back at him. Thirty-five years later, he lies gravely ill and in the sunset of his life. For me, this was a transforming moment. Again, I was forced to face my own mortality and the realization that everything and everyone changes.

Chapter Fifteen

A Day Remember

Alise was not in the bedroom, when I returned in a blue funk and began dressing. I passed the dresser and sneaked a quick look into the mirror. Do not ask why. Perhaps I was seeking a second opinion or suspected the bathroom mirror had been less than honest, playing some cruel joke on me. Nothing had changed. I got dressed and stood at the window, looking twenty stories down onto the awakening street below.

The morning light, filtered through overcast skies, filled my eyes. I could smell the aroma of fresh croissants, Canadian bacon, and freshly brewed coffee wafting through the apartment, from my kitchen downstairs. I finished securing the links in my French cuffs and adjusted the less than perfectly tied knot in my necktie. I never could get those blasted knots right. I envied guys who could tie a perfect one every time. Of all my many accomplishments, that was not one of them.

Just then, I felt Alise's arms slip around my waist. She rested her head against my back and squeezed tightly. I grasped her arms gently and turned around to face her. Her eyes sparkled in the soft light. Her strawberry blonde hair had an unusually bright glow. I pulled her to me and kissed her, lightly at first. After a passionate minute or two we both opened our eyes. Alise smiled and gently stroked my face.

"I love your face, just after you've shaved," she said.

"And not before?"

"Stop it. I know you understand what I mean."

"Just kidding"

A moment of silence passed. Suddenly, Alise began softly singing the words to a song I hadn't heard in years: Doris Day's Que Cera.

When I was just a little girl,
I asked my mother, what will I...

"And what did she tell you?" I asked, before she could continue. She did not hesitate, smiling broadly and tossing her head back.

"That I would grow up to be a successful author, marry a rich, handsome, lawyer, mortgage-banker farm boy from Texas. At least I'm a fairly successful author person."

"There's still time," I said.

"What do you mean?" She asked.

"Nothing," I answered.

I found myself hoping I had not inferred too much and quickly looked away. The last thing I wanted to give Alise was false hope about my desiring marriage soon. I was not at all sure I wanted to get married—ever. And it was not fair that I did not make that absolutely clear to her. Yet, there were also signs marriage was not really what she presently wanted. Why we have yet to approach the subject head on, I do not know. The word fear comes to mind.

Still, I always equivocated, whenever she would make those little suggestive statements. I would respond with as few words as possible and try to change the subject without appearing to do so. Alise was not deceived. I have come to believe that women are equipped with an intangible something that makes it impossible to best them in any kind of mind game having to do with their own emotions.

I was aware Alise sensed my deep, reflective mood, as she always seemed to do, despite my attempts at masking it. Throughout breakfast, she repeatedly stared at me with questioning eyes, even as she spoke of other things. I found it impossible to hold her gaze. That is another of those special traits many women have.

They can engage you in the most detailed of conversations, while staring at you intently—their minds riveted on a totally unrelated subject.

Mother was the absolute best at this I have ever seen. She could make you think you had her rapt attention glued to whatever you wanted to talk about. Suddenly, like a swooping eagle, she would pin you with a riveting question about something you were praying she had forgotten. Alise was the same way.

After breakfast, Alise stood near the kitchen's island counter with her back arched slightly, her right hand on her right hip. I walked up behind her, kissed her gently on the nape of her neck and turned to walk away. She turned, grabbed by left arm at the wrist, forcing me to stop. I turned back to find her eyes pinned to mine like darts. I offered a smile for sale. She was not buying.

"After all your successes, this day tops it all for you, doesn't it?"

"It does."

"Then, why the glum face?" She asked.

"What glum face?"

"As if you had to ask."

"Oh?"

"Don't obfuscate," she said.

"Don't what?"

"Come on," she said.

"I'm not obfus... whatever you said."

"Oh! Don't lie."

"What are you saying?" I asked.

"Be honest," Alise said.

"Alright. I guess I didn't realize I was looking glum," I said, launching immediately into spirited and defensive denial. Alise persisted.

"What's the...," she started and stopped in mid-sentence.

"What's what?" I asked.

"I almost did it," Alise said.

"Did what?"

"We promised never to ask each other that question and I almost...Anyway, I was about to ask what the matter was. But the truth is, I know."

"What could possibly be the matter? I have been looking ahead to this day for a long time. I'm ecstatic. Honest!"

"Uh huh. Sure."

Alise was not buying it at all. I really did not want to get into one of those deep, never-ending, soul-searching discussions about full expression—getting in touch and all that. Although I consider myself quite expressive and in-touch, I honestly was not sure I understood what I was really feeling. I was in uncharted territory.

I had not awakened expecting to find someone else in my mirror staring back at me. Was this some sort of male menopause I was going through? No way, I thought. I am too young for that. Besides, that whole thing about male menopause was just something women dreamed up. Misery loves company, I thought. It is one of those Oprah topics or something.

"Hey! Top of the world," I effused, stroking the air with a clinched fist, to add an exclamation point.

"Alright," Alise said grudgingly with a touch of suspicion.

"Which means I'm happy beyond belief," I said, then realized I was laying it on a little too thickly. I had already gone too far.

"And you should be on top of the world. That's my point," Alise said.

"So, like on most things, we agree."

"On many things. We agree on many things," Alise said, tilting her head and flashing a girlish smile.

"Correct," I conceded. "I tend to be a bit imprecise so early in the morning."

Alise smiled again, kissed me softly and again slipped both arms around my waist. I could feel myself pressed against her and backed away a quarter step.

"I was only kidding," she whispered. "I know we are quite different in many ways, but I tend to smile effusively, find it hard to stop bouncing off the ceiling, whenever I'm happy beyond belief, like last night. Right?" She winked. I winked back, having heard nothing I disagreed with regarding the night before.

"Last night was fantastic," I added, slipping my arms around Alise. She nodded agreement.

"In fact," I continued, "I have absolutely no feeling below my waist. I am numb."

"Let me check," Alise said, slipping her right hand down my side and toward my crotch. I flinched and stepped back a full step this time. She laughed softly and stepped toward me with her hand outstretched.

I grabbed both her hands, pulled her to me and held her tightly. She nested her head against my chest. A silent moment passed. I could feel my heart beating against the side of her face.

"Don't worry about me. I'm fine," I said. Alise tilted her head back and looked up at me.

"It's my forty-second," I said. "Plus, yesterday Forbes estimated my net at 6.8 billion. I do not know where they got that. I wish they were right. I really do wish they were right."

"So, they're off by a few million."

"A few hundred million. And today, I'm being named a full partner in Sarrazin, Jacobs and Carrazzo. After all this time, I finally get to play lawyer. It's like something I heard Johnny Mathis say once. Somebody was interviewing him. I forget who it was; perhaps it was Dick Cavett. I forget. In response to a question, he said his main goal, now that he had achieved the success he wanted, was to seriously study music...to learn to read and write music. I thought that was amazing. Isn't that amazing?"

"I'd say so," Alise agreed.

"That's sort of the way I feel, too."

"I understand. I do."

"Do you?"

"Of course."

"The last time I remember talking to father about what I do; he wasn't so much impressed with my financial success as he was with my job—my profession. He repeatedly asked me: 'Son, when you gonna start lawyerin'?"

It was as if he was asking when I was going to get a real job. I chuckled and answered: "Soon. Real Soon." I recall he seemed very pleased by that.

Alise tilted her head to one side slightly and gave me one of her patented squeezes that said she understood exactly what I was trying to say.

"No one is more deserving," said Alise. "Everyone knows you could buy the firm, if you wanted to. Then old man Sarrazin could afford to buy a new toup. I mean, you'd think the man could afford a better rug than that, for god's sake," Alise said with a chuckle. "Sorry," she apologized. She had nothing for which to apologize. She was absolutely right.

"It's true," I agreed. I needed a good laugh. Alise's smile faded slightly. There was that gaze of hers again. She instantly saw beyond my words. She was reading me like a book. We both knew it.

"Sweetheart, for some people, not all but for some, it's when they are swimming in success—when everything is going their way, that they're forced to look long and hard at where they are, who they are, to take inventory and ask questions there are no ready answers for. That's what is happening to you. I can see it. I can feel it. And it is okay. It really is. Don't be too analytical, right now," she said.

A long moment of silence followed. We just stood there, locked in a long embrace. Alise was right. I was being far too analytical, but I could not help it. She took me by the hand, walked me over to the sofa and returned to the kitchen. Seconds later, Alise brought me a fresh cup of coffee.

"I suppose, I should be seriously concerned about Crane," she said. "He's probably standing on some ledge, right this minute."

Alise was referring to one Crane Vanderpool III, a very bright lawyer for Sarrazin, Jacobs and Carrazzo. He was certain he would be offered the full partnership. The two of us were not bosom buddies and everyone knew it. Crane had let it be known he was not impressed with my wealth or me. As far as he was concerned, I was buying the partnership.

The truth was, I was not buying the partnership. The firm was only looking out for its interests. After all, I was not exactly raw hamburger. My appointment could only benefit the firm in myriad ways, while fulfilling my dream at the same time. I hate to use a trite phrase, but it was a win-win situation.

"Crane will be alright," I said, coming weakly to his defense. "He's not quite the inveterate jackass he appears to be."

"I'm sure he thinks he should be in your shoes today. The guy has campaigned for partner for years. He's almost made this a test of manhood."

"He'll survive," I assured Alise.

"I suppose you're right. Reptiles have been surviving for centuries. Just watch your back."

Alise said it jokingly, but I knew she was serious. I loved the way she put things. Alise had a knack for putting things just so. Her take on Crane fit him perfectly. She had met him on several occasions and knew him to be bright, pompous, obnoxious, cunning, quick-witted, elitist, annoying, and downright full of himself. There's more but let this suffice.

Crane was also a brilliant lawyer. He exemplified more conflicting aspects of the human condition than any single human being either of us had ever met, except for the late Richard Nixon. The former President and Alise had shared a publisher. I met him several years ago at a private party hosted by the publisher. I digress.

I sipped my piping hot coffee and stared at Alise. She looked so beautiful and radiant, even at this early hour. I could not help wondering if she now saw me any differently than she had the night before. The thought did not make any sense to me, but there it was, stuck in my mind like gum to a whorehouse-bedpost. Considering my experience with the mirror, I was certain my face must reflect some obvious change.

Just then, my temples seemed grayer, the lines in my forehead deeper, my voice less steady. It was dumb, but that is what I was thinking. It occurred to me, men are not supposed to think about things like this. Alise took note of silence—my pensive look. I answered her before she asked a question.

"All my adult life I have heard older guys talk about reaching that point in their lives, when one morning they look into the mirror and find their father gazing back at them." Alise just stared at me for a moment.

"Is that what happened to you this morning?" She asked, stepping closer.

"It was unbelievable. Suddenly, it was not just I in the mirror. I could see father. I could see his face. Then, it wasn't so much his face as it was my resembling him in a way I never noticed. It was startling. It didn't happen yesterday or the day before or the week before that. It's like...I had crossed some invisible line. All of sudden, there I was. Just like that. There was no warning."

"How's it make you feel?" Alise asked.

"Mortal."

"Mortal?" Alise asked.

"More mortal than I have ever felt before," I confessed. "At last, I am forced to accept that this life will not last indefinitely."

Alise stared at me lovingly and perhaps with a tinge of pity. She then reached out and grasped my hand. I looked at her and smiled.

I somehow got through our morning good-byes without renewed probing from Alise. I could tell she wanted to press me further, but let it go. However, each time I headed toward the door, she managed to extend the good-byes with a mention of one more thing that required much more than a simple yes or no. It was as if she was trying to keep me from leaving.

"I have been neglecting my place, lately, thanks to you," she said. "So, I'll probably be at home until I see you for dinner tonight."

"Alright," I answered.

Alise had a very elegant apartment several blocks away. She spent very little time there, except when she worked on some deadline and needed the isolation.

"I'll call you," she promised.

We kissed again. Finally, we stood at the front door. I gripped my briefcase with one hand and embraced her with the other. Alise gently pried my hand from the case, took it in her own and placed it on the floor near the partially opened door.

Neither of us spoke. We stood embracing each other for the longest time. Something in her eyes reached out to me, pleading for me to stay. I kissed her again, stepped into the corridor and started slowly for the elevator. It was a much longer walk than ever before.

When I reached the elevator doors, I glanced back to find Alise still standing in the doorway. She looked lovelier than I had ever seen her. The longing glance she cast was one of sadness and resignation. It was the look of someone seeing a loved one for the last time. A shiver coursed my entire body. I could not figure it out. It prompted a feeling of guilt, on my part. I blew her a kiss, which she returned. She then leaned her head against the doorjamb, remaining there until I was out of view.

When I reached the lobby, Jared, the 26-year-old doorman was all grins. I could not remember a time when he was not exactly this way. He had great potential as a spokesman for some dental office. That morning, however, I found myself preferring to be greeted by someone with a demeanor more like my own. In hindsight, I owe Jared a debt of thanks.

"Morning, Mr. Phalen, and happy birthday to you," he barked good-naturedly. I answered good morning and thanked him for his good wishes. He made a habit of knowing things like that.

"I see you're riding in even higher style this morning than is your custom," Jared said, pointing through the thick, brass-framed, glass doors. A white limo sat parked at the driveway curb. A uniformed chauffeur stood next to the opened rear door.

"The firm sent it over this morning," Jared informed me, displaying a remarkable grasp of the obvious. I rather expected they would, though I did not let on to Jared. I had earlier looked forward to driving the new 560SL I had treated myself to a few days earlier. It was the first car I had purchased in years, and mainly for those weekend trips to Connecticut.

The trip to the Towers was almost over, by the time I settled into the limo's familiar comforts. As we pulled away from the apartment, I thought of calling Alise, then quashed the idea. I was not sure what I would have said that would have made sense.

The look I saw on her face, as I waited at the elevators, was still troubling me. I closed my eyes and imagined her slumped on the living room sofa, communing with her favorite Chagall. The painting hung on the wall directly opposite the sofa. Perhaps I would surprise her and have her meet me for lunch. She would not expect that. I loved surprising her.

The limo pulled in front of the World Trade Center and headed for the underground garage. I had the chauffeur stop and I climbed out, having decided I wanted to walk in through the front door for the first time in ages. Perhaps I would spot J.J. spinning one of his famous stories, which he often did in return for a couple of quick bucks. I had not seen him for several months and was wondering what happened to him.

J.J. was an engaging fellow, a homeless man who was not at all typical of most of New York's down and outs. He spoke in a more articulate manner than did most of the highbrows I associated with. He was clearly more insightful and more amusing in a non-self-deprecating way.

For almost three years, J.J. had been a fixture, standing near the entrance, dressed in a soiled but well-fitting, once beige suit. He always wore a wide grin and greeted me in a manner that never changed.

"Morning there, Mr. P. Have you heard this one?" He would ask, then launch into his tale. When finished, I would either give him a thumb-up or a thumb-down or offer him a few bucks. If I gave him a thumbs-down, and still offered the two bucks, he would refuse the money vehemently.

"Only if you like it," he would tell me. "I insist you only pay me if you like it." I respected him for that. He was an honest and very proud man.

One morning six months earlier, I invited J.J. inside for breakfast at one of the upper-level restaurants. With great reluctance, he agreed. I understood. The gawking, the remark we received inside the elevator, and even more inside the restaurant were vile and disgusting. Nonetheless, we had a great breakfast and an even greater conversation.

I learned J.J. had a degree in business and had hit the skids six years earlier when his wife died. He also lost his job and succumbed to illicit drugs and alcohol. It stunned me to discover this man, who appeared to be near 60 years old, was only forty-five.

"My God!" I thought, "We were almost the same age."

I found myself staring at him and thinking but for the grace of God go I. It was a humbling experience. Then I committed, what was for most wealthy persons of goodwill, a sin of the heart. I offered J.J. a substantial amount of money to help him get back on his feet. Had I been thinking clearly, I probably would have anticipated his reaction.

He rejected the offer. It was not money he wanted, although even he acknowledged it was money he badly needed. What he most wanted was a chance to work and rebuild his life in an honorable way.

So, I pulled my philanthropic boot out of my mouth and made several calls to local charities J.J. had expressed an interest in working for. I suggested to him his knowledge represented greater financial benefit to him if offered to a commercial enterprise. I then received yet another valuable lesson from this unassuming man. He said what he most desired, in addition to making a decent living, was a chance to give back. That made a tremendous impression upon me. What a concept!

I reached the fiftieth floor and made my way to the massive double doors leading to our suite of offices. Three steps from the door, I had the urge to turn around, go back to the apartment, get Alise, pile some things into the car, and head for Connecticut.

No sooner had I opened the door and stepped inside than this chorus of voices erupted in a rousing rendition of For He's a Jolly Good Fellow. There were at least three hundred-fifty people standing underneath streamers, banners, balloons—the works. Ruth, my secretary, dressed in her favorite red ensemble, looked on with the pride and admiration of a mother. Others were tooting on kazoos, clapping their hands. It was bedlam.

All I could do was smile while standing there like a potted plant. I had not expected anything like this. I looked behind me, expecting to find someone else standing there—perhaps the real honoree. There in front, leading the raucous cheering were Sarrazin, Jacobs, and Carrazzo themselves.

"Congratulations, J.P.," said Jacobs. It was as if I had stepped onto the set of some 1940s movie about corporate life.

Then began an endless round of backslapping, hugs, congratulations, and toothy grins. Someone near me shoved a brimming glass of champagne into my hands. Still, someone else crowned me with one of those silly, multicolored party hats. I was five years old again and mother was putting that silly little sailor's cap on me. Only this time I did not have to take it. So, after a respectable ten or fifteen seconds, I removed the hat and stuffed it in my pocket. I drank the champagne, though.

Amid all the well-wishes, I felt self-conscious. Contrary to popular perception, I am a very private person. At times I tend to be withdrawn and cerebral. I seldom have an opportunity to be true to my own instincts, on that score.

I often find myself to be a contradiction. I am a natural introvert with strong extrovertish tendencies, nurtured through practice and conditioning. Except for mother and Rosie, only Alise knows this to be true. By necessity, I have to be gregarious and engage with all kinds of people in all kinds of business situations. This was one of them.

There was one person absent from the throng. I did not see Crane Vanderpool, until I happened to look toward the rear of the room. There he was, leaning against the doorframe clutching a coffee mug and wearing a scowl. Our eyes met briefly. He turned and stalked away.

The whole thing with Crane seemed so juvenile to me. At this level, one might reasonably expect the players to know you win some and you lose some. There was always a new game to play. Unless you burned a very important bridge behind you, you would always be in the hunt. Apparently, Crane did not see it that way.

The celebration continued at length. After speaking with virtually everyone in the suite, I simply slipped off everyone's radar screen. The party had a life of its own; it did not need me. I soon made my way to the edge of the throng and stood looking on like a casual observer. It was akin to an out-of-body experience. Any second, I expected to see myself standing there in the middle of it all, being congratulated.

I turned, walked the short distance to my office, past Ruth's empty desk, and noticed a brightly wrapped gift bearing a card with my name on it. It was just like Ruth. I had hinted loudly that I did not want her spending money on presents, but like always, she had done what she wanted to do. That was Ruth alright.

I entered my office, closed the door behind me, flipped the light off, and stood there. The relative darkness fit my mood well. Natural light from the still overcast skies streamed in through the lightly tinted windows, casting a surreal glow across the room. I could even see the pea soup mixture of mist and clouds right outside the window. At times, I prefer darkness to light.

At home, I often enjoy sitting in a comfortable chair in absolute darkness. It allows me to think with my eyes open, without the distraction gazing at 'things' can bring. Alise would always tease me about showering with the lights off. I always responded that since I knew where all my private parts were, there was no problem.

I sat at my desk for a time, then flicked on a small Tiffany lamp. I glanced at mother's picture on my desk and thought of just how far away from home I was. The thought struck me in a manner it had never before. I began feeling estranged—even prodigal. Maybe it was the Champagne, on top of a very eclectic breakfast and the compote of emotions I had indulged in that morning.

I stared at mother's picture, lifted it, and turned to the window, until the outside light illuminated and caressed her face with a soft glow.

"Here I am, mother," I whispered, "Top of the world." And it was true. I was on top in every conceivable material way. Still, I had this sense of emptiness that all the successes, all the attaining of long-held goals had not filled. I had my cake, but the icing was thin.

I made a quick mental summary of my accomplishments, my holdings, my awards, my degrees—my things.

"So, is this it?" I asked myself.

I looked slowly about the office. There were priceless works of art and artifacts collected over so many years. There were other mementos and trinkets acquired along my way from somewhere to here, wherever here was. What was I doing here? Except for Alise, Ruth, and John Turret, I did not really know any of these people.

Sure, I had associates I had known for years and called friends, but they were not really friends in the true sense. Friend is a word bandied about all too loosely these days. But, why on earth was I being so maudlin—so disgustingly introspective?" I wondered.

"Cheer up stupid!" I cajoled myself. "This is what you always wanted. All of it! So, what's going on with you? Don't tell me you are one of these people who is not happy reaching a goal, only in the quest for goals." I was not. I was not that type, or was I? I had always managed to reach one summit and immediately begin another ascent. Never one to tread on dead moss, I had to keep moving. What was so different now? What had changed?

I rested my head on the desk listening to faint sounds of the festivities going on in my honor. What were they really celebrating? I wondered about that. I was under no illusion. Though I am certain their well-wishes were heartfelt, they likely were simply thrilled to have any reason to take a break from the normal grind. They would have been just as eager to help celebrate the grand opening of a new elevator.

Sitting there, still cloaked in a gray mood, all I could think about was what happened that morning in my bathroom. Talking with Alise had certainly helped, but there was no way to fully explain how I felt. I was not completely certain myself. In a way, I felt at war with myself. I was finally compelled to acknowledge that the sum of my successes was less than fulfilling.

My feeling downcast was nothing new. There had been times before when I felt uncertain—perhaps even a little depressed. But it would always last only a few minutes. Even in the throes of these emotions, I knew that it was only a passing phenomenon. Somehow, this time was different.

I raised my head and again stared at mother's picture. Her eyes seemed to say what I had heard her say so many times:

"Everything's gonna be alright, son." She would then press my head to her and caress me gently. Nothing before or since has ever showered me with such of a feeling of peace and security. I also embraced thoughts of father, whose face I kept seeing, whose voice I kept hearing. Without warning, a geyser of emotion filled me with an inexplicable longing. It was then I knew.

Chapter Sixteen

Lookin' For the Summer

I cannot tell you the precise moment it occurred or why my decision evolved with such speed and resolution. All I know is that I came to my eleventh hour and had to choose a direction in which to take the rest of my life.

The weight of all the uncertainty, the unhappiness, the confusion, missteps, regrets, and sins of my existence seemed to descend upon me like a net. I felt besieged. There was a moment of reckoning to contend with. Days of my life were passing by with seemingly greater and greater frequency. I could no longer pretend all was well with me.

So, with all the revelry still in high gear, I sat at my desk and wrote a one-paragraph letter of resignation. After all the fighting and clawing to reach the top of the heap, I wanted out. The realization that what I had been chasing was virtually illusory, in substance, was inescapable. I had surrendered my freedom, becoming a captive.

I was captive to my daily pursuits; captive to my need to maintain the image of me that others and I had cultivated. I traveled prescribed courses, day after day, seldom veering from the beaten path. Never mind that I traveled these paths in a gilded carriage, I traveled them, nonetheless.

Of course, I do not mean to suggest everything I had done was meaningless or of questionable value. It is just that for the first time, it was clear to me I was missing something. There was an emptiness to my life that could no longer be disregarded. I needed something more than I had. Maybe there was still time for me to find it. I had to try.

With a new century and a new millennium approaching, I was becoming increasingly introspective and philosophical. I felt as if I had only a few years to prepare myself to cross some Great Divide connecting past and future. What would an audit of my life reveal? I had never truly taken one. I could not shake these new feelings.

I felt compelled to alter the course of my life in an unselfish way; to divorce myself from the numbing sameness of my familiar. Although I could not fully understand how I had come to this moment, there I was. The hardest part of all would be pouring all this out to Alise. What would it mean for us? I expected a long, tortured night.

Ruth entered the office, carrying a present for me, and saw me sitting in the dark, surrounded by empty boxes and open file drawers. When I calmly informed her that I was resigning and leaving New York, she reacted with shock. Tears filled her eyes. She grew very emotional.

Ruth was only one of a handful of people I truly considered a friend. Within minutes, we were both crying like babies, recalling all the happy times we had shared. I insisted we would still have good times. The tears gave way to laughter, then more tears.

"I'm not leaving the planet," I joked amid the tears. She responded, saying leaving New York was tantamount to leaving the planet. Ruth loved her New York.

She had saved my rear end many a time. There was no way I could ever repay her. I assured her of lifetime employment, but that was not paramount in her mind. She confessed to having long ago sensed I was not where I wanted to be and apparently had lost my zest for the Wall Street life. Apparently, Ruth knew this even before I knew.

Ruth and I were in the middle of discussing what the probable reaction of the partners would be to my announcement. Suddenly, a gunshot blast rang out! There was no doubt what it was. Shrill, marrow-chilling screams erupted. I bounded to my feet, as a frantic woman of about 20, thrust open my door and all but collapsed inside.

She had been shot, we thought. I dashed to her. Tears streamed from her eyes. She ranted incoherently. Some crazed gunman had burst through the doors with an AK-47 and begun killing indiscriminately, I imagined.

A crush of humanity stampeded past in the corridor. I was able to make out Crane Vanderpool's name in her babble. Had Crane finally snapped? Moments later, the horror was vivid beyond reality. Crane was dead.

Even as I write these words now, it all seems more fiction than reality. I was only one of six people who entered Crane's blood-splattered office. We found him face down on his desk, blood still oozing in a pool around his head. His bloody hand still gripped the chrome-plated .38 caliber revolver. Frantic calls to 911 were made earlier, but there was little need for medics to hurry. Believe me, no one should have to see something like that. I still cringe and grimace when I think about it.

It was the most horrific sight I have ever witnessed. Brain matter lay splattered across open file folders on the desktop and on a photograph of his wife Julie and 4-year-old son Colin. The stench of human feces filled the room, causing a couple of us to vomit. To this day, I deeply regret entering that office. Whatever possessed me, I do not know. Perhaps I thought there was something I could do. There wasn't.

Pandemonium and disbelief reigned throughout the sprawling suite and other SJ&C floors. What was a cheerful, celebratory atmosphere had transformed into a gory death scene. It was all too surreal to comprehend. Staff, who earlier had been cheering and partying were now weeping, comforting each other while expressing shock and wondering why.

Crane's office door was closed and barred, while we awaited the arrival of detectives and the coroner. Meanwhile, the media and other ambulance chasers were soon barking at the gate and being held at bay by our security people.

Shortly after the police arrived, several of us were questioned. Others and I had observed a folded sheet of paper next to Crane's gun hand. We were all careful not to touch anything. When the questioning by the officers ended, we were left to confront our own unanswerable questions.

Sarrazin hastily called a meeting. He asked the firm's crisis management team to deal with potential psychological effects on employees. I left the meeting after the first five minutes and locked myself in my office. I refused to feel any sense of responsibility for what Crane had done to himself and the rest of us.

"Stupid fool!" I kept whispering over and over again, pounding my desk. "How could he do this to his wife and his son?" I yelled out in anger and frustration. Surely this had to involve more than being passed over for partner. Even Crane Vanderpool would not commit suicide just to ruin my day.

Later, police and the medical examiner's people were everywhere. The lead police detective, without mentioning details, informed me the paper we saw was a suicide note. I did not want to know what it said. Right or wrong, I had my own suspicions and did not want them confirmed.

How does it get to this? How does failure to attain some position trigger such feeling of hopelessness in a man with so many reasons to live? What leads him to see suicide as his only alternative?

With one muzzle flash, an eternal shadow fell over my memory of time spent at Sarrazin, Jacobs, and Carrazzo. Given Crane's obvious state of mind, I suppose I and others were fortunate he had not taken out his anger on the rest of us. He could very easily have walked into my office and taken my life.

I had known of only one other person, my dear Rosie, who attempted to take their own life and only one who had succeeded. It was so long ago, I had either forgotten or forced the memory of it from my mind.

Dr. Theodore Davies, everyone called him 'Fessor' Davies, killed himself when I was not more than 8 years old. He was the much respected, much-beloved principal of Crawford High—a man we all loved and revered.

Professor Davies would often visit our third-grade class to reprise historical speeches. He looked an awful lot like Abraham Lincoln, except he did not have a mole on his cheek, was not very tall and did not have a stovepipe hat. He did have a beard, which he kept neatly trimmed.

Suicide was such an alien notion for us kids to grasp. Grownups refused to talk about it. During those days, adults treated such trauma with abject silence. Today, counselors and psychologists come in and kids are encouraged to talk about such events. Such was not the case way back then and most certainly not in Rosedale.

I later learned details of Professor Davies' death, by eavesdropping on the conversations of grownups and from talking to other kids who had done the same. Professor Davies, a lifelong bachelor, was found one Saturday morning by Sariah Penfield, owner of the small house he rented in town.

When she could not arouse him, hours past the time he would normally stop by her place for Saturday morning coffee, Miss Sariah called the Sheriff. Forcing the door open, they found him in his bedroom, sprawled across his bed fully dressed. He had placed a pillow over his head and shot himself in the temple.

The whole town was in an uproar. Everyone wondered why such an intelligent, educated, successful, and well-liked man as Professor Davies had blown his own brains out. I suppose in the minds of many, only dumb, uneducated, disliked failures ever committed suicide. Wrong.

Word was Professor Davies had spent late hours in his office the night before. Duncan Stoddard's father mentioned passing the school and seeing a light on in the Professor's office as late as midnight. While that was a little unusual, Mr. Stoddard assumed he was working late. It was in his office that a one-line suicide note was later found. The contents were never released.

It was not until a month later we learned that over fifty thousand dollars in school funds, under the Professor's control, were missing and unaccounted for. We soon learned a strange word—embezzlement. Months later, we learned 'Fessor sent the money to his family in Philadelphia to care for a brother who later died of cancer.

The fact he had not taken the money for himself mitigated in favor of a less hostile view of 'Fessor Davies. I am sure the town would have forgiven, understood, and done whatever possible to help him make restitution. Precious few were willing to forgive him for taking his own life.

For us kids, suicide was hard to understand. Our teacher, Miss Calin, told us our friend would no longer be coming by our class to recite the Gettysburg Address. Peetie asked if we had done something to make him not want to live any longer. Duncan asked if being dead was like being asleep for a long time, or like...forever. Miss Calin started crying.

I did not call Alise for lunch, as planned. Instead, I went to some dumb movie. I cannot recall what the movie was about. I went to the theater to escape the harsh glare of reality. Besides, it was dark inside. I purposely chose some mindless, banal fare to be lobotomized by. I did not want to think, although I do some of my best thinking in the dark. God knows I needed to do some serious thinking, but not that day.

There were hordes of business decisions to make, and I did not want to give myself an opportunity to change my mind. Whether my eyes were open or closed, all I could see was Crane face down on his desk.

Other thoughts persisted. I was not intending to completely divest myself of all business activity; only those things that demanded a day-to-day, hands-on approach. As long as I had a laptop computer, a modem, and other electronic gadgets, I would be in-touch at will.

Suddenly, every thought about myself seemed selfish and disrespectful. I did not attend Crane's funeral, which was held a few days later. I could not bear the thought of staring into the grief-stricken faces of his wife and son. I signed the firm's letter of condolences with my initials only.

Despite her earlier comments about Crane, news of his suicide floored Alise. She found it difficult to believe he could end it all with no one watching. Crane had often demonstrated a talent for staging events for maximum impact. Thank God this time was an exception, or was it?

What surprised me was that Alise was not at all shocked by my own big decision. Again, she showed she knew me better than I knew myself. A silent Alise looked at me and took a deep breath. We spent the next hour sitting on the sofa embracing.

Alise spoke of having seen a change envelope me. She somehow knew I was nearing a transforming moment—a major turning point. The gravity of father's situation and the devastating effect all this was having on my mother was awakening me to a new view of what was truly important.

What this all meant for the future of our relationship remained an unanswered question, even though we talked throughout the evening and well into the early morning hours. Alise seemed determined to not frame things in a way that would make me feel a sense of obligation to her. But I could not help feeling obligated. I cared very deeply about her and knew how she felt about me.

Still, I felt as if I were proposing to abandon Alise and the years we had spent together. However, there was no way I could ask her to set aside her life pursuits. I did not expect, nor would I suggest she join me in some uncertain search for something even I was not sure existed. So, we agreed to leave all our options open.

My leaving New York was in no way a walking away from Alise and certainly not a walking away from whatever the future may yet hold for us. I knew Alise favored marriage and at least one child, before my sperm count dropped and her biological clock ticked to a stop.

If I had asked her to marry me, she would have said yes, and we would have been married that weekend in the picturesque little white, A-framed chapel we had passed so often on our trips to Connecticut. Alise had taken several pictures of it and even had greeting cards made featuring it on the front flap.

If the truth be known, I wanted to be a father. I did not want to live my life without having a chance to be both the father my father was and was not. However, the last thing I wanted was to become a parent without having committed myself to the time and effort raising children demand. I also knew none of those things could happen, until I had followed this star leading me to God knows where.

I persuaded Alise to sell her apartment and move into mine. She did not own a car and saw no need for one, but I persuaded her to take the Mercedes anyway. I finally relocated all my files and equipment from the Trade Center and stored most of the incidental items.

I relocated my business nerve center, including a staff of fifty, to a less opulent suite of offices in a Manhattan building I owned. The day-to-day oversight of certain aspects of my business was entrusted to a handful of key associates and my lawyers. Chief among them was John Turret. John was and is a longtime Harvard friend, legal and financial genius, and a true confidant from Simon, Wachtler and Evans. Since the majority of my business activity was conducted by telephones, faxes, videoconferencing and computers, my executive suite was effectively wherever I happened to place my laptop.

We spent almost every minute of the next few weeks at each other's side, joined at the heart. During that time, Alise and I returned to practically all our old haunts, relived precious moments shared over the years. It was a very emotional time for both of us, but we promised to restrain the tears. It was not as if we would never be together again.

We even braved an official tourist tour of New York and loved every minute of it. It provided a liberating feeling, a transformation in my take on everything, which amazed even me. I looked forward to beginning a new phase of my life. At the same time, I felt reluctant to leave Alise. I must say, without her understanding and selfless support, I would have been unable to embark on my journey with the clear mind I needed.

"At this point, your parents need you, even more than you need yourself," she'd often say to me. "If you don't do this, you'll never forgive yourself and I don't want you to be able to point to me as the reason you didn't."

She was right. After all this time, I would finally be going home. I would be returning to a place that held so many wonderful memories and had helped form the person I had become. In a way, I was about to venture back into the past—back to a time that perhaps only still existed in my mind.

Although I knew Rosedale would likely not be a final destination, for the first time I felt apprehensive. I hoped I was not building myself up for a huge emotional disappointment, regarding what I expected to see and feel.

The truth is youth can never be recaptured. Life presents us with a certain view of things unique to the point and place in time we happen to be. Often, we grow older and become easily enamored of a past airbrushed by time and bathed in the forgiving afterglow of self-indulgent retrospective.

There was always the possibility my returning to Rosedale, while important to my folks, would rob me of the storybook images I had of being a kid in Rosedale. I was sure to have a different perspective of the physical surroundings than I had as a child. Many of the familiar faces I had known would no longer be there. So many of the grownups I had known as a child had passed on.

I recall that on many occasions, during calls to mother over the years, she would inform me of the death of someone I had known. Often, I could not recall the face. She would go on to describe the person or mention a relative of theirs. That would jog my memory and she would continue, describing how dignified the funeral was, how peaceful the deceased looked.

It occurred to me that in Rosedale I would again be amongst down to earth, honest, unpretentious people. All they would care about was that the youngest Phalen boy, Jimmy T., was home to see about his mama and daddy.

"He sure does favor his dad," They would tell each other. I would smile, say how good it was to see them all, and I would be telling the truth.

Three days before my scheduled departure, I got a call from J.J. He said he heard I was leaving and had a good-bye gift for me. I agreed to meet him for lunch. As fate would have it, I met him just outside the entrance to the restaurant where we had shared breakfast before.

This time, I hardly recognized J.J. He looked like a Philadelphia lawyer in a New York state of mind. The rapid transformation was startling. The same waiters who had scoffed and scorned him before were now smiling and treating him like the human being he always was. I am sure they did not recognize him.

I was happy to learn J.J. now worked for an international charity organization and was making plans to launch an exciting business venture with his family and friends. He was a completely changed man. I kept looking at him, awed by what I saw.

J.J. knew about Vanderpool's death. He had also read that I was lowering my profile. I explained everything to him. He listened carefully and said he envied me. I assured him he had no reason to, that during the time I had known him, he had taught me important lessons.

Then came a moment I shall never forget. J.J. reached into his jacket and handed me a small, nondescript, rectangular box. He had this incredible look on his face—a look that one has when one knows the gift they are giving will blow the recipient away. It did.

I opened the box slowly. What I saw set me back on my heels. I stared in shock at the contents. There, enclosed in a clear plastic protective sleeve, lay an unused ticket to the first game of the 1955 World Series. The historic game, between the New York Yankees and the Brooklyn Dodgers, was played at Yankee Stadium.

J.J. just sat there with his chin resting on his interlocked fingers and his elbows resting on the table. He wore this incredible look of satisfaction.

"What...where did you get this? It's got to be priceless," I garbled.

"It is. There are two of them. I have the other at my mother's in Queens. My father bought them. We were supposed to go to the game that day."

"What happened?"

"He up and had a heart attack—he died."

"I'm so sorry to hear that," I said.

I sat back in my chair, took a long deep breath and stared at the ticket. I found it hard to believe.

"I guess you must have been about..."

"Six. I was 6 years old."

"J.J., I really appreciate the thought, but there's just no way I can accept this. This ticket is part of your family history, part of your life; it's—an heirloom from your father," I told him. J.J. shook his head and smiled.

"The love of baseball is something we both share. It's yours, Mr. P. I want you to have it."

"Call me Jim," I insisted."

"Can't do that," J.J. insisted. "I still have to call you Mr. P. That's the way I know you. I don't mean to sound formal, because I consider you my friend, but..."

"Alright," I conceded. "Alright."

J.J. insisted I accept his gift. He said it was a very modest thank you, for the encouragement and friendship I had offered him. I could clearly see he was not about to take "no" for an answer and I accepted.

"It's gonna bring you something very special," he said.

I looked at him, wondering just what he meant by that. In my mind, the fact I had been given such an unbelievable gift was special enough. I had no desire to know its actual value. I already knew it was priceless.

We left the restaurant, took the elevator down to street level and stood outside talking for several minutes, before J.J. hailed a cab. He said good-bye, shook my hand and rode away.

I watched the cab disappear into heavy traffic and stood there clutching the box with both hands. I remained rooted to the spot, looking around, hearing the constant buzz of activity, and feeling a peace I had not felt before.

An hour later, I stood outside the entrance to an empty Yankee Stadium. It was something I had to do. The Yankees were in Chicago that day and the place was all mine. I stood there staring at the timeworn facade of the legendary 'House that Ruth built.'

For a moment, I expected to hear a voice boom out over the public address system announcing the starting lineups for that 1955 World Series game. A tingle ran down my spine. I removed the box from my coat, removed the ticket and stared at it for the longest time. I could not take my eyes off it. I read every single word on it—front and back. Right down to the Printed in the USA on the last line.

It was 1955 again. Although I was only a year and a half old, I was there. I was at Yankee Stadium. Father held my hand, as we waded through the crowd. The excitement, the thrill of it all was more than a young heart could take. We were carried along like flotsam on a wave. Everything looked so big, so... overwhelming.

I reminded myself that on that day in 1955, real people stood where I was now standing. Perhaps a young boy had stood there with his dad clutching his hand tightly.

Then there was the game. Never mind the Yankees won that first game by a score of 6 to 5. Most importantly, the Dodgers won the series, 4 games to 3. Of course, the Yanks got revenge in '56. In game 5, the Yankees' pitcher Don Larsen bested 'Sad Sal' Maglie and entered the history books by pitching a 97 pitch, perfect game. It was the first no-hitter in a World Series. But my beloved Brooklyn Dodgers reigned supreme in '55. That was enough for me.

I imagined being in the stadium that day, sitting on father's lap and gazing excitedly down onto the field. There they all were, my longtime baseball heroes: Robinson, Reese, Furillo, Gilliam, Snider, Hodges, Campanella, Amoros, Drysdale, Labine, Erskine, Newcombe and the rest. I knew I was dreaming, but that was alright. Dreams are the building blocks of all realities.

"Thank God for dreams," I whispered aloud. "Thank God for dreams and dreamers who never grow weary of dreaming."

Four days later, following a long night of soul-searching conversation, many tears and sinew-sapping lovemaking, I was now only minutes from leaving New York. I was traveling light, having packed only a clothes bag and a small suitcase. I loaded them into the red Corvette convertible I had purchased a few days before. I was taking only one suit and was wearing the first jeans and tee shirt I had worn in decades.

Alise and I went through more tear-filled good-byes. It was the most difficult and emotionally draining departure I have ever made. She refused to walk down with me. I understood. Instead, she remained curled on the sofa, asking only that I tell her I would see her later in the evening. I did as she asked.

With my heart beating furiously, I opened the door slowly and glanced back at her, just as she brushed tears from her cheeks and smiled.

"I'll be alright," she said.

I wanted to believe that, but her voice was filled with emotion, even as she tried to sound calm.

"I know you will," I said.

Then came the inevitable silence and the feeling that if I did not leave at that moment, I never would. I stared across the room and found myself drawn back to her. The pull was irresistible. She must have felt it too because she stood and loosened her sheer robe. I started to her.

We fell immediately into embrace and kissed with a passion that quickly enslaved us both. Without relenting for even a second, we found ourselves again immersed in torrid activity that threatened to virtually devour us. Suddenly, there was no world beyond that room, no time beyond the moment, no life beyond the one we shared there together.

An hour later, with the veins in my forehead still throbbing, I again stood at the door, trying to say good-bye. Alise blew me a kiss.

"What do I say, when those who have not heard about what has happened, ask me where you've gone? What do I say to them?" I hesitated for a few seconds.

"What should I say?" She asked again.

"Tell them.... Tell them I have gone looking for the Summer."

"Looking for the summer," she repeated with a soft smile. I nodded yes.

"I love you, James T. Phalen," she said barely above a whisper. I heard her clearly.

"I love you, Alise Tomei," I said.

Alise looked away, for only a heartbeat. "I think you should go now," she said. "Please, go. Please."

I backed away, until I reached the doorway. I glanced once more at Alise and walked slowly into the corridor, leaving the door ajar. Seconds later, I started for the elevator. It seemed five miles away.

Chapter Seventeen

Charlie

I did not inform mother, Rosie or anyone in Rosedale I was coming home. I doubted they would have believed me. What's more, I wanted to surprise them. Of those I really cared about, only Alise and my secretary, Ruth Wiesenthal, knew of my decision. Beyond that, neither they nor I knew how long I would remain there or where my journey would ultimately lead me. I was not thinking that far ahead and had no compulsion to do so.

For the first time in my recent adult life, I had no indelibly written schedule to adhere to. I felt like a captive bird at last set free and ready to fly. What concerned me was my being able to leave New York with some degree of anonymity. I did not want to wake up and find my face and my plans splattered on the front page of the Times, the WSJ, The Post or even The Weekly Reader, for that matter.

My concern along those lines had its origin in the experience of a famous friend of mine who had endured a real horror many years earlier. His simple plan to spend a month relaxing in Monte Carlo became a story of escape to avoid prosecution for tax fraud and drug charges.

A doctored photo of him with his reputed mistress appeared on the front page of this yellow rag. The entire story proved to be absolute garbage—fiction of the worst kind. Yet it ruined his business, destroyed his career and his marriage. Later, the real facts emerged, appearing on page twenty.

Not surprisingly, a major financial newspaper referred to my single day as a partner at Sarrazin, Jacobs and Carrazzo as: "...the capricious meanderings of a billionaire brat still in search of another mountain to climb."

I fired off a letter, knowing they would not have the balls to print. I was right. Alise suggested I give them a 'Bronx Cheer' and ignore them. She was right, but I could not resist sending the letter.

The long-awaited day arrived. I left New York, without fanfare or notice and thought: Now, if I could just keep things this way, that would be fantastic. I wanted to disappear and be free to cruise the highways and byways like any other recent retiree searching for lost youth.

This was a day of mixed emotions and feelings of immense uncertainty. Earlier in the morning, I had stared long and hard into my mirror and asked myself if I was nuts or just plain stupid. What was I doing? Was I sure I wanted to do this?

I had already asked myself those questions a hundred times, since making my decision. I still had doubt. But the decision was irreversible—cast in stone. What was compelling me was more than the desire to go. I felt a burning need to escape my present confines. Ready or not, I had reached a turning point.

A few days earlier, Alise and I had driven to Cooperstown to visit the Baseball Hall of Fame. My first visit had come during my first year at Harvard. For me, it was more a pilgrimage to Mecca than a casual trip.

I remember how magical and awe-inspiring that experience was for me. John Turret, my former classmate and closest friend, whom I mentioned earlier, had offered to accompany me. I felt hard put to tell him I did not want company. As it turned out, I was spared this task, when his girlfriend from Des Moines paid him a surprise visit.

Having been raised in Rosedale, where one of the most exciting things I had ever done was attend the State Fair of Texas, in Dallas, visiting Cooperstown was a dream come true. There it all was, right there in front of me: the history; the faces; the uniforms; the gloves;

the shoes, sensing the hallowed aura. I remember feeling like a kid and promised myself I would come back again. I kept the promise.

I think Alise, though not exactly a baseball fan, enjoyed the trip as much as did I. She seemed thoroughly amused by my insistence she take my picture from at least a dozen angles in front of the building. She later told me I reminded her of a certain 9-year-old boy I had often told her about.

I suppose we must have really looked like a couple of tourists to one elderly gentleman. He approached us, while we stood near the entrance. Alise had just snapped off a couple of quick takes, when he stepped over to me and whispered loudly:

"Where 'ya from?"

"New York, by way of Texas," I whispered back.

"Been here long?" The man asked.

"About an hour or so," I said.

"Oh, I see. So, you folks just arrived in The Big Apple and already you found your way to Cooperstown. You must have baseball in your blood, alright."

I did not have the heart to interrupt and tell him that I thought he meant how long we had been in Cooperstown. As it turned out, I would not have had much of an opportunity to interrupt anyway. He hardly came up for air.

"I bet you use to play baseball as a kid, right? Dreamed of ending up here someday yourself, right? Bet you use to worry your dad to death about buying gloves and balls and playing catch and everything. I know my son did. You kinda' remind me of my boy, Charles, Jr. We lost him in Vietnam almost thirty years ago. He loved baseball. He was nineteen years old. 'Course he was little taller than you, though not by much."

Before I could respond, Charlie continued. "This place is like magic—a time machine, as I call it. I get a little bit younger, every time I walk through those doors there."

Just as he was getting warmed up, a petite, grey-haired woman in a pantsuit, whom I took to be his wife, stepped over to us and interrupted him in mid-sentence.

"Excuse me, I'm Ann," she said with a warm smile, a turn of her head and a hand placed on her husband's arm.

"Charlie, for god sakes, let the young man get inside so he can see all this magic you been talkin' about." Charlie looked briefly embarrassed, cupped his right hand to his mouth and took a few steps back.

"Forgive me," Charlie apologized again and again, despite my insistence his apology was not necessary. He explained he had visited the Hall so many times, he had become a self-proclaimed ambassador. It was his calling in life, as he laughingly put it, with a twinkle in his eyes.

Before Charlie finally strode away, he removed a frayed, brown wallet, and despite his wife's look of disapproval, showed me a picture of Charles, Jr. at age ten. The young, cherub-faced kid had on a little league baseball uniform and held a Babe Ruth, Louisville Slugger across his shoulder.

I looked at this young boy. I peered deep into his face and his eyes. I recognized the excitement there. I had seen it all before, in my own mirror. I must admit, Charlie, Jr. did bear an uncanny resemblance to me at that age. The small picture prompted many thoughts of days long gone. For some reason, my mind recalled the time Mr. McCloud called on me to pitch my first game.

"Me?" I asked. I was as surprised as anyone. Not that I doubted I could pitch. What was no secret to Mr. McCloud or me was that I did not have the strongest arm in the world.

For almost a month, during my second year on the team, Mr. McCloud had on several occasions had me pitch part of batting practice. I was excited and shocked. After all, my position was third base. Even there, it took solid effort for me to get the ball to first base with some zing on it. I managed. Why I was not positioned at shortstop, I do not know.

My real advantage was that I was quick. I could get to the ball fast and took delight in making lunging dives, springing to my feet, or throwing from almost any contorted position.

That day that I pitched, we were opposing the Dayton Pirates. The Pirates were a very strong team with a lineup loaded with powerful hitters. We all thought our pitcher, Sheb Dugan, could keep the Pirates off balance with his blazing fastball and his Luis Tiant windup. Tiant was a rather paunchy major league pitcher, with a Fu Manchu mustache. His notoriety sprang from his twisting and turning his back during his delivery to home plate.

When the game started, I began at third base, as usual. Things quickly turned sour. The Pirates went through our pitching roster like Grant went through Richmond. Balls were popping out of the park like popcorn. It looked totally hopeless. Fortunately for us, our big hitters were connecting too. We were still in the game.

By the time we limped into the bottom of the fourth inning, the score was Pirates 8, Dodgers 5. An anguished Mr. McCloud called me over, stared me in the eyes, laid one of his heavy, lead-like paws on my shoulder and said:

"I want you out on the mound."

"Sir?" I was not sure I had heard right. He removed the huge wad of chewing tobacco he kept tucked in his right jaw, spat, and repeated: "Look at me. Go pitch. I want you and Peetie to go back there behind the dugout and throw a few."

Peetie was as shocked as I. Yet, we did as told and sneaked behind the dugout. When the top of the fifth inning rolled around, I took to the mound and began my warm-up tosses. A buzz went through the crowd. For the first time in my short career, I knew what real fear was.

There I was out on the mound, the focal point of everyone in the park. It had never occurred to me that when you are the pitcher, everyone has their sights trained on you; the fans, your teammates, the opposing team, the umpires, everyone, including God. Your every move is closely scrutinized.

I was not sure I was ready for this. "I'm a third baseman," I thought. "What am I doing here?"

I tossed my final warm-up pitch. The home plate umpire signaled for the game to resume and Peetie trotted out to the mound with his gut hanging like a feed sack over his belt.

"Okay Squirt," Peetie said. "Just watch my signals and throw your pitch." I looked at him curiously. My bottom jaw dropped to my waistline.

"Peetie, I got a question."

"What is it?" He asked.

"What's my pitch?"

Peetie just laughed, turned away and headed back toward home plate, leaving me more confused than before.

"Play ball!" The ump shouted. The surly batter stepped into the batter's box with what looked to be the trunk of a Sequoia in his hands. I almost choked. I just stood there, while Peetie went through a series of signals, trying to tell me what pitch he wanted.

The trouble was, I only had one pitch—two at best. I figured Mr. McCloud must have had some reason to bring me on in relief. I made up my mind I would just pretend I was in batting practice and do my best.

After staring in at Peetie for what seemed like a week, I started into my windup and prepared to deliver my first official pitch as a Dodger hurler. This was history in the making. I raised my left leg, lifted then lowered my right arm, dipped my left shoulder, and followed through with my pitch.

The instant the ball left my hand, I wanted it back. I wanted to chase it down and start all over again. When I saw Peetie come out of his crouched catcher's stance, remove his mask, and look skyward, I knew I was in trouble.

The batter never got a chance to swing. The ball sailed a mile over the plate, over the backstop and into the bleachers. I was so embarrassed, I wanted to burrow underneath the mound. Pirate fans hooted and laughed. Dodger fans gasped. I just stood there.

Seconds later, I was surrounded by my teammates, Mr. McCloud and could see mother, Rosie, and Carter in their seats, dying for me. Mr. McCloud put his big hand on my shoulder, leaned down and told me:

"Son, settle down. Everything's gonna be alright. Just consider that your last warm-up pitch. Put 'em in there! Let's go!"

With that, Mr. Mac clapped his huge hands together resoundingly and trotted off the field. I took to the mound again, trying to forget my first pitch.

Things improved considerably. My second pitch was a ball, low and outside. In fact, every pitch I threw from that point on was either low and outside, low, and inside or just plain low. The result was Pirate after Pirate who found themselves struggling to get a handle on my pitches.

It was not that my pitches were blazing or that they arrived with extraordinary movement or anything. That was the problem, especially for the Pirates. Every ball I threw had a different speed. What each pitch had in common was the fact they were all low.

While I struck out only three of the batters I faced that day, there were no walks, and no one got past first base. Every ball hit was a ground ball and directly at someone. You could see the disgust on the faces of Pirate players and coaches as well. Dodger Fan frustration became fan elation.

My confidence grew with every pitch, and I was thrilled to see these terrific hitters tripping over their own feet and lunging all over the place trying to hit my pitches. It was a thrill I remember to this day.

While we still lost that game by one run, we were not losers. I was perhaps the biggest winner of all. The final score was 8 to 7. I managed to hold the Pirates scoreless, and we almost won the game.

Mr. McCloud explained he had me pitch precisely because he knew my pitches lacked the speed and consistency of those thrown by his regular pitchers. I suppose he chose me because of what I could not do, as much as for what I could do.

It was then I recalled the negative reaction of my teammates, whenever I was asked to pitch batting practice. The decision was not welcomed. The guys always complained I barely got the ball to the plate with enough speed for them to time their swings. It all made sense.

All this made it even more clear to me, that baseball existed as a game for everyone; the strong, the not so strong, the tall, the short, the thin, the not so thin—everyone.

By the way, the week following our 8 to 7 loss1, we faced the Pirates again. Once more, I pitched the final three innings. This time, we kicked their tails, 9 to 5. As the season progressed, I resumed playing third base, mostly. On occasion, I got the relief call. Eventually, I developed a strong arm and a few variations to my slow, sinking, not so fastball.

I found myself staring at Charlie and seeing the pain that still rested with him. I was moved, seeing the glint in his eyes. I heard the emotional tremor in his voice, when he spoke fondly of his deceased son. I somehow felt a connection with both. Baseball was the common link. I did not have to know everything there was to know about them. It was enough to know how much they loved baseball. We were kin.

Searching Charlie's face, I imagined the pain and heartache he and tens of thousands of other Charlies, whose sons and daughters never came home from Vietnam, must yet feel.

For a moment, my thoughts turned to Carter and that day he stepped off the greyhound bus on crutches and minus a leg. Some wounds never really heal completely, despite our desire and need to move beyond them.

At Alise's suggestion, I asked Charlie and Ann if they would pose for me. They eagerly agreed and Charlie spent the next several minutes making suggestions regarding the best spot to take a photo. I waited. When he had settled on a location, Charlie stood proudly with his arm around Ann and smiled.

Ann turned to face him and began straightening his shirt collar. Alise looked at me and smiled. Ann patted his hair into place and generally made quite a fuss over him. Charlie grew a little impatient and gently grasped her hand.

When they were finally ready, I snapped the shot. We then shook hands and said our good-byes. Alise and I stood holding hands and watching, as Charlie and his wife walked away arm in arm. It was very easy for me to imagine he and Charlie Jr. had spent many hours together, doing all the wonderful things fathers and sons do.

It was also heartwarming to see the deep love Charlie and Ann shared for each other. They seemed to know each other's thoughts, each other's expectations, and needs. They were one. I recall them telling us they had been married forty-five years. It appeared to me they were still enjoying their honeymoon.

I have since come to regret not exchanging phone numbers with Charlie. It would have been great to have had further opportunities to talk to him about baseball and about life. I am sure I could have learned a lot from him.

I discovered many years ago, that many old men are like walking repositories of knowledge and wisdom that they happily impart to all who will listen. I suspect Charlie was such a man. I also suspect were I to return to Cooperstown and spend enough time wandering around the Hall of Fame, I would run into Charlie for sure.

I will never forget Charlie or Ann or the photograph of his son, Charlie, Jr. or that wonderful, sunny afternoon in Cooperstown at the Hall of Fame. Someday, I will return.

Eighteen

The Long Road Home

I do not mean for this chapter to read like a travelogue, but I must share a few thoughts about those thousands of miles, some memorable events that took place, and some unforgettable characters I met.

This trip was a new experience for me. I had never traveled alone by auto on any trip remotely approaching this distance. I viewed this not only as the journey of a modern-day prodigal son, but as an opportunity to perhaps meditate on things I normally gave only scant thought to. I was both excited and somber.

Father was uppermost in my mind. Were it not for him, this road trip would never have occurred. I was anxious and impatient to see him. Yet, I recognized my fear of what I would find; fear of what I would feel. My circuitous route was proof of that.

One part of me wanted to get to Rosedale quickly. Another wanted to take a meandering route to afford time to think and benefit from the therapy the driving would provide. After all, if getting to Rosedale quickly was my main objective, I could have taken the Gulf Stream.

Tucked away in my cavernous mind was the illogical notion nothing undesirable could happen before I arrived home. It was just a silly notion in my head. Still, I concluded if I took my time, I could perhaps forestall any possibility father's condition would worsen. I knew that line of thought did not make sense, but that is the way I felt.

I left upper Manhattan, taking Park Avenue to 97th Street, east to Franklin D. Roosevelt Dr. and began my southwesterly drive en route to I-278. The skies were partly cloudy, the air unseasonably cool. David Sanborn's lusty saxophone was blasting from the CD. I cranked it to the max momentarily, just for the heck of it. And why not? I felt twenty-one again, despite that middle-aged guy staring back at me in my rear-view mirror.

I had not gone a dozen blocks, when the realization hit me that I was really leaving. There I was, actually in the car with my actual clothes in my actual bags and my actual foot on the gas. There was no turning back now. I was leaving New York.

Then out of nowhere, I was rocked by this overpowering urge to call Alise, tell her to pack her bags and meet me in the apartment lobby. I could still see her sitting there on the sofa where I had left her. I imagined her feet curled underneath her; her head resting on her left hand. I could see her, with her left elbow on the armrest, as she toyed aimlessly with tassels on the corner of one of the pillows.

Already, I missed the sweet, soothing sound of Alise's seductive voice, the sweet subtle smell of her sensuous aroma. I longed to feel her baby-soft skin and her taut, sculpted body next to me. I craved having her so close I could feel the beat of her heart; feel her sweet breath against my face. I bit my lower lip, took a deep breath, pressed on the accelerator, and struggled to force the urge to pass.

Strangest of all, I hardly noticed or cared about the crush of heavy traffic. It was as awful as always, but I did not care. For the first time in a long time, I was not rushing someplace and was not in a headlong dash to get to some boring meeting attended by even more boring people. I did not even mind being cut off by demolition cabs and fist-flailing, fanatical drivers hell-bent on getting nowhere as fast as they could. I was free at last.

I continued on FDR to the Queens Midtown Tunnel and onto the Long Island Expressway. From there I jumped to I-278, otherwise known as the Gowanus Expressway, which took me across the Verrazano Narrows Bridge. I crossed the bridge, dodging more than a few potholes, continued farther on I-278 to I-95, otherwise known as the New Jersey Turnpike. By the time I reached I-287 and neared I-78, I was getting a little dizzy from all the transitions.

A few miles beyond the town of Somerville, I turned onto I-78 and headed toward Bethlehem and Allentown, Pennsylvania about 60 miles away. It was not until then I was free to give the 'Vette its head and let it run. I could feel the raw power rumbling beneath me.

All those years in New York, I had not owned a car until I purchased the little Mercedes, I gave Alise. Owning a car in New York is not the same as owning one in Los Angeles, or Dallas, or even Rosedale, for that matter. Whenever I needed a car, I rented one or had my driver take me wherever I wanted to go. Not having a car meant eliminating one more headache. In New York, if you can eliminate a headache, you do it.

Now, I felt like a teenager with keys to his first car and a full tank of gas on a Friday night. There was nothing in front of me except miles and miles of more miles and miles. I had money, checks, credit cards, an ATM card, a driver's license that proved I was over 21, and no curfew. I suppose my grungy appearance did not quite rival the image of Malcolm Forbes in a black leather jacket riding on a custom Harley, but this was still living free.

I breezed down the Interstate, staring ahead with laser intensity, then realized I had a death grip on the steering wheel. My hands ached. I was unaware I was so tense and sitting hunched forward in my seat. My jaws were clenched, and my temples throbbed. I loosened my hold and took a deep breath, slowing to the posted speed and easing into the right lane. I kept reminding myself that with so many miles in front of me, I had to learn to relax.

Getting past my conditioned need to be in the fast lane was not easy, but I was determined to try. I forced myself to stay in the slow lane. Meanwhile, traffic blew me away as if I was standing still. After a time, it did not bother me. I was relaxed. It actually felt good, even therapeutic.

The drive down I-78 took me through a treasure of scenic and semi-wooded terrain. This was a part of the country I had not seen before but had always wanted to. I took it all in hungrily, wishing I was in the passenger seat instead of behind the wheel. The drive, the scenic view—all this was causing the stress to fall away with every succeeding mile. It was wonderful.

By the time I reached Allentown, around two in the afternoon, I had logged less than 150 miles, although I had been behind the wheel for almost three hours. I decided to stop, top off the gas tank and get my first Big Mac of the trip. I had spotted the signs long before seeing the city limits. I think the hunger was more psychological than real.

Alise had told me the trip would not be official until I had enjoyed my first Big Mac, fries, and chocolate shake. Eager to have this beginning made official, I had my ceremonial meal. Within forty-five minutes, I was back on I-78 and trying to stay under 70 miles per hour. It was not easy.

My goal was to get as far as Roanoke, Virginia before packing it in for the evening. I planned to rise at 5:30 am, get an early start and drive as far as Memphis or maybe Little Rock by evening the next day.

Roanoke was approximately 350 miles away which would take me about six hours if I did not give in to urges to take side trips. I knew there were numerous historical points of interest along the way and gorgeous scenery to take in by leaving the beaten path. The most direct route would take me past much of this scenery and would not be quite as interesting.

Despite the surrounding beauty, thoughts of father hung over me like a cloud. I would at times be breezing along, listening to the music—my eyes taking in the countryside, then it would hit me. A feeling of foreboding and sadness would strike me like a lightning bolt. Once, I pulled off the road and sat there for a full half-hour staring into nothingness.

I had the distinct feeling my decision to leave New York had been dictated by something or someone far bigger than me. It seemed ordained—dictated by a greater power. It also seemed it was happening at the only time it could have. It was as if I had arrived at the station, just in time to catch the last train home.

Just north of Jonestown and Lickdale, I-78 transitioned into I-81, a fact that almost went unnoticed by me. I thought I'd taken a wrong turn. The gorgeous scenery of deep green woods, rolling hills and level fertile farms were mesmerizing, captivating, and liberating. I envied those who had the good fortune to enjoy this view every day.

Before long, I blew by the capital of Harrisburg and headed for Strasberg 130 miles away. I took a swig from the remainder of my diet Coke, now mostly water, reached for an Everett Harp CD and gave David Sanborn a well-deserved break.

Following a brief stop in Strasburg to remove the Coke from my kidneys and stretch my legs, I continued 80 miles to Staunton. This section of I-81 took me through the beautiful, scenic Shenandoah Valley with its splendid views across rolling terrain, and paralleling wooded mountains.

I knew there were several caverns in the area, but there would be little opportunity to explore them on this trip. In Staunton, one of the oldest cities west of the Blue Ridge Mountains, I refueled, grabbed a few junk food items, and decided to alter my course.

Instead of returning to I-81, I took I-64 to the Blue Ridge Parkway and stayed on it all the way into Roanoke. I knew the route would be very winding but gorgeous. It did not disappoint. I only wished I had timed my arrival for a few hours earlier, to catch the sunset.

The Parkway followed the crest of the Blue Ridge Mountains and other beautiful ranges providing breathtaking views of the beautiful Shenandoah Valley and Southern Highlands. The route took me through peaks, across lakes, through tunnels and past vista points too numerous to count. At times I found myself trying to look to my right and left at the same instant. If I had stopped as often as I wanted, I would still be on the Parkway.

As beautiful as the drive was, I was happy to arrive in Roanoke minutes after a stunning sunset. It was not until I was about 12 miles from Venation that I realized both my still and video cameras were inside my suitcase.

I found a place to stop, grabbed my still camera and caught the last glimmer of the sun, as it dropped out of sight just beyond a distant ridge. I cranked off a half dozen exposures, before climbing back in the car and continuing to Roanoke.

There was absolutely no mistaking Roanoke, the so-called Star City, for any other city, as I approached. The nickname comes from the huge electric star positioned atop Mill Mountain that, itself, rises 1000 feet within the city limits. I entered the city, taking the Blue Ridge Expressway to Orange Avenue and to downtown. Before securing lodging, a hot meal and much-needed sleep, I had to see this star up close. I took Jefferson Street to Walnut Avenue and followed the signs up the mountain.

When I arrived at the top, there were dozens of other people in a city park located at the mountain's peak. They too, were taking in the fantastic views of the city on this clear summer night. The star was well over a hundred feet high and almost as wide. I strolled around the area for about fifteen minutes, took a few snapshots, using the star's light, and started back down to the lowlands.

To this day, I have no explanation for failing to call ahead and reserve a room for the night. I guess I had been so caught up in my excitement, the thought escaped me. I did not think I would have difficulty getting a room. The only question was where I would find one. I had grown accustomed to five-star hotels and knew that anything much less would be roughing it just a little too much.

Having thought this, I deemed it a touch elitist and decided to head back down Williamson Road to see what I could see. I remembered spotting an attractive little place called the Roanoker Motor Lodge and pulled in to have a look see. As it turned out, it was only a one star. It was clean but had only very basic accommodations with exterior corridors.

I passed on the Roanoker and after a couple of calls on my cellular phone found a vacancy at the 8 story Marriott-Roanoke Airport. It was just shy of 9pm, when I arrived feeling a little worn and ready for a good meal. I registered, emptied the car, took everything into the room and headed for the restaurant. It was scheduled to close at 10pm and I only had minutes. When I shuffled inside, I noticed only a few other patrons remained.

While waiting for my dinner, I called Alise. Hearing her voice was like hearing the soothing song of an angel. It was like we had been apart for a month already. She wanted a mile-by-mile account of the whole trip, and I wanted to know about her day in about the same level of detail. We were like young lovers separated for the first time. That must have been apparent to the waitress who brought my dinner, serving it with a never-ending smile.

My conversation with Alise ended, with less than ten minutes left before the restaurant's scheduled closing. I kept glancing at my watch, when my waitress, who noticed me checking the time, mouthed: "It's alright."

Alise reluctantly informed me she would be leaving in two days for a week in London. Her agent had arranged a European leg for her new book tour and insisted she not pass it up. I agreed she should go. I did so, knowing full well I wanted the comfort of knowing she was still curled up on the sofa in the apartment. It was an admission I made grudgingly to myself. We soon ended our conversation with slurpy phone kisses and softly spoken good-byes.

I gulped my food, chased it with hot tea and spent thirty minutes talking with Anitra McDavid, my waitress. She was a character, extraordinaire. Anitra was a 62-year-old grandmother, who looked 50 or younger. She possessed an airy personality and a penchant for conversation. When I told her I was from New York, she smiled, touched my hand, and promised not to hold that against me. She wanted to know where I was headed. I told her home—to Texas.

"My first husband was from Texas, also" she said.

"First?" I asked.

She smiled, placed one hand on her hip and poured my coffee with the other.

"Tell me if I'm wrong," she said with a twinkle in her eyes, "But do I detect a little prying into a lady's business in the tone of that question?" She asked. I kept quiet.

"Well?"

I pleaded innocent and we both had a good laugh. I learned Anitra not only worked at the hotel's restaurant but was also a part-time student at a nearby Jr. College. She explained that getting her college education was a promise she had made, at the age of 23, to her mother who lay on her deathbed. Although it was a struggle, she was at last making good on her promise.

Anitra was very attractive, though a little over made-up. She was eager to have me guess her age and glowed with delight when I wisely understated it by fifteen years. She exuded an effervescence and energy I had not seen in women half her 62 years. I remember watching how hard she worked, trekking back and forth. What a toll nine hours of that must take, I thought.

I recalled how many times I had been in restaurants and given scant attention to the persons serving me unless they screwed up. Something about this woman made me appreciate how difficult and demanding the job was. It was clear she felt tired, and her feet must have been killing her. Still, there she was, smiling and bubbling.

As I talked, or rather listened, I could not help thinking this woman deserved to be living her senior years in the comfort of her home, enjoying her grandkids, and playing bingo. Instead, she had to work withering hours, suffer insufferable customers. Yet she somehow had the motivation to seek a degree. I was awed.

Then, it occurred to me I should not ascribe to Anitra my own antiquated conception of what 62-year-olds should be doing. She seemed happy enough. Besides, I could not envision her glued to a rocking chair or playing bingo.

Before I left, Anitra thanked me for a generous tip and made me promise I would come down for an early breakfast the next morning. I hedged a bit. She insisted. Having learned she was twice divorced, and on husband number three, I figured Miss Anitra McDavid was not one to take no for an answer. I said yes.

I arrived at my sixth-floor room with plans for the evening that included a trip to the exercise room, a half-hour in the sauna, a shower and sound sleep. I did not want the trip to serve as an excuse for abandoning my daily exercise program. Nevertheless, despite good intentions, I only got as far as the shower and bed.

I slept like a baby and awoke at about 5:15, feeling as if I'd slept for twelve hours. Maybe it was the wine I had enjoyed with dinner.

Maybe it was the pleasant though exhausting conversation with one Anitra McDavid.

I awoke, found myself in the hotel room and for a second had no idea where I was or how I had gotten there. I gathered myself quickly, showered, shaved, and grabbed some breakfast. That all went quite fast, owing in part to Anitra's absence. I sat for a while, drinking coffee, and enjoying the first morning following the start of my trip. I felt great. Then, thoughts of father suddenly flushed my mind, leaving my heart racing. I took a few minutes to gather myself.

As I was leaving the restaurant, I asked about Anitra. I learned she was ill and had taken the day off. A young female co-worker confided she had been pushing herself too hard. Anitra's strenuous schedule included working six days and going to school four days a week.

She had also recently suffered the tragic loss of her 5-year-old grandson and was struggling to conceal her grief. What made the tragedy unbearable was the fact her youngest daughter was charged in the child's death. Considering all that. I was amazed she could still present such a warm and selfless attitude. I asked the young woman about Anitra's new husband.

"What husband?" She asked. "Annie hasn't been married since her first husband died fifteen years ago. She likes to tell people she's had several husbands. That what she told you?" I nodded yes.

"That's just her way of putting people on. She was pulling your leg. Between school and this place, she ain't got time for a boyfriend, much less a husband. Excuse me."

With that, she answered the cook's bell and hurried to deliver food to her customers. I stepped to the end of the counter, removed my checkbook, and penned a short personal note to Anitra then placed it and a modest check in an envelope. After addressing the envelope, I waited until the woman returned. I asked her to make sure Anitra got the letter and she assured me she would.

As I was leaving, it dawned on me I had only met Anitra the night before. Already, I had learned so much about her—personal things that now affected me. I had spoken to her at length; had developed great empathy for her and admired her determination. Of course, there was so much more I did not know about her. But I knew enough to know she was a good person. I wish I could have said good-bye.

Chapter Nineteen

Plan "B"

I returned to my room and called mother.

I had not spoken to her in a couple of days and knew she would be wondering why she had not heard from me. I definitely did not want her to call New York, speak to Alise and have Alise feel compelled to lie about my whereabouts. Lying was the one thing Alise did not do well.

I spoke to mother. She was surprised I was calling so early in the morning. It had not dawned on me it was about 5:30 in Texas. Normally I would not call her until ten or later, EDT.

Nothing escaped Bonnie Phalen. Mother's query put me in the awkward position of obfuscating—lying. I tried to deflect her question by saying I had gotten up early, was not going to work and longed to hear her voice. It was all true, but I chose not to elaborate.

I asked about father. Mother hesitated ever so slightly, which prompted me to ask again. She insisted he was doing about as well as could be expected. Translated, that meant he was not improving. I asked the question again, in various ways, hoping to get her to be more straightforward.

Then Mother's voice dropped. There was this long silence. I could sometimes read her silence better than I could her spoken words. I knew father had long ago lost his lucidity and from Carter I had learned he grew more and more detached and distant with each passing day.

When I last spoke to Carter, I asked him if he thought I should come home right away. He said he did not think father's condition warranted it. Clearly, he was still holding out hope father would have a complete recovery. We all were.

Mother went on to say father's appetite was fairly good. However, he was not sleeping as much during the day as he had been. She saw that as a good sign. I offered no contrary view. We were all being very careful to keep her in a positive frame of mind.

My parents had been together most of their lives and had not spent a single night apart. It had to be very difficult, for mother to face the real probability the only man she had known and loved would not celebrate another Christmas with her. It was difficult for me to deal with that. It had to be much harder for her.

Mother began reminiscing about the things father used to do—how long it had been since he had done this or that. There was a faraway quality to her voice. It offered an insight into how she had perhaps already begun to prepare for what appeared inevitable. It touched me. I remember sitting on the edge of the hotel bed and leaning over with the phone pressed to my ear. Even after we said our good-byes, I sat there holding the receiver in my hand, staring into nothingness.

"So, what now, Mr. James T. Phalen," I derided myself. "What now? What good does all your things do now? Your father is dying, your mother is in pain, though she won't admit it. There is not a thing you can do, except pray." So, I prayed. And I prayed.

An hour later, I checked out, using the room TV, and buzzed the bellboy who arrived quickly and took my luggage downstairs. I followed. With keys in hand, I exited into the cool morning air, took a deep breath, and stretched fiercely, before continuing to my car.

With my eyes riveted on the ground, I walked about halfway down the first row forward of the entry driveway facing Hershberger Road. Suddenly, I realized I must have gone too far, turned around sharply, and retraced my steps.

I then honed my sight on the space where I was certain I had parked my car. The space was empty. My car was gone. I did a three-sixty turnaround and looked again. It still was not there. I again surveyed the row from end to end. It was not there.

I walked across the drive-thru to the other side, thinking perhaps I had parked there instead. No luck. My car was definitely gone. I could not believe it. If you have ever had your car stolen, you know there is an initial refusal to accept the fact. You look behind trees, around the corner, even in your pocket. That is what I was going through. Had I arrived earlier, I could have valet parked.

"My car has been stolen," I whispered over and over to myself, still in shock and disbelief. I just stood there.

All those years in New York, I had never been mugged, never been accosted in any way, never had one thing stolen from me, except my innocence. I am in Roanoke less than 10 hours and my $50,000 car was history, heisted, gone. Poof!

"Ain't that a pain in the...," I muttered.

The young officers who took my report were only doing their job. However, I admit I was irked, when they asked to see verification, I indeed owned a 1995 Corvette. Being personally aware of my purposely grungy look, I obliged them. Appearance is everything when no one knows who you are.

Once satisfied, the officers completed their report and informed me that for the past six months, there had been evidence of a car theft ring operating in the area. They seemed to have a fancy for Corvettes and 5.0 Mustangs. My timing had been perfect.

The Marriott people and the Roanoke Police were most understanding. They pleaded with me to not judge their fine city by this unfortunate incident. I promised to try very hard. After offering me a free additional day's lodging and a discount on the rental of a GM, Ford or Chrysler car, the hotel management repeatedly apologized. I assured them I did not blame anyone except the thieves and respectfully declined their generous offer.

There was no way I wanted to continue my trip in some rental car, and I was not about to wait around until my insurance company replaced mine. That would have to wait. I am sure it is a fine city, but I wanted out of Roanoke as soon as possible. So much for an early start. Now it was on to Plan B.

~

During the next two hours, I became well acquainted with the hotel lobby, restaurant, and restroom. I received consolement from the young bellhop who stored my luggage in the Concierge's office.

However, it did not take long for the kid to begin to grate on me. I am normally laid back, easy-going, gregarious. But I was not in a very good mood just then.

On at least three occasions, the kid expressed his lifelong fascination with Corvettes. He had me describe, in excruciating detail, my brief experience as the owner of one. He kept peppering me with dumb questions. I wanted to scream. I considered getting him Chevrolet's 800 number and off my back.

I waited impatiently for nine o'clock to roll around, having decided I would buy another car and be on my way. At nine o'clock, I boarded the hotel's courtesy van and rode a few miles to the showroom of a local Cadillac dealer. There, I entered unmolested and headed straight for a Midnight Blue, Seville STS sitting in the middle of the showroom floor.

After about ten minutes, one of a handful of salesmen who had apparently tagged me as some lookey-loo greeted me. I was being judged by my appearance and was enjoying it. Obviously, the guy who approached me had lost the flip of the coin. He was friendly enough, even appeared to have taken a bath, flossed his teeth, and combed his hair that week, but his opening line irked me.

"Like to own one of those someday?" He asked.

I looked at him for a long second, then the car again. Already, I knew I did not like this guy. But I am a forgiving sort.

"I'm Jim," I responded, ignoring his question, extending my right hand, and applying a viselike grip to his. He flinched and grimaced.

"Oooh! Quite a powerful handshake you got there, Jim. I'm Glenn Wassole," he responded. For a brief instant, I could have sworn he said something else.

"She's a beaut, huh?" He continued, "Got that Northstar engine you probably heard about. Runs rings around the Lexus, the BMW, the..."

"Looks good, great reviews, excellent specs," I interrupted.

"Oh! You been readin' up on Sevilles, I see. Everybody in my family drives one. What 'cha drivin'?"

"Nothing, at the moment. That's why all my luggage is sitting over there. That's why the van dropped me off."

With that answer, I observed Glenn glance over his shoulder at his compadres, who were all smiling and paying very close attention.

"What 'da 'ya do, Jim?"

I knew I was about to get the quickie qualifying treatment and I wanted no part of it. I was in a hurry and in no mood to be handled.

"I'll take this one," I said pointedly. Glenn's eyes widened, swallowed hard. I thought he might need CPR.

"Excuse me?"

"I said, I'll take this one," I repeated.

"Right," he said, with transparent disbelief. "Aaah...check, cash, or charge," he joked, reaching out and slapping me lightly on the back.

"Charge," I said, without smiling. Glenn's own smile faded. The corners of his mustachioed mouth turned downward.

"You're kidding," he said.

"I have no time for kidding. I am in a big push, alright? All I have on me are out-of-state checks. I do not carry $51,675.16 around with me. So, I'll have to charge it."

Glenn looked dumbfounded. His jaw dropped several inches below what would be considered normal. I calmly removed my Platinum American Express Card and tossed it onto the hood of the car. Glenn took a step back to maintain his footing and picked up the card on his second try.

"Hey! Are you serious?" He shouted.

"You could say that."

"I take it you don't want to test drive it or anything," he managed, with a higher vocal pitch.

"Listen, Glenn," I said. "Just relax. I want the STS. A test drive is a selling tool. I am already sold. I want the car. I will test drive it on my way to Texas."

Within an hour of paperwork and a brief conversation with the dealership owner, who to my regret recognized my name, I sat behind the wheel of my newest new car. Glenn took me through the obligatory salesmen's dribble about the car's operation, most of which I tuned out automatically.

It was not until he mentioned the car had an auto locator system already installed, that he got my attention. He mentioned it much earlier but, for some reason, it did not click. I was eager to get on the road again.

I declined the owner's request to have a picture taken with him standing in front of my car. The last thing I wanted was to have my photo wind up as the centerpiece of some regional advertising campaign. It is not that I have a suspicious or cynical mind. I have suspicious and cynical thoughts. There is a distinct difference.

After the deal was done, I spent fifteen minutes sitting in the parking lot pushing buttons, twisting knobs, reading the manual, programming seating positions, and adjusting the balance and fader on the CD player. Once I was familiar with where everything was, I buckled up, adjusted the mirrors, and pointed the well-crafted carriage toward the Interstate.

Chapter Twenty

Moment of Decision

As I recall,

I was too busy appraising the ride and inhaling that new car smell, to notice I was fast approaching the Blue Ridge Expressway transition. I had to make a quick decision.

I could take the transition to the Expressway, as I had planned, and go on to Asheville, North Carolina almost 300 miles away. I could then make a stopover to see the Great Smoky Mountains National Park, go on to Atlanta, Montgomery, Mobile, New Orleans, Houston, Waco, and finally northwest to Rosedale.

My other option, which would save time but was less scenic, would be to take I-81 to Knoxville and I-40, then to Nashville, Memphis, Little Rock, Texarkana, and Dallas. I would likely stop in Dallas to visit Rosie, go on to Waco, and from there to Rosedale. With less than a mile to the transition, I decided to take the Parkway to Asheville, jump to I-40 just north of the Smoky Mountains Park and go on to Knoxville and beyond.

Cruising comfortably, I raised the volume on my Mike and The Mechanics CD, leaned my head against the headrest, and continued to the Parkway. I felt good, considering my exciting morning. The noonday skies were brilliant, forcing me to bring out my sunglasses. I had more than 1300 miles in front of me and was leaving my Roanoke experience behind.

One song on the CD touched me in a very special way. It still does. I pressed the repeat button and played the track again and again. The name of the song was In The Living Years. It is a very powerful and meaningful song that every son and father should hear. Whoever wrote those lyrics surely wrote them from a very personal experience.

I arrived in Asheville shortly after seven. I then took Interstate 40 to Knoxville, stopping only for gas and food at truck stops, then kept on to Nashville. I had no idea these mammoth truck stops were as big and self-contained as they were. These things were more like small villages than anything else. I found them fascinating.

One especially memorable character I met there was an amiable, but scruffy gentleman, of seventy or so, with the unlikely name of Oscar Nepniddle. His nearly shoulder-length, snow-white hair was gathered in a ponytail. He had an unhurried manner about him that was engaging.

I envied this man's fit physique and carefree attitude. He sat next to me at the counter, eating what looked to be half an apple pie and drinking a carafe of coffee. Oscar wore tattered jeans, a faded jean jacket pasted with corporate patches, cowboy boots, and sported a Raiders cap. Although he ate continuously, he talked nonstop. I took deep breaths for him.

During our conversation, Oscar confided he lived only five miles away. That struck me as a little odd. I asked him why he chose to eat at a truck stop. He grinned, then pointed out he was a widower and hated eating alone. Besides, the double-crusted apple pie was great. More importantly, he explained, he had grown damn weary of eating three frozen-food meals every day for over a year.

However, this lament was quickly followed by a boast that his culinary habit had resulted in his prized collection of microwave dinnerware. For no logical reason he could offer, Oscar had saved all the plastic dishes from all those frozen dinners. He was clearly proud.

"They don't make them the way they use to," he complained. "They used to be rigid and thick. Now, they are flimsy and thin."

Oscar railed on like some anti-tax crusader. He declared that the deteriorated state of microwave dinnerware called into question America's claim as the only remaining world superpower. Amazingly, I found myself mesmerized by the conversation.

Sitting around listening to truckers speaking their own special lingo was likewise different. I spent some time, downing coffee, apple pie and talking to a trucker hauling commodes from North Carolina to Los Angeles. He told me I should get a portable CB radio and if nothing else, stay awake listening to truckers up and down the Interstate. I admit to having found that suggestion tempting.

I looked at the fellow and could not imagine spending twenty years pushing one of these behemoth vehicles cross-country. I just could not see doing that day in and day out, trying to stay awake, pumping my veins with caffeine, clogging my arteries with greasy cuisine.

Still, I envied their spirit, their camaraderie, and their obvious attraction to the open road. The last thing the guy asked me was what I did for a living. I told him I had sort of retired.

I purposely did not call Alise that day. I missed her terribly, but I did not want to establish a precedent of calling her from every major city or even every day. I knew once I started down that road, it would be difficult if not impossible to explain not doing so, for whatever reasons.

I left Knoxville and drove on to Nashville, arriving there just after 1 am. When I gassed up, it was raining blue dogs. I spent a few minutes parked under the canopy, sipping on a soda, and munching corn nuts. By the time I paid my gas tab and returned to the Interstate, it was pouring blue dogs and puppies.

Driving in the rain did not bother me at all. There was almost no difference in the handling, cornering, or anything else in the car's performance. It was cozy inside, and I felt a sort of comfort I had not felt earlier. I was in a cocoon. As I stated before, I have a fascination for inclement weather and have no idea where it comes from. I have been that way since I was a child.

I eased into the truck lane, cruising at about 65 mph, and was repeatedly blown away by big rigs. They passed me like I was standing still, covering me with spray and disappearing. I remember glancing down at my speedometer and shaking my head. These guys and gals must have been doing 80 mph, in the rain no less. They had more guts than me. I held my speed and gave them all the room they needed.

If everything went as planned, I figured to arrive in Rosedale early the next afternoon. The very thought sent a tingle up my spine. I had not been home in over ten years, for any amount of time. I could only imagine what it would be like.

The swirl of thoughts kept me wide awake, as the miles melted away. At times, I would look to the front, back, and both sides and not see a headlight or taillight anywhere. At times, I felt completely alone out there.

I was surprised I was not the least bit sleepy when I reached Memphis at 2:15 in the morning. I exited downtown for a brief, self-guided tour and found the streets deserted, except for a police cruiser. It came up behind me like a comet and blew by me at warp speed. I caught a quick glimpse of a TV cameraman in the rear seat, lights, and all. "Cops," I mumbled aloud. They must have been filming an episode of the TV series Cops or something.

I continued my slow drive around the city, past the Lorraine Motel, site of MLK's assassination, down Beale Street, and over to Mud Island. Minutes later, I returned to I-40 and continued on my way. Too bad I had not arrived earlier. I had wanted to tour Graceland, and other sites, and sample some of the fantastic food and music for which Memphis is famous. I had grown weary of fast food and was dying to sink my teeth into some genuine home-style cooking. I say home-style because real home cooking would have to wait until I reached mother's table.

I still was not sleepy. And as long as I was not, I felt I could continue on to Little Rock—maybe even to Texarkana. Then, it happened. Just like that, I found myself opening my eyes, as the sound of my tires hitting the warning reflectors on the outside of the slow lane shot me wide awake. I gripped the steering wheel and kept the car under control. I had dozed off and had no recollection whatsoever of having ever closed my eyes.

The experience scared the hell out of me. My heart was in my throat and my sphincters were having a spasm. I pulled immediately off the freeway and started looking for the very first motel with a name I recognized. No luck. Failing that, I stopped at the first motel with a name I could read.

Minutes later, I found a place and parked at the curb, in the drive-thru this time. I was determined to have a car the next morning. I checked in, took a long shower, and collapsed onto the bed. Sleep came instantly. I slept like a baby. I awoke refreshed at 7am, had breakfast and was back on the Interstate by 8:30am.

Driving straight through Little Rock, I transitioned to Interstate 30 and continued to Texarkana. There, I refueled, grabbed a home-style burger at the Whataburger on Stateline Boulevard and returned to I-30.

I was determined to reach Dallas by early afternoon. I had made excellent time, by drafting for hours on a black big rig owned by Dick Simon Trucking. The trailer sported a skunk for a logo. I never figured out the significance of the skunk. Anyway, the rig kept on hauling, as I made the exit. The driver looked toward me, gave me two friendly blasts on his air horn and waved. Friends are made quickly on the open road.

It was just shy of 3:30 in the afternoon when I rolled into Dallas and registered at the Doubletree at Lincoln Center. Tired does not begin to describe how I felt. All I wanted was a hot shower, a few minutes in the sauna and some real Texas beef.

I had not had a good, thick, juicy steak for years, thanks to Alise. It was not that we were trying to be vegetarian or anything. She convinced me that unless I wanted to die of cardiac arrest instead of old age, I had better watch my diet. Alise suggested if I had a taste for meat, I should eat chicken, turkey, or fish. I fell for it. How can a real Texan fall for something like that?

The truth is, there is only so many ways to eat chicken, turkey, or fish. It all made good sense, but I was a Texan. Eating beef was like a religious experience. Anyway, Alise was not here. I had one of the best steaks I had eaten in my life, complete with all the trimmings.

I tried reaching Rosie, late into the night, to no avail. I spoke to mother for only a few moments and casually asked if she'd spoken to her. She said no and did not expect to until she and her family returned from New Orleans. They had gone there for the week and were to return on Saturday.

Although it was Friday, I decided not to wait in Dallas through Saturday. I would remain the night, drive to Waco then to Rosedale the next morning. It turned out to be a very long night.

Shortly after midnight, with my heart racing, I awoke with a start and sat straight up in bed. Beads of perspiration covered my brow. My pajama shirt was thoroughly soaked. I sat there for a moment, catching my breath, trying to figure out what was wrong with me. It was the dream—an awful nightmare. It was not my never-ending dream this time. It was worse. I had a nightmare more real than any I had ever experienced.

I rose from the bed, weak and dazed, staggered to the restroom in the dark and washed my face with cold water for several minutes. With the water still running, I sat on the toilet seat—my head buried in my lap. It all began coming back to me. I had dreamed father died, and in her profound grief, mother had taken her own life. The dream seemed so real—as real as my sitting here at my computer.

In the dream, which I will never forget, father had died. To our surprise, he had asked that his body be cremated. Cremation was not embraced in the tenets of the New Redeemer Christ Church and mother had decided against it. Afterwards, she agonized over her decision. Her grief over father's death took a profound and visible toll on her.

In the dream, I returned from spending the day with Carter, found mother had overdosed on pain pills and was not breathing. Frantic, I carried her in my arms to the car, rushed her to the County Hospital, but they were not able to save her. She died, without regaining consciousness.

When I wrenched myself free from the clutches of this awful nightmare, I was shaking, perspiring, gasping for air and thankful it had only been a dream. My heart throbbed. I felt a sharp pain in my chest. That really scared me.

After settling down, I struggled to figure out what could have led to such a dream. What subconscious thoughts and fears had contributed to this frightful nightmare? Was it my deep fear father would succumb to his illness? There was not a day when this was not on my mind.

I sat thinking and shaking. I wanted to call mother but did not want to risk alarming her. I wanted to be sure both she and father were fine. I tried to convince myself they were.

There had to be something symbolic in the dream—some non-literal meaning to it all. I knew mother deeply loved father, but there was no way she or any of us would even consider taking our own lives. I had no sooner thought that than I remembered Rosie. Before her suicide attempt all those years ago, I would have said the same thing.

With my eyes now adjusted to the dark, I returned to bed. The only illumination entering the room was a faint strip of light visible at the base of the door. I fixed my gaze on it until it became a blur. I then buried my head in my lap and began praying. Even as I did so, I was sure it would take the Almighty a moment to adjust to the sight and the sound of me praying.

Praying was something that had all but become perfunctory for me over the past number of years. Only after the onset of father's condition a couple of years ago had I returned to my faith as a way of coping. All else was failing. Rather than my faith being my first resort, it was my last. All I could hear was father's voice in my head repeating a verse that said:

Train up a child in the way he should go. And
when he is older, he will not depart from it.

Feeling guilty, I found myself struggling with a serious question. Was I praying because I believed God would hear me, or because I felt father would have expected me to pray? I alternately prayed and talked myself asleep.

I later awoke to find only a half-hour had passed. I then tried counting sheep; that did not work either. For some weird reason I cannot explain, the sheep turned into bouncing basketballs. I have no idea what that meant.

Fading in and out of sleep, I kept seeing myself in an open field. Two headstones were in front of me. A white dove circled overhead. This was hopeless. It was clear I was not going to have a night of peaceful sleep.

I got up, took a shower, packed, and left. Everything was eerily quiet, as I made my way to the elevators, down to the lobby and checked out. I had to arouse the young desk clerk who was inside the office. He finally came out, wearing red lip prints on his face and missing a belt. Minutes later, by 3:45 am, I was on I-35 and headed for Waco.

There was no point my waiting for sunrise. I wanted to reach Rosedale as soon as I could. I had hoped to see Rosie, but I would have plenty of time to visit with her and her family in the weeks and perhaps months to come.

Five miles before I reached the Waco city limits, all traffic came to a halt. Two eighteen-wheelers had tangled. One had jackknifed, spilling a load of watermelons. A half dozen cars had piled up. Traffic was backed up for more than a mile. Texas DPS (Depart of Public Safety) Officers were rerouting traffic at a Spur exit 500 yards ahead of the accident site. It took almost forever. I finally cleared the area, reentered I-35, and continued on into Waco.

I stopped in Waco only long enough to top off my tank and grab a cup of coffee at Burger King. While there, a young hitchhiker wearing faded Army fatigues and tennis shoes spotted me, took me for an easy mark, and tried to engage me in conversation. He had a huge backpack, a wooden staff, and about four days of grit, grime, and road dust all over him.

Just as I was about to leave, he asked how far I was going. I told him not far enough to do him any good and out of curiosity asked where he was headed. He answered: Australia. I wanted to laugh but managed to resist the temptation. I explained Australia was just a little out of my way and wished him well.

It was 7:45 am when I finally saw Waco in my rear-view mirror. I was now less than two hours from home—two hours from the place where my journey had begun more than forty years earlier.

With each passing mile, I grew more and more anxious. My excitement mounted. I wondered what familiar faces remained in Rosedale. I visualized returning to hallowed places, where my young footsteps had long since been erased by time.

All those years and I had returned only three or four times and then never for more than a day or two. Often, I would arrive late in the evening or night and be gone by mid-morning. There was always an urgent need to rush back to New York.

A few times, I had flown mother and father to Miami for summer vacations, holidays, and other occasions, but was never able to persuade them to visit New York. Father would always decline, without offering a reason. I think his reluctance was due to all the salacious stories he had heard about New York City.

I often wonder why I never chose to return home more often and for longer periods. I suppose I was avoiding the possibility of having my lifestyle called into question by a place and an environment reminiscent of a simpler life. Perhaps. Yet here I was going home because not only was I eager to see father, I felt drawn by memories. It was a paradox for sure.

Chapter Twenty-one

A Familiar Place

Less than an hour after leaving I-35 and turning onto U.S. 74, I had left one world and slipped into another. There was a more direct route to Rosedale, but I purposely chose the all-but-abandoned stretch of U.S. 74. I drove for miles down the narrow two-lane highway, without seeing another soul.

The summer sun was already beating down on the rolling hillside that sloped gently on either side of the roadway. Long stretches of weathered, wooden fence lay like a skirt along the brilliant green fields running up to the roadbed. I slowed to less than forty miles an hour and took in the gorgeous sight—a sight more beautiful than any I had seen in a long time. I was almost home.

Several minutes later, I spotted a familiar landmark in the distance, pulled to the opposite side, well off the road, and stopped. My heart fluttered. I sat staring for a time, with the engine running, and turned down the music to get a better view.

Seconds passed. Minutes passed. I killed the engine then got out of the car. The caressing warmth of the morning sun, the sight, and smell of bluebonnets, the feel of familiar ground underneath my feet embraced me. I felt as if a thousand pounds had been lifted from my shoulders and my heart. I could not absorb it all quickly enough.

Bending down, I slipped my fingers into the warm soil, then stood with a small amount in my hand. I sifted it through my fingers and watched as it fell back to the earth. Still taking in the wonder around me, I walked across a shallow, grassy area leading me up a slight embankment and onto the fence. The fence stretched as far as the eyes could see. I glanced up at lofty clouds miles high and saw the bluest sky I had seen in a very long time.

I had finally reached the spot—a bucolic setting overlooking endless, rolling fields carpeted with wildflowers and tall, green, willowy grass swaying in a soft summer breeze. In the distance, under skies dotted with birds and scattered cumulus clouds, several towering oaks leaned slightly to the east, standing out in bold relief.

It was a view most will see only in their dreams, if at all. It was a picturesque sight once very familiar to me. One towering tree atop Heritage Hill stood out above all else. It was Carter Oak, which meant I was gazing at a part of Phalen Farm. I was home. I took a deep breath of fragrant Texas air and felt tears welling in my eyes.

I could stand right here for a hundred years, I thought, rooted deeply in this land, my head turned to the sky, just like those old oaks over there. I would have nothing to fear, nothing to escape from or to, and nothing to envy or be envied by. Thank God, some things never really change. If angels are not still hovering nearby, it is clear they passed this way.

I stood gazing past the rustic, weathered fence, lost in thought and fond remembrances. I focused on the Ol' Oak tree, while remembering my 7th birthday and the trip Carter and I took to that spot.

For a moment, I could almost see father and me standing way out there under those sprawling branches. He sometimes brought me there to make a point about the wonders of God's creation. I listened respectfully and pretended we were going fishing or camping. I did a lot of pretending back then. I only wish we had taken more time to do simple but memorable things like that.

I loved and respected father, then and now. A man more dedicated to providing for and rearing his children in a godly manner was never born. Thank God, father married a saint—my mother. She was and is a gentle, caring, cheerful woman who never complained. She performed her duties, as a wife and mother every day, without murmur or mention.

Of course, the world was not perfect then, but it was very different—wonderfully different. As far as we knew then, it was perfect. We had no sense of being isolated from the rest of the planet.

We suffered no ill effects from much that was wrong with the world. All that was too far away to matter, even if we had known about it. We played, went to school, attended church, dined like royalty on food grown ourselves, and had great friends. Did not everyone? I now know they did not. I have since learned our Father's Knows Best world was the exception, not the rule. Too bad.

At long last, I ripped myself from the spot and made my way back to the car. Just as I did, an old, faded blue pickup carrying an elderly man and a teenage boy passed by. The man honked. Both grinned and waved at me enthusiastically. I waved back and wondered who they were.

One thing was certain: I was home. That act of good neighborliness between apparent strangers would not have happened in most places outside the south and outside Texas in particular.

I recall that not long after I arrived at Harvard my freshman year, I passed a khaki-clad, bearded guy on the walkway approaching the administration building. Being fresh off a Texas farm tractor, I spoke to him.

"Hello," I said.

The guy looked at me as if I was speaking Martian. He kept walking, glancing back curiously as he did. I never forgot that. The man turned out to be one of my law professors.

By the time I reached New York some years later, I had prepared myself to be just as aloof and distant as the next humanoid. As it happens, you can take the boy out of Texas, but you cannot take Texas out of the boy. I remained an outgoing, friendly sort.

Shortly after returning to the car, I continued down U.S. 74 to FM Road 18 where I slipped over to U.S. 71 and continued the next 5 miles to my beloved Rosedale. A mile before the city limit, the two-lane highway widened. It was the first difference I had noticed in addition to the fresh road striping.

I drove farther a short distance and there it was—a gorgeous sign, reaching for the sky: CARTER PHALEN OLDS, PONTIAC, CHEVY-GMC TRUCKS. My chest swelled with pride. I slowed, pulled onto the driveway, and found a parking space at one end, near the front of the main building I just sat there. Even at 10:30 am, there was a buzz of activity all over the dealership.

I got out and walked around for a short time. A young woman in jeans, cowboy shirt, and boots approached and introduced herself as Candy. She told me she had seen me drive up and wondered if I was ready to trade my car in for a real Cadillac—a GMC pickup.

I laughed and joked around for a few minutes, then told her I was there to see Mr. Phalen. She informed me he had not come in yet and was most likely out at his mama's *place* west of town. I thanked her and left. As I walked out, she pleasantly insisted I consider trading up to a truck. She was dead serious. I promised her I would consider her suggestion. It was only then she permitted me to leave.

I drove hurriedly through town but was still able to spot significant differences in the way Main Street appeared. For one thing, there were new street signs. The street also seemed a tad wider. And there were new stores with unfamiliar names. I kept looking for Paine Brothers Men's Store but did not see it. It had to have been there somewhere. I figured I had been driving too fast to spot it. Later, I would take my time and walk through the whole town.

Something else caught my eye. Main Street now boasted full-fledged traffic signals. All I remembered was a couple of blinking caution signals, one four-way red and one red/yellow. Now, we were practically suffering from urban sprawl. The next things I expected to see were shopping malls, tattoo parlors, and sushi bars.

Turning onto West Road, I drove slowly past my alma mater, Crawford High School. I considered stopping but decided not to. Curiously, the place looked as if it had been standing unoccupied for at least a century. I thought I saw a posted sign on the large double doors and detected several broken windows along the front row of classrooms. I hoped I was wrong. Surely, they would not let the place sink to such a level of disrepair.

Several bends and turns later, I was coasting down Sennett Road and could finally see home, on the left side, in the distance. A lump rose to my throat. My eyes strained to make sure these first images of my long-delayed pilgrimage home imprinted my mind without the slightest distortion. I knew that at some point in the future they would join the many memories I already had of Rosedale. I wanted to get it right.

I reached the turnoff, pulled slowly past the freshly painted gate, and started down the long asphalt drive to the main house. At first blush, it appeared very little had changed. The house, though still quite some distance away, appeared to be the same color.

The wooden fence paralleling the drive also sported fresh paint. The grass looked as green and freshly manicured as always. The stand of grand oak trees, forming a loose sentry around the house, seemed only slightly shorter than before.

The rust-colored barn with white trim, just off to the right and a couple hundred yards from the house, looked freshly painted as well. I was certain all this painting and maintenance resulted from Carter's efforts.

Carter was determined father's illness not be a reason for the deterioration of one single aspect of the farm. He and the many neighbors and friends saw to that. That is one of the many wonderful things about living in a place where people know and care about each other. Small town people tend to share each other's suffering as well as their joy.

As I got closer, I could see father's brand-new car, a dark blue, 1975 Ford Galaxie, parked under the carport and partly covered by a tan-colored tarp. Father never drove a car that was not at least four or five years old. This one was pushing twenty real hard. He had never owned a new car in his life and professed never to want one until it was well broken in.

A new, red GMC pickup truck with dealer tags, which I assumed belonged to Carter, sat just off the main driveway that now circled in front of the house. That was different. I eased alongside the truck, parked, turned off the engine, and sat there. A moment later, I could see someone partially open the screen door and peek out. It was Carter. I could see him, but he could not make out who I was.

He appeared only slightly heavier than his usual hundred sixty-five pounds. Big Brother wore jeans, a brown leather vest, a long sleeve western shirt with fancy do-dads on the pocket flaps and a tan cowboy hat. He cut quite a handsome figure indeed.

I took my sweet time opening the car door and eased out with my back turned to the house. I closed the door and turned around. Carter stepped out, shutting the door behind him, He yanked the hat from his head, as he started toward me. Suddenly, he let loose a yelp, slapped his thigh with the hat, and tossed it twenty feet into the air.

"Jimmy! Jimmy! Is that you?" He screamed. "What in the world! I'll be damned! What you doing here?" Carter then cupped his free hand to his mouth and glanced back toward the front door. It was no doubt a conditioned reaction to father who years earlier would have heard the 'd' word and been ready to tan his hide for sure.

Carter was walking and moving just fine, as if he had his own natural right leg. Right away, I could see he showed no sign of a limp. I hurried toward him. The two of us stood hugging each other and pounding each other on the back excitedly. It was good to see him looking so good—so alive. I had not seen my big brother so animated and so vocal since we were kids.

The last time I saw him, shortly after father's first trip to St. Luke's in Houston, he seemed withdrawn, distant, and very depressed. At that time, I hardly recognized him as the brother I had known and loved all my life. Now, Carter looked every bit the successful businessman he was. With the hat on, he looked like J.R. Ewing, but I did not dare tell him that.

And I could not wait to meet his wife and see my two-year-old nephew. I had only seen pictures of both. Carter and Elizabeth had gotten married without telling even mother or father. What is more, they told no one they were expecting, until Elizabeth was almost five months along.

That was the old Carter. The wonder was that he had considered marriage at all, so soon following his prolonged period of depression. Carter had great difficulty rebounding from the trauma of losing his leg, from seeing his buddies die in his arms. He had truly come a long way. I was very proud of him.

We carried on like kids, for what seemed an eternity. We were making enough noise to wake up Sam Houston. Just then, a gorgeous, 5'-5" angel with beautiful white hair pulled back, wearing a flowered dress, and flashing the broadest smile I ever saw, appeared like a vision in the doorway. As we moved toward her, Carter whispered to me under his breath.

"Father is not at all well, Jimmy. Mother keeps insisting he's getting better, but he's not. I don't think he's gon' make it. And I just know She's gon' take it real hard, whenever he passes on."

I was not quite prepared for Carter's frankness, given his previous avoidance of the reality of father's condition. I gave him an acknowledging glance and gripped his shoulder. When I neared mother, I could see streams of tears on her cheeks. She shook her head from side to side, her eyes smiling all the while.

"Oh, my god. My god, boy! Look at me. What are you...you should have called me. I look a mess and don't you try to tell me any different, James Theodore Phalen."

Mother fiddled with her hair and tugged at her dress. I had been home less than five minutes and already she had called me by my full name. I assured her she was beyond a doubt the most beautiful woman in all of Texas and gave her a hug and lifted her in the air. All the while, tears streamed down her face.

Mother leaned her head against me, sobbing and bawling me out for not telling her I was coming. I knew those tears symbolized more than the joy she felt seeing me. They were tears long held inside. They were tears no doubt flowing from a lifetime of self-denial. Mother had always subjugated her own desires.

When the tears ebbed, mother asked me for the second time why I had come home so suddenly and unannounced. I explained it all over again, to her and Carter. I told them the decision was prompted in part by my need to give my life sorely needed new direction—some new meaning.

The explanation still did not quite register. The look of disbelief on both their faces was profound. I understood and expected as much. All those years, my business activities, and my dogged pursuit of the big deal dominated my life. It served as my elixir, my refuge, my aphrodisiac. They were seeing a new me for the very first time. It would require some time getting used to.

Carter said he envied me the freedom to do what I had without having to answer to anyone. I confessed I envied him the fact he fell in love, got married, and had a young son.

Just as I said that I observed his fallen expression and a furtive glance at mother who looked away briefly. I suspected there was a lot for me to catch up on. I moved on to another subject.

Although I was eager to see father for myself, I was somewhat reluctant to go inside. When I did enter the house, a pall came over me. It is impossible to describe it here. Even now, the sensation has not diminished. There was a pervasive quietness, a stillness. Flowers of all descriptions seemed everywhere. The smell filled every room.

I love flowers. Only this time what I saw was a bit much. I learned later that friends and strangers alike stopped by often, bringing flowers. You name the species, it was represented many times over. The place reminded me of a well-stocked flower shop. My first thought was to take most of them and toss them onto the compost pile out by the barn. Better judgment prevailed. I opted to wait a reasonable time before thinning them out.

Father's nurse was a very stern-looking, robust, laser-eyed, Mary Dell Slaney. She stood in the doorway leading to the sunroom. One look at her told me that she was not a woman to trifle with. Mother introduced me as her baby boy from New York. In that instant, I knew I was home, alright.

From the outset, Mary's demeanor identified her as warm, friendly, and not likely to take guff, when it came to doing her job. She was in charge and father's welfare came first. I learned it was she who personally shaved him daily and gave him his bath.

Father was sitting in the sunroom with his back to us, nestled in his wheelchair. He was facing the window and had a view of the fields. As I approached, I could see his head listing to one side. My heart sank and I struggled not to show my apprehension. I bit into my lower lip and took a deep breath to steady my emotions.

Before I reached him, mother stopped me, gripped my right arm, and looked up at me with eyes reddened by her crying.

"Son, he probably won't say anything. But I'm most sure he'll recognize you, though. He'll know it's you."

The words struck me like a hammer. Apparently, no one thought to tell me how weak and feeble father had grown. Carter stepped to father's chair and turned him away from his view of the southwest fields. I then saw him as I had prayed I never would.

A brown and white, plaid blanket covered father's lap. His brow was furrowed with lines deeper than I could have imagined. His hair was almost completely white. I observed his curled right hand. He held a crumpled handkerchief in his left hand. I stood less than two feet away from him, struggling to recognize him, picturing him side by side with the father of my childhood.

I turned and saw mother lower her head and bring a hand to her face. I could never stand the sight of my mother crying. I looked away from her and knelt in front of father. My eyes brimmed with tears, as I put both arms around him and embraced him for a long moment.

Father seemed so small, so frail, so childlike—hardly there. I gazed at him with quiet disbelief and ran my fingers through his white hair. I could feel him shaking slightly, although I knew he could not be cold. Mother and Carter quietly left the room, leaving the two of us alone.

I leaned down and looked up into the face of this wisp of a man. I had to keep telling myself this was the father I had known, loved, feared, and obeyed all my life. This was the very same man. This was father. I felt the need to say it aloud, again and again.

"Father," I whispered.

I took my left hand and touched his shoulder. Through his long-sleeve shirt, I felt his protruding collarbone and the sunken space around it. He was once so tall, so strong and vibrant—his back as straight as an arrow. I wanted to hold him in my arms and rock him gently, as he had most likely done me when I was a child. I wanted to breathe new and vibrant life into him but realized I was no god.

"It's me," I whispered. "James, your son, James." I waited for a hint of recognition—just the slightest. Father bobbed his head a couple of times, looked in my direction but appeared to be staring right through me. It was one of the most emotional and most difficult moments I will ever experience. Again, I felt powerless and found myself longing for the past.

More than ever, I stared at him and feared growing old. I found myself hoping when the moment came for me, I would have the strength to end my own suffering. That thought ran counter to everything I had been taught, but I could not help it. That is the way I felt.

I touched father's chin and raised his head a bit. Again, he appeared to glance into my eyes ever so briefly. Again, I thought I saw a glimmer of recognition. Perhaps I only imagined it because I wanted so much for it to be true. I wanted him to know I was home and at his side. He had to know, and I needed to be sure he was aware of it. For me, it was important he realize that, at last, his son decided to forsake his own selfish pursuits and come home to be with him.

I pulled up a rocking chair and sat near father for almost an hour and a half, talking to him as if he were fully cognizant. Indeed, I had no way of knowing he was not aware of what was going on. According to experts with whom I have since spoken at length, it is highly likely he was cognizant, though unable to articulate.

I told father all about my decision to leave New York. I spoke of finally becoming a partner in a major law firm, about the long trip home. Several times, I had to stop and wipe away the drool from the corner of his mouth and straighten his head. His neck muscles were no longer strong enough to keep his head erect for long periods of time.

Meanwhile, Carter returned to town promising he would return for dinner in a few hours. Shortly after he had gone, Nurse Slaney reentered the room. She apologized, but said it was time for father to take his medicine and his afternoon nap.

While father slept, I sat in the kitchen watching mother prepare dinner. This was something I had done a thousand times, as a kid. The cook arrived and mother once again introduced me as her baby boy from New York. The lady was also a rather stout, handsome woman of sixty named Jennie Lee Rafer. Apparently, she loved sampling her own cooking in substantial portions. It showed.

Jennie Lee prepared father's special meals. Mother insisted on cooking mine: homemade dinner rolls, mashed potatoes, spicy fried chicken, corn on the cob and peach cobbler. That brought to mind the day I complained of having to eat corn, chicken, and mashed potatoes two days in a row. That was the day mother brought out those Depression Era photos.

I made faint pleas for mother to not bother cooking. She knew I was not sincere. While I had always been a glutton for pastries, she knew I would walk a mile for her spicy fried chicken and homemade rolls. The one thing I was concerned about was mother's cooking exploding my waistline.

Chapter Twenty-two

A Love to Remember

Mother finished preparing dinner.

We then strolled outside, sat on the front porch swing, and waited for Carter. The late afternoon breeze, aided by the surrounding canopy of trees, afforded us an unbelievable porch temperature of about seventy-two degrees. For mid-July, this qualified as a cold front, as any Texan will tell you. Even the humidity was an exceptional seventy percent. El Niño was truly unpredictable.

Mother and I talked about almost everything you can imagine. I found myself again having to try to convince her I had indeed altered the course of my life. I think she just wanted to be sure, before allowing herself to accept it as gospel.

In her own manner, mother had often lectured me about putting too much store in the things of the world, as she put it. I made it clear my decision did not mean I would be spending the rest of my life in Rosedale. Her response? "Son, you could do a whole lot worse," she reminded me. I had to agree.

As expected, mother got around to asking about Alise. She chided me for not bringing her.

"When you gonna get married, son...give us some grandkids?" She asked, with a twinkle in her eye. "Seems to me you're the only one who hasn't. Do you love Alise?"

I was unprepared for the onslaught, and for that question. I hedged, but mother likewise was not prepared to let me off the hook. Whenever she latched onto something, she was as dogged as a bloodhound. Nothing was going to shake her off the scent.

"Do you love her?" She repeated, doing a half-turn to face me. Her move altered the swing's smooth movement and caused it to swing wildly for a moment. Once we were back on track, she resumed the inquest.

"I'm waiting."

"She's really the most wonderful woman I've ever met."

"Do you love her?"

"I care about her very much."

"But do you love her?"

"Sure, I... I do. I love her."

"Hmm. You don't sound too sure,"

"I know. It's just that I've tried to avoid labeling how I feel about

her, you know?"

"In other words, you've never told her the words."

"I've told her many times. She knows how I feel, though."

"She love you?"

"I believe she does. I know she does."

"And she's told you?"

"Many times."

"Son, a woman wants to know she's loved. She wants to hear the words. There are no substitutes for the words sincerely spoken. So, if you really love Alise, you should tell her. Say the words and say them often."

This went on for several minutes. I listened like the dutiful, respectful son I was. Mother would not allow me to change the subject. At one point, she began to talk about father—how they had met. I was stunned to learn she did not love him when they married. She told him so.

"I respected him more than any man I knew, except for father," she said with a distant look in her eyes. "I grew to love your father. Don't know if that would work these days, though. That sort of thing was commonplace, back when we were coming up."

A glow descended over mother, as she reminisced about first meeting father. I could not remember ever hearing the story before, not in this detail.

The two of them met at a church-sponsored dance. That stunned me. Father? Dancing? I could not paint that picture at all. I could not imagine father near a dance floor, much less dancing.

"Son, your father was quite a dancer, back then," she said. "He could 'cut the rug' with the best of them, even though his folks were very strict and kept a very tight rein on all their kids. All the girls wanted to dance with him, but whenever he'd ask me, I kept saying no. I think that was what kept him coming back. He just couldn't believe I could resist all that Phalen charm.

"To tell you the truth, I liked his brother, Raymond, more than I liked your father...until I got to know your father, that is. He never knew that. Truth is, I never told this to a solitary soul, except for my sister Callie. I swore her to secrecy and as far as I know, she took our secret to her grave. So, now I'm swearing you.

"Anyway, your father and me were at this dance. Back then, New Christ Redeemer Church would hold these dances once a month for young folks—teenagers. It was alright, the dancing I mean, as long as we didn't allow ourselves to enjoy it...that is in a worldly sort of way."

Mother winked when she said that. I got her meaning.

"So," she went on, "We all told ourselves we did not enjoy it, in that way, and just kept on dancing up a storm. Later, your father got tired of asking me to dance and getting turned down, so he asked my older sister, Callie, to dance. She said yes. I was flabbergasted. Can you imagine that? I was fit to be tied. I got so mad at her, I wanted to smack her one.

"Every time your father would bring her back over to her seat, he'd give me this smirky look. I'd turn my head, pretend I didn't see them and didn't care how many times they danced. They could have danced until their fool legs fell off, for all I cared.

"Pretty soon, this boy named Erastus Pitts, a very homely looking fellow, asked me to dance. I said yes. It wasn't easy to say yes to Erastus, but I said yes. Poor Erastus couldn't dance. He kept stepping on my feet. It was downright painful, you hear me? Painful!

"During one song, Erastus and I were dancing, and your father and Callie were sitting, talking and laughing, having themselves a grand ol' time. I got really steamed, just watching them. So, when I saw your father watching *us,* I stepped really close to Erastus.

"The poor fellow got excited. I could tell he was getting pretty worked up, you know? He was breathing hard, and sweat was beading up on his brow. I could feel his grip on me tighten and everything. I started to ask myself why I'd done a fool thing like that. I smiled and pretended I didn't notice anything, but before I could back away from him, up rushed a dance monitor. I 'bout fainted."

"Dance monitor?" I interrupted, totally unfamiliar with the term.

"That's right," she went on. "Way back then, we had these grownups who would make sure we all kept a certain physical distance between us. In fact, they would carry a twelve-inch ruler with them, and if they thought some couple was dancing too close, they rush up to them and thrust that ruler between them. If it happened to you more than once, you were asked to leave the dance, and your parents would find out and you were in serious trouble.

"That night, before I could back away, the monitor rushed up to us with the ruler. I was so embarrassed, I ran out of the hall and stood outside crying up a storm. A few minutes later, someone tapped me on the shoulder. I thought it was Callie come to rub it in. I had my fists balled up and I wheeled around ready to sock her one. To my surprise, it was your father. I was shocked, although I tried hard to pretend I was not. He looked so serious and concerned. He had a big glass of fruit punch, which he gave to me. I should've poured it all over his head and those curly locks of his.

"Anyway, I did not. He even apologized and I could not understand why. He insisted everything was his fault and kept on apologizing and apologizing. I drank the punch and even shared some with him. He was a charmer alright. He was not flashy or anything, just cute, in a cutsie sort of way. He would just look at you with those big eyes and... Anyway, that night was the beginning of a relationship that has lasted more than fifty odd years. Fifty years." Mother took a deep breath and looked away.

"My God," she said. "It doesn't seem like it, but it's been over half a century. Imagine that. Half a hundred years."

I sat profoundly speechless. Mother smiled and stared far beyond the distant tree-line—back fifty years. I looked at her. She turned quickly to me.

"Why did I tell you all that stuff? I plum forgot."

I had never known mother to lose her train of thought like that. It bothered me a bit. She laughed it off.

"Alise. We were talking about Alise; about growing to love someone," I reminded her.

"Right," she said. "And it's true. Sometimes, love is right there all along. You're just a little slow to recognize it and even slower to confess it. Here comes Carter."

I looked around to see Carter's pickup heading toward us. Mother stood and started toward the door.

"I'm going in to set the table. I want the two of you to come right along, now. I'm gonna' call Rosie a little later."

"Yes ma'am," I joked. She took a big playful swipe at me and took a step backwards.

"Alright, James Theodore Phalen," she said with her hands on her hips. I laughed. There it was again. I had been home only a few hours and twice she had called me by my whole name.

Twenty-three

Full Circle

My first night home was filled with joy, sadness and mixed emotions. I was thrilled to be in Rosedale, and excited to see Carter, my mother, and my father. Just being under the same roof with them gave me a feeling of belonging—of being connected again, of having come full circle.

It saddened me deeply, seeing father this way. Except for the fact he was not sitting in his usual place at the head of the table, dinner was wonderful—like old times. Then again, without father at the head of the table, it was impossible for things to be like old times.

After dinner, I called and spoke to Rosie for the better part of an hour. She sounded so excited and apologized for not being at home when I had passed through Dallas. Rosie could not believe I was in Rosedale and promised to arrive there by the weekend for sure. We said our good-byes and I handed the phone to mother. The two of them talked for at least an hour.

Although the sun was beginning to set, Carter and I went for a long walk and got a chance to talk. It was he who brought up the subject of Elizabeth and their son William. I could hear the pain in his voice, when he told me they had separated, and that divorce was inevitable.

Elizabeth was a native of Chicago and had lived in Dallas with a sister for several years, before meeting Carter there. They had a whirlwind courtship, fell in love, and found they could not live without each other. However, four years later, Elizabeth had still not embraced the notion of spending the rest of her life in a place like Rosedale.

Things came apart. She insisted Carter sell the home he had built for them near Fall River. She further demanded the dealership be sold or moved to Dallas, Houston or anywhere there was at least one mall and a modern movie theater. Elizabeth gave Carter six months to decide what to do. Rather than take six months, it took him more like six seconds. He refused the ultimatum. Elizabeth packed and left without a good-bye or anything, taking little William with her.

Carter explained in tortured detail, that the day she left, he had been working all day. He arrived home in the evening, just as Elizabeth was driving away with little William. He saw them, waved, and honked his horn. She even honked back. Carter erroneously assumed she was driving into town and would soon return. He was wrong. It was the last he would see of her in Rosedale and for at least three months anywhere.

When Carter entered his house, he discovered at least half the furniture and all of Elizabeth's and the baby's clothes were gone. Apparently, movers had come earlier in the day, while he was at work. He kept saying: "A few minutes earlier and I would have gotten there before she left."

I asked him if that would have made any difference. He admitted it probably would not have. Carter looked deeply hurt. I did not think he could ever forgive Elizabeth for not saying good-bye face to face. That had to be a cruel blow. I also had to realize that I did not know everything about their relationship.

Carter insisted there was no reason for her to fear him in any way, whatsoever. While they had their arguments, he had always listened and seldom ever raised his voice. He said he would often leave and take a long drive into the countryside to avoid arguing in William's presence.

Carter was exactly the same way when we were kids. He almost never became vocal during an argument. His quiet demeanor always made me and Rosie appear to be bullies, even though he was bigger, older, and—he says—wiser than were we.

The only things of real value Carter found in the house were photographs, family videos and William's birth certificate. He had always kept those things locked in a bookcase. Apparently, Elizabeth had either overlooked them or chosen not to take them. The key to the bookcase was where it always was—in the den, inside a hardbound copy of War and Peace.

While he was telling me all this, I could hear the tremor in Carter's voice. I could see the anguish in his face. It was difficult listening and knowing I could not really help. But Carter needed to talk about it; he desperately wanted to get it out of his system.

When he found her months later, Elizabeth was living in Dallas only a few blocks from her sister. However, not only did she refuse to see him, but she also refused to let him see William. That was the harshest blow of all.

"She knows how much I love my son," he told me. His voice kept breaking "This was her way of hurting me even more than she had already."

I had known male and female friends who had had similar experiences. I could never understand the reason for denying a child the chance to maintain a relationship with the absent parent. Such act was a selfish and condemnable attempt to cause pain for the other parent.

From what Carter told me, reconciliation was definitely out of the question. The divorce would be final in a few months. Perhaps the one good thing about it was that he expected liberal, shared custody. He would finally get a chance to be with William again.

I knew how much Carter loved his son and could tell he still loved Elizabeth too. When I was in New York, we would often talk on the phone. He would boast William was already showing signs of being a major league pitcher someday. I told him he sounded like a boastful father and asked him how he could tell. He said, by the way William tossed his pacifier and later his bottle across the room. I would laugh, but he was serious. He then went on to describe the velocity and arc of the tossed objects.

Carter was and is a very proud man. He does not accept assistance easily. I learned that when I first offered to buy the GM dealership for him. I simply wanted to be of help. However, Carter resisted the offer for years. Only after I presented the idea as a long-term loan, did he agree.

To help with this present difficulty, I offered to help relocate the dealership to Dallas or any place else he wanted. Carter would hear none of it. He changed the subject and refused to talk further about it. He had a way of changing the subject faster than anyone I know.

My first night home, I slept in my old bed. It still fit me comfortably. Only the tips of my toes hung over the edge when I first stretched out. Finally, I figured it out and removed three of the six pillows mother had stacked against the headboard. It worked.

Earlier, I called Alise at 1am E.D.T, a fact she drowsily reminded me of. We talked for almost an hour, though it seemed like only a few minutes. Alise's business trip to Europe was canceled. She sounded disappointed. However, she informed me she might be traveling to San Francisco within a couple of weeks.

I could hear an undertone in her voice that belied her insistence she was okay. She kept telling me she was fine and changed the subject. Everyone was changing the subject on me that day.

Alise asked me about father's condition, about his prognosis, about mother, how well she was coping. I tried to sound as upbeat as I could but expressed my concern. I told her about the dream I had experienced the night before in Dallas. Her immediate reaction was that it was too explicit to be taken as some omen. She felt it was likely a result of conscious worrying and stress. I did not disagree.

I missed Alise a lot and told her so. However, I did not tell her about my urge to call her only minutes after I had left. She said she missed me too and confessed to having trouble getting to sleep with me gone.

Alise also thanked me (tongue in cheek) for the vibrator I gave her, as a parting gift, then asked what device I was using. My answer? I was too tired and stressed out to think about much of anything.

There was heavy sigh and a pause from Alise that I thought curious. My suspicion was it indicated she doubted my last declaration. I said as much and drew a quick and spirited denial. Following a few more minutes of adult conversation along those same lines, we said goodnight, closing with mushy phone kisses. It left me feeling like a teenager.

The ensuing days were filled with rediscovery. I renewed my familiarity with the Phalen farm and spent long hours talking to father. I wondered just how much, if anything, he heard and understood. I prayed it was most, if not all, and searched for signs of recognition in his eyes. Often, I would simply sit next to him, holding his hand and watching over him. I would ask him questions and pause, as if expecting his normal response.

There was little doubt father was growing more feeble and was slowly slipping away from us. Notwithstanding my growing resistance to logic, this was the logical conclusion to draw. In my heart, I continued my fervent cling to hope.

It was so hard to watch father, but there was no place else I wanted to be. We were doing everything possible. Still, it did not seem enough. All agreed the most important thing was making sure father was comfortable and pain-free.

Despite the apparent realities of father's health, I found giving up on miracles an anathema to me. I had not come home to participate in a death vigil. One morning I suggested to mother we re-hospitalize father for a short time. I felt that new, specialized treatment could be explored. I had been researching hopeful advances in stroke treatment, consulting with specialists around the world. No one could make any promises, but several new treatment protocols, still viewed as experimental, were showing great promise, both in Europe and the U.S.

Mother listened patiently but was foursquare against the idea. She felt father's being away in a hospital would only hasten his decline—rob him of precious moments better spent with loved ones. Mother described my suggestion as the voice of my heart. She was right, but I did not want to accept that then.

An awful lot happened during my first week home. I discovered I knew only a fraction of the people remaining in Rosedale. Many had drifted away, after Texas's oil economy went sour in the eighties. I learned old man Paine died of emphysema five years earlier, and no other relative surfaced to take over his business. Mother thought she had long ago informed me of his death. I did not recall she had.

Dunphy's Diner was still named Dunphy's, but not a single Dunphy had anything to do with it. The new owner was some up-and-coming restaurateur from Waxahachie. I had been gone a while, but never knew Waxahachie to have up-and-coming restaurateurs, or much of anything. I could be wrong. If I am, I am sure I will hear from the Waxahachie Chamber of Commerce. Please address all communications to my publisher.

To my dismay, I learned from Carter, my unofficial tour-guide, Crawford High had closed more than three years earlier. I did not recall being informed of that either. My thoughts turned to my vow made years earlier, to restore my alma mater to its former glory. I suppose that idea was now moot.

The main building was now condemned as an asbestos hazard. State and Federal Inspectors had discovered dangerous levels of carcinogenic material in the ceiling, walls, insulation, and even in the aging mechanical facilities. Clean-up cost was prohibitive, requiring a long-term tax levy, recently voted down. Voters and residents had decided to merge with other nearby school districts with similar problems. They had hurriedly constructed an array of temporary buildings out near Ridgecrest.

The Rosedale Chamber of Commerce and Crawford County officials continued to wrack their brains trying to figure out how to attract new business and industry. That was revealing since voters failed to approve a crucial tax for schools. I was not surprised. It happens all over the country. Because school tax measures are one of only a few such measures voters get to vote on, it receives the brunt of their anger and frustration.

There was no way to attract business, industry, and new families without being able to showcase sound, safe and effective schools. I understood their need to widen and deepen the tax base. Good schools do not just happen.

Rosedale was not dead, but it was not really growing either. Some argued it was on life supports. Except for its close proximity to Waco and the fact its picturesque surroundings attracted tourists during summer, Rosedale certainly would be suffering even greater economic depression.

Young people were not staying around after graduation. Once their diplomas were clutched in their fists, they headed straight for the city limits and hardly looked back. That describes what I had done as well. Maybe now, all these years later, I could do something about it. Perhaps it was long overdue.

Rosie and her family arrived on Saturday. Seeing her was very emotional and special for both of us. We shed more than a few tears. She and her family got there early that morning and stayed until long after sunset. Was it almost like old times? Not really.

What was difficult for me to absorb was the sight of my dear sister Rosie all growed up. There she was, with a husband, a son and looking like the beautiful middle-aged mother she was. When you have spent so many years watching a grimy-faced, rough and tumble kid in jeans and boots climbing trees and fences, the sight I saw made for quite a contrast.

I suppose seeing me took some getting used to for Rosie as well. I thought about my experience with the mirror in my bathroom and wondered how much older, and like father, I appeared to Rosie and even mother. Neither they nor Carter had made mention of any change in my appearance. I began to think it was all in my mind, just as Alise suggested.

My fondest memories of Rosie were of her outfitted in jeans, tee shirt and the worst looking sneakers (that is if she was not wearing cowboy boots) you ever saw. Those days were long gone now. It is difficult to acknowledge, but we were all now at or near the ages mother and father were then. That was a very sobering thought. What child imagines ever getting that old? No one ever gets that old.

Late that afternoon I convinced Rosie and the others, except for mother, to join me in a brisk hike to Crawford Lake. Robert, Rosie's husband, was a little reticent but agreed to join us. All during lunch, he wanted to talk business. He hinted his boss, Perot, had plans to divest some of his business interests. I made it clear I recently engaged in some divesting of a sort myself and had no interest in acquiring anything except peace of mind. I then quickly changed the subject.

The hike turned out to be a more ambitious an undertaking than I had counted on. However, it was the most fun I had enjoyed in ages. Except for my brother-in-law, we all behaved like kids on a school outing without chaperones. Robert had considerable difficulty relaxing and being himself. Then again, perhaps not.

Within seconds of beginning the hike, I could tell this was perhaps the most non-corporate, impromptu thing Robert had ever done. Initially, he wanted to delay leaving until he had located some sunscreen. No problem. I fully understood the precaution. After all, he was fair-skinned, a pale fellow lacking a hint of pigmentation.

That aside, we all were well advised to take the same precaution. Still, it was not like we had planned a quick safari across the Serengeti. I like Robert a lot, but that day he complained mournfully of the heat; the humidity, the rocks, the dust, the butterflies, the grasshoppers and almost everything you can think of. What a wus, I thought.

One irksome offense he committed was repeatedly asking if we were there yet. That is a pet peeve of mine, as anyone who knows me will tell you. It is a simple matter to know when you have arrived at a known destination.

Just think about it. As I figured it, a big lake was hard to miss, for a supposedly intelligent, sighted person such as Robert. I was even willing to lay odds that everyone would likely know when we had gotten there. A big lake with water and everything stands out. By the way, Robert is really a great guy. We have gotten to know each other much better since our first meeting. I consider us to be close friends now, at least before this chapter.

Attending church provided the best chance I had to see old friends, to say hello to people I had known as a child. Many members, older grownups when I was a kid, were dead now. And there were far fewer young people than I remember. The fact the minister was only a year older than me struck me as amazing. The fact I made note of it at all was telling.

After some time, I observed almost all the professionals; the police officers, the doctors, ministers, and others were either my age or younger. I was barely younger than the President of the United States. That is a true sign of growing old. You find when you interact with these people, they are calling you sir and being deferential, because of their perceiving you to be their elder.

Sadly, since I had arrived, I had not seen a single classmate of mine. Being there at New Christ Redeemer brought back a flood of memories, especially when Carter and I sat in the same pew we sat in as kids. Thankfully, mother had not insisted I wear a sailor suit. And luckily, no little old ladies rubbed my head or even told me how cute I was.

Following the service, almost everyone who approached me recognized me prior to my recognizing them. Just what the importance of that was, I am not sure. It was often embarrassing to be standing nose to nose with someone whose name you were supposed to know, only to find yourself struggling to recall it before the conversation ended.

Most asked where I had lived all those years and what I had been doing with myself. It pleased me they did not know already. My stock answer was that I had lived and worked in New York.

That seemed enough explanation to satisfy the curiosity of most of them. A few confessed they could not rightly understand why anyone in their right mind would ever choose New York City over Rosedale. But, since I had come to my senses and acknowledged the error of my ways, they were willing to forgive my transgressions.

During several of these conversations, I learned father had for years proudly boasted that his youngest boy was a lawyer. To him, it was not important I had not practiced law, I was a lawyer. I had made something of myself.

"Son, your father was and is very proud of you—of all you kids," they would say. I kept hearing that, over and over. It was good to hear.

Chapter Twenty-four

Revelations

It was not very long before the predictable occurred. The doggedly determined media learned of my whereabouts and lay siege with a vengeance. Why me? I wondered. C'mon! I was not a movie star; not a celebrity, a hot Rock musician, or even one of America's Most Wanted. Apparently, most national reporters had somehow milked all the Whitewater, Hillary, Newt Gingrich, and O.J. stories. No one had come forth recently to claim having had a tryst with the President. That left me as the obvious choice.

The phones rang at all hours of the day and night. I received calls from almost every major media from both coasts and the Midwest. Voice mail and messaging were installed on mother's phone, so we could all have some peace.

I turned down requests for interviews, from all media except The Rosedale Courier. For once, the hometown paper had an exclusive denied the majors. It made the most of it. After more than a solid week of intense pressure from the national media, things began to taper off.

However, just before that week's end, a couple of overzealous and enterprising journalists in a rented Range Rover drove right pass our farm's hastily installed barricade. They motored up to the front door and climbed out with cameras and boom mikes. A polite Carter asked them to leave. When they exhibited some reluctance, he cranked off a few quick rounds into the air with his AR-15. They hauled butt, leaving behind a length of cable and a size 11 Reebok shoe. They almost left the Rover.

The two later tried to file a complaint with Jim Weston, our Sheriff. J.W. refused their complaint, telling them if they ever came back out to our place, he would supply us the ammo. He concluded his lecture, as was his custom, by tipping his cowboy hat and telling them to have a nice day.

I both celebrated and grieved at what I found in my beloved Rosedale. One of the most heartbreaking moments came one early afternoon. Carter and I went to Dunphy's and ate a healthy lunch of smothered chicken, dumplings with light-brown gravy and half an apple pie. We then strolled around town for a while. We should have jogged. A half our later, we returned to his truck and headed down West Road. A few miles down, we turned off onto mostly deserted Delaney Road. It was overgrown with high vegetation and had heavy undergrowth on both sides.

Another quarter mile down, Carter pulled onto the right shoulder and stopped. I looked at him curiously. He pointed through the windshield toward what appeared to be the remains of some collapsed structure. It was obscured in a heavily overgrown area. I stared blankly for a second, then my jaw dropped. Carter killed the engine and we both got out of the truck. I just stood there, looking around and shaking my head.

I was looking at all that remained of my beloved Alston Park. This place was at one time my home away from home—home of the Rosedale Dodgers, my little league baseball team. It was hard to imagine this horrible looking, dilapidated, rotting, overgrown dump was the site of my greatest triumph as a baseball player.

I looked around, sickened by what I saw. Before me were abandoned sofas, refrigerators, a broken commode stool and worse. Every imaginable refuse was strewn about. The place had become a dump.

"What happened?" I asked, both dumbfounded and shocked.

"They just let it go," Carter said.

"That's an understatement. Why? What happened? What happened to little league?" It surprised me I had not heard anything about this.

"It's a long tale."

"I've got time."

I could see Carter was not too eager to talk about whatever had led to the awful demise of my beloved baseball park. I walked forward, past the rusting, half-buried chain-link gate, and fence—once an entrance to the place. I noticed a fallen For Sale sign lying face up on the ground.

"What happened?" I repeated.

Carter relented and told me the story, albeit reluctantly. He explained he took no pleasure in destroying memories, altering my fond recollections. I told him I understood, but from where I stood someone had already done just that. It seems Rosedale had been keeping a dark little secret from me. I had now stumbled upon it.

When I was a kid, playing baseball was my life, my dream. It was all I wanted to do. I did not ask where, who, when or what. I just wanted to play baseball. And I did. We knew that our team, like other teams, had sponsors; organizations, businesses, individuals, and the like, who provided moneys. That was all we knew. It was no big deal. All we wanted were our uniforms, our equipment, and a field to play on.

I knew sanctioning came from the Little League organization in Williamsport. Whether we were or were not officially sanctioned never really came up. It would not have mattered to my friends and me anyway. All we wanted to do was play baseball.

The years went by. Fifteen years ago, the largest and most generous group of sponsors formed an organization benignly called The Rosedale Men's Association. It was supposedly nonprofit and made up of just about every influential businessman, civic leader, and man of note in Rosedale. They contributed more than eighty per cent of the total moneys used to support the team and provide maintenance for Alston Park.

Many of their members helped to establish and operate concessions, provided team awards and trophies at season's end.

These were men kids looked to and respected. They were so-called pillars of the community.

According to Carter, about seven years earlier, several black and Hispanic families moved into and around Rosedale. Almost all the families had young children. Many had sons eager to play little league baseball. As all-American as that was, it posed a problem—a major problem for many upstanding and respected citizens. Many were members of The Rosedale Men's Association.

Many otherwise neighborly, well-meaning, bible-toting, god-fearing members of the Association adamantly opposed permitting nonwhites on the team. It caused quite a buzz around Rosedale and surrounding towns.

One Sunday afternoon, a local Minister and Association member, Rev. Filus Demby, along with two or more town fathers met with most of the minority parents to discuss the matter. However, instead of joining with them or at least acting as a neutral arbiter, the minister and his cohorts tried to persuade the parents to withdraw their sons from team consideration. Carter said the minister had reportedly gone as far as to quote from the bible and Proverbs, telling the parents:

Blessed are the peacemakers, for
they shall inherit the kingdom of God.

I was disgusted, listening to Carter's account of these sordid and shameful acts. This was 1994. There had been a black family or two on the outskirts of Rosedale, when I was a kid. They had sons my age. I recalled once talking to one of the kids. I asked why he didn't play ball with us. He seemed surprised by my question and offered an answer I only now understood.

"I can't," he said. "I can't."

All these years, I had understood him to mean he did not know how or had no interest in doing so. In retrospect, he probably knew more about his realities than I knew about my own. He and his parents no doubt knew he would not be welcome. Therefore, they never made the attempt. I now wish I had known what he had meant. I wish he and his parents had tried to force the issue. That is easy for me to say now.

Carter went on to tell me that during the meeting with the minister, the parents unanimously rejected efforts to pressure and intimidate them. They later contacted Little League Headquarters. When pressure from the Little League came down to grant the boys a tryout, the 'Association' appeared to relent and granted the tryout.

Although all but one of the kids performed with above average proficiency, they still faced rejection based on, allegedly, woefully poor performance. Carter said those were the exact words.

The parents appealed to the Little League. The organization responded, strongly suggesting the kids be accepted. Their decision was rendered, after they reviewed surreptitiously recorded video of the kids' tryouts. Even to this moment, Carter says no one knows who made the video.

It amazed me that neither mother, Carter nor Rosie had bothered to tell me about this, assuming Rosie knew. Carter said it was their conspiracy hatched to protect my rosy memory of my beloved Dodgers and Rosedale. I think it was because they felt too embarrassed and wanted to forget the whole thing.

When the sponsors, dominated by the Association, still refused to rescind their ill-advised action, the Little League issued an ultimatum threatening expulsion. Astoundingly, they opted to withdraw from the national organization and formed their own.

They were able to convince several teams in Crawford and nearby counties to join them, arguing that what was happening in Rosedale could happen to them. They even conjured up the hackneyed argument that outsiders were interfering, trying to tell law-abiding taxpayers what to do. Even in the 80's, that argument fell on receptive ears.

Carter informed me that one of the most vocal and strident members of the Association had been Mr. Dunphy. I could not believe it. He was always so friendly to everybody—to everybody white, I guess. He and the others had argued to other members and other teams that if they did not stand together, they would fall together. It was as if Mexican General Santa Ana had just crossed the Rio Grande with a million Mexican troops, tanks, Blackhawks, and Cruise missiles.

It appeared the minority families were outmaneuvered. The team remained lily-white, although many parents made it clear they did not oppose having green kids on the team, as long as they could play. However, the Association pressed on. It appeared nothing could change the results.

The editor of the local paper, Mr. Earl Sanders, editorialized in favor of the kids playing, and he paid the price. Many advertisers stopped advertising. Vandals even attacked his paper. In the wee hours of one Friday morning, a bucket of horse manure sailed through his front window. Fortunately, not much damage resulted. He continued to print his conviction.

Shortly thereafter, on the advice of a lawyer hired in Dallas, Black, and Hispanic parents threatened a lawsuit. A white representative of the NAACP office in Waco threatened a demonstration. He pointed out that the Rosedale association and many other nonprofit organizations, enjoyed certain state, local and federal tax exemptions. They concluded these were subject to Civil Rights and nondiscrimination laws.

The Association had a choice. Either they would provide equal opportunities to all kids or provide them to none. Unbelievably, and to their eternal shame, the group chose *none*. They officially ended little league in Rosedale.

When I heard that, it astounded me. So virulent was the racism of several of the group's leaders, these men chose to punish a whole generation of kids who would no longer have a chance to play official little league baseball in Rosedale. What was even more regrettable was that they presented these kids a very ugly and repulsive lesson. I prayed they had not learned it.

By now, Carter and I had made it through the tall grass out to where I imagined third base once was. I stood staring toward the collapsed remains of the dugout. I then turned toward the fallen chain-link screen behind home plate. It was a wretched sight that pained me to see.

I allowed my mind to take me back to when I was nine years old and playing in my very first baseball game. That entire last inning flashed before me like a movie. I could hear the crack of the bat, see the runners break. I could see that hot ground ball streak through my legs and into left field.

I could even hear the roar of the crowd, feel the adrenaline rush through me. There it was—the whole thing, just as I had seen it a million times before. I must have had a distant look on my face. Carter walked over and stood staring into my eyes.

"Are you okay?" He asked, shaking my shoulder vigorously. I quickly came back to earth.

"Sure," I said, rather mechanically. He knew what was going through my mind and said as much.

"I know what you're thinking about," he said feigning a throw toward where second base should be.

"Right."

"I wish father could have seen you that afternoon," he said. I turned to him and smiled. "So do I."

Carter was right. He did know what I was thinking. He knew very well. He and mother and Rosie had been there that day. Carter indeed remembered. I should not have been surprised he did.

A long period of silence followed, as we continued surveying this abandoned field of dreams. I started on a diagonal toward where I estimated first base used to be. Halfway there, I came upon a slight rise in the earth. It was the old pitcher's mound.

From where I stood, home plate did not seem as far away as it once had. That is what happens when you grow up; things look smaller, shorter, closer. I glanced over my right shoulder. Carter was standing only a few feet away, observing me like the watchful big brother he was.

"I'll race you to the truck," I yelled. The look on his face was one of incredulity. We both broke out in uproarious laughter that sent birds scurrying from nearby trees. Before he could compose himself, I wheeled around and tore off the mound on a dead run for the truck, moving as fast as I could.

"That's cheating," Carter yelled, tearing out behind me. I am glad no one was taping this contest. It was not a pretty sight. I hit a couple of rough spots that almost sent me flying on my butt but managed to stay upright.

I reached the truck only a few strides before Carter. We both collapsed over the hood, laughing, and gasping for breath. I hurt all over. I managed to look in his direction to say something cute but erupted in uncontrollable coughing. It was truly an ugly sight to behold. Believe me, Carter was in even worse shape, though not because of his prosthetic leg.

"Man, you are insane, he managed between gasps. "Know that? You are nuts! We're too old for this."

"Speak for yourself," I snapped. Perhaps snapped is a bit of an exaggeration. I did not have the strength to snap.

"Look at you," Carter yelled, pointing, and still gasping.

"Look at you," I said.

"I guess you realize we could both go into cardiac arrest. No one would find us for a year out in these damn weeds. Even buzzards wouldn't circle out here. Know that?"

He was right. After we finally caught our breaths and dragged ourselves into the truck, I took another look at what had been a wonderful, exciting place for me. I looked real hard and made a silent promise.

We had only driven a short distance when I posed one more question to Carter. I wanted to know; I had to know what if any role father had played. What had his reaction been to the whole shameful episode? The moment I asked, a broad smile flashed across Carter's face.

"Jimmy T., you would have been very proud of him," he said, beaming. "He didn't say much at first. One Sunday morning, before church dismissed, he rose and walked down to his usual spot in front of the elders' table. The place was so deathly quiet, you could hear a mouse drooling on cotton, I swear. He had his say, told them all how he was ashamed to be a part of this town, that he could not see anybody claiming to love God and behaving that way toward innocent children. He said what was happening was wrong and they would all have to answer for it someday.

That Sunday, I left church with my head held higher, my chest stuck out farther than ever before. I was proud of him. It was a lesson in putting principle before popularity, about being willing to speak out about what you believe is wrong. Mother was so proud; I cannot tell you. I wish you could have been there." I wish I had been there too.

That night following my nostalgic but disappointing trip to Alston Park, I spent hours going through old steamer trunks mother had stored in Rosie's old room. One contained a dozen five-pound metal cans containing my marble collection. The trunk must have weighed a ton. The mystery of how mother got them in the room had to rank right up there with questions about the Pyramids and crop circles.

I emptied several of the cans onto the middle of the bed and raked them into a pile. There were at least a thousand of them there, sparkling in the light. There were cat-eyes, swirls, solids, bolies and more. I knew I was behaving like a kid, but I did not care. That was the whole idea.

When I was kid, I used to play marbles all the time, especially in the summer. My favorite game was holes. That is where you and your opponent both put up an equal number of marbles, sort of like a poker bet. We would stand around this clean, smooth, hole about the size of an inverted cereal bowl. The shooter would hold the marbles in a closed fist and drop them into the hole.

The object of the game was to end up with an even number of marbles inside and an even number outside the hole. If that happened, you were the winner. You would collect all the marbles and call out a number to shoot again.

For an example you might say:

"Shoot four!"

That meant you would put up four marbles and your opponent would put up four for a total of eight. You would then shoot again as described above. If you were lucky, you would win more marbles than you lost. If you were extremely lucky, you would clean out your opponent's marble stash. He would leave as a vanquished soul, promising to return someday.

There is a very critical technique to shooting holes. One would not simply drop the marbles in the hole unless you were shooting twenty or something. Then, you had to hold forty marbles in your hand. You would have to hold the marbles in both hands and drop them.

I had a special technique. I would snap my wrist as I released the marbles, aiming at a point just inside the rim of the hole. The marbles would land with a loud crack and fly everywhere. I always tried to land more marbles outside than inside.

I got to be doggone good at this. It was great fun as well. Father did not like us playing marbles this way. He said it was like rolling dice—like gambling. Mother saw it as the harmless game it was, but father had different ideas. He pointed out that although we were not gambling for money, we kept whatever marbles we won. He may have had a point.

At any rate, I tended to play only when father was not around. Of course, I had to make sure he did not discover my holes, so I played behind the barn. That turned out to be the best place anyway, because the sun caused the barn to cast a long, fat shadow, from early morning to just before noon. In the afternoons, from about 2pm on, it was not bad either, because a big oak tree was not too far from that side of the barn.

In all the world, one of my favorite people to play against was a soft-spoken, pock-faced boy named Iggy Davenport. Iggy was a tall, lanky, Ichabod Crane-looking kid with hands much too big for his skinny arms. His feet were far too big for his spindly legs; even his teeth were too big for his mouth.

Iggy was a friendly kid. Best of all, he had all these brand new, shiny marbles. I think I may have sinned because I truly coveted Iggy's marbles. He was an only child and his folks, who lived down Sennett Road around the bend from us, gave him almost everything he asked for.

Iggy would show up with two five-pound buckets of marbles on the handlebars of his heavy-duty Murray bike. I used to love to see him coming. That was not only because of the marbles, I genuinely liked Iggy. What I liked most was the fact he was very determined to win and never became angry when he lost, which was quite often. The truth is, he almost always lost. I would win so much, I started to feel guilty, but I did not stop playing.

Often, when I had Iggy on the ropes and down to his last twenty marbles, I would shoot twenty. I would cram the forty marbles into my hands, with Iggy's help, and go into my ritual. I would fix my steady stare on the hole, take a real deep breath, and let them go. Then the critical count would begin. Nine times out of ten, the results were in my favor.

Iggy would rise, dust himself off, pick up his bike and stand there watching, as I packed my winnings away in my empty Brer Rabbit Syrup cans. That was the brand of syrup father used to buy all the time. It came in these metal cans with a picture of a rabbit dressed in a coat and pants on the label. Once you peeled the label off the can and removed the remaining syrup with lots of boiling water, you could use them to store all kinds of neat things inside.

Anyway, Iggy would stand there absorbing the sting of his loss and gathering his empty buckets. A few seconds later, he would turn to me and say:

"Be right back," he would always declare. Then off he would go on his new bike, heading for home. A short while later, he would return with dozens of new marbles, still in the original plastic bags. We would then start all over again. Carter sometimes watched, but seldom played. After a vanquished Iggy left, we would both roll on the ground with hysterical, eye-bulging laughter.

So, as I stood staring at the bed full of marbles, I thought about Iggy. I wondered whatever happened to him. I also wondered if people were still calling him Iggy. Probably not. He had the kind of personality that bode well for his ultimate survival. He never let things get to him. I cannot recall ever seeing him blow his cool.

I opened the next trunk. There, lying right on top of the pile was my baseball glove. It was my very first baseball glove—the one dad had bought for me at Western Auto that Saturday morning long ago. I sat down on the floor next to the trunk and slowly lifted the glove. I held it like it was the Hope Diamond. Slipping it onto my hand was a little difficult, but it looked the same. Willie Mays' name was still visible over Mickey Mantle's, and I again whispered an apology to Mickey.

Also in the trunk was the treasured game ball my teammates had presented me, following my very first little league game. I clutched it with both hands, turning it over and over. The grass stains and scuffmarks were still visible on it.

I then found my old uniform, neatly folded, and wrapped in plastic near the trunk bottom. I lifted it, removed the plastic and stood up. To my surprise, both the pants and the jersey were starched and ironed. I held the pants against me, then heard someone snickering in the background. Looking up, I saw mother standing in the doorway laughing at me.

"I think they're a little short," she teased.

"Hmm. Right. And I see someone starched and ironed them."

"No! You must be kidding," she said.

"Nope," I said

"That's not really starch," she said with a wink. "It's more like a preservative."

She broke into a laugh and cupped both hands to her mouth. It was great to see her laugh. I went to her and gave her a big kiss and a bear hug.

"Thanks for keeping all this," I said.

"These things belong to me too. Your memories are my memories—all our memories," she said. I embraced her again.

Chapter Twenty-five

Native Son

A week later,

I was still steaming over the little league mess when Carter invited me to accompany him to a Chamber of Commerce meeting. At first, I was reluctant to accept, having the night before decided I was going fishing. The last thing I wanted was to attend a boring Chamber of Commerce meeting and find myself obliged to suffer fools with a smile.

I went anyway. The meeting was held at the Rosedale Country Club. What Rosedale Country Club? I asked. That is how long I had been away. I did not know Rosedale had a country club and presumably a golf course to go with it. Yet, there it was, located roughly two miles east of town in a beautiful, wooded area. It was accessible via an asphalt road that snaked through gorgeous oaks and gently sloping hills.

The complex was less than three years old, attractively designed, well-built and well maintained. The nine-hole course was laid out beautifully. The main house, though relatively small, had three banquet/meeting rooms and a great view of the course. I was impressed.

The meeting started promptly. I positioned myself in the rear of the room with Carter, content to be a silent observer. Following the pledge of allegiance and a short prayer, old man Dunphy introduced me to the gathering.

That was my first surprise. I had yet to speak to him since returning home. He had arrived late, and we had only exchanged nods and smiles from across the room. I rose, nodded politely, and sat down. Dunphy insisted I have a few words. I graciously refused with a smile and wave of my hand. He went on.

Routine agenda items were dispensed with. The subject then turned to the need to stimulate business growth and attract industry and jobs to Rosedale. One salient point made was that Rosedale and surrounding environs had great promise for attracting both low- and high-tech firms. Everyone agreed.

Located within the broader region were well-respected universities, colleges, transportation arteries and other amenities. The State of Texas was actively supportive of efforts to woo industry from other states. They were willing to encourage relocation through several incentives. It all sounded very interesting.

It was during this discussion, that I was drawn into the conversation. A young man, who introduced himself as Jeffrey Paine, grandson of Mr. Finneas Paine and recent graduate of the University of Texas, stood to pose a question to me. I had no idea there were Paines left.

"Mr. Phalen," he began.

"Jim," I corrected him.

"Thanks, but that will take me a moment to get used to. If you don't mind," he said.

I shrugged my shoulders and invited him to continue.

"Some of our members," young Paine went on, "are aware of your stature and position within the corporate and financial communities." I nodded and wondered what would follow this glowing preamble.

"You're C.E.O. and I believe also the majority stockholder in IDM, the leading edge, Silicon Valley software and peripheral manufacturing company."

"That's correct," I said.

"According to detailed reports, published yesterday in the Wall Street Journal and Newsweek, you're planning to relocate this 12-billion-dollar company from California to Arizona. I was wondering if you could confirm this for me."

I hedged at first, saying I did not intend to either confirm or deny the stories. It was the answer I would have given a reporter. When all eyes trained on me, I quickly realized coyness and evasiveness might work in New York, but in Texas it was about as welcome as a skunk at a picnic. I relented.

"The story has some factual inaccuracies but is basically true. IDM's board has been in serious discussions with Arizona officials who have presented us with some very attractive incentives," I answered. I knew the points the young man was trying to make, so I shut up, sat down, and let him make them.

"I was wondering," he continued, "if you might reconsider that option and consider relocating IDM to Rosedale instead."

The room erupted in applause. It was clear everyone thought that was the best question they had heard all day. Young Paine smiled like a freshman-debating student who had just posed the killer question. I hesitated for a second. The room went silent.

"Sure," I said. My one-word answer caught Jeffrey and the others off guard.

"Sir, you will?" He asked, his voice ringing with excitement.

"Sure, I'll consider it."

Another resounding applause erupted, drowning out the continuation of my response. I waited several seconds before continuing.

"I will consider it. But I must tell you it is a long shot. I do not want to mislead anyone on that score. Many, many, rigorous conditions would have to be met, for IDM to make a positive decision. The company's autonomous board would have to see a properly constructed package of incentives, including tax, zoning, and land considerations. Also very crucial is the status of the prospective employee pool. This requires thorough evaluation. Of course, my heart and my emotions naturally lead me to want to do whatever I can reasonably do to benefit my hometown. After all, I am a native son."

"Our most famous," a voice belted out. Then came more applause. I was growing embarrassed by all the clapping. So, I figured since I had their attention, I should point out a few things that had to be a part of any consideration to invest in Rosedale.

One option I discussed was that IDM may, instead of relocating its headquarters, consider using Rosedale as an expansion site. Serious thought was warranted. Presently we were operating in California, Massachusetts, and North Carolina, and planning three more sites over the next four years.

However, that timetable could be advanced. Debt was low, productivity was up, and market share had increased three hundred percent over the past five years. Overall, the company was enjoying a phenomenal growth rate of 25% per annum and showed no signs of slowing.

I also discussed the need for an educated and educable work force and quality residential housing, something I knew was lacking in the area. Furthermore, I made it clear IDM was an equal opportunity employer, not only in word but also in practice. We went beyond the word of the law, in that regard.

No one would suffer discrimination based on race, creed, color, origin, gender, sexual preference or physical impairment. The only requirement was that they have the desire and be capable of performing the job. Period. I made it clear that if anyone had a problem with anything I had said, they should withdraw their request IDM consider opening a facility in Rosedale.

I paused several seconds. For the first time since the start of the meeting there was roaring silence. I scanned the room and saw more than a couple of highly arched brows, but no one voiced a single objection.

The meeting lasted for almost three hours. When it was over, I had not only promised to consider locating a new IDM plant in Rosedale but had decided to try to stimulate economic growth. My first step would be transferring 100 million dollars in deposits from New York and dividing them between two Rosedale area banks.

I was practically mobbed afterwards. I asked myself why I had chosen to not go fishing that morning as planned. I then answered my own question. I knew this would happen and felt thrilled to even be able to return home and make a difference. It's a feeling I wish for everyone.

Carter and I started to leave, when I was introduced to a white-haired, impeccably dressed, elderly gentleman in a dark blue, pinstriped suit. He was James T. Barnwell, a former Waco resident. Barnwell owned thousands of acres in Crawford County. He was just the man I wanted to see.

The only one of Barnwell's many properties that interested me was the parcel including Alston Park. Within ten minutes, I made him a generous offer. With a simple handshake, he accepted. The deal was sealed as simply as that.

That is the way much business is done in places like Rosedale and other parts of Texas. No lengthy conferences or 'doing lunch' was necessary and the only lawyer involved was I, but I never let on.

Barnwell and I spent the next ten minutes discussing the best fishing spots. He insisted I visit him and his wife at their little 20,000-acre spread near Irving. I promised I would. That one brief transaction was the beginning of my realization of a dream I had not dared even dream.

Later, Carter and I sat in his office recounting details of the meeting. My mind locked onto one thing—bringing Alston Park back to life. It began to dawn on me, that I now owned what was for me, and those starry-eyed kids I once knew, hallowed ground. I cannot tell you how I felt thinking about it. Carter, as always, knew what was going through my mind.

"Jimmy T., you are not hearing a doggone word I'm saying," he complained mildly.

He was almost right. I was already thinking about getting crews out the next day to begin cutting away the growth, hauling away garbage and debris. I could not wait to hire an architect and a construction company. I did not care where I found them, I wanted the best for this project. Money was no object.

When I told Carter what I was thinking, he laughed. He said he had not seen me that excited since I was nine and father let me play baseball. He was right. I felt at least that excited, if not more.

"Little brother, you own this town, stock, barrel, and bullets. You know that?" Carter half-joked. I assured him, I had no desire to own Rosedale, either literally or figuratively.

"I know, but you do anyway, and I couldn't be happier about it," he insisted. I asked what he meant.

"For once, I can be assured Rosedale won't die like a lot of little towns around this state, this country. It's gon' live. What you're doing is gonna change people's lives. I've never been so proud to be a Phalen."

"It's going to take everyone's help."

"Yeah, but I was looking around the room and I thought to myself, If Jimmy wasn't who he is and didn't have the means to do what he's doing, there's no way these folks would be willing to stand on their heads like this," he said, laughing. "There wasn't a soul there who doesn't think they won't somehow benefit from your doing all this. Did you see old man Dunphy? I swear Jimmy, you could have farted, and they'd have all sworn it was perfume or something."

We both doubled over, laughing like fools for at least five minutes. Tears rolled down our cheeks. We started coughing. It was insane. In retrospect, the line was not that funny. It's the way Carter said it and the look he had on his face. You had to be there. Several of his employees must have thought we were nuts.

Three weeks later, things were taking shape rapidly. The town fathers along with county officials had prepared a liberal package offering IDM incentives to locate the new plant. They had also formed an impressive alliance with the state of Texas. Several key politicians were keen to fulfill campaign pledges to attract new industry to the State. This all happened with amazing speed.

I had spoken extensively with IDM management. All had concurred in my decision to seriously consider the idea. The fact I was Chairman/CEO, as well as eighty-two percent majority stockholder, in no way abrogated their principal responsibility to make autonomous decisions. I insisted upon it.

As important as the IDM project was, I admit my primary focus was on the resurrection of Alston Park. Already, that was fast becoming a reality. The property was cleaned, surveyed, debris removed, and construction plans for phase one submitted and approved.

When I spoke to Carter, Rosie and mother about the progress being made, I told them I had decided to rename the park, The John Q. Phalen Park and Recreation Center. Mother was certain it would thrill father to know that.

The next day, during my daily conversations with father, after reading him the paper, I told him of our decision regarding Alston Park. While I cannot say I observed any visible reaction on his part, I thought I saw a twinkle in his eye. Perhaps that was because I wanted to see it. It made me think I had at least conveyed my excitement to him.

Phalen Park would be more than a baseball field. There were fifty-two acres in the parcel of land I had purchased. There would be other phases constructed over the next few years, whether I remained in Rosedale or not.

Part of the additional construction would include an Olympic-size swim center, a gymnasium, plus exterior facilities for volleyball and tennis with seating. There would also be exercise, banquet and meeting facilities for kids and seniors.

When completed, expenditures would total over 12 million dollars—a bargain, considering what the cost would have been elsewhere. More significantly, residents of Rosedale and surrounding areas would have employment during and long after project completion. Rosedale desperately needed jobs.

I made a special arrangement with the town and county governments. They would provide the funds for maintenance, and I would lease the entire complex to them for 100 years at one dollar per year. They happily agreed and offered to pay in advance.

When word got out, the whole area teemed with excitement about the project and for good reason. It meant much-needed jobs, increased tourism, and an influx of capital. The project became a source of pride for the entire county. Everyone would be a winner.

My greatest difficulty, as all this took shape, was being able to move about without having to stop and engage in long conversations with everyone I saw. However, after a time, people sensed I needed a little privacy. They began affording me the solitude one expects in a small town.

I knew construction of the baseball park phase would not be completed in time for the last of the normal little league season. Still, I hoped to at least play an inaugural game dedicating the park before school began in mid-September.

The problem, even with that idea, was that Rosedale no longer had a baseball team. That meant we had to quickly begin holding tryouts and launch a training camp. The idea was laudable, but it was probably the most demanding of all the ideas I had come up with.

Putting together a team meant having to find a temporary manager—me. I was now knee-deep in the baseball business, determined to keep it less business and more baseball, somehow.

I found people in and around Rosedale who were more than eager to get involved. Many of them were also part of the clique that had promoted the stupid actions of the Association years earlier. I used them anyway because I needed warm bodies.

I asked one of them, Joe Bright to act as manager. He readily accepted, with the understanding that I wanted every kid to play. Tryouts would be open to all. That meant every race, male and female. It was that last part (female) that clearly stunned him. He did not object, but I could see his bottom lip quiver and the startled reaction in his face.

These were new times. I thought back to when I was a kid. It occurred to me Rosie could have qualified for our team without breaking a sweat. However, the idea of her playing baseball never even came up. The assumption was girls did not play baseball.

Baseball was and is, in the minds of many, a boy's game—a man's game. The truth is, it is big business, not just a game. I suppose that sort of socialized thinking accounts for the fact that before Jackie Robinson, modern baseball was considered a white man's game. While I am no slave to political correctness, I wanted every kid to have a chance.

Meanwhile, I had to convince the contractor I was not insane; that demanding he complete his work in record time was not a sign of lunacy. No problem. I simply offered him a healthy bonus as a financial incentive. It worked. Suddenly, my relentless insistence on a rigorous, around the clock construction schedule made a lot more sense. The truth was, I was not about to take no for an answer.

I was prepared to hire another contractor, if he had not been able to do what I wanted done.

Chapter Twenty-six

Rosie, All Growed-up

It was 5:35 am on an unbelievably cool Saturday morning in late July. Only the slightest hint of a coming sunrise appeared on the distant horizon, as night fled the approaching day. In Texas, cool and July are mutually exclusive, but this day was different, for a short while at least.

Rosie and I sat quietly on the edge of our pier at Crawford Lake, barely fishing, if results were any measure. Only thirty minutes had passed since we had arrived. We were both quite snug in our down jackets and faded jeans and sneakers. That would soon pose a serious comfort problem. I had been away for a long time, but not so long I had forgotten the capriciousness of Texas weather.

After many minutes of staring into the water, it became clear the fish were not keen to accept our offering of the best bait in Texas. Perhaps someone farther upriver was offering them a tastier menu, but I doubted that. Everyone in these parts of Texas, including the fish, knew Phalen bait was second to none.

The air was unusually crisp, and the sun seemed a tad tardy. We were both aware that in a short while, the heat would force us to peel off our jackets. We would later wish we had dressed in cutoffs and t-shirts instead.

Suddenly, there was a tug at my line. Then just as quickly there was nothing. I lifted the line carefully and discovered some thief had stolen my bait. I quickened my resolve and rebaited my hook, driven by the desire for raw revenge.

Rosie, usually very talkative and expressive, hardly said a word for the longest time. When we were kids, she would talk to the fish to get them to bite, or so she claimed. Since she always seemed to bag the most fish, we grudgingly accepted her claim with only a small grain of salt.

Rosie had driven down from Dallas alone the night before. All during dinner, she seemed quiet and pensive. Even mother noticed it. During our entire trek to the pier, she had hardly said two words.

I caught her up on what had been going on since I arrived. She listened attentively but had nothing to add. No questions. No challenges. That was a dead giveaway something was wrong. I wanted to ask her what was bothering her but decided she would tell me when she was ready. I was right.

The sun finally rose with a vengeance and the down jackets came flying off. Neither of us had caught a single fish, but that was fine. I had already delved into the picnic basket for one of mother's leftover barbecue sandwiches and a Big Red soda.

"I remember how much you use to love those Big Reds," Rosie said with a short-lived laugh. "I remember daddy used to buy us each one. You somehow made yours last longer. I always wondered how. You drank just as fast as we did. I never could figure it out."

"I stretched it," I said.

"And I found out just how you stretched it."

"What do you mean?" I asked, as innocently as I could.

"I learned you would drink down your soda about halfway, then add water and sugar to fill it up again."

"Who me?"

"Mama told me all about it years ago."

"That was supposed to be a secret," I said.

"I understand why you wouldn't want anyone to know about it. It must have tasted awful."

It did and it was a dumb thing to do. The carbonation had dissipated, the flavor...everything. All I had left was a pink liquid. At least it was sweet. And I had plenty of it."

Rosie and I laughed about that for a while. Soon, she was silent again. I turned and looked directly at her. Before I could pose a question, she opened up and began talking again.

I was happy to learn there were no problems with her marriage or Robert, Jr., as I had feared. What I discovered was troubling Rosie also troubled me.

"I think I've waited too long," she said, her voice tinged with sadness. She kept saying it over and over. "I've waited too long. I've waited too long."

Rosie seemed on the verge tears. I rested my pole and moved closer to embrace her.

"What do you mean?" I asked.

"I'm talking about dad. I've waited too long to talk to him about things that happened when we were kids. There are so many questions I never got answered. He was a good father, provided for us, taught us right from wrong, sheltered us. Perhaps he sheltered us far too much."

I knew then that Rosie and me, and even Carter, shared many of the same feelings. Rosie perhaps more than the rest of us. It was that morning I learned how much she harbored dislike or even hatred of some of the ways father had dealt with her. Then and now, she saw these things from a view neither Carter nor I had or could ever have.

Rosie recalled that from the very beginning, she was made to feel she, and all women, were inferior to men and boys. It was simply a given. No one looked her in the eyes and said those words explicitly. It happened implicitly, by society at large and amplified by her childhood experiences at home.

There were the constant biblical references father made, that made Rosie feel women were not highly thought of or respected. She wondered if God really meant for the bible to portray those things. Rosie even wondered aloud if God was a misogynist. She then felt guilty and blasphemous, for having entertained the question.

Rosie recalled father's insisting she always dress like a girl and behave like a lady, when all she wanted to do was play with her brothers. She simply wanted to do the same things we did. Maybe if she had had a sister, she mused, perhaps she would have felt differently.

Rosie felt expected to automatically do things like; clean the house, wash the dishes, cook, help mother around the house, keep her fingernails clean. While some girls may have favorably viewed such treatment, Rosie loathed them.

She also felt that Carter and I were judged and treated by a different standard. What bothered her was the insistence she set her sights on more traditional women's goals. It was one of the reasons she majored in education in college. Though she acknowledged teaching was an honorable and much needed profession, she recalled only being taught limits.

On the other hand, Carter and me, and boys generally, were encouraged to be all we could be. Implicit in that was the notion we could be anything from acrobats to doctors—even President.

There was also the matter of her high school prom. For the first time I could remember, Rosie talked about how embarrassed and humiliated she was that night. She felt sorry for poor Jonah Beck, her date. He was already a nervous wreck, from just having to ask father if Rosie could go to the prom. Then to learn father would be driving them to and from the prom poured salt into an open wound.

I have since concluded Jonah wanted to take Rosie to the prom very, very badly. Look at what he went through. There is no doubt had I found myself in his position, I would have taken some other girl or stayed at home.

On Prom night, father returned to the school an hour early to pick up Rosie and Jonah. And at one point, tired of waiting, went to the gymnasium door and asked one of the coaches to bring them out. Rosie learned that the man, coach Stennis, had prevailed upon father to be patient and to wait. Thank God for coach Stennis.

Things had gone badly enough. All night long, several kids razzed her and gave her a hard time. I did not know Jonah got into a brief scuffle after having had his fill of the teasing they had endured. I asked Rosie if she knew whatever happened to Jonah. The last she heard five years ago, he was a Marine Corps Lt. General, stationed at the Pentagon in Washington, D.C.

"J.B.?" I asked, mouth agape.

"Right. J.B.,"

"Do you mean, the J.B. I know?"
"J.B.," she repeated.

Finally, the subject of her first pregnancy, and the baby we had all lost, came up. Even at 43, it was extremely difficult for Rosie to speak about it without growing emotional. As she spoke, she paused often to compose herself, while gazing out across the lake. I suggested she did not have to talk about it, but she insisted she wanted to. For years, she had held it all in. Not even Robert knew exactly how she felt about that experience.

Rosie recalled the night she first revealed she was pregnant, describing it as the hardest thing she had ever done in her life. At one point, she considered taking an overdose of aspirins. All she thought of was how father would react, what he would say, what he would do.

She had disclosed everything to mother earlier, before we left for Christmas Eve service. I never knew that. Mother then revealed the dream she had about the pregnancy. She felt God had prepared her for Rosie's dramatic news. Mother and Rosie decided it best to wait until after church to tell father and the rest of us.

What hurt Rosie so deeply was the fact father's reaction made her feel dirty—unclean in his sight and the eyes of God.

"Not only had I angered and disappointed my father," she said with a trembling voice, "I had sinned against God. So, now God was angry with me. I mean, where do you go, what do you do when you anger God, and you care about that sort of thing?" She asked.

I hunched my shoulders. I did not have an answer. Still, I could feel the pain in Rosie's voice and knew she would likely feel that pain for the rest of her life. There was no question she relived those traumatic moments every day of her life.

I asked her how father had responded to Robert, Jr. or Robbie, as they called him. Rosie told me that before his stroke, father had been the quintessential, doting grandfather with Robbie. The same was true of Carter's son.

Rosie recalled that once, when Robbie was only ten months old, she watched from a doorway as father held the baby. He sat with him in a rocker, staring down at the baby, rocking gently back and forth and humming a lullaby.

When Rosie eased over to them, she noticed tears on father's cheeks. Neither ever made mention of it. She always wondered if he was thinking of the grandson he never knew. Perhaps he was.

Rosie made clear she did not hate father, just the opposite. It was her love for him that made her blame herself all these years. She hated herself for causing pain and embarrassment for the family. Rosie mused that it was a good thing those were not Old Testament Days. Both she and the baby's father would likely have been put to death.

I assured her the only pain and embarrassment she had ever caused me resulted from beating me in the Main Street Foot Race in '66. The race was a featured part of Rosedale's Founder's Day celebration. The embarrassment took place in front of the whole town.

She laughed and appeared to take a step back from her melancholy gaze into the still water at our feet. After the laughter subsided, Rosie again spoke wistfully of her first child.

"I still love him," she whispered.

"I understand," I said. But I did not understand. How could I? I could only imagine the true nature of the timeless bond between a mother and her child. Never mind that the baby never breathed a single breath outside his mother's womb. For Rosie, he was her first son, James Aaron Phalen. To her, he was and would always be a real person.

What man can ever fully understand, that for many women, that bond forms the instant she realizes there is the hint of another life inside her. For others, it comes much later. For Rosie, that bond still existed.

To this day, Rosie has never told us who James' father was. Despite father's demand made in the name of "God," she refused, saying that since God already knew, and had not struck her dead, there was little need to tell anyone else. I admired her for that.

It was Rosie who brought up the subject of her attempted suicide. She spoke about it as being an out of body experience. For her, the memory sprang more from a dream than reality. That's exactly the way she put it.

Rosie said that in retrospect it did not seem as if it ever happened. Only when she glanced at the faint scar on her left wrist, did she think about it. While it was a horrible time, she made it clear she never wanted to forget it, and never wanted to deny what happened.

I mostly listened. Rosie explained she had not really wanted to die as much as she wanted to escape. She wanted to escape the pain, the fear. She wanted to escape the look of shame in father's eyes and the self-condemnation in her own heart.

Rosie also wanted to avoid lingering stares of judgmental townspeople as well as the overcompensating, saccharin-laced kindness of others. Most of all, she acknowledged wanting to escape the person in her own mirror. That was as much as she wanted to say. I put an arm around her shoulder and squeezed really tight. Sometimes, a good hug is all any of us really needs.

What both Rosie and I feared was that the moment to share feelings about growing up under father's stern hand had passed. It was now too late to tell him, that although we loved and still love him, we had regrets and questions.

I would like to think even father had regrets. But were we being selfish? Were we focusing too much on what was undoubtedly only a part of childhood? I think not. We were being honest about what we were feeling, trying desperately to keep everything in perspective.

We had both come to understand parenting is not an exact science. Certainly, no childhood is perfect. Neither of us was dysfunctional, by today's lurid talk show standards. Rosie and I were simply desiring to reconcile aspects of childhood.

How does a child in his or her forties, with a father nearing death and unable to communicate, have such a conversation with him? Should we move on and let it be? What real choice did we have? What if he could hear and understand what we were saying but could not respond—could not defend or explain his actions. That would be extremely painful for him. Neither of us wanted that.

Following a great deal of soul-searching and a lengthy conversation with mother, we both learned for the first time, that she had spoken of this to father years ago. She had urged him to have such conversation with the three of us. While father had not ruled it out, he made it clear he did not see the need for it. However, he did promise to think about it. I suppose he did.

Mother had shouldered the burden of all our disappointments and heartaches in her bosom. She knew of our hurts and wounds and tended to those she could, never laying them at father's feet. In hindsight, perhaps that was a mistake. I will not judge her.

I have learned that a mother's role is a precarious one. Often, there's the pull of love and devotion to her husband and the tug of love, devotion, and connection to her children. Often, what is demanded in her is the wisdom of Solomon, the power and strength of King David.

Mother explained that she shielded father because he was often too busy with work and church. He had the weight of other responsibilities on his shoulders. It was a view held by many women of her generation. She deserved no ridicule for that.

What was bold for her was her pointing out to father that his children needed his close involvement and fatherly attention, "especially the boys," as she put it. She told of wishing he had spent more time playing with us than lecturing us and said as much to him.

Father's response was that he was no longer a child. Housework and tending kids were woman's work. That response typified father's world and an attitude he had acquired as a child. I recall mother reasoning that father's childhood, the values, and attitudes of his own father, had molded and shaped him long before she met him.

Rosie and I decided not to say anything that would cause father any consternation or pain. That was the last thing we wanted to do. It was clear we should have spoken to him years ago, when he could have fully understood and responded. The time for that had passed forever. We wanted the time remaining with father filled with pleasant remembrances and the joy of being together.

Before Rosie returned to Dallas, she posed a simple question to me that I could not begin to answer.

"How long are you staying?"

I had not really stopped to consider a timetable. The truth was I had not set one and had no plan to do so, short term. However, Rosie's question had made the correct assumption. The day would come soon when I would move on from Rosedale. It was never my final destination. I just did not know when. And that was okay with me. Time and circumstances would provide the answer.

My conversation with Rosie had focused my thoughts on just how much time had passed. Remembering conversations we had as kids, about subjects that seemed so important then, caused me to wish my prayers to quickly become an adult had gone unanswered.

Twenty-seven

A Day of Healing

September 7th is a day that will live always in my heart. It was an eventful day of wonder, a day of healing, and the beginning of closure for me.

It began as had most of my days, since returning to Rosedale. I had an early breakfast with mother and Carter, then sat reading the morning paper to father, who was by now confined to his bed. He was too weak to sit up in his wheelchair in the sunroom, as had become his custom.

During breakfast, Carter brightened our day when he informed us there was a growing probability he and Elizabeth would reconcile. It was great news. He had spent the weekend in Dallas with her and William. Things were looking decidedly better. Both had confessed they still loved each other and both loved William more than anything in the world.

Both mother and I were ecstatic. There was a glow in my big brother's face, not there since I had arrived. He looked the picture of health. He appeared younger and exhibited a more youthful bounce in his step. Carter was even more talkative and animated than either of us could remember.

Alise called later, from a television studio in Chicago. She had just concluded an interview and was scheduled to do a book signing later in the afternoon. She sounded so excited. The two of us had not realized just how much we really cared about each other. We were both spending a small fortune in phone bills.

Later in the day, I received a photo Alise had taken of every room in the apartment. She had written a caption beneath each, which read: "Empty without you, but I'm OK!" I got the meaning. The feeling was mutual.

Alise had also included a surprise thank-you note, sent me by Anitra McDavid, the waitress I met in Roanoke. Anitra said my gift was a godsend that assured her of funds to complete her last two years of college. She concluded, saying I was an angel disguised as a man. That was very sweet of her, though greatly overstated. I was touched.

Alise was eager to hear about the park's construction. It was nearing first-phase completion, and in record time. I told her it appeared we would get in the dedication game, as planned. We were also well under way with efforts to reestablish our affiliation with the national Little League Organization.

Everything appeared to be falling into place with amazing speed. However, my suspicions were that things were going along much too smoothly. I had always felt when that happens, one should be prepared for the other shoe to drop. This time, I hoped my fear was without merit.

Alise was equally thrilled to hear that a perky 10-year-old girl, Ellen Parker, had made the team. I had to repeat it several times, then listen to raucous cheers and applause at the other end of the line. After promising to nominate me as Honorary Woman of The Year, Alise gave me a loud, slurpy phone kiss and said good-bye. I felt buoyed by our conversation and missed her even more.

Later, while I was reading to father, he appeared to tire faster than before. Furthermore, he was hardly making audible sounds at all now. For weeks, doctors had been telling us he was slipping rapidly. Father's heart was weaker and his pulse increasingly unsteady. I did not want to hear or even know of these things, but I had to know.

We had all observed his deterioration, but I kept telling myself he would bounce back, that it was still possible he would fully recover. For weeks, I saw him go through periods of weakness, then rebound, somewhat. I expected, or rather hoped, that his period of rebounding would somehow grow longer and more pronounced. I still believed in miracles. I had no choice.

Once more, I raised the question of having father moved to a major hospital in Dallas. Mother again expressed her opposition to the idea.

"I don't want to chance him dying away from home," she said firmly. "I just don't want to chance it. If there was any possibility they could make him well, then I would. But all they want to do is experiment on him 'til he passes on. We've done too much living between these walls. I want him here."

She was right. Mine was only the voice of a son wanting to be certain he did everything—spared no expense in the care of his father. Father had always done what he thought was right. In the future, I wanted to be able to look into my mirror and not be ashamed of myself.

Yet, I knew even this desire sprang from a degree of self-concern. I admit that and find nothing wrong with it. I had no desire to grieve. I was still having great difficulty facing the fact I could lose father.

Being in Rosedale and at home did not soften the pain of seeing him as he now was. Every corner of the house, every acre of land reminded me of growing up and seeing my father as a robust, healthy, strong-voiced man. Never mind that he would often say things I did not want to hear. I would have given anything to hear him chew me out about some undone chore. I was now forty-two and still longing for the past.

I spent the late morning of the 7th with the contractor, inspecting work at Phalen Park. We discussed details, regarding painting and padding the outfield walls. Several merchants had suggested we sell panels to advertisers. I declined. Instead, we received permission from major league teams to paint their logos on the walls, just above the lower padded sections.

My point of personal privilege was having the Brooklyn Dodgers positioned in center field. The Los Angeles Dodgers logo appeared a short distance away. I confess that when the team left Brooklyn, I no longer considered them real Dodgers. They are a class-act franchise alright; it is only a matter of loyalty. Forgive me, Mr. Lasorda.

Everything about the park was as perfect as it could be. The artful sign naming the park had gone up the day before. Both Carter and mother, along with a few Rosedale officials and a local news photographer, were on hand. I cannot describe the feeling of pride we shared. It was a very moving experience.

The Media Pro Production company I had hired to document the construction project arrived from Dallas a little late. We had to pose again. Since much of what I had experienced as a child was memorialized only in my mind, I wanted to take complete advantage of present technology.

Not only were we using broadcast Beta-Cam video cameras, but we were also using still cameras and 35mm film as well. Additionally, I arranged for aerial shots. I did not want one moment or photo angle to go unrecorded.

Everything was falling into place. What was once an awful eyesore had been transformed into a point of great pride. In nine days, the first little game was scheduled to be played to a sellout live crowd of over eight thousand fans. We would likely have a standing crowd of thousands more, thanks to the media focus and word of mouth.

The Rosedale Dodgers were about as ready as could be expected. They would oppose a larger, faster, much more experienced team from Waco, but that did not matter. What they lacked in size and experience, they would have to compensate for with grit and determination.

I had spent a great deal of time watching our energetic but inexperienced youngsters trying to master the fundamentals of baseball. Fortunately for us, some of the kids had been playing baseball on other area teams and formed a sound core group. Still, there was a long way to go. Watching the practice sessions had not inspired much hope of a win. Nevertheless, I remained an eternal optimist.

The excitement in Rosedale was at a fever pitch; it was palpable. You could not turn anywhere without seeing a sign or banner or something trumpeting the celebration. Everyone was joining in the spirit of the occasion. Town fathers had gotten together and formally declared September 17, John Q. Phalen Day, in honor of father. The gesture touched us all very deeply. We issued a statement to that effect.

I learned this was the biggest thing to happen in Rosedale's history. I appreciated the sentiment. However, I respectfully disagreed. I remembered that long-ago Saturday when Carter and other servicemen returned to Rosedale from Vietnam. I remembered the band playing; the DAR members providing dinners for the boys; the tears in the eyes of my mother, the look on father's face. Nothing could ever supplant that day in importance and sheer emotion.

I wrapped up my tour of the park and headed home. When I arrived at the front door, mother was waiting for me. The look on her face gripped me. It was one of foreboding and dread, I thought. I froze, stopping just short of the door. My heart paused mid-beat. I had never seen such dread on her face.

Before I could say a word, mother beckoned for me anxiously. I hurried to her and was all but pulled through the doorway.

"What is it?" I asked. My voice trembled.

"It's your father, son."

"Is he alright?" I asked, expecting the worst. Nurse Slaney stood observing us from the door leading to the sunroom. Mother motioned me to follow. I did and stepped through the open doorway. There was father, sitting upright in his wheelchair, staring out toward the fields. I took a deep breath and offered a word of thanks to the Almighty.

"Can you believe it?" Mother asked, clasping both hands together. I moved to where father sat and knelt next to his chair. He turned his head slightly in my direction, although he made no direct eye contact. I turned toward mother who was smiling and crying at the same time.

"He just...sat up in bed a half hour ago and started grunting really loud to get our attention," she said. "We went into the room, and he had this look on his face. I remember seeing it many times before, like when he used to call me, and I couldn't get there fast enough."

I also remembered how, as a child, those piercing looks made me quake in my boots. Father could be a very impatient soul.

"I just could not believe what I was seeing," mother kept on repeating "Stunned, is what I was. That's the word for it. I kept on trying to figure out what he wanted. I didn't understand. And then, I understood exactly what he wanted. He wanted out. He wanted to get out of that bed. So, we put him in the wheelchair and brought him in here. He still doesn't seem satisfied, though. At least not to me. Not to me."

I pulled up the rocker and sat down next to father. Over the next few minutes, I told him all about the park and all the celebrations planned in his honor. At first, he frowned. His brow furrowed and his eyes narrowed. He then closed his eyes, squeezed them shut for a few seconds. He repeated this for a while, as I continued talking to him.

I told father all about the new little league team, about the game scheduled in his honor. When I mentioned how I felt standing on that field again and recalling when I played little league, he closed his eyes for an even longer time. Soon thereafter, he began grunting. I asked mother to step inside and see if she could understand what he wanted.

Mother felt father was trying to say something, but we could not figure what it was. We kept asking him whether he was hungry or tired or if anything hurt him. Each time, he grunted again. He seemed to be trying to speak.

I could see the frustration and the pain in his eyes at not being able to say what he wanted to say. It was so painful watching him and wishing I could understand him. What happened next was something I have not since been able to explain. It was as if someone spoke to me in a loud and clear voice.

Without saying a word, I bounded to my feet and returned the rocker to its usual spot. I then walked behind father's wheelchair and turned him around. With mother looking on questioningly, I began pushing his chair toward the doorway. Mother followed. We reached the living room and instead of heading to the bedroom, I started for the front door. Mother stepped in front of us. I stopped.

"Son, where are you taking your father?"

"Out there, mama." She looked at me as if I'd lost my mind.

"Out where?" Mother asked.

"Outside, on the front porch," I said.

"The porch?

"The porch," I said.

"Why?"

"That's where he wants to go."

"How do you know? I mean..."

"Mama, I just do," I insisted.

I did not want mother to see the emotion welling inside me. There was no doubt in my mind father wanted to be outside. He wanted to feel the wind in his face, see the trees without peering through windows and screens.

"It's kinda hot out there," mother fretted.

"I'm just taking him out on the porch. It's not so bad on the far end. Wind's blowing...smells like summer and everything. Don't you think so, mother?"

Mother turned to face Nurse Slaney, who hunched her squared shoulders and remained quiet.

"If you think about it mama, being outside is what he would be missing more than anything. He was always outside, even when there was nothing to do. You used to say he would paint an already painted section of fence just to be outside."

Mother smiled and stepped back. She knew I was right. Father was the type who was always outdoors. If he was not building something, he was in the fields with his vegetables or patching a hole in the barn roof. The disrepair was often little more than a raised nail or something. He would be out there just banging away. You could hear his hammer for God knows how far.

The hammer had not sounded for a long time now. The vegetables were doing well, thanks to Carter and several neighbors. Father was never one to spend long periods of time cooped up inside a house. It was unreasonable and illogical to believe he had changed now.

I eased him out onto the porch. Father's face seemed to light up right away. His white hair ruffled in the strong breeze whipping down the length of the porch. Mother followed us outside to the swing. A look of concern still covered her face. I secured father's chair then took mother's hand, guided her over to the swing and motioned her to sit. She did. I could see the emotion building inside her.

Father had built this porch swing long before Carter was born. He had even carved his and mother's name on the underside of the last piece of wood he installed. Mother first told me about the carving when I was in high school. She said it was one of the few and most sentimental acts father had performed, since their marriage.

She would mention it with a slight quiver in her voice, followed by a quick disclaimer. That being, she did not mean to ever suggest father was not a sentimental fellow. Even when she voiced her own disappointment regarding father's actions or inactions, she was always the first to leap to his defense. That was real love.

She sat in the swing and leaned over, touching father's hand affectionately. What I saw then and had always seen was a rare kind of love that hardly exists anymore, except in fiction.

Theirs was not a love that ebbed and flowed based on the ups and downs that occur in a marriage. It was steady, unwavering, and sure, unaffected by temporary emotional reactions and disagreements. I envied them and still hoped to know even a semblance of that kind of love someday.

While mother sat there, I left her and father and went inside for a moment. When I returned shortly and started toward them, mother stood and took several steps toward me. A look of surprise covered her face and for good reason. Clutched in my hands were my trophy baseball and the baseball glove father bought for me all those years ago.

I reached her and she just stood there looking at me. She did not say a word—did not ask me any questions or anything. I turned father's chair until he faced the opposite end of the long porch, knelt beside his chair, and placed my hand atop his.

For the first time since coming home, father seemed to be looking directly and cognitively at me. I peered into his eyes and could see my own reflection in his pupils. I felt as if our hearts were beating in unison.

Without saying anything, I lifted his left hand and gingerly placed my glove on it, as far as it would fit. I glanced up at mother. She had taken a step back and now stood with her arms folded, looking on with the warmth only a mother can exhibit.

I continued with great care. Once the glove was on father's left hand, I took the baseball, stood, and took a few short paces backward. My heart rose to my throat. All the while I kept hearing a distant voice urging me on. I looked at father, whose gaze seemed fixed on me. I prayed he was aware of what was about to happen.

It was then, time and place seemed to shift. No longer was I forty-two, I was only seven or eight. No longer was my father weak and ailing, he was tall, strong—reaching every bit of his 6'-5" frame. I still had to tilt my head back to gaze up at him.

We were all standing in the wide-open space, in front of the barn playing and having a great time. Father was wearing his favorite, faded 'Mule Jack' coveralls, a wide-brim straw hat, and those thick-soled, brown leather ankle boots he loved. We had just finished playing hide and seek in the barn. I handed him his glove and grabbed my own, as Carter and Rosie stood watching from nearby.

Then, as magically as it had appeared this image, of things that never were, faded slowly from view. So absorbed was I in this moment of fantasy, I did not hear Carter drive up and park his truck in the driveway. I honestly do not recall hearing a sound. I must have stood there staring at father for a full three or four minutes. I lost track. I felt at once like a kid and again much too old to be playing make believe. But this was not make -believe. This was real.

I clutched the baseball, stared at it for a long moment, then at father. Suddenly, a calm came over me. The sensation was unlike any I had felt before. There was no need to hurry anymore. There was no need to worry about ticking life clocks, unfulfilled desires, or anything else.

I stared at the baseball in my hand, then at father. When the moment seemed right, I leaned over and gently tossed the ball into the glove he wore. It landed cleanly. Mother sighed and clasped her hands over her chest. I just stood there for moment, absorbed in the meaning of it all, then started toward father.

I had not taken two steps when, to our collective amazement, father began moving his right hand. I stopped still. This was a miracle. Father had not moved his right hand, since before his second stroke. Mother, Carter, and I all gazed in disbelief. However, the real miracle was yet to come.

Seconds later, father's fingers moved. I recall thinking, that what I was witnessing would likely not rank very high amongst all-time miracles. But for us, it could not have been more dramatic.

With tortured effort, father managed to get a thumb, index, and middle finger around the ball. Mother cupped both hands to her mouth and shook her head from side to side. I watched intently, unable to move. Father held the ball for a time, then began to inch his hand forward. The ball slipped from his fingers into his lap.

Tears filled my eyes, blurring my vision. I brushed them away. Just then, father somehow summoned the strength to repeat his labored effort. This time, he managed to lift the ball a full inch or so above his lap and struggled to extend his arm as best he could.

It was then his strength failed him. The ball fell from his hand, tumbled onto the porch deck, and rolled toward me. I stood there waiting, staring down as it reached my feet. I reached down, picked it up and squeezed it in my hand. I looked up at father. His head had tilted slightly to one side.

By now, mother was crying, and I was wiping away even more tears. My eyes were riveted on father, the glove on his hand, the look on his face. Carter stood shaking his head, finally turning away to conceal his own tears.

Taking the few steps, I reached father and again knelt in front of him. I took the ball and, while opening his glove with my free hand, tucked it snugly inside the webbing. I gazed up into his eyes. It was then I saw a lone tear beginning to trickle down his right cheek.

I immediately knew he was much more aware and alert than we had thought. Father desperately wanted to make known what was in his heart. I put my arms around him and embraced him for a long while. I pressed my cheek to his and felt the beating of his failing heart against my chest. At that moment, I truly felt I was a part of him, as never before.

For the first time, since becoming an adult, I felt like a child again. I cannot explain it. I felt more than just my father's son. I felt connected to him in a way I never had before. My only regret was that it had come so late. My one lasting joy was that it had come at all. I would have given all I had for this moment.

Mother was still in tears, standing next to me. She placed her hand on my head and tousled my hair. I turned to see Carter. He too, was overcome and stood looking on in teary silence. At one point, he turned and stepped away briefly.

A stranger looking on, may have viewed this same scene, and concluded hardly anything took place on the porch, that summer day. They perhaps would say father never really threw the ball, that his movement was random, involuntary, not indicative of intent or desire. They would be so wrong. I know better. They might even suggest the tear he shed was not a result of any specific emotion he felt. We all know better.

Father's toss was not a sizzling strike that caused me to flinch from its velocity. That was not the point. The meaning of what happened goes far beyond the act itself or even my interpretation of it. It was a moment branded in my mind and on my heart. I will never forget it, as long as I live. For the first time in my life, I had played catch with my father. What's even more important, I had connected with him in a way so vital to fathers and sons.

Chapter Twenty-eight

Farewell

At 5:50, on the morning of September 8, 1994, my father died. My father—died. I will remember that day, that hour, that exact minute as long as I live.

If you have never suffered the death of a parent, there is no way you can understand what I felt and still feel. Something profound happens deep inside you, changing you forever. You cannot prepare for it. You just cannot.

Carter, who had spent the night, Rosie, mother, and I were all at father's side. Mother had called Rosie at 1 a.m., having awakened from a prophetic dream. She had seen an angel, bathed in light, standing at the foot of her bed with arms outstretched. Shortly thereafter, a soft voice had spoken to her, and she woke up.

In a calm voice, mother told Rosie to come home as soon as she could. Rosie arrived just before 5:30, while we slept. Minutes later, mother grew concerned about father's labored breathing and summoned us all to their room.

We all stood quietly around father's bed, holding hands, and fighting back the tears. Mother prayed softly and held my father's hand gently in hers. At 5:50, my father opened, then closed his eyes, heaved a heavy sigh, and slipped away. He was gone. His pain, his suffering, his travel through this life was over. My father's leaving was as dignified and as framed with love as one has a right to hope for.

This is not an easy chapter for me to write. Something inside me wants me to end my story here, but I still hear the voice and there is much more to tell. I miss my father much more than I ever imagined I would. There's an emptiness that seems larger than even my father's enormity in my life justifies. And it grows.

Ironically, my father took with him my own fear of dying. I no longer fear death. Like so many instances during his life, my father had cleared a path and gone on before me. And I knew I would someday follow him. It is very difficult to explain.

As I said, something profound happened deep down inside me, the day my father died. I sensed it immediately; it coursed throughout my body, and I knew it went far beyond the emotion resulting from his loss. Everything that had mattered to me the day before was now insignificant, not even worthy of thought.

As a child, it was as if I had stood in a slow-moving line behind my parents, awaiting my turn to face life and death as they had or would. All that once seemed an eternity away. Now, it felt like I had taken a quantum leap forward toward my own mortal demise. The wonder of it all was, it no longer mattered.

What did matter was the living yet to do. Amid the inner turmoil, there was a surprising calm that grew out of my resignation to the inescapable realities of life and death. I felt as if I was now irrevocably an adult, not only in theory but in practice. There was no longer the luxury of slipping easily in and out of my adult role at will.

You see, no matter how old you are, as long as your parents live, you can feel free to retain some semblance of a juvenile spirit, if not behavior. I realize this may not be true of everyone, but it was true for me. As I have said, parents are not supposed to die. Parents live forever.

Mother remained in father's room for most of that fateful day. Even after his body had been removed, she refused to abandon her high-back rocker near the bed. She sat there clutching her tattered bible and rocking gently. At times, she could be heard singing hymn after hymn.

One song she kept repeating was: Softly and Tenderly, a beautiful hymn. It's the theme song to one of my all-time favorite films; The Trip To Bountiful, starring the talented, and wonderful late actress, Geraldine Page. Bountiful is a touching, heartwarming story that brings both laughter and tears. If you have not seen it, do so. Every time I see the film, I think of my father, my mother, and that September 8.

After a time, mother's tears ceased to flow outwardly. I was certain they flowed inwardly and would not soon end. We were all concerned, but knew mother needed to be alone. I felt I knew what was going on in her mind and heart. Yet, there was no way I or anyone else could know. How could I? Sure, I had lost a father, but mother had lost her lifetime partner—the person to whom she had entrusted her heart and love for most of her life. What does that feel like?

Carter, Rosie, and I tried to be as consoling as we could for each other. We spent hours recounting the things we all loved about father. Funny how, despite the bad memories, the good ones always rise to the surface. And that is as it should be.

In the middle of our talking, I suddenly wondered why we were speaking about father in the past tense. Then, reality quickly returned. He was gone. This would not be the last time I experienced this slipping in and out of reality. By day's end, I felt emotionally spent. I just wanted to close my eyes for a year and awaken to find father well.

On the morning of Saturday, September 10, 1994, following funeral services at New Redeemer Christ Church, my father was laid to rest in our family plot at Evergreen Memorial Cemetery. He was placed next to the graves of James, my infant nephew, father's brothers Silas and Raymond and his own dear mother and father.

On that day, the hot, unforgiving Texas sun shone more brightly than ever. There was not a single cloud in the brilliant blue sky. It all belied the dark reality of the loss we all shared. Father would not have wanted us to be sad and tearful. Still, it was very difficult not to be sad. I did not feel like a mature adult. I did not want to behave like a mature adult. I felt like a child. I felt like a son who had lost his father.

The service at New Redeemer was brief but emotional. Many of the hundreds of mourners spilled out of the small church onto the surrounding grounds and even the narrow roadway. Their presence was a clear and visible testament to the esteem in which my father was held.

Elizabeth and William had arrived the night before. Robert and Robert Jr. had arrived earlier that day. Our family sat on the front pew and listened, as the new chief elder and other speakers eulogized my father. He was described as a god-fearing father and husband, a man loved and respected by all with whom he came in contact. They were right. Even those who differed with him respected him and were there to pay their respects.

Because he was a U.S. Army veteran, The President of The United States sent a letter of condolence that was read aloud. Afterwards, it was returned to the large envelope bearing the Presidential seal and given to my mother.

Mother later asked me how in the world the President knew about such things. She thought it most considerate of him, to take time out of his demanding schedule to send a letter to her. I considered explaining how those things are done, then decided against it. I even expressed my own surprise at the gesture.

I recall sitting in the middle of the service and briefly wondering why these people were standing there talking about my father. I even glanced around and wondered where he was, why he was not there. I could not recall a single time that I was in the church and my father was not standing in his usual place or seated on the Row of Elders.

Later in the service, I walked to the podium and spoke for our family. I tried to speak about my father from my heart, without breaking down, but my words felt inadequate, and I failed in the latter. I did manage to thank those who had come, many from great distances, for their friendship and their caring. I was sure my father had known how they all felt about him.

Sadly, father's funeral came only one week before all the festivities in his honor were to be held. No one thought the events should be postponed. To the contrary, that day now took on an even greater meaning for us.

It was mother, who was a tower of strength for all of us, both then and now. Even at the cemetery, she remained somber, but not emotional. Her composure held firm, until the contingent of Army Reservists from Waco fired their twenty-one-gun salute.

That ritual was followed by the ceremonial removal of the U.S. flag from the casket, and its presentation to mother. It was a very emotional moment that brought tears to all our eyes. It made me think of that day father proudly wore his faded Army jacket to the bus depot. Mother must have remembered that day, as well.

I was certain that later in the night, once we had all gone to bed, mother's steady exterior would likely give way to expression of grief and sadness. Finally, she would grant herself a moment to cry aloud, bury her face in her hands and let her emotions flow freely. At that present moment, she appeared to be restraining those emotions.

It was at the cemetery, I suddenly realized something about Carter and Rosie and even myself. Except for her lasting memory of father, we were now all that remained of mother's fifty-year relationship with my father. He was the last person—the last connection—to a past they both had known. They had shared an era and time in history each remembered and understood.

None of mother's own family remained. Now there was no one with whom she could reminisce about the past. That is what happens when you live a long life. You outlive your spouse and family and friends. It is a bittersweet reward.

I remained at the cemetery long after everyone had gone, except the caretakers. Carter, Rosie, and their families went home with mother. I found it extremely difficult to leave. Something was keeping me there. As I absorbed the sights and sounds of everything around me, my senses seemed sharper. Nature's aromatic fragrances were more pronounced than ever before. The trees appeared greener, even taller than usual. The sky looked bluer, the clouds whiter. A choir of songbirds, nestled in nearby branches, seemed to sing a more melodious chorus than I could recall having ever heard.

My thoughts turned to Alise. She had wanted to come, but I had suggested she not do so. I did so, because I did not want to introduce her to the family at such an emotional moment. At least that is what I told myself. To this day, I do not feel Alise yet understands what my thinking was, although she has never mentioned it to me. I am sure it was my fault for not explaining myself more fully. At the time, it did not seem the thing to do.

I stood at my father's grave and stared for the longest time at the matte, grey casket festooned with a huge bouquet of flowers. My eyes traced its shape; the height of it; the length of it and the width of it. I refused to let myself accept that it represented a resting place for my father.

The man I had known was much too big a man to fit into such a small space. I represented my father. Carter and Rosie and mother represented my father. He was in the wind, in those trees around me, on the wings of every bird. He was a part of all things good, decent, and honest.

What hurt most, as I stood there entranced, was the stark fact that I would never again see him in this life. It is during moments like this you think of a thousand and one things you wish you had said during the living years.

After a time, I walked over to my father's casket, removed a white carnation, and placed it in my lapel. It was then I heard the voice again. Only this time, it was clearer than ever. It was not a voice I recognized. It was fearless, mature, resonant, and projected the tenor of unquestioned authority.

"He was so proud of you," the voice said. "Jim, there is no doubt, your father was proud of you; you heard him say the words with his eyes and the touch of his hand. His voice was weak and failing by then, but you heard him clearly. You must also know that, had he to do it all over again, he would do many things differently." I still hear those words ringing in my ears.

Moments later, I took several steps back from father's grave, turned and started for my car. It was then I spotted her—a woman dressed in black, standing in front of a large headstone some distance away. I could hardly see her.

I almost did not notice the woman at all and had no idea who she was or why she was there. I could see a black veil covered her face and guessed she was more than fifty yards away. Still, there was something warm and familiar about her—something that beckoned. I could not walk away.

I stood still for a moment, staring unashamedly in her direction. She must have sensed my gaze, because she turned briefly toward me, then away. I started in her direction, and she began walking away. Her pace quickened, with each passing second. I hurried to catch up to her.

"Excuse me!" I called out.

She continued, without the slightest look back. I called out again.

"Excuse me!"

This time, she slowed to a gradual halt and waited, as I approached. When I reached her, I was desperate to know who she was, and was prepared to follow her as long as necessary. Only steps away now, and still behind her, I spoke to her as calmly as I could.

"I'm sorry for yelling out, but do I know you?"

"It depends on who you are and who I am," came her tentative and softly uttered reply.

The velvety voice touched something inside me, quickening my pulse. I walked around to face her. She lifted her veil slowly and my heart fluttered. My jaw dropped. I would never have guessed who she was, except for her eyes—those unbelievable eyes. The woman standing before me was Rachel. It was Rachel! My Rachel!

I was struck mute. My heart pounded wildly. This could not be, yet it was. It was Rachel. I saw her face, the way her lips turned down slightly, the hazel eyes that still danced, the raised cheekbones. This was really Rachel. There was no doubt of it.

"I know you. I know you," I said, slowly finding my voice. My mind was spinning like a merry-go-round. I even lost the familiar sensation of my feet being planted firmly on the ground.

"I know you, too," she answered. It was her voice I heard. It was Rachel's voice.

I knew I was staring, but I did not care. We were both staring. There was a decided awkwardness to it all, but that did not matter one bit. I wanted to embrace her immediately and at the same time I wanted to back away several feet to fully observe her. I was desperate to take in this dreamlike vision before me. I whispered her name, again and again. Time slowed to a crawl.

"Rachel. Rachel"

"James," she answered.

There was plenty of staring between us, during those first few nervous moments. Neither of us could believe our eyes. Rachel had matured much more gracefully than I could ever have imagined. There was only a hint of grey in her hair. Her skin seemed more like that of a 20-year-old. I soon felt self-conscious and wondered just how I appeared to her. Was she disappointed? Did I look old?

Abruptly, it was as if a celestial light had shone down and enveloped us both. I reached for her hand and drew her gently to me. Rachel smiled. I embraced her, kissed her lightly on her cheek and stepped back to look at her. I just stood there, riveted to the spot, taking in the sight of her.

There were tears in her eyes—tears Rachel wiped away with her gloved hand. I grasped the hand, held it to my lips.

"It's been a long time," she whispered.

"Several lifetimes," I agreed.

"And you still look very handsome, James T. Phalen. And so distinguished, too."

"And you're even more beautiful now than I remember you, Rachel ahh..." I paused and waited for her to fill in the blank.

"Summers. It's still Summers," she added. I smiled with a level of relief that I immediately recognized but was unable to explain. More silence followed.

"I suppose you're wondering why I'm here."

I nodded yes. Rachel looked away momentarily, then away toward where she had been standing earlier. She spoke slowly, with measured emotion.

"This is the first time I've been back here in all those years. I heard about your father when I arrived a few days ago. I'm so sorry."

I thanked her and grasped her hand.

"My uncle's property has years of back taxes. I came to sell it. And since I was here, I decided to visit his grave, pay my respects to your father at the same time," she said. I nodded my thanks and kept staring.

"Why didn't you call the house?" I asked. "Surely you were not going to leave without saying hello. Were you?"

"Probably yes," she admitted with a smile

"Why?"

"I thought it best. But now I'm glad I didn't."

"I can't...I find it hard to believe I'm actually looking at you standing right here in front of me. You broke my heart, you know."

"Did I?" She asked. Her gorgeous eyes flashed.

"Yes, you did."

"Forgive me. I didn't mean to break your heart. I'm sure it mended years ago and it's probably been broken a few more times since."

"I don't know if it mended. I think I just grew accustomed to the pain."

Rachel smiled widely. I loved it when she smiled. I always did. I could see her dimples when she smiled.

"A man of your means and your fame must surely have a family to share so much with. Your family come with you?"

"I'm not married," I answered. Rachel looked at me pointedly. She seemed genuinely surprised.

"Are you serious?"

"Of course."

"That surprises me."

"Why?"

"Because you come from such a close-knit family. I always thought you'd get married and have a real brood. I recall you were supposed to be President of the United States, too. Remember?"

We both grasped each other's hands and smiled. I kept on staring at her. I could not help it. There was just something about Rachel, beyond the fact that she was now a beautiful and mature woman. There was something I could not quite put my finger on. She looked as stunning as ever. Her skin was youthful and taut, as smooth as a peach.

"I'm truly sorry about your father's death. Please convey my condolences to your family," she said. With that, Rachel released my hand and seemed prepared to leave.

"Look. I just know you are not going to leave me again so quickly, are you?" I asked.

"I really should be going. I hope to have everything completed by Monday. I'll be leaving then," she said.

That is not what I wanted to hear.

"Leaving for where? Where do you live?" I asked.

Rachel hesitated before answering and considered not telling me. My eyes conveyed my insistence on knowing.

"California. I live in California."

"California's a big place. Where in California?"

"North of San Francisco, not far from the ocean and the wind and the sound of surf pounding large rocks. I call it heaven on earth."

"I've always wanted to see heaven," I answered as smoothly as I could.

"Live a good life and you will."

"I am serious. You cannot just leave. There is so much for us to catch up on. I only have one lifetime, you know. Besides, I never knew why you left all those years ago. I understood you went back to Beaumont. I wrote you at least a hundred letters but never heard back. Nothing. The letters never came back, either. So what happened? I never forgot you for a moment, you know."

"And I never forgot you, James Theodore Phalen. Our friendship was the best thing that happened to me."

"So, tell me why you left."

Rachel again hesitated before responding.

"That's all in the past. I left because I had to."

"Because of your uncle? Because people were concerned about your staying there alone with him? That was the rumor at the time."

"People had their reasons and their rumors and..."

The subject was something Rachel was clearly very uneasy talking about. Apparently, there was a great deal of pain associated with those distant memories and she was fearful of reviving them.

As sensitive as I was to that fact, I could not chance her leaving without answers to questions I had carried with me all those years. It was pure chance that had brought us face to face again. I doubted once she left, I would ever see her again. No matter what, I simply had to know.

"Come out to mother's with me," I said, changing the subject as smoothly as I could. "We can talk later, and I can help you settle your business on Monday. You'll get a chance to see Rosie and her family before they leave. She would love to see you. She has a little boy now. Carter is married too; he has a son who looks just like him. A lot of folks are coming by you know...bringing food and everything. The custom hasn't changed."

"I see you haven't changed as well, James. And you are still trying to charm me."

"Me?"

"Of course, you."

"Is it working?" I asked.

"You are very persuasive," she said.

"Thank you, but is it working?"

"Not many people knew way back then, just how charming and persuasive you were, James Phalen. And you still are."

"I must not have been too persuasive. I couldn't prevent your leaving."

"As I recall, you never asked me to stay."

"I did."

"I remember your saying you wished I wouldn't leave, but you never asked me to stay. I would have remembered."

"Would it have made any difference, if I had?"

"No. I had to leave."

I found myself staring at Rachel again, thinking about that last time we were together. I remembered the two of us sneaking out of the Christmas services and stealing kisses near the water fountain. I remembered being scared to death that someone would find us standing there pining for each other with moon eyes.

I did not want her to leave, then or ever. And I did not want her to leave now. Exactly what was I feeling? Was it simply the excitement of seeing Rachel after so many years? Was it possible that seeing her had rekindled the love I was certain I felt for her so long ago? I was not sure.

"So, will you come with me?" I asked once more, putting on my best puppy-face and smiling. I had not expected to smile at all that day. Rachel smiled, pondered my offer for a few seconds and nodded yes.

Twenty-nine

Rachel, Rachel

Rachel accompanied me to the farm that afternoon and stayed until late evening. I could not keep my eyes off her and made no attempt to conceal the fact. She looked so radiant, so alive, so regal. We did not have an opportunity to talk one on one at length, but it was just wonderful having her there. It was as if she had been sent by angels to soften the pain, we all felt.

Not only did I treasure Rachel's presence, but she and Rosie were also like longtime friends, behaving as if it had only been weeks since they last saw each other. For me, there was a dreamlike quality to the evening. Mother remembered Rachel as well and remarked about how little she had changed. Carter introduced Liz and William and kept looking at me, raising his eyebrows. At one point he whispered to me:

"Marry this woman right now, or I'll divorce Liz and marry her myself. She's gorgeous."

I had to agree. Rachel was a picture of ageless beauty. From across the room, I found myself ogling and had to force myself to look away from her for a moment. I was waging a losing battle to appear unaffected. At one point Rachel observed me watching her, smiled knowingly, winked, and continued her conversation with Rosie.

One thing that gave me pause was the fact Rachel took care to avoid other guests who could best be described as the 'Old Guard' of Rosedale. However, I understood her reaction to them.

These were people who would have been adults during the time she was here and most likely to have been the gossips spreading rumors then. It was strange to see a few white-haired mavens cloistered in the corner in whispered conversation and curiously observing Rachel from a distance.

Alise called later and spoke to mother again, offering her condolences and promising to keep all of us in her prayers. When I spoke to her, I noticed her voice sounded different. She told me she had a touch of laryngitis and was taking prescribed medication. Her doctor had ordered her to get some rest and keep her mouth closed. So far, she was doing neither.

Hearing of her prescribed silence, I cut our conversation short, made her agree to get some rest and promised to call her later that night or the next morning. We said playful good-byes and hung up. I stood there for a moment, wondering why I felt so guilty and not quite sure why. All I had done was say hello to an old friend, bring her home and spend time reminiscing about old times.

Perhaps the guilt I now felt flowed from the undeniable excitement I was feeling just seeing Rachel. Maybe it was because I could not erase the thought of holding her in my arms and making love to her for the very first time. No doubt the guilt sprang from the fact I should have been feeling only grief, and here I was masking it with thoughts of Rachel. I was quite confused.

~

An hour before sunset, as most others began leaving, Rachel graciously refused my offer to drive to Crawford Lake to view the sunset. She complained of being tired and wanting to rest. Rachel informed me she was staying at a recently built Quality Inn, just outside Rosedale, and would be happy to see the sunset on Sunday, if the offer still stood. I assured her it would.

An hour later, everyone had gone and for the first time since arriving in Rosedale, there was only family in the Phalen house. Most of the medical equipment and remaining supplies were gone, except for my father's wheelchair. Mother said she wanted to keep it. Carter tried to persuade her to get rid of it, but she insisted.

Just as the sun was setting, we all gathered behind the house and watched until only a glow along the horizon remained. It was the most spectacular sunset any of us could remember seeing. I rushed inside and grabbed my still camera. I took several shots, with mother in silhouette in the foreground, outlined against the reddish-orange sky. It was a beautiful, captivating scene that ended far too soon. I later had the picture enlarged and framed. I carry a wallet size copy of it with me and gave framed enlargements to Rosie and Carter.

My greatest concern then and now is for my mother. She and father were like one—inseparable. She had known and loved only one man all her life and now he was gone. How does one cope with that inevitable feeling of emptiness? How does one lie in a bed shared with a spouse for over fifty years and survive the deafening sound of silence? How does one deal with the sight of that vacant pillow lying well within reach? How does one accept that so familiar a voice will never be heard again? I do not know. Perhaps it is my imagination or perhaps my fear, but even now when I speak to mother, her voice sounds more and more distant. I am afraid.

To my surprise, as everyone prepared for bed that night, mother persisted in quizzing me about Rachel. I attempted to discourage the conversation, but to no avail.

"She still looks so beautiful," she noted. "Is she single?"

I said I thought so. Mother wanted to know why I had not asked, to be sure. At first, I thought she was just making conversation to keep upbeat. I soon changed my mind.

Mother only wanted what every mother wants for her children, that they know the happiness they themselves have enjoyed. It is only natural. In retrospect, it was not so much that she favored Rachel. She wanted to see me married and finally raising a family. Remember, only a few weeks before, she had been encouraging me to tell Alise how I felt about her.

It was an hour later, as I passed mother's room, en route to the kitchen that I heard her crying. I stood at her door, torn between knocking on the door and walking away. I recognized this as a painful but necessary part of her confronting her new reality. There was nothing we could or should do, except embrace and love her.

By Sunday morning, Rosie and Robert had decided to remain at mother's through the next weekend's celebration. Then, after breakfast, we all received some much-welcomed good news. Carter and Elizabeth announced they were reconciling and planned to repeat their marriage vows at New Redeemer Christ Church on October 9, the anniversary of their wedding. It was wonderful news. Mother was moved to tears, and we all offered hearty congratulations. I had only one burning question:

"Does that mean we have to give gifts again?"

"Absolutely," Carter answered. Everyone laughed. Elizabeth was beaming, clinging to Carter like grapes to a vine.

Later that morning, at mother's insistence, I called Rachel and invited her to dinner. Surprisingly, she accepted, and I drove out to get her. When I arrived at Quality Inn, my heart was beating a mile a minute. I waited in the car a few minutes, to allow myself time to get a grip. I was hard put to rationalize the degree of my excitement.

Rachel was waiting for me in the lobby. The instant I saw her, it reminded me of that first day I met her. Even the fragrance she wore was startlingly reminiscent. A warm glow of expectation covered her face, and I am sure mine as well. I felt like a schoolboy picking up his first date and it no doubt showed. I had made up my mind to be cool, calm, and laid back. I am not so sure I was successful.

~

The day spent at the farm was absolutely 'storybook' in every way. Still, my father's absence was never far from our consciousness. Any minute, I expected to see him walk into the room and dominate it with his presence.

Mother insisted on preparing the dinner alone, despite repeated offers of help. While she was in the kitchen, we could hear her singing hymns and talking aloud. She even laughed occasionally at our antics and wide-ranging conversations. At one point I sneaked into the huge kitchen, slipped up behind her and put my arms around her waist.

"Sometimes, your father used to do that," she said.

"Father use to do this?" I asked. My voice apparently conveyed my surprise. It did not seem like something the father I knew would do.

"Hmm, you sound surprised," she observed.

"I am."

"Don't be. Elder Phalen could certainly exhibit a romantic flash, every now and then, especially when we were first married. Sometimes he could get downright frisky."

"Father?" I again remarked. Mother looked surprised.

"Of course," she said.

"Father? Romantic? It's just that I'm having a little difficulty imagining father being romantic," I said.

"He certainly was. In fact, even after you kids were born, I would sometimes have to shoo him away, whenever I heard you kids poking around. You really are surprised, aren't you?"

"Quite."

"Son, you have to figure he was romantic sometimes. After all, we did have you three children. Right?"

I had to agree. You never imagine your parents being romantic, much less intimate. You simply do not. Mother found all this humorous and laughed uproariously at my expense. Carter heard all the commotion and came into the kitchen to see what was so funny. Neither of us told him.

Mother soon ordered both of us out of her kitchen. She was smiling alright, but she was serious. On my way out, I passed her mixer loaded with banana-nut bread mix and dipped some with my finger. She threw a potholder at me, but I ducked just in time. It was really great to see her in such a playful mood. I wondered how long it would last. I wondered what would happen the first time she found herself at home and truly alone?

After dinner, I did what most boys do on their first date. I showed Rachel my toys. More specifically, she received permission to see my treasured memorabilia mother had stored in those old steamer trunks. It was like going on a scavenger hunt. We even ran across several notebooks of additional poems and short stories I had written in junior high and high school. I had overlooked them earlier.

Rachel seemed to thoroughly enjoy sitting on the floor, rummaging through all that stuff with me. I had a great time watching her, very discreetly of course. The time went so quickly—more quickly than I wanted it to go.

It was late afternoon when I borrowed Carter's truck and drove Rachel down Miles Road to the northern shore of Crawford Lake. We seldom saw the Lake from this side when we were kids. The eastern shore and a part of the southern shore were more accessible to us from our farm.

From the northern shore, our view of the sunset would be partially framed by long, sloping tree lines that converged on either side in the distance. It was as if the trees existed for precisely that purpose.

The waters were exceptionally calm, in contrast to the turbulence I felt inside. I was quite nervous and could not understand why that was. I had been in the presence of beautiful, intelligent, alluring, radiant, beguiling women before. Why was being with Rachel so different?

Rachel was very quiet during the drive, permitting me to do most of the talking. I reminded her of the day Moose Strunk made his big move on her. Moose had expected Rachel to faint, and fall awestruck into his burly arms. She remembered the incident as well. We both laughed.

Not long after, I parked, and we walked along an isolated stretch of lakefront. The area was populated with mostly knee-high grass, a few trees, scattered rocks, and wild birds.

The scene was extraordinarily beautiful. If you stood there and allowed yourself to dismiss all modern notions, you could easily imagine being transported back a hundred years. You would feel, as did I, this was the most important place—the only place on earth. Time no longer mattered.

For a long while, I left the speaking to the sounds of water flapping against the shore; birds chirping, the distant call of one of nature's creatures and the sound of the wind whistling through the trees. There was so much I wanted to know about Rachel and very little she wanted to tell me. I was determined.

Once more, I asked her why she had left Rosedale. She avoided the question deftly, and commented on how much Rosedale had changed, how excited the whole town seemed. She wanted to know more about construction of the park complex. It was a subject I was eager to discuss and did ramble on a bit. In fact, she got me to talk about not only Rosedale but myself, having me account for almost every year of my life from graduation to present.

"Hey! That is not fair at all." I said, realizing what was happening to me. "I've told you almost everything about me and you haven't talked about yourself at all."

Rachel smiled, but remained silent for almost a full minute, before responding. She began by telling me she was once married to a doctor she met while earning her degree in psychology at UCLA. That was in 1979. They remained married three years, before divorcing. She never remarried and they had no children.

After earning both a master's degree and a Ph.D. in psychology, Rachel turned to writing, lecturing, and consulting. Presently, she was writing her third book and doing occasional clinical work, mostly in San Francisco. She was Dr. Summers. Rachel Summers, Ph.D.

I had always wondered what Rachel had done with her life. I had imagined all sorts of professions she might have gone into, but psychology had not been one of them. Rachel told this to me in a very matter of fact way, without much emotion or detail. I asked why she never remarried.

"I never fell in love again," she said.

"Never?"

"Not even once."

It was an affected response I took note of. Something in her voice, in her manner, told me she was both unhappy and alone.

"What about your family?" I asked, "The sister in Beaumont."

That turned out to be a pivotal question. Rachel thought about it for a very long moment.

"We were half-sisters. When I left Rosedale, I went to live with her for almost three months. Her husband and I didn't get along.

So, I moved to New Orleans to live with an aunt—my father's sister."

Rachel did not elaborate. Instead, she fell silent. I was not sure if I should press her. I was disappointed that just when she was beginning to talk, she suddenly stopped. I pressed on.

"Did you graduate from high school in New Orleans?" I asked.

"No. I ended up moving to Los Angeles and lived with my father's oldest sister through high school and to my junior year at UCLA.

"I'm sure she's proud of you," I said.

"She was. She passed away, not long after the beginning of my senior year. After that, I moved onto the campus. Fortunately, I received several scholarships. Otherwise, I'm not sure what would have happened to me. I'm sure college would have been completely out of the question, though."

I was listening very carefully and from what I heard, it seemed likely that no family member attended her UCLA graduation. I asked and she confirmed it. I could not imagine the sadness and the disappointment that must have caused her.

"What about your mother?"

The instant I asked, I knew I had touched a raw nerve. Rachel's half smile disappeared completely. She drew a deep breath.

"What about her?" Rachel asked.

"I just wondered if..."

"I haven't seen my mother since I was eight years old. She left my father and me and I haven't seen or heard from her since. My dad tried to raise me, but he couldn't. The alcohol wouldn't let him. The pain wouldn't let him. He died when I was twelve."

The details were finally coming in fits and starts. All this was so painful to hear. I offered my heartfelt, yet meaningless I'm sorry.

"It was a long time ago," she added.

"Was the alcohol the reason your mother left your father," I asked, fully realizing I was prying deeply—more deeply than I or anyone had any right to do.

"No. The alcohol was a result of her leaving. She left for other reasons, mostly pressure from her relatives. They were very disappointed and angry with her for marrying him in the first place. When I was born, they turned their backs on her completely."

I realized I had led her into a painful area. I had barely opened my mouth to change the subject when Rachel spoke up. She turned to face me squarely.

"Look at me, James."

Her directness caught me off guard, but I did as she asked. I turned to face her and looked deeply into her eyes. We were less than a foot apart. I could almost feel her breath and felt an almost uncontrollable urge to kiss her.

"I'm looking," I said.

"What do you see?"

"What do you mean?" I asked.

"What do you see," she asked again. I stared more deeply.

"I see a warm, wonderful, very intelligent, and beautiful..."

"Thanks, but there's something else," she said. "Look again. Look closely. I'm not the person you think I am."

I was confused. I had no idea what she had in mind.

"I don't understand," I said. "I don't understand what you mean. Tell me what you mean."

"I'll try to explain it," she said.

Rachel drew a deep breath and looked away for the longest time. I waited. At last, she turned to stare at me as she had never before. There was interminable silence. This time, I was determined to remain quiet. She would be the first to speak. I waited and waited. Finally, the silence was broken.

"When I was a little girl, I used to love playing with dolls. Most little girls did, back then. I would look at them, hold them, dress them, comb their hair. I used to think if I closed my eyes and wished really hard, I could make them come alive. Then, I would have someone who was truly my friend. I thought my beautiful, perfect dolls were a lot like me. They had the same hair, the same, softness, the same..." Rachel stopped talking.

"What's wrong," I asked.

"I'm dancing around the point. Maybe I should just put it simply," Rachel answered.

"I agree," I said.

Rachel looked away then back. "My father was black," she said.

My jaw dropped. Every syllable of every word seized me. It seemed I lost all sensation of being inside my body. I saw her lips move. I heard the words.

"And my mother...was white," she continued. "I'm not white, James. I'm not the hazel-eyed, auburn-haired, Anglo you've thought I was all these years. I am black, African American, formerly colored, back when I was last in Rosedale."

Rachel's eyes never blinked, as she spoke those words. I felt reduced to granite. I am certain I stopped breathing, for a moment.

"Truth is," she went on, "I passed, as they call it. Until I was eighteen years old and even older, I passed—denied who and what I really was. After a time, I almost fooled myself. There was the me I knew I was, and the me I led others to believe I was. And it worked. For a long time, it worked."

Had there been more of a breeze blowing, I am positive I would have been leveled. I was just that frozen with disbelief. I gasped and stared at Rachel, unable to force a single word from my mouth. I knew I had heard her correctly, but I was wanting her to repeat what she had said. I must have looked like a pillar of stone.

"You don't have to say anything, James."

"No, no. That's not it. I just..."

I was stuttering like a fool and must have looked thoroughly dumbfounded. I was. The truth is, the confession rocked me down to my shoes. There is no other way to say it. I grasped her hands and held them. She pulled away.

"That's why I was forced to leave Rosedale," Rachel went on. Her look was drawn and distant. I wanted to stare at her but dared not.

"Forced? You were forced to leave?" I asked. My voice broke.

"Yes, forced," she said. "My uncle and aunt were the only relatives on my mother's side who, quote unquote, accepted me. I came to live with them. At the time I had nowhere else to go. I even took their last name. But somehow, just after my aunt died, the school superintendent and others found me out. My uncle was told that if I did not go quietly, the word would go out that he had a blossoming, nubile, young colored girl living alone with him. Of course, they assured him they were only thinking of me and his reputation."

"What did your uncle..."

"Do?"

"Yes. I'm sure he was furious," I said.

"He was more than furious. His first reaction was to get his shotgun and go shoot somebody. I pleaded with him, told him I just wanted to leave. And I did. There was no way I could stay. I would have left even sooner than I did, but I knew I would see you at the church that last time. To tell the truth, I'm surprised the truth about me never leaked out, especially in a town like Rosedale."

I listened to Rachel, dazed, and numbed by what I heard. I could not believe what I was hearing. Once again, I had another view of the dark underside of not only Rosedale specifically, but America generally. I felt drained, just listening to her.

I could not imagine the burdens Rachel had carried for most of her life and how they affected her view of herself. What could I say that would sound the way I wanted it to sound? What reaction did she expect from me? What did I expect from myself? For purely selfish reasons, I briefly wished I was not standing there. The odds of me doing and saying the right things were practically zero, I thought.

Only in my adulthood, had I learned what passing was about. To learn now, that the Rachel I had known had endured that, was hard to comprehend. It was futile for me to even try to imagine what it must have been like. And what of the Rachel standing in front of me? She had to be the sum of all her experiences. We all are.

Rachel understood my stunned surprise and said as much. She wondered aloud how it must have been to hear what she had told me. I apologized to her incessantly, as if I had been personally responsible. Rachel assured me I had no need to feel in any way responsible. Further, she made it clear she viewed the relationship we had enjoyed as the one redeeming thing about her entire stay in Rosedale.

"I'm sorry for having to destroy your pristine memory of me," she apologized.

"Nonsense!" I responded, making it understood I would have none of it. I tried desperately to convince her my view of her had not changed. It was then, I realized such a declaration should not have been necessary. Again, she understood and did not count that against me. I was beginning to second-guess everything I said. I had not done that earlier in the evening. Why was I compelled to do it now?

Without my articulating it, I wanted her to believe that her being African American made no difference regarding how I saw her. I wanted to believe that myself. The truth was it did affect the way I viewed myself with respect to her. It had to. Would I have thought about her the way I had from the moment we first met, had I known? All this was a new reality that had to supplant the old reality that had been a part of my life for so long. In the process, new realities emerged without my seeking or welcoming them.

Another question I asked myself was: "Now, would you want to take Rachel back home and reveal to your mother, Carter, and the others what she had just told you? Did you still want to take her in your arms and make love to her? If you had known this all those years ago, what difference would it have made?"

At that moment, all my liberal, 'We are The World,' colorblind notions were being put to the test. No matter what I said or did, I knew Rachel would doubt my sincerity. Perhaps she would have good reason to doubt them. As much as I tried to ignore what I had just learned, it was impossible to not be affected in ways even now I cannot define. I would be lying if I said anything different.

What I did know is that at my core, my emotional connection to Rachel had not changed. If anything, I felt even closer to her, in an indefinable way. What I did not want to feel was benevolent. I do not feel I did. That was a worry for me. It is often too easy for well-meaning whites to appoint themselves caretakers for nonwhites whose situations we empathize with.

"I think we should go now," she said, turning and starting back for the truck. I ran to catch up to her, jumping quickly in front and grasping both her arms.

"Why?" I asked.

"It's getting late."

"What? And miss a gorgeous sunset two days in a row? No way," I said, guiding her back to the shore's edge. She offered no resistance. Still, the atmosphere had clearly changed. She had changed. Had I? In my mind, I cursed both her damn secret and her need for it.

The sunset was almost as beautiful as it had been the day before. While we watched, I told Rachel all about the colorful history associated with Crawford Lake, about our secret pier on the other side, about fishing there as a kid and skipping rocks in the summertime. All the while I wondered if I was telling her all this in an effort to downplay what she had just told me. At the same time, I wondered if she was thinking the same thing. I went on.

I even shared with Rachel the thinking process I had gone through, before deciding to leave New York; of my having left to go looking for the summer, whatever that meant. We spoke often of our Crawford high experience. I revealed my longing for those wonderful carefree days of long ago. Rachel acknowledged that she too, was searching; she was searching for herself, for real love, for a family she could at long last call her own. I felt deeply moved.

I gazed at her unabashedly and saw the sun's final glow reflected in her face—in her eyes. I felt drawn to her and leaned over to kiss her. She turned away. I did not pursue. Rachel turned slowly back to me. I kissed her and held her tightly in my arms. Her response was somewhat reserved and unsure, but I understood that. I could not blame her.

Many, many years, and countless sunsets earlier, I could only have dreamed of being alone with Rachel. Now, here we were, accompanied only by sun-soaked clouds, a sinking sun, and a caressing wind. Rachel's arresting aroma filled my nostrils and I held her even closer to me.

Still, I could not shut out the knowledge of what she had just confided in me. I regretted her having told me this secret, though not because it affected my feelings for her. I felt strongly that it erected a barrier in her mind. I could see it in her eyes, hear it in her voice. The most difficult thing was there was nothing I could do about that.

We remained at the lake, until the sun disappeared. Only a faint orange and red glow remained. The air-cooled considerably, the sky darkened, and we soon began hearing night sounds all around us. Moments later, we both fixed our sights on the moon, pointing it out almost simultaneously. That brought a brief smile to Rachel's lips.

At that instant, in that place, it seemed either the whole world was at peace and in harmony with itself, or civilization had vanished. Only we remained. Either scenario was okay with me. This was what I had missed all those years. Or was it?

Many times, I had longed to be some place where nothing was demanded of me except silence and my simply being. I felt that here. I was sure Rachel felt the same way. All around us was an enveloping quiet that seemed to demand reverence. I turned to face Rachel and observed the faint moon-glow on her face and in her eyes.

"I've never seen you in moonlight," I whispered. She smiled and looked away briefly.

"That's true," she said, glancing skyward again. "It seems so...far away, yet so close." I nodded agreement and stepped closer to her.

"Right now, you seem that way to me. You seem so close, still so far away. Seeing you here is the best of my dreams come true. I mean that."

"James..."

"It's true."

"James, it's been...at least twenty years. How could I have remained more than just a... a faint recollection in your mind? I know who you are, what you do, how..."

"Don't say it," I interrupted. This was not one of those times I needed reminding of who I was. A long silence followed. We walked a little farther along the lakefront. By then, the full moon was much brighter. Its liquid silver reflection shone on the water.

"It looks so dreamlike," Rachel observed. I agreed. Looking out over the lake, it was hard to imagine there was even a tinge of sadness and pain anywhere in the world. I could even imagine my father was still with us. I allowed myself to imagine he would be waiting when we returned to the house. What would he say? What would I say to him? I had no answer.

Even as these thoughts cascaded through my mind, the echo of what Rachel had revealed earlier kept reverberating in my head. It produced a strange cacophony. Despite all my efforts, I could not help seeing her considering what I now knew about the pain she had suffered as a child. I also wondered if that suffering had ever ended. My guess was that it had not.

We arrived back at the house. Rachel stayed only long enough to say her goodbyes and we left. Once we were back at the inn, I repeated my offer to help her conclude her business transactions the next day. She thanked me, but declined, saying that what she had to do should not take long or pose any problems.

I then confessed that the offer of help, while genuine and heartfelt, was also a poorly veiled attempt to insure being able to see her again. Rachel smiled and thanked me for my refreshing honesty. I waited...and waited.

"I want to see you before you leave," I said.

"Why?"

"Because I don't want you to suddenly disappear on me again. Once in a lifetime is enough. Don't you think?" I asked. Rachel placed her hand on mine, leaned over, and kissed me softly on my cheek.

"I hate good-byes," she said, as her probing eyes carefully engaged mine. "I've said too many good-byes. I loathe goodbyes."

"I hate them too. What about tomorrow?" I asked.

Rachel looked away, then back again. "There is only the moment," she said.

"Moment by moment, tomorrow always comes. It always comes." I said, then smiled and made a face.

"I would like to believe that" Rachel answered, fighting off a laugh. "I will promise to write to you at your mother's. Question is, will you write back to me?"

"Sure. I'll write."

"Are you sure? Hardly anyone writes anymore. Everyone wants E-mail," said Rachel.

She was right, but I had plenty of experience writing to her.

"I wrote before," I reminded her. She smiled.

"You did. And I still have all your letters," she said. Rachel's revelation set me on my heels.

"You what?"

"I still have your letters—all of them."

"Then, you did get them."

"Yes."

"Why didn't you answer?"

"I never answered because there was no way anything could ever have happened between us. I didn't want to invest in impossibilities. But I promise to answer this time."

"What about telephones?" I asked, knowing she was testing me by suggesting we write each other.

"I'll send my telephone number in my answer to your first letter," she smiled.

"Give me your number while you're here. I'll still write to you."

"I believe you. But I will send it to you. Then, I will have no unreasonable expectations of phone calls that may never come. Without any expectations, I'll write you, to see how you're doing. If you choose, you may answer me. Deal?"

"Deal," I agreed.

Having sealed our deal, I escorted Rachel to her room and waited until she opened the door. She turned back to me, and our eyes met. I held her gaze. She looked away briefly then thanked me again for a wonderful day and evening. I expressed my great joy in seeing her and hoped to see her again.

An awkward moment of silence followed. Rachel smiled, said goodnight, planted a quick kiss on my cheek. As she turned away, I caught her hand and drew her close to me. She seemed genuinely surprised but offered no resistance.

I kissed her firmly and held her close to me. I felt her arms tighten around my waist and heard a soft moan escape her lips. We stood there, locked in a quiet embrace for the longest time. Even so, I kept wondering if I really wanted more.

Finally, Rachel took a step back, peered deeply into my eyes. She had a look that suggested there was much she wanted to say. She kissed me gently on the cheek, then opened her door.

I wanted her to invite me inside. Even after the door closed shut, I stood there for several long moments, as if I expected her to open it again, like in the movies. It did not happen. Several times, I started to knock and ask Rachel to let me in. I did not.

Many times since, I have imagined her there, inside the room, standing at the door with one hand gripping the knob, ready to open it, should I have knocked. However, I did not knock. Instead, with great reluctance, I turned and walked away. Only once did I glance back over my shoulder. The moment still lives with me.

Chapter Thirty

Serenade Highway

I did not see Rachel the day she left Rosedale.

At 11:30, Monday morning, following a brief meeting with my contractor, I called the Inn. The clerk said she had checked out but had left something for me.

"Damn!" I muttered, disappointed with myself for not contacting her earlier, as I had considered. Again, Rachel was gone, and I felt empty inside. It was Deja vu.

I drove over quickly, roared to a stop outside the hotel and raced inside. The desk clerk handed me a white envelope. Inside was a short, fragrance-laced, handwritten note that read:

"Dear James: Thanks for being a wonderful friend and for having created so many precious memories that will last me a lifetime. I treasure all those moments we've spent together over the past couple of days. May God bless you and your family. I will value our friendship as long as I live."

—Rachel.

I sat outside in the car reading the note over and over, trying to determine if it meant good-bye forever or good-bye, for now. I would have to wait for the answer to that question.

Later that night, I told Alise virtually everything about my seeing Rachel. She already knew about our friendship in high school and her having left so suddenly, back then.

Someone reading this may think me nuts for telling her, but she deserved to know. We had promised to always be honest with each other and I had always tried to do that. I valued our relationship very much and could do no less.

I prepared myself for a thousand questions from Alise. They did not come. She asked me to describe how Rachel looked after all these years. I did. I admit I probably provided a description slightly less glowing than the reality, but I tried.

Alise wanted to know how I felt about meeting Rachel again. I told her the truth—that I was not sure. All I knew was that I felt attracted to her. I assured her I had not acted on that attraction, although the thought had crossed my mind.

After a long silence, Alise said she would have been surprised if I had not thought about it and heartbroken if I had acted upon it. I also knew our relationship would have been history. Alise understood and candidly admitted to passing by men every day and wondering how they would be in bed.

After that confession, there was an even longer silence. My first thought was that her comment was reactionary. This was an admission I had not heard her make before. It never occurred to me those thoughts ever crossed her mind. I know that sounds chauvinistic, but it is true. Now I was being the silent one. Alise tapped the phone with her finger.

"Anybody there?"

"I'm here," I said.

"Good. I thought we had been disconnected."

Later, Alise admitted she was only half-joking by her last comment. She amended it to say she only had those thoughts about men she knew. I did not laugh. It was not funny. However, she had made her point.

Mercifully, the subject changed. We talked at length about the upcoming weekend's festivities, which were fast approaching. We talked, until Alise's voice began breaking up again. At my insistence, we finally said goodnight.

During our conversation, I did not tell Alise about Rachel's startling revelation. The words just would not come out. Even as we spoke, I thought about it and even started to tell her but backed away. Why?

On Tuesday morning, Carter, Rosie, and I trekked out to the southwest fields, reaching Carter Oak well before 9 am. We had convinced mother to let us prepare breakfast for her for a change. She gave in, reluctantly. I must say Rosie did most of the cooking, although we were all equally willing, if not equally gifted helpers.

Elizabeth and William remained at home. Robert and Robbie were still fast asleep. I could tell that Robert, Sr. was becoming slightly stir-crazy. He had taken to working on his portable computer several hours each day. I suggested we awaken him and invite him to join us. Rosie quickly nixed the idea.

The three of us had not had an opportunity to talk since the funeral and this place offered the most gorgeous setting possible. Bluebonnets and sunflowers appeared everywhere, arrayed like a blanket stretching as far as the eye could see.

Our discussion centered on mother and speculation about how she would fare without father. There was obviously no way to know for sure. We all agreed time would provide the answer. We would provide the love, support, and attention. Rosie promised to try and get mother to spend some time with her in Dallas. Neither of us held out hope that would happen. Then again, mother could be full of surprises, when she wanted to be.

We all remembered the time she accompanied Mrs. Strunk, Moose's mother, on a Saturday drive to Waco. The two simply wanted to get away for a while and see some place with real traffic signals. I was no more than 8 years old, at the time. The three of us were at the church that morning, participating in a Saturday morning grounds cleanup. Mother and Mrs. Strunk were only gone for a half day or less, but father was fit to be tied.

As it turned out, mother had not told father where she was going. Unable to find her, he became very upset with her. She insisted she had left him a note when she was unable to find him. It so happened, father had gone into town to the hardware store and had not told mother. Mrs. Strunk stopped by, and mother agreed to accompany her to Waco. It was most unusual for mother to act so impulsively, but she did it anyway.

When she returned, father gave her a piece of his mind. It was the only time I can really remember the two of them arguing. Well, it was not really arguing. Father was doing most of the talking. Mother just listened for a while, anyway. Father shooed us out of the living room, but we remained in adjoining rooms with our ears pressed firmly against the walls.

Father said his unannounced trip to town should not be compared to mother's traveling to Waco. Even then, that argument seemed to be a distinction without a difference. However, father said it with such authority and conviction, it had to merit acceptance. Mother had only one thing to say:

"John, you only have three children: two sons and a daughter I am not your fourth child." She then stalked out of the room and never said another word on the subject.

That was the strongest show of independence I saw mother demonstrate. In many ways, it was very much out of character for her. On the other hand, it was the true expression of her suppressed character—her too often subjugated personality.

We were all very proud of her, though we made no open expressions of that sentiment. We just looked at each other with raised eyebrows and widened eyes. Even at 8 years old, I knew what was fair and what was not. Besides, I did not like father shouting at my mother.

Before we concluded our sibling discussion, we agreed to make household help available to mother on a permanent basis, whether she wanted it or not. Mother had clearly grown accustomed to having the assistance. However, she was subject to change her mind without official notice to anyone.

There was the strong likelihood she would want to return to being the master of her own house, especially her kitchen. Deep inside, mother never became fond of having someone else piddling around in her kitchen.

We agreed to try to persuade her to travel, since she had always expressed a desire to do so. Rosie pointed out that mother's desire to travel had been predicated on father traveling with her. She was probably right. One thing was certain. Mother would have whatever she needed and wanted, whenever she needed or wanted it. If it were possible to spoil her, she would be spoiled. We all had high expectations she could be persuaded to give in. Only time would tell.

Friday morning came much sooner than any of us expected. The ballpark was finally ready for its grand unveiling. Every detail had been attended to with great precision. Amazingly, there had been no delays. The around-the clock construction schedule had been grueling, but well worth the additional cost.

Taking care not to tread on the baselines, I strolled onto the infield, out to the edge of the pitcher's mound and stood in awe. It was beautiful—absolutely beautiful. Even a non-baseball fan could not have denied being impressed. I wished my father could have seen it.

The skies were a hazy blue and the temperature had fallen to the low eighties. Everyone was hoping the weather for Saturday would be just as gorgeous. The weatherman was promising it would be, but we all knew the reality of Texas weather. There was an old Texas saying that; if you do not like the weather, just wait a minute or two. The weather was sure to change, and sometimes very fast and dramatically.

I walked over almost every square inch of the field that day, more than once. I found myself reliving the memory of all the glorious times I spent there at practice, enjoying those heart-pounding game days.

I remembered Mr. McCloud gathering us all around home plate after each game. He would tell us that whether we won or lost, if we had done our very best, he wanted us to leave the park with our heads held high. As I looked around the park, I could not help remembering all my Dodger teammates: Peetie, Jed, Duncan, Twenty-one Smith.

Twenty-one Smith. We actually had a player named Twenty-one Smith. I swear! We called him Smitty. Twenty-one took well to his name. What he did not like was kids calling him Smitty. Only his very best friends could call him that. He was a big kid, strong as an ox and occasionally temperamental. No one teased him. Smitty was the last of his parents' twenty-one kids.

Word was, after kid number 20, the Smiths ran out of names they liked. When Smitty was born, they named him *Twenty-one.* It was to have been only temporary. However, on the day his mom was released from the hospital, they had decided to leave his name as it was. I suppose such a thing could only happen in Texas. By the way, Smitty was a fantastic southpaw pitcher. I understand he owns a construction company in Baytown, just east of Houston.

Instead of driving straight back to the farm, I drove for miles down beautiful Serenade Highway. Every town, every city, every place should have a Serenade Highway. There should be a national law requiring it.

Although it is too narrow to officially to be considered a highway, no one cares. It goes nowhere, yet it goes somewhere very special. Serenade Highway is open only to residents of an area of Rosedale that includes our farm and about a dozen more parcels of property. The very complicated reasons for that, stipulated in specific land deeds, dates to the mid 1800's.

There is a posting at the turnoff onto the highway that says: Person's Caught Using This Highway Illegally, May Be Subject to A $25 Fine (big bucks back in the 1800's) And 30 Days in Jail—still significant today.

Serenade Highway is a beautiful, twelve-mile, tree-lined road which snakes its way through breathtaking countryside to within a mile of U.S. 71. It then loops back onto itself. Trees on either side are home to thousands of serenading birds. Fortunately for one's ear, they disperse themselves well, along the entire route.

If you roll down your windows and drive slowly, you will hear the serenade every mile of the way and back again. It is an experience that is truly unique—almost ethereal. You feel as if you have entered another world.

The moment you turn onto the roadway, the first thing you notice is that it is quite narrow. Two cars can pass each other, but not without both using a portion of either shoulder.

The next thing you're aware of is a tunnel of shade that produces a noticeable drop in temperature. That is because these majestic oak trees on both sides of the road provide a canopy. Rays of sunshine create beautiful streams of light that cascade through the branches and crisscross the roadway.

I drove slowly, listening intently to nature's endless concerto. I could suddenly feel the stress; the pain, the crushing weight of all that had happened, magically peeling away from me. It was almost a feeling of rebirth.

Only a few minutes en route, I pulled to the right shoulder, stopped, and exited the car. I walked ahead a few yards, stood still, and closed my eyes. I imagined I was the only person in the entire world. Here, I felt free to think. The place seemed like an open-air cathedral. It was like nature's cathedral and the choir was in great form that day.

An hour later, I reached the loop and pulled off the roadway. It was so quiet and peaceful. All I could hear were the sounds of birds singing and the grass growing. A cornucopia of natural fragrances abounded. I sat there mesmerized by my surroundings. After pausing to take in the beauty of all those flowers covering the sloping hills beyond U.S. 71, I began my drive back.

For some reason, retracing my route was not a replay of the drive out, as one might expect. Instead, it was a new experience in itself. The feel was just as wonderful but quite different. Perhaps it was the way the sunlight came through the trees. Maybe it was because during the return trip, the different time of day cast a new light upon everything. I reached my starting point, eased to a stop, considered repeating the trip, but resisted the temptation.

Friday night was filled with great anticipation and raw excitement about what Saturday would bring. Following dinner, I noticed mother had slipped away. I found her sitting in her bedroom browsing through old photo albums.

At first, I considered joining her then opted not to. I felt it best to leave her alone with her thoughts, her photos—the memories. It was important she begin to come to grips with her new realities in her own way. What I did not want to do was smother her. So, I closed the door and rejoined the others.

The rest of the night found Carter, Rosie and me swapping childhood stories, and discovering we all had varying memories of some of the more embarrassing moments. Nothing unusual about that, I dare say. One of the more embarrassing stories involved me. Carter's version was not as I remembered, although it was substantially correct. What happened was this.

When I was in junior high and high school, I earned quite a reputation for being fleet of foot, (as well as a brilliant student, I might add). Almost every day at noon, several of us boys would race each other, beginning at the door exiting the main building. We would dash across open ground, behind the rear of the cafeteria to the side door leading inside the cafeteria. The total distance was roughly two hundred-fifty yards or so.

On this ill-fated day, all the sprinters stood just outside the main building's rear exit. Someone yelled "Go!" and the race was on. We all streaked across the yard and into the open field like a herd of gazelles. I took the lead.

I confess I had a unique running style. I ran with my head tilted back. I do not know why, but I did. I seemed to generate more speed that way. The only problem was that running style tended to cause me to squint my eyes. Not a good technique at all. It was also quite dangerous. The course led between two buildings that were not very far apart—the cafeteria and the combination Wood Shop and Music building.

I was in the lead by a good three strides, as we neared the cafeteria and the other buildings. My head was thrown back, and my arms and legs were pumping like well-tuned pistons. I had just blasted through the breezeway, with my mind flush with the thought of declaring victory and retaining my crown, when I descended into the bowels of purgatory.

Suddenly, near-tragedy befell me. In the words of Moose Strunk, who was in second place, I disappeared off the radar screen.

I was there one second, then I was not. What happened was an embarrassment I have not outlived to this day.

Just as I was halfway through the breezeway, I decided to split a pillar by darting to the right of it. I then ran right past the back door of the cafeteria, which landed me chest deep into its grease and slop pit. The cast-iron cover should have been over the hole, but it was not. Were that to happen to some kid today, the school would be in serious legal trouble.

Anyway, the only thing that saved my butt from going under was the fact my elbows held me up on both sides. The result of this embarrassing experience was lasting humiliation. The next thing I knew, a huge crowd of giggling morons gathered around me and stood watching me as I struggled to climb out.

Finally, I saw Carter wading through the crowd and fighting to get to me. He and another boy pulled me out. I stood there covered in slop and grease, feeling like a complete idiot.

I skipped lunch that day, having been summoned to the boy's locker room. There, I had to hear it from the coach who was not at all angry. I would have preferred he had been. Instead, he and his staff laughed their fool heads off. I stood there with my legs spread apart, my arms held out like wings—slop and grease dripping. They all laughed.

Presented the option of going home and facing father right away or wearing gym clothes the rest of the day, I chose the latter.

Carter and I differed on this story. He claimed I fell all the way down in the pit. He says slop was up to my chin. I disagreed.

I distinctly remembered being saved by my elbows. They supported me, until Carter pulled me out. Either way, that experience ended my participation in the Great Noon Day Races forever.

After we'd exchanged stories and arguments to the point of insanity, I tried reaching Alise. I called her a half dozen times and got no answer. The last time, I left her a message stating I would call before leaving for the park next morning.

I tried not to worry. Alise was a big girl quite capable of taking care of herself. More than likely she had gone to one of those parties her publisher was so fond of throwing. With that comforting thought, I went to bed.

Sleep did not come easily that night. I lay awake until almost two in the morning, staring up at the ceiling and listening to crickets chirping outside my window. While these little creatures were annoying, I was thankful I did not have to cope with those demons of summer nights—mosquitoes.

I remained deeply concerned about Alise, and I was also experiencing butterflies about the big day. I even went through dress rehearsal, in my mind, trying to assure myself all would go according to plan.

Fitful sleep resulted in my pounding the pillow into at least a hundred configurations. I doubt I remained in one position for more than five minutes. Finally, I got up, retrieved my Willie Mays glove from the dresser, tucked it under my pillow, and fell fast asleep. Some things never change.

Thirty-one

Day of Honor

The big day arrived with the breathtaking sight of a big orange sun rising majestically, amidst scattered cumulus clouds, nestled in a sea blue sky. It was a day made for baseball; a day made for a family gathering; a day made for fond remembrances and a day of honor.

The Phalen clan enjoyed a big, wonderful breakfast, got dressed for the day's events and gathered in the living room. Mother looked sensational in her white denim, designer, pantsuit. She wore a red rose in the jacket lapel and even wore a pair of white Reeboks.

It was the first time I had seen her dressed so...so hip. Rosie helped her with makeup and styled her hair beautifully. The transformation amazed us all. Mother was naturally beautiful, but now she looked youthful and alive. She was like a woman with more living in front of her than behind her. Just looking at her made me feel twenty years younger.

I insisted on taking pictures and video as well. I gathered everyone for a portrait in front of the fireplace, then ushered them all out onto the front porch. There, the photo session continued. Rosie kept glancing at her watch and trying to keep us all on schedule as best she could. Her experience as an elementary school teacher came in handy.

At 10am, we arrived at the Rosedale Town Hall, to the applause of hundreds already gathered. A milling horde of press greeted us.

We resigned ourselves to tolerating all the close attention as best we could.

The minute we exited our vehicles, escorts quickly guided us inside and offered us a delicious-looking breakfast. We were all too stuffed to eat. However, Robbie and William managed to down most of a shared cinnamon roll and half a glass of milk, within a span of about ten minutes. Mother was afraid they would get stomachaches by forcing themselves to eat so quickly. They did not.

A short time later, we walked out the rear exit into the courtyard where parade vehicles and designated drivers were waiting. These cars were all gorgeous vintage motorcars; the likes of which I had seen only at vintage car shows. I resisted the temptation to make an offer to buy several. It was difficult.

Once we took our seats in the cars, the other parade participants including the high school band, the DAR, the VFW, local merchants' entries, the mayor's car and others positioned themselves behind us. It was time to go.

Banners draped over the car doors proclaimed it John Q. Phalen Day. It was a proud moment for all of us. After a couple of false starts, the band finally struck up. The parade officially began with the release of hundreds of balloons outfitted with colorful streamers.

The lengthy procession—with mother and me in the rear seat, and the mayor in the front seat of the lead car— majestically wound its way down Rosedale's brightly festooned Main Street. The sustained cheers and roar of the crowd, lining both sides of the street and numbering more than Rosedale's population of 11,126, grew ever louder.

It was an exciting, colorful, and wonderful parade. And I have seen my share of parades. Banners and streamers decorated stores, small shops, restaurant facades, and even trees. There was nothing like a parade involving the entire town, to bring out the best in people. The thrill of seeing my father honored in such a public way was overwhelming for all of us.

When we reached the sparkling new John Q. Phalen Park, a boisterous crowd of over 3,500 people, already in the bleachers and cheering wildly, greeted us. Once all the parade entries made their way into the parking area, the band ended their playing with a tumultuous flourish.

We exited the vehicles and were quickly escorted into the park by the honor guard. Another wave of applause erupted. Soon, the 8,500-seat facility filled to overflowing amidst a 4th of July atmosphere. Everyone was caught up in the excitement. There was no way to escape the contagion.

Ushers took us to our reserved seats a couple of rows up, just behind and to the first base side of home plate. The crowd, now swollen to standing room only, cheered as the teams completed warm-ups and returned to their respective dugouts. You could feel the electricity in the air and knew this was a very special moment, a very special place.

I kept focusing on my mother. We had never seen her so excited, so alive. Her eyes danced and sparkled. She was looking all around, enjoying herself, taking it all in. I knew she had to be wishing my father was there with her. Perhaps he was.

While we waited for the opening ceremonies to begin, I reached inside my fanny pack and removed the small box containing my treasured ticket to the opening game of the 1955 World Series. I well-remembered J.J. telling me the ticket would cause something very special to happen to me someday. Perhaps it would bring our Rosedale Dodgers a bit of good luck.

As far as I was concerned, something special had already happened. There I was with my wonderful family, in an honored place—the hallowed ballpark where I had known my greatest childhood triumph, a place now named in honor of my father. What could be more special? Nothing.

We were now only minutes away from the opening ceremonies. Before they could begin, however, there was just one more item awaiting installation in the new park.

The public address announcer asked for everyone's attention and had the crowd stand. They complied. A short distance away, a young man approached our seats carrying a velvet pouch. Mother and the others looked at me curiously. I looked away, pretending not to notice them.

The kid stood next to mother and removed a solid brass plate, with father's name inscribed on it in bas-relief. While the announcer informed the crowd of what was taking place, the young craftsman, who had designed and made the plaque, carefully attached it onto a section of bleacher next to mother. When he had finished, he embraced her. We were all a little teary-eyed.

I stood there, remembering all the baseball games I had played, and my custom of selecting a spot in the stands for my father. It was a very emotional moment for me. The crowd applauded, but only Mother, Rose, and Carter knew the deep meaning it held for me. From that moment on, a permanent seat would be reserved for my father.

After the playing of the Star-Spangled Banner, by the band, the starting lineups for the Rosedale Dodgers and the Waco Giants were announced. The teams took their positions along the first and third base lines. The crowd cheered the announcement of both teams with equal enthusiasm. Of course, as the game progressed that was bound to change. And it did.

Then, to mother's total surprise, I took her hand, had her stand, and escorted her down onto the field to throw out the ceremonial first pitch. She was thoroughly outdone but could not back out. There was nowhere for her to hide. Everyone looked on, as cameras whirred.

I gave mother the new baseball, returned to home plate and donned a catcher's mitt. Returning to my place behind home plate, I knelt, ignoring my creaking knee joints and a very audible grunt. Looking out toward the mound, I flashed mother a couple of quick signs, which she never saw. Even if she had, she would not have known what they were.

With the urging of the crowd, mother took her version of a pitcher's windup and fired her imitation of a fastball. It reached me in only two bounces. Raucous cheers went up.

Grinning ear to ear, mother threw both arms straight into the air in triumph and started toward me. You would have sworn she had just heaved a 100-mile an hour, Nolan Ryan fastball. I dropped the mitt, winced in mock pain, and started toward her. I gave her a big hug and she slipped her arm underneath mine. The deafening applause matched the pounding of both our hearts, as I escorted her back to our seats.

With the ceremonies now completed, the Dodgers took the field to the cheers of a standing crowd. It was a proud moment for all of Rosedale. Whether they would play well or not, the kids looked fantastic in their new uniforms. After all the rigorous preparation, the game was on.

However, there was still one more surprise in store for everyone. The crowd gasped, when 10-year-old Ellen Parker headed for the pitcher's mound, with her braided ponytail bouncing in the breeze. You could feel and hear the ripple that raced through the entire park.

I looked over at Rosie. She looked at me and gave me a thumb's up and a wide grin. Seconds later, I heard a disparaging male voice a few rows back.

"Oh, my god," he said. "I thought we were playing to win." I wanted to turn around and confront him but elected not to. I also observed several players on the opposing team point toward the mound and laugh derisively. We all said a prayer for Ellen and hoped she was up to the task before her.

Ellen Parker was one of those rare, fiercely competitive kids who had no idea what self-doubt was. Already she had overcome the skepticism of the boys on her own team, as well as the poorly disguised doubts of some of the team coaches. She seemed unaffected outwardly but had to be affected inside. Just how much all this would bother her would be known very soon.

We did not have long to wait. The final strains of the Star-Spangled Banner had barely died down when Ellen peered in for her sign. Her calm demeanor belied any nervousness she may have felt. All eyes were on her. Some were no doubt hoping she would fail.

Ellen sailed her first three pitches past the leadoff hitter for called strikes. That was just the beginning. She went on to strike out the first six batters she faced and blazed into the top of the third inning with a shutout and a no-hitter going for her. It was unbelievable. Rosedale fans were as stunned as the opposing hitters.

The jeering from the opposing sidelines had long since stopped. I heard no more derisive comments from those in the crowd either. Instead, the crowd was chanting Ellen's name and cheering her on with every pitch.

I do not think any of us had dared dream things would start out this way. Through it all, Ellen's facial expression remained constant and unemotional. She was out there taking care of business and she knew it; never doubting herself for a moment. The rest of the Dodgers were playing a fantastic game as well. So far, our defense had performed superbly. I nevertheless had an apple-sized lump in my throat.

I watched a little black kid, Kenny, playing third base for us. This youngster reminded me so much of myself. Kenny appeared to be about the same size as I was at nine and was bouncing up and down on his toes, waiting for the ball to come his way.

During the throw-arounds, I noticed it took all Kenny could muster, to get the ball to first base, but he got it there every time and right on the money. That was I at the age of nine, in every detail. I would have preferred he play shortstop, but I was not the manager.

We were all frankly amazed at how well our kids were playing against the more experienced Waco kids. Through the first three innings, the game was scoreless. The Dodgers had three hits, although no runner had gotten past second base. It was a pitcher's duel all the way. Ellen was taking her time and being careful not to overthrow. She was pacing herself and staying well within her capabilities.

Looking at this game was pure excitement for me and was full of wonderful recollections. This was what real baseball was supposed to be about. As I looked around the field and up and down the benches, I could see kids of every shape and description. These were all just kids with a real love for the game and a desire to just play. It was fantastic.

I was told that in the fourth inning, the Giants finally scored the game's first run. It was on a full count—three balls, two strikes, two-out pitch with a runner on second. He had made it there by virtue of a walk and a pitch that got away from the catcher.

The next hitter slammed a hard double to straight away center, scoring the first runner. He later died on second base, when Ellen struck out the next batter. We were behind now, but she still had one-hitter going. There was still time to pull the game out.

I had to be told all this later, because somewhere between the top of the fourth and the bottom of the fifth innings, something happened to me that defies all logical explanation. I am even hesitant to mention it here, for fear of being discounted as a nut.

While I sat watching the game and munching on a hot dog, I was suddenly whisked back to the summer of '62. It was no longer 1994. For a brief period, I was nine years old again and being ordered into the game by Mr. McCloud, just as I had all those years ago.

There I was, taking to the field, almost tripping over that very same blade of grass. The palpable excitement I felt was causing my heart to punch a hole in my chest. The pulsing sound beat in my ears like a big bass drum.

As before, I stood at third base, pounding my glove, bouncing on my toes, waiting for the ball to come, and come it did. Just as before, I was unable to field it and it streaked between my legs into left field. The crowd yelled. I knew I had blown the game and the rest of my life too.

I wheeled around and darted into short left field as fast as my little spindly legs could carry me. Everything that followed was exactly as it had happened on that magical summer day in 1962. I cocked my right arm and fired a rifle shot to second base.

Only seconds before a runner slid into home plate, the second baseman took the throw and applied the tag to the runner sliding into the base. The game was over! We had won! I was a hero! Once again, my jubilant teammates buried me underneath their human pile. Again, I crawled out and stood there beaming with pride, admiring my thoroughly dirty uniform.

With my chest exploding with joy, I glanced up into the bleachers and saw Carter, Rosie, mother, and… my father? My father was there! He had seen the whole thing and was jumping up and down just like the others. I could see a wide grin on his face. I saw him turn to the man standing next to him.

"That's my boy down there," he said, boasting. "That's my kid who made that play. That's my kid right there!" He was proud of me. My father was proud of me. I heard him say the words. I was far away from where he stood cheering, but I heard him as clearly as if I were standing next to him. He was there!

So consumed was I by what I was experiencing, I had not heard Carter yelling out to me excitedly. When I realized what was going on, the hotdog was at my feet, and I was probably the only one still seated. I looked up at Carter and asked him what was going on.

"Fantastic! Amazing!" He yelled. "That little kid playing third base just hit a two-run homer."

I heard him, sure enough, but I was not certain I heard right. He was referring to Kenny. I bounded to my feet in time to see this half-pint rounding third and heading for home. All his teammates were waiting there with high fives and pats on the back. My chest swelled.

I knew exactly what that kid was feeling. I knew that regardless of the outcome of the game, he would treasure what had just happened to him for the rest of his life. I prayed his father was there, watching.

Now all Ellen and the Dodgers had to do was hold the line and get the Giants out in the top of the sixth. It sounded easy enough, but reality was another thing. These kids from Waco had not earned their reputation by rolling over and playing dead. This game was not over.

The sixth inning started off with a walk on four straight balls. Ellen, still under the 75-pitch limit, appeared to be tiring a bit. It was only a matter of whether or not she had enough steam left to hold on. We had a tough hurler up in the bullpen, but everyone was hoping Ellen could finish the game.

With nothing to lose, the Giants manager had the first base runner bouncing up and down on the base pad. He was clearly hoping Ellen would be distracted. She did her best to ignore him.

The next batter was a very short, stocky, right-handed kid who offered Ellen a very compact strike zone. On top of that, he was crowding the plate. The runner took his lead again. The Dodgers' manager brought the infield well-in onto the grass. The outfield was also waved in closer.

On the very first pitch, the batter grimaced and took a healthy swing. "Strike!" Bellowed the home plate umpire. The infield was immediately moved back to the edge of the grass. The batter was swinging away. I did not think moving the infield back was a good move, but I was not managing.

We awaited the no-balls, one-strike pitch. Seeing the infield back and a hit and run on, the runner squared around and laid down a perfect bunt down the third baseline. Everyone appeared safe. My thinking was vindicated. Small comfort for me. However, the third baseman charged in hard, grabbed the ball, and threw to first base, just nabbing the runner.

The first base runner advanced. Now there was one out, one on second. Up stepped the Giant's strongest batter and hardest kid to get out, a big lefthander they called 'Brute.' The Dodger pitching coach called time and trotted out to the mound. I could tell he was seriously thinking of relieving Ellen. She was breathing hard, and the velocity of her pitches had clearly fallen off. I could see her pleading with the coach to keep her in the game.

The coach relented and Ellen's face showed renewed resolve. The umpire broke up the meeting on the mound and the game resumed. The time-out had bought Ellen some much-needed time to catch her breath. She took her time, gazing in for her sign and going into her windup.

The first pitch to 'Brute' brought everyone in the park to his or her feet. He got around on a high fastball and tagged it solidly. The ball sailed high and deep toward right field. The outfielder streaked toward the right-field corner, as the second base runner rounded third and headed home.

The right fielder reached the wall, stared straight up and watched helplessly. The ball was still climbing, as it went over the wall, barely foul. We all fainted a little.

Having escaped that scare, the Dodger manager decided not to take any chances. He had 'Brute' intentionally walked, much to the displeasure of the Giants' fans. It seemed a very smart move, at the time.

Without hesitating, the Giants' manager made his own tactical move. He recalled the right-handed batter waiting on deck and substituted with another lefthander, who looked just as menacing as the Brute.

Ellen had her work cut out for her. If the Dodgers were lucky, she would get the batter to keep the ball in the infield and increase the possibility of a game-ending double play. That was the strategy. However, it was not to be.

The batter swung on the very first pitch and launched a weak fly ball to left field. It was too well hit for the third baseman to reach and too weakly hit for the left fielder to get to in time. With the ball sinking fast, the left fielder wisely played the hop and held the runner to third base. We were in deep doodoo.

Many of the Dodger faithful were now yelling for the manager to yank Ellen. Adults and parents take these kids' games very seriously. Manager Joe Bright removed his cap and scratched his head. I could see the agony in his face, as he stood perched on the steps of the dugout. He was on the verge of adhering to the demands of the crowd. I was hoping he would stand his ground.

Bright started out and toward the home plate umpire to announce a change. My heart dropped. Suddenly, he stopped dead in his tracks and held his ground. He then turned, gazed out toward the mound, and yelled out much-needed encouragement to Ellen.

With sheer grit and determination, Ellen got the next batter to take a called third strike. Dodger fans went hog-wild. Everyone was on his or her feet now, jumping up and down. It was nail-biting time for sure.

The next batter was a big surly, burly kid with considerable girth and forearms the size of my thighs. He was truly huge. It did not look good for us at all. If this youngster could just manage to get the bat around with any speed at all, we were doomed.

The batter quickly got ahead in the count. And as rapidly as you could blink your eyes, it was two balls no strikes. Our catcher walked out to settle Ellen down. Two of the infielders gathered near the mound to cheer her on as well.

When the next pitch, a fastball in the dirt, almost got past the catcher, a collective groan shot up from the Rosedale faithful. The kid did a fantastic job blocking the ball and keeping it from going to the backstop. Had he not done so, the third base runner would have scored, and the other runners would have all moved up for sure.

Disappointed with herself, Ellen shook her head and stepped off the mound. She stared at the runners then stepped back on the mound. Ellen shook off the next three signs, before accepting the fourth. Her jaws clenched. She grimaced.

Everyone in the park held his or her breaths. You could almost hear heartbeats. Ellen summoned all her remaining strength and went into her windup. She uncorked her best pitch. Everything seemed to slow to half speed, as the ball streaked toward home plate.

The batter was ready and waiting; his eyes were riveted on the white sphere. He started his bat motion perfectly. The muscles in his forearms rippled. He let out a yelp. In the twinkling of an eye, bat and ball collided with awesome force. The batter crushed the ball solidly, with the part of the bat hitters call the sweet-spot.

The sound of solid wood colliding with ball was resounding. It was explosive. It's what every batter dreams of. I do not know if you have ever played baseball, but when you hit a ball like that, you feel it from your hands all the way down to the bottom of your feet. You want to just stand there and watch it fly.

All runners broke with the pitch, but the hitter barely moved toward first. He just stood there watching the ball, the way Reggie Jackson used to stand there admiring his handiwork. Hardly anyone had any doubt about where this ball was going. The only question was what county it would finally come down in.

We all watched with resignation and sinking hearts, as the towering fly ball headed for straight away center field. Dejected Dodger infielders tossed their gloves to the ground in disappointment. The jubilant Giant dugout emptied onto the sidelines. They were ecstatic, yelling at the top of their lungs and jumping for joy. A five to two score would be very difficult to overcome in a half inning.

With the crack of the bat, the center fielder turned his back and raced toward the wall as fast as he could go. The ball climbed like a Saturn rocket leaving the pad at Cape Canaveral. My heart sank to my Reeboks.

The poor outfielder looked over his shoulder briefly and kept running as fast as his legs could carry him. I saw him reach the warning track still going full speed with his head strained skyward. I knew he was headed for a crash. We had padded the walls and hopefully the kid would suffer no injury.

The ball just kept sailing. The kid reached the wall and never slowed—his legs churning so, his feet landed halfway up the wall. With his glove handheld high over his head, his free hand grabbed for the wall.

In one fluid motion, he yanked himself upward with half his small body extending above the wall and his back turned to the infield. With breaths held, we watched in awe and disbelief. As improbable as it sounds, the kid did the impossible. He leaped skyward and snared the ball. Miraculously, it landed only partially in the webbing of his glove—a *snow cone.*

I could not believe it. No one could believe it. He teetered on the verge of falling over the wall for a second, then fell at least 6 feet backwards onto his back, with the glove still held high. Just then, the ball began to tumble out. The tumultuous crowd noise was unbearable, the bleachers rocked. It seemed we were in the middle of a 7.0 quake.

From where I stood, I could see the ball fall out of the glove and onto the kid's chest. My gut was churning, and I was not alone. At the last instant, he reached for the ball. Miraculously, he managed to grab it with his free hand, just before it rolled from his chest to the ground.

The umpire, who had dashed toward the outfield, had a great view and signaled a good catch. Phalen Park erupted all over again. The little guy jumped to his feet, with the ball held high and made a mad dash toward the infield. The tumult rose. He kept running, as the crowd cheered him on.

The kid ran and ran. He reached second base and kept on running. He reached the pitcher's mound and continued running. He ran until he reached home plate. There he stepped on the plate and jumped up and down repeatedly. The entire Dodger team immediately joined him.

Even the manager and coaches joined him around the plate. It was an amazing sight to see. He had made a truly impossible catch reminiscent of my hero, the great Willie Mays. If I had not been there and seen the play for myself, I would never have believed it. I was there and I still found it hard to believe.

I know it is cliché, but words are totally inadequate to describe what we witnessed that day. Nothing I could say here can possibly explain what it felt like to be there. You will have to imagine what it was like to witness such heroics by a bunch of kids full of heart and determination. They all played like champions.

The game was over. The Dodgers had won. The crowd went insane. Bedlam reigned. We were just standing there, letting it all sink in. The cheering seemed to go on forever. After an interminable period of celebration and restoration of modest order, each team lined up on the first and third base lines. Each player shook hands with members of the opposing team. Afterwards, every player and coaches on both teams were presented a commemorative baseball bearing a special inscription engraved on it.

It was decided that instead of naming one Dodger the game's most valuable player, every Dodger player would be named most valuable player. That meant we would have to purchase and inscribe more trophies, but no one was going to object to that.

Before the players left the field, the crowd gave both teams a standing ovation. They truly deserved it. What each of these kids took away was the memory of a baseball game they would be talking about in Rosedale and Waco for a long time.

A half hour later, several hundred people remained in the bleachers. Many found it difficult to leave. I was one of the many who just wanted to sit there and let it all soak in. There was no reason to hurry. There was no place else to be that would have been half as exciting.

An hour later, only a dozen persons, including a couple of media people, remained in the park. Carter, Rosie, and the others had taken mother home. I had promised to arrive in time for dinner. I found it impossible to leave immediately.

Still later, I realized I was the only one left to savor what had happened that day at Phalen Park. I walked down to the infield and stood on the mound clutching one of the commemorative balls. I turned a full three-sixty, to take in the view around me.

It was almost five o'clock and the sun was still beating down. I stepped onto the mound, removed my baseball cap, and wiped my brow. The wind had picked up considerably and was blowing hard toward center field. Thank God it had not been blowing that hard earlier. We would likely have had a different outcome.

I stared toward home plate, assumed a pitching stance, and peered in for my sign. Just as I went into my windup, I caught a glimpse of someone dressed in white, seated high in the bleachers on the first base side behind the backstop. I assumed it was someone who, like me, still found it hard to leave the park.

I resumed my windup and fired a high fastball. It streaked toward home plate then disappeared. The ball simply disappeared. I do not mean this figuratively; I mean it literally. The ball just disappeared. There is no other way to say it. I stood there on the mound and watched with my mouth open. From where I stood, I could see the ball was nowhere in sight.

I fully understand the inference of what I am writing. I know it may cause many raised eyebrows. Nevertheless, I know what happened. I released the ball, watched as it reached home plate and immediately lost sight of it. It did not land on the ground, and it never reached the backstop. I would have heard it crash into the chain link fence and fall to the ground. It did not.

A minute later, I trotted toward the plate. The person in the bleachers stood and started down toward the field. The minute I got there I could see the ball was nowhere to be found. I was dumbfounded. There had to be some logical explanation, I thought. There had to be. Things like this do not happen in real life. This was not some Hollywood movie.

I continued to the backstop and searched the entire area to no avail. I walked the complete length of the fence and looked everywhere possible. I carefully examined the fence and found no possible way a ball could have passed through to the other side. There was no baseball to be found. I tried to think about it logically, applying all my rational thinking skills. Nothing.

To this day, all I have is my own private, very personal explanation of what happened. I choose to keep it that way. There is little doubt in my mind and my heart, that for an instant, I was not the only person on that field. It is not important whether anyone else understands this. All that matters is, that I know. The event defies all logic and reason, but it happened.

I had all but given up on my search for the ball, when I turned and saw a very beautiful and familiar face standing at the fence, staring at me. I rubbed my eyes repeatedly, to be sure I was seeing correctly. It was Alise. My jaw dropped. All I could do was stare at her. She seemed an apparition.

"I had to come," she shouted out to me. "I had to."

"Alise!" I called out.

"I love your pitching form," she said.

"What are you doing here? I don't believe this!"

I hurried toward her, reached the backstop on the run. We stood there, kissing through the holes in the fence. It did not take long to figure out there was a much better way to accomplish our goal.

We both made our way to the end of the fence and stood kissing and embracing each other. I was thoroughly stunned. It was so good to see her. No wonder I had not been able to reach her on the telephone; she had been en route to Rosedale.

"How long have you been here?" I asked, still absorbing the fact she was actually there in front of me.

"All along," she answered.

"All along?"

"I was the first one here. I saw it all."

"Everything?"

"Everything," Alise said, "including the ball you threw to home plate, just then."

"You saw that?"

"I did," she whispered. "I did. It disappeared. I can't believe it, but I know what I saw. Just when it reached the plate, I didn't see it anymore."

We were both silent for a long moment.

"He was here," I whispered."

"I believe he was here," Alise said. "I do."

She squeezed my hand firmly and smiled through the tears forming in her eyes. I then patted my pocket and removed the object I had placed inside. I raised it to show Alise. It was the box containing the 1955 World Series ticket J.J. had given me. Could what had just happened have been what he had meant?

Alise and I soon lost all track of time. We sat up high in the bleachers, holding hands and watching the sunset. Finally, the park lights came on. All that remained of the sun was a long, red-orange sliver of light stretching forever along the distant horizon.

There were so many things yet to contemplate, so many decisions to be made. However, at that moment, all we wanted to do was simply exist; to simply realize being alive. So, we sat there speaking to each other, even through our silence. I looked at Alise and drew her even closer to me.

Just then, thoughts of Rachel washed over my mind. I could not shut them out. I tried but could not. I felt guilty and squeezed Alise, while whispering her name over and over. Several moments passed. I decided I had no choice but to surrender to whatever thoughts chose to invade my mind.

Alise and I soon found ourselves talking about where our lives would take us from here. I admitted my uncertainties and we agreed to talk about them. All I knew was that the time had come for me and for us to make whatever commitments we were going to make. I was not getting any younger; neither of us was. Before too long, we would both be a half-century old. Unreal! Besides, it was time I finally began dealing with Alise from the top of the deck.

Did I truly love Alise? Did, after all these years, my heart really belong to Rachel or the Rachel I thought I had known? Was I destined to spend the rest of my life lookin' for the Summer—a summer that could never be again? Was there some other voice calling me to move on, to try changing the lives of others for the better? I had to know.

With father gone and mother in her declining years, I felt more connected to this place than ever before. Since leaving Rosedale as a college freshman, I had never lived anywhere that gave me the sense of belonging I realized at that moment.

Still, I felt compelled to move on. Perhaps it was only the wanderer in me. I suppose what I had discovered is that life can never be reduced to searching for a single answer to a single question. I was at last where I had longed to be. Yet, my gaze was still far beyond the next rise—beyond the next turn in the road.

Perhaps my calling was to somehow find all those young faces I had once known and said sad good-byes to on a commencement night long ago. There were promises made then that were yet to be fulfilled. Inside my mind and heart was a longing to bring all the disparate aspects of my life together and make them harmonious. Then again, perhaps all this soul-searching was further evidence of my undying idealism. I would like to think it was my recognition of the brevity of life and the need to make sure my life truly counted for something.

My mind and heart were swirling with questions and very few answers. There were life-altering decisions to be made. On some mornings, all I wanted to do was find a quiet stream somewhere deep in the woods, lean back against a shade tree, and be serenaded by songs of silence.

After all the footsteps I had laid down, I had now fully come to understand and appreciate the often-quoted line in poet Robert Frost's poem: "Stopping By Wood On A Snowy Evening."

"The woods are lovely, dark and deep,
but I have promises to keep,
and miles to go before I sleep.
And miles to go, before I sleep."

There is still so much more my heart wants to say—so many more memories to recall. But for now...

Rest well, my father.
Your loving son, James.

Reflections

A Year Later

It has been over a year since my father died.

Alise and I have spent most of that time traveling back and forth between Rosedale and New York to see each other. Working on the book and following through on construction of new IDM facilities here in Crawford County have consumed my every minute. Alise and I have been engaged for two months now. We have not yet set a wedding date, but we are both filled with excitement and expectation.

One of the most difficult moments our family faced was the day mother reluctantly removed many of father's personal belongings from their bedroom. Much of his clothing was donated to charity. The rest was packed away, except for an old blue suit father wore to the dance where he and mother first met.

Carter and Rosie each selected items they personally wanted; Carter, a pocketknife, and Rosie, a wallet father carried all our childhood photos in. It was atop the nightstand, next to his bed, the morning he died.

I chose an old pair of father's work boots. They are dirty and caked with mud; the soles have holes in them; the laces are broken, and it is impossible to tell their original color. I have made no effort to clean or restore them. I prefer they always remain as they are. These boots are the most important possession I have. They speak of a strong, largely private man, who was always close to the earth and who reveled in hard work.

I visit my father's grave often when I am in Rosedale. However, I prefer honoring him and remembering him, during frequent walks out to the towering oak on top of Heritage Hill. Whenever I am there, I feel his presence and remember the talks he used to have with me.

While I still remember with regret not having my father's involvement in so many of my childhood experiences, those final months with him provide treasured memories I will take to my grave. I miss him terribly and will forever wonder if he understood what happened between us, during his last days. I felt, and would like to believe he felt, a passionate father and son connection that had never existed before.

I ask myself if I ever thanked him for being the father he was. Had I told him I loved him? Sadly, I do not recall I did, at least not explicitly. And I deeply regret not doing so. If you can honestly say those words to your parents and have not done so, please do. Once they are gone, it is too late. Be sure to make the living years count.

I am thrilled to write that mother is doing well, although she misses my father and still grieves for him. She is surrounded by love and caring that sustains her in her darkest hour.

Mother recently shared a writing she found, called Spring Love. She says it expresses her own thoughts and memories about her life with father. I have included it in the following pages.

She is also thrilled Alise, and I are now engaged, and only reluctantly gave me a handful of letters that arrived recently from Rachel. I wrote Rachel several times, after seeing her a year ago. For some reason, I have resisted opening the letters and am yet unable to throw them away.

Many wonderful and some not so wonderful things have happened during the past year. They involve many of those individuals I have written about here and many I have since encountered. While I will not enumerate those things here, perhaps I will in the future.

However, I will mention my visit to the county cemetery. It came days after our inaugural baseball game and was a very emotional experience. I spent about a half hour there. A month later, I had the old, nondescript marker replaced with a custom headstone. On it were engraved five human images, without facial details. This was a long overdue tribute to the friend I never knew.

In addition to quietly searching for old friends, I have been persuaded by my trusted friend John Turret, to speak to father and son gatherings. John is my trusted friend and business associate to whom I entrusted many of my day-to-day business responsibilities.

Upon learning of this book and reading earlier drafts, the idea occurred to him that others could benefit from my experiences. I resisted the idea at first, but John is very persistent. John, it so happens, is an African American of enormous talent, intelligence, and business expertise. He is a man who has never forgotten his humble roots in Harlem. He insists that countless inner city and suburban youth alike could draw great benefit from my input and my financial resources.

The new nonprofit organization he's formed, F.A.S.T (Fathers and Sons, Together) seeks to intervene in the lives of youngsters, especially males. The goal is to alter their life-course before tragedy strikes. The principal focus of the organization is strengthening the relationships between fathers and sons.

A father's role is as important to a daughter's development as it is to a son. However, I want to speak to fathers about the relationship between fathers and sons.

Fathers, it is imperative you give freely of yourself and your time to your sons. Nothing is more important. Please do not become so consumed by your career that you neglect setting aside time to embrace, to listen to, and to PLAY with your sons and all your children.

Roll up your sleeves! Get down on your hands and knees and PLAY! The seemingly simple things you do, or fail to do, help to shape, and mold your sons for a lifetime. It helps determine the kinds of husbands and fathers they become.

I realize that many non-custodial fathers, who are unable to provide adequate monetary support, feel they need not give of themselves and their time. That is wrong. Unfortunately, many custodial mothers foster this notion by using the child as a wedge or a blunt instrument. Fathers, give whatever you can, especially of yourself. Stay involved in your children's lives. Both parents must focus on what is best for the child.

Sons and daughters need their parents. However, there is a special need each son has for a caring father who respects and honors women, and all life. That need cannot be substituted for, no matter how caring and supportive others are.

Fathers, remember this. Every positive memory you create with your son is like a powerful building block in the development of his character, and his view of himself.

A Poem

SPRING LOVE

by Marie Cartwright

It is a beautiful Spring Day.
In our hearts it is always Spring.
Me and my fellow, we are walking together,
talking together, sharing dreams of life together.
How happy and alive we are, walking through the woods in Springtime.

Flowers are blooming today.
Birds are singing too, hopping from limb to limb.
Our faces are reflected in a stream. The blue water flows through green woods, splashes on a big white rock and moves on. Hand in hand, we stroll on through the woods in springtime.
How happy we two must be.

We walk on, laughing aloud, remembering childhood days—days so long past. We laugh at little things, silly little things, just the way we used to do. I feel so young. I always feel young, alive and in love this time of year. Our memories recall our youth, as we walk through the woods in springtime.
We laugh and skip along, often humming songs of long ago.
How happy we two must be.

How blessed we are to have the chance to walk together, talk, laugh, and share our lives together in the springtime of the year.
Every now and then, we stop and look into each other's eyes.
Words are not needed.
When I look into his big brown eyes and he looks into mine,
we see each other's reflection—and smile.
We are always happy, walking through the woods together
in the springtime of the year.

And though we see signs of approaching winter in our lives, in our hearts it is always spring. It is forever Spring.

Where The Winding Road Ends

© 1998 From Gene's book of poetry, *Still Dreaming*

Who can say where the winding road ends, where the dark night fades, and the light begins to reveal the path to places unknown, and the promise of harvest for seeds long sown? Who can say where the winding road ends? Who can say?

Who can say where the winding path leads, where the cold heart cries, and the blind eye sees the arc in the road give way to a view that confounds the many and rewards the few? Who can say where the winding path leads? Who can say?

Teach me, of leaves of gold, crimson and yellow–once green. *Inform me,* of naked branches and limbs laden with virgin snow. *Enlighten me,* of ice that clings stubbornly to bending bough. *Humble me,* to glorious Spring that emerges triumphant, then soon gives way, in the inexorable march of seasons that ends where it all began, yet never ends until...

Who can say why the winding trail bends,
why the songbird dies, and the silence descends, muting the eternal cries of countless lost souls, leaving fools and the wise to only suppose? Who can say why the winding trail bends? Who can say?

Who can say where the winding road ends, where the dark night fades, and the light begins to reveal the path to places unknown, and the promise of harvest for seeds long sown but not forgotten? Who can say where the winding road ends?

Who can say?

EPILOGUE

This book was written before I learned of my father's lung cancer, from which he would not recover; it is dedicated to both his and my mother's courageous struggle and their determination to fight. Both are now gone. She passed away on her birthday, August 13, 2001.

The afternoon of April 29, 1995, in Baytown Texas was overcast and gray. By late evening, rain threatened as the sun began to set, stealing the final rays of muted light. Despite the dreariness, I invited my ailing, 78-year-old father into the front yard of our childhood home. While my 10-year-old son, Patrick, and my brother, George, stood watching, I played catch with my dad, for the very first time. George recorded the emotional event with my video camera.

Mother looked on from the doorway, with tears streaming from her eyes. It was a sight she never expected to see. My father appeared to be deeply touched. We all were. Although his weak physical condition only permitted him to stay a short while, the moment will last me forever. After all these years, I had finally played catch with my father.

—Gene Cartwright

GMW-MOTL

For other titles by the author, and for the author's bio,
Author Site See: https://genecartwrightbooks.com/

Author Biography

Gene Cartwright, a native of Texas, often says it was his great fortune to be born at the right address— the home of his parents. He insists his love of writing, and learning was sparked by his mother, who taught him to read when he was barely four.

He is a former electrical engineer, inactive Marine, a former Oprah guest author, past Pulitzer nominee for fiction, author of 14 books, numerous screenplays, and short stories, and director of two film shorts.

For two years, his book tour for 'I Never Played Catch With My Father,' took him from coast to coast: He has appeared on numerous television and radio programs, including Oprah, NPR stations, and countless TV morning shows, news, and sports shows. He has been the subject of numerous newspaper and magazine articles

Please, see the author's complete works of books and screenplays at https://genecartwrightbooks.com/

Publicist: Nancy Eddy - Novato California 415-883-0174

Made in United States
Orlando, FL
24 June 2024